THE

KILLER'S FLAW

A NOVEL

NATALIE GRIFFIN

Windy Owl Press
Yukon, Oklahoma
nataliegriffin.com

Editing: Shayla Hale
Cover Design: Melinda Martin
Interior Formatting: Melinda Martin

ISBN: 979-8-9868738-2-4 (hardcover)
          979-8-9868738-3-1 (paperback)

To Elizabeth, or "Bee," as I knew you.
I will forever miss hearing your voice
and I will always wish I could give you that well-deserved hug.
You will always be my number one fan.

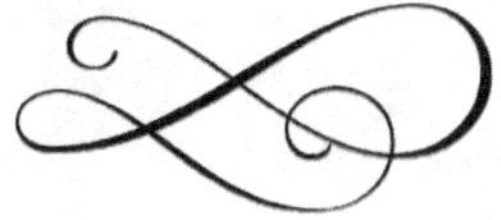

CHAPTER ONE

Job Announcement

New songs will always daunt me. The notes on the page blur into one solid blob, making it impossible to differentiate an E and a G. The process of turning the tangled mess of fingers and keys into meaningful music is arduous. The challenge is both thrilling and comforting at the same time.

It was on one of these days when they told me.

"Petronella!" Mama shouted from the kitchen. "I don't hear you! I told you, one more song. Get to it!"

Stifling a grumble, I placed my fingers on the black and white keys and squinted my eyes to make sense of the individual notes. At least I had chosen a song with power behind it. Unlike certain pieces that just flowed back and forth like a lullaby, I could pound my feelings out onto the keys.

But there wouldn't be enough time to perfect the piece, and I didn't need to sound like I was bent on destroying the beautiful instrument.

It was one of the last items of any worth in the small house.

The sale of our belongings was a slow process. First, the paintings my family had acquired over generations were sold. Soon after, the servants were let go, and the slaves sold to family, neighbors, and friends. When nothing else remained, my father sold the little trinkets on the various shelves, shattering the façade of financial security.

I truly didn't realize it was a farce. Not until the last porcelain bird of my great-grandmother's was in the hands of the snooty, upper-class Mrs. Westers. She turned it over in her hands, lip pulled in a kind of scowl as she debated whether it was worth shelling over the money for such a trinket. Her eyes rolled over me, showing exactly what class she thought we belonged in.

That was the moment I knew that my father's gambling debts were common knowledge. We were officially as good as dirt.

We never were upper class. But we could always live a comfortable life. Stress-free as far as I could tell.

Or at least it seemed like it. Until, that is, the gambling debts my father accumulated were labeled Past Due.

All those delicate items that told of our financial security, our happiness, were gone.

That piano was the last piece of my crumbling world.

And I wouldn't let it go without a fight.

"Petronella!" Mama snapped. "Stop your lollygagging. Get through that song, then come help me in the kitchen."

I traced the keys, feeling the cold ivory against my fingertips. This was the only dance that could transport me from one place to another. With a resigned sigh, I let the sonata pull me away from my reality.

They would be here soon.

Every hoofbeat on the street drew me from my trance. Was that them? Had they finally arrived to take it from me?

The runs on the third page swept me into their comforting embrace. I tilted forward and back, transformed by the ebb and flow of the eighth notes.

The knock on the door wrenched me from my paradise in the most violent way. "No," I whispered. I tucked my fingers under the lips of the keys, wishing I could pull them inside me for safekeeping.

"Petronella, get the door. Hurry now," Mama said. She sounded as if she were in a distant land.

My breath caught in my throat, and I let my nails scrape against the base of the keys. "Is there not anything we can do?"

Mama clucked her tongue, fixing me with a quick, disapproving stare. She brushed past me, skirts sashaying with every step she took. She smoothed her apron down and straightened her shoulders before pulling open the tall oak door.

"Welcome, welcome," she cooed, instantly transformed to a hostess. "Right this way, gentlemen."

Two suit-clad men made their way into my increasingly bare home, eyes taking in every inch just as I would imagine they would in a brothel.

"Is that it over there?" The taller one inclined his head in the direction of my precious piano.

My hands slipped from the keys, playing the mournful sound of dissonance before they landed in my lap.

"Yes, that is it." Mama narrowed her eyes further at me, silently warning me not to make a scene. "Petronella, head to the kitchen. The potatoes need peeled for supper."

Every inch of my soul ached at the thought of leaving the bench for one final time. My place to hide, to feel truly safe . . . it would be gone. Forever. I didn't want to move. I wanted to fight. I wanted to yell and scream at my father, demand that he come up with his own solution.

The men took heavy, purposeful steps toward me.

I imagined what would happen if I refused to move. I'd hold onto the piano with all my might as they tried to separate us.

"*Petronella.*"

My legs made of lead, I stood obediently and stepped away from my beloved instrument.

Their hands were too rough against her beautiful wood. Their fingernails were dirty, their hair loose and unkempt. They could never love her the same way I had. In such an environment, she would be miserable—

"*Petronella, now.*" Mama grabbed my arm with enough force to haul even the most devout nun from a reverie and pulled me into the kitchen doorway. "Stop your dawdling and get busy. You have no time to pine over such things."

Teeth grinding against the pleas that rested on the tip of my tongue, I nodded and stepped into the hot kitchen.

The door swung shut behind me, a final blow to my emotions. Tears pricked at the corners of my eyes. Before Mama could see, I wiped them on my sleeve.

It wasn't fair. No part of it was fair. But there wasn't a thing I could do about it.

Except for peel potatoes.

Every thump from the sitting room made me flinch. Did they hurt her? Did they scratch that elegant finish I loved so much?

At one point, the thump was occupied by her mournful cry, a low note chiming through the air.

"Petronella, dear. It's just a piano," Mama said, tapping my hand with her pointer finger.

I uncurled my fist, potato skins falling onto the countertop, grateful to be free once more.

"Yes, Mama," I whispered.

The thumps and thrums from my piano faded into the hustle in the street. My shoulders sagged, and I breathed deeply, fighting to control myself. I couldn't break. Not just yet.

"Good morning!" My older sister Miriam pushed her way into the steamy room, a basket of scones over one arm.

"Oh, good morning, dear!" Mama gave her a one-armed hug and a kiss on the cheek. "How's the little one?" Her hand fluttered over Miriam's protruding bump as if it would ensure the little thing would come forth, begging for snuggles from his or her grandmother.

Miriam made a face. "Wouldn't let me sleep last night."

Mama tsked. "It doesn't get much better as time goes on. Pretty soon and—"

"I know, I know," she muttered. "But I made scones. Woke Timothy a little early to make them, but I couldn't stay idle."

Mutely, I took the basket and set it on the table. The smell of the heavenly pastries wafted to me, threatening to break through my sadness.

"Hey." Miriam nudged me with her elbow. "Cheer up, okay? You won't find a good man pouting like that."

"She's right." Mama cut through a potato with such force that the resounding *thump* startled me.

I sighed. "I'll find a man when I'm ready. Right now, there aren't any good ones." I would likely have to say those very words a million more times before they finally listened to me.

Mama shook her head back and forth, tutting to herself as she rapidly sliced the potatoes into tiny chunks. "The world doesn't wait for you to be *ready*, Petronella. You already had one proposal, and you turned it down."

I held my breath to keep myself calm. It wouldn't pay to speak my true feelings. Tom would control my every waking moment and then go off to do whatever he pleased. That was certainly not going to be who I married.

We fell into the rhythm of our work, not one of us saying another word.

Papa sat with a grin plastered to his face, like a child bursting with untold secrets.

I felt queasy watching him. He had done something. I just knew it. Something, anything to fix "our" situation.

My younger brother, lovingly called "Little" Chris despite his towering height, nearly vibrated with the urge to reach across the table. "Pass the butter?"

Mama stopped mid sentence. "Christopher, you couldn't wait just a few seconds? You *had* to interrupt?"

He set his jaw, his stubborn streak shining through. "You weren't exactly giving me an opening."

Mama opened her mouth to rip into him, but Papa jumped in first.

"Claire, everyone . . . I have some exciting news," he said, pressing his chest against the tabletop, his eyes sparkling.

Miriam's shoulders slumped. My expression probably mirrored hers: dread.

Mama sighed deeply. "Go on," she prodded.

Anxious energy radiated around the small table. We all knew what was coming—some sort of grand plan that would likely make things significantly worse.

"I was at the bar today—"

"Christopher!" Mama gasped. "You *promised*!"

Papa shot her a reproachful look. "You can't limit a man. Besides, I met someone who offered to help us out."

Little Chris's groan was audible.

"Really?" Mama did her best to sound encouraging, but the doubt was as plain in her voice as if she'd painted it on a sign.

I eyed him, doing my best to keep my expression under control. Meeting someone while at a bar couldn't be a good sign.

"Yes! He owns a vineyard in Tennessee and is in need of help."

Were we moving to Tennessee so he could work? Miriam's hand found mine, squeezing it. I didn't have a clue why she seemed so concerned until he continued.

"This is a big change for you, my baby bug." His eyes found mine, that proud, loving smile lighting up every inch of his weathered face. "He agreed to take Nella on as a kitchen maid. Let her start her own life."

I choked on my potato.

Little Chris pounded my back until I stopped my sputtering.

"No!" I squawked, eyes wide as I frantically searched my parents' faces. "We aren't . . . I can't be a maid." I misheard him. There was no other explanation.

Mama stared at him, mouth open in a little "O" of surprise. "Are you sure?" she whispered.

"I know it's hard, dear, but it's time for her to do her part to help this family. She declined Tom's proposal last year and shows no interest in entertaining any other suitor. Besides, she's getting a little old to get many offers. In times like these, she can't just be a spinster. This will *help* her."

I bristled. "Papa, no . . . please!" My fingernails cut little moon shapes into my palm. "I'm just fine here. Mama needs my help! Little Chris is working, right? If—"

"Your father is right," Mama declared. Lines of sadness stretched from the corners of her eyes. "You can't stay home forever. You're twenty-four, Petronella."

I went mute with shock, staring at them all. No one offered a single shred of help. "But Tennessee? Papa!"

"I'm sorry, Nella." He truly didn't look the least bit remorseful as he stared at me. "It's already done. You leave in the morning."

"The morning!" I squeaked, standing abruptly. My temper boiled to the surface, let out by the panic. "No! You can't just sell me like some slave to the highest bidder! You sold everyone else already. You got rid of Jed, the servants . . . and now me? Papa! Please!" I whirled on Mama. "Please! Don't let him do this!"

Her voice went an octave lower, the threat level rising. "Petronella, sit down. Now. What your father does, he does for the good of the family. That includes you."

I gripped the edge of the table, tears blurring my vision. "But Tennessee! I can't leave here! Please! Papa! I'm your *daughter*! Do something!" *I'm your baby . . .*

"If you're going to behave like a child, you need to go up to your room," Mama said in her "don't you dare cross me" voice. I pushed the chair back with my thighs, not caring that it squeaked dramatically before crashing to the floor.

"Petronella!" Papa scolded, launching to his feet, hands firmly on the edge of the table. "Go to your room. Now! And get to packing."

"Pack what's left, you mean?" I snapped. "After you *sold* everything?"

I hadn't seen Mama get up from her place and make her way to my side. A few inches taller than me, she easily grabbed my ear and hauled me to the door. "Room. Now." She released me at the doorway with a swift swat toward my rear.

I sidestepped her advance and trudged my way up the steps, my humiliation growing.

I should've behaved, listened, not squandered away my last dinner with my family.

But on second thought, my father practically sold me off like some discarded slave. Did he really deserve anything from me?

CHAPTER TWO

The Train

I didn't say a single word to any of them.

If they were going to let Papa sell me off like a common household item, they didn't deserve my affection.

My heart shattered in two on the train's platform, but I did my best to hold my head up and stay strong.

"Come on, Nella Bug, at least give him a hug. You never know what might happen," Miriam said as she wrapped me in the biggest hug she could manage with her protruding belly.

I sealed my lips in case my true feelings came pouring out. Papa didn't seem to notice my stony mood. He gave me a one-armed hug before he handed my trunk up to the stocky man waiting just inside the passenger car.

"I love you, Baby Bug," Papa started, reaching to trace my arm with his fingertips. I flinched away from his touch. "You deserve your own life, you just needed a little push. Change isn't always something to run from." His lips quirked in the hint of a smile, lost in the memories of my childhood.

I ground my teeth as I fought to keep my mouth shut, my fingernails digging into the palm of my hand. Father or not, I would never forgive him. *Never*.

"Are you ready to go, then?" my new owner asked, his wide smile barely hiding beneath his mustache. Did he not realize how much this decision truly cost?

I took a deep breath, set my jaw, and stepped inside. Back and neck straight, eyes forward, I strode out of sight and headed for my assigned seat.

Serves them right. But I had to admit, I didn't fully believe that myself. My entire soul felt broken into a million pieces. I had cried all night long. I had skipped breakfast. Miriam even had to pack for me.

I knew my broken family could see through my furious front, just as I could detect their brave façade. Especially from the train window. Every one of them looked on the verge of tears. Even Little Chris and Papa.

Especially Papa.

I was a daddy's girl. *He* taught me to play the piano. *He* taught me to live, breathe, think piano. But then he turned on me.

Earnest Murray was my official captor.

Well, in my mind at least.

An older man, somewhere between my papa and grandfather's age, with a little too much padding and in desperate need of someone to neaten his chaotic gray facial hair. He seemed harmless enough. A little excitable, but I doubted he'd do anything to hurt me. At least not purposely.

This man owned an entire vineyard. And now me. I couldn't fully let my guard down, and I knew it.

For a stranger from the saloon, he didn't look as dangerous as I had expected. That didn't make me any less angry with my father. Every clack of the train on the tracks only fueled my fury.

By the time the station disappeared into the morning fog, Mr. Murray had fallen headfirst into a happy monologue about his land, the success of the vineyard, and far too many details about the house. I only partially listened, letting my thoughts stew into what was bound to be a permanently angry mess.

When he mentioned he wanted a drink, I only nodded and continued my study of the rapidly passing landscape. My eyes threatened to close, the lack of sleep from the night before finally catching up with me.

Dwelling over him controlling my future in some despicable way wouldn't change a thing. As foolhardy and unforgivable as Papa's decision was, at least it didn't seem like the burly man would hurt me. The most harm he could cause would be to talk until my ears bled.

Or possibly get drunk on the other side of the train.

He must've been gone a half hour. Though the absence of his constant chattering made time pass a lot slower. He only left for a drink. How long could that take?

It certainly wasn't my responsibility to locate him, but the unbidden thought of the man careening from the walkway to the track below caused me to stand with an unladylike sigh. He could've easily been torn to shreds. With a delicate clearing of my throat, I smoothed my skirts and began my mission.

He was sure to be in the dining car with one too many glasses of wine. That was what strangers from saloons did, right?

Crossing from one car to the next sent shivers down my spine. My fingers gripped the railings with all the strength I could muster. I would *not* be one of the unfortunate souls who perished in such a way. With a shaky breath, I made the little hop to the next platform. One down.

The comforting smell of biscuits and gravy greeted me before I even opened the door to the dining car. He would be inside. I would just ensure he was okay, perhaps get some water, then go sit back in my own peaceful seat.

The possibility of him not being there never entered my mind. The only people in the room, other than the man behind the counter, were a couple whispering in the corner. There was no sign of Mr. Murray.

Perhaps they had a different car for the alcoholic beverages. I shoved down the worry and headed for the next crossing. If I hesitated too long, I'd lose my nerve.

"Miss! Miss!" The waiter waved his arms wildly to get my attention. "Passengers aren't allowed that way. There's nothing to see, only storage."

I hesitated, brow wrinkling in confusion. Trains weren't magic. He couldn't have transferred himself from one side to the other without my at least seeing him. "I'll just be a moment, I need to check for someone." Was it even proper to be on the hunt for my employer? Wasn't I supposed to simply let him live his own life and stick to my own duties?

Before I could lose the nerve for yet another crossing, and before the waiter could decide to come after me, I escaped through the door and hopped the space to the next car.

He hadn't been wrong. The next car *was* storage. But that was where the normalcy ended.

In the corner, a tall man stood above a heap, his chest heaving with the intense effort it took to remain calm. Parts of his long brown hair had broken free of the ties and stuck to the sweat on his face, his unbuttoned jacket only adding to the disheveled appearance. But my eyes wouldn't leave the knife in his left hand. Ever so slowly, a thick droplet of blood balanced on the tip before falling onto the still body beneath it.

My mouth worked before my brain. "You killed Mr. Murray."

The heavy-set vineyard owner was that heap, his clothing absorbing his own blood—drop by drop. Or at least doing its best. No haggard breathing came from him, not even the smallest movement.

I remained rooted to my spot, eyes glued to the young man. He stared right back at me, absolute horror ripping its way across his face.

He took one solid step in my direction. My brain snapped back into working order. I turned on my heel and raced back the way I had come, both my breathing and the click of my heels loud in my ears. The coupler between the cars rattled under my feet, making my palms grow sweaty and my heartbeat reverberate in my throat. One wrong step, and a fall to my imminent death would end any chance of fleeing.

I ran through the dining car, reaching the opposite door just as he came in—no sign of the knife, no hint of what had happened. His loose hair was casually pushed behind an ear. He didn't look any worse than an irritated husband.

"Miss? Miss?" the waiter called as I dashed from the dining car.

Get help! Tell him. Scream! Something! But the panic threatened to choke me, eradicating the words before they had a chance to form.

I only slowed when I reached the coupling, gripping the railing like a lifeline. His slow, measured steps sounded behind me, disappearing only as the door slammed shut between us. I knew one very specific thing: there was no need to run, because I had nowhere to go.

That didn't mean I wasn't going to try.

CHAPTER THREE

The Mountain

Rushing as fast as my skirts allowed, I retraced my way through the remaining cars, ignoring the raised eyebrows from the other passengers. I could only hope he gave up the chase long ago, choosing instead to settle down in his own seat. The thought of screaming never entered my mind. All I wanted to do was hide, let everything disappear, and let this memory become a mere dissonance in an ink-stained sonata. I could catch a train back home when we reached the next station.

As long as I went unnoticed.

Like a child racing to base after a rowdy game of tag, I practically dove into my seat. I could hardly breathe from the panic that swelled in my chest. There really was nowhere to go. I couldn't fit into my trunk, though I certainly considered the option. With a sinking finality, I slumped deeper into my seat and struggled to focus on controlling my shaking.

He'd seen me, sure. But had he really seen enough to grasp what I looked like? Perhaps he was just looking to corner the running girl at the end of the train and wouldn't notice the other passengers in their seats.

I did my best to neaten my appearance and stay calm. If luck was on my side, he would simply walk past me and look for someone distressed. But he knew what I was wearing. How could he miss the girl with the wide, pink checkered skirt and matching ribbon in her bonnet?

The wait was interminable. My back was to the door, so each time it opened, I flinched and had to fight the urge to turn around.

When it finally happened, my eyes were shut as tightly as possible. All I heard were the heavy, purposeful footsteps and then the sound of someone sitting across from me.

Some tiny part of my brain fought to convince me that it was someone else. The man from the kitchen checking on me, perhaps. Or maybe I had imagined his blood-soaked body, and it was Mr. Murray coming back from his meal.

The thudding of my heart didn't lie. I forced one eye partially open, then shut it almost instantly. I hadn't even seen his face yet, only how bone-straight he sat.

It didn't matter how much I wished him away; he simply wasn't going to disappear. With a deep, shaky breath, I forced my eyes open again.

Lo and behold, there he sat. He had neatly buttoned his vest since I had seen him last, though there was no sign of the jacket. His eyes narrowed a smidgen as he studied me, one brow raised.

My body trembled, despite my best attempts to keep steady and meet his gaze. The goal was to become some kind of woman that he could not hurt. My shivering form was certainly not that.

My voice mimicked the shake. "You can't hurt me here." Saying it aloud was supposed to convince myself of it. The smirk that appeared on his lips did the complete opposite.

"No." There was no shrug to accompany it, no movement apart from the finger that traced the edge of the table.

"I could scream." I eyed him carefully, hoping for any kind of reaction.

Worry shot across his face for a mere second before his smirk transformed into a half smile, his teeth just barely showing. He leaned forward as if to tell me a secret, then lowered his voice. "Do it."

I gritted my teeth. It was my only ticket out. I took a deep breath to prepare myself, but nothing happened. The would-be scream sizzled out before it could even begin.

"What are you waiting for? Do it." His voice was a low purr that made my stomach swim.

He was toying with me. Like a cat with a mouse. I knew it. But I couldn't make a noise.

A laugh rumbled from his chest, a sound that made the bile rise in my throat, effectively choking out any potential cry for help. He settled deeper into the seat and turned to watch the countryside pass outside the window.

Time ticked on. I couldn't jump off the train to freedom; I knew very well he wouldn't let me get help. That perilous moment of walking from one car to the next would be the only opening he needed to slit my throat and let me fall.

I had no escape route. But the silence was more than I could take.

"What are you going to do to me?" To my dismay, he didn't respond. He glanced at me out of the corner of his eye, but otherwise didn't react.

I wanted to vomit. *Needed* to vomit, rather. I couldn't come up with an acceptable answer to what he wanted to do with me once we got off the train. The end result was always the same: death.

I didn't *have* to follow him. I could simply start my caterwauling and hope someone would figure out what was wrong.

But all he had to do was claim I was some mentally unstable wife and that he was only trying to protect me.

A cluster of staff paced the aisle, worry written plainly in their furrowed brows. "Found 'em in next ta the flour. Blood everywhere," one said to the other.

"Did the blood get into—" The second went silent, as he likely realized that every eye was trained on him.

Like a flickering flame leaping from one timber to the next, every passenger went stiff and silent.

The train slowed, the screeching brakes making the change in plans all the more obvious. We certainly weren't anywhere close to our next scheduled stop. The train ride was supposed to last all day, and it couldn't have been much past noon.

I scanned my surroundings, as if they would provide the perfect opportunity to bolt. Questions from the other passengers reverberated around, concern not missing a single face.

A booming voice came from the end of the car. "Attention, ladies and gentlemen, there has been a mishap that we needed to address. Everybody will leave the train for now. We will be back on our way shortly. We have stopped in the town of Chattanooga, so for those who would like to get off here, you may take your belongings. I have been informed that there is a stagecoach route that comes through here daily." He didn't wait for the questions that popped up from nearly every seat. He simply waltzed straight through to repeat his message to the next car.

My companion stood and stretched, the movements slow and leisurely. He watched me out of the corner of his eye the entire time. I didn't budge. We all had to get off the train, but I certainly wouldn't be going with him. I would walk off with the crowd and disappear with them instead.

He, of course, had other plans. Ignoring the luggage above our heads, he took my upper arm. His grip likely appeared tender to any onlookers but was certainly uncomfortable to me. He pulled with just enough force to bring me to my feet. My body obeyed him, listening only to the pain that came from his fingertips as they dug into my skin.

"Come along, darling." He led me to the exit, the other passengers crowding all around us. "We will just take the coach to the next town." He had the perfect amount of scorn in his voice to sound like some pompous rich man.

I tried to stop several times, but with the number of people pressing around us, and with how tightly he held onto my arm, there was no way to halt our progress.

My new captor had it all planned out. There was a man at the door, helping the women step to the platform below and taking note of who would return when the train was in working order. As I opened my mouth to alert him to my predicament, my captor simply talked over me. He droned on about how improper it was to make people like us take the coach.

He never let me go as I stumbled onto the platform. When the man called after us, my captor picked up his pace, forcing me to take two steps to his single stride.

"Sir, you forgot your bags!"

The crowd engulfed us as he pulled me forward. My heart raced as I searched for a savior. No one so much as glanced in our direction. They were all too preoccupied with their own travels.

At the edge of the weathered station, he veered away from the main street, choosing a nearly silent one that rambled toward the mountain. I gripped a wooden hitching post with both hands. My efforts were pointless. He pulled on my arm a little harder, the splinters from the post embedding into my palms as my hands slipped free.

I caught sight of a middle-aged man watching us, brows raised in suspicion. Desperately, I reached for him. "Please sir, help—"

"Mind your manners, woman!" my captor snapped. He stood still, holding me securely to his side. "I'm sorry, sir, you understand, it's our responsibility to keep *them* in line when they get a little too promiscuous." He glared at me.

If he managed to get me into the woods, that would be it. He'd end my life to be free of a witness. I had to make this stranger understand! "Just let me go—"

Satisfied, the man smirked, tipped his hat at us, and disappeared back into the crowd.

There was no time wasted as my captor dragged me on, becoming one with the shadows behind the buildings. As we reached the edge of town and started the ascent into the forested area beyond, it finally occurred to me to scream.

I opened my mouth wide but only managed a small squeak before his hand firmly clamped my mouth shut.

"I don't give chances," he growled, his face so close to my own I could feel his breath. "I wouldn't open that mouth of yours again. Got it?"

My body trembled of its own accord, but I nodded.

He released my jaw and resumed the trek through the forest. The slope of the mountain did nothing to dampen my nerves. The trees stretched for the sun, seeming to grow taller with each passing one. My stuttered footfalls rustled the undergrowth, scaring birds and alerting rabbits with every crunch of the leaves. His footsteps, on the other hand, were completely silent.

I strained my ears, but all I could hear was the way my breathing grated against my parched throat, the melody of the breeze through the branches, and my own faltering steps.

He pulled me along tirelessly, the bustle of the town fading into the distance.

How far are we going to go before . . . The mere, unfinished thought froze my limbs, sending me spiraling to the ground of decomposing leaves. *You will join them soon enough* . . .

The man grumbled something that almost sounded French and hauled me to my feet again.

When he stopped moving, a sob shattered my body, sending me straight to my knees. The sudden release of my arm re-awoke the bruising pain deep inside. My entire body curled toward its inevitable resting place, crumbling in my own misery.

He would kill me. One swipe of his blade would be all it took. Would it hurt? Would it be quick? Would he have his way with me first? Or worse, would he satisfy his sadistic desires with the knife itself before the final blow?

Each thought broke me further, evicting more sobs than my lungs could handle. I gasped for air and choked on my cries, over and over again.

Without making so much as a sound, he knelt beside me. He rested one arm over my chest, pressing my back against his torso. Each movement was a soft caress, the sweetest of farewell songs. I could feel his steady heart beating against my back. His other hand snaked around, bringing the clean blade to rest against my neck.

My crying stopped, self-preservation taking over. My body refused to so much as breathe, for fear the movement would be the end of me.

His voice took on a whole new tone. No longer was it harsh and reprimanding. Every ounce of the stress was gone, replaced only by sorrow. "I'm sorry. I must do this."

I pressed into his chest with all my strength, as if it would get me farther from the offending object. Why didn't I scream while I could? Why didn't I cause a scene?

In the bushes beyond, something rustled. Everything stopped. He didn't breathe. When there was a second sound, he got to his feet, releasing me. "Stay put," he muttered before making his way to investigate.

I practically vaulted up. Before I was fully standing, I was running. My feet tangled with my skirts and the leaves, but I moved on. The muted pink of my traveling dress wrapped around my right foot, refusing to release it. Time came to a standstill as I tipped forward, falling.

The ground I landed on wasn't nearly as flat as the area he'd chosen for my demise. The mountain scooped me into its grasp, yanking me down faster and faster with each passing moment. I grabbed for whatever I could see. A passing branch, a boulder, my legs, my arms. Anything. Like a doll, the mountain knocked me around until there was simply nothing under me. No leaves, no dirt, no trees. Just air.

My scream echoed through the nothingness.

As soon as I hit the ground, the pain disappeared into black.

CHAPTER FOUR

The Family

The pain returned before my eyes fully opened. Red, burning pain that radiated from my leg, all the way up my torso. It pulsed relentlessly, making my vision swim.

The scene that met me was not that of the forest sky, the mossy ground, or anything closely related to heaven or hell.

I'd envisioned their entrances would either be festooned with fluffy white clouds or roaring balls of fire.

This place was roofed in wood. Nothing celestial about it.

With an involuntary moan, I fought to sit. The room was hot and stuffy. There were a few dusty trunks shoved in one corner, crates in the other. The only light came from the tiny window, sending long shadows across the floor.

I was in an attic.

The debilitating pain overtook my entire body as I swung my feet over the edge of the small settee. The pain emanated from under my filthy skirts. I gritted my teeth and powered on. Perhaps, if I completely ignored it, the injuries wouldn't become real. At least not yet.

The moment I tried to stand showed exactly how wrong I was. I collapsed to the ground in a heap, the pain evolving to a new intensity. A cry escaped my lips, and my hands curled into fists as I prayed for the agony to subside. It was the kind of anguish that took over every tiny part of my body, crawling like fire ants to immobilize me.

A thud from the center of the room startled the pain into a temporary, tolerable submission. I nearly stopped breathing.

Footsteps thudded through my ears as the unwelcome visitors joined my attic prison. Slowly, as if they would transform into the angels I craved, I turned my head to watch them.

Two people stood beside an open trapdoor. A broad man of medium height with a salt-and-pepper beard and matching hair stood beside a teen with nearly identical facial structures. I could only assume they were father and son. The father looked nothing short of furious; the boy stood aghast, his mouth hanging open.

It took no time at all for their number to double with the addition of two men in their mid-twenties. One of these men had ashy blond hair and a strong, angled jaw. I could see the muscles through his undershirt, only adding to his large stature.

They didn't scare me nearly as much as the fourth and final man who appeared through the trapdoor. I knew all I needed to know: I wasn't in heaven.

This was hell.

My captor stood under the older man's gaze, head bowed in submission. His shaggy, coffee-brown hair fell forward, covering most of his face.

Without warning, the father took complete control of the situation. In one fluid movement, he cleared the space between us, gripped the hair at the base of my neck, wrenched my head up, and pressed a knife to my neck.

"No!" my original captor said, leaping past the youngest brother and frantically reaching for his father.

The knife pressed tighter against the tender skin of my throat. "And why shouldn't I?"

He hesitated, eyes wide as he fought to come up with a reason. He looked so harmless next to his father and brothers. He had freckles spanning across his cheeks and nose, and his face had a softer, rounder appearance.

"She needed my help," he said.

Despite the puppy dog illusion, the muscles were obvious on every inch of his body.

His father set his jaw, his teeth bared in a near snarl. There was *nothing* soft about him. "She needed your help, eh? You were on that train for *one thing* and *one thing* only. You told us it was taken care of. Now, what is *this*?" With his nails digging into the skin at the base of my neck, he shook me. The pain shot through my body with every movement, causing me to cry out.

"She's my responsibility," the puppy-faced captor said, his head drooping again. "She didn't deserve to go like that."

The older man made a noise somewhere between a laugh and a cough. "No one gets to choose." He hauled me up with a mixture of my hair and shoulder before dropping me back on the settee. "You get to clean up your own mess." He released me and took the single step to his son. He pressed the knife into his hand. "You have five minutes."

The father herded the other two men back down the ladder, giving us one more firm look before disappearing, shutting the trapdoor behind him.

My young captor stood in the middle of the room, pale, still, hardly breathing. He looked so much younger than he had on the train—enough so, he resembled a newly chastened schoolboy.

When he took a step forward, I whimpered and dragged myself as far back as I could. My leg sent desperate messages to the rest of my body with my every effort. He sat next to me, running his finger up and down the shiny steel of the knife.

"I *am* sorry," he said. His touch was gentle as he brushed away the hair that had stuck to the nervous sweat on my neck.

"Please," I whispered. My voice was a squeak, hardly audible even to myself. "Please, just let me go."

He gave me a sympathetic half smile. "I can't do that. I've already let this draw out too long."

I met his blue gaze, fully aware I looked much like a terrified puppy myself. "I don't even know what all of this is. I couldn't turn you in even if I wanted to!" I knew begging was futile, but what else was I to do?

Sadness flickered through those blue eyes before they went blank, completely emotionless. "I'm sorry." He took a deep breath and readjusted the knife on my throat.

"Please," I whimpered. "Please don't."

And, with a shout of frustration, he threw the knife at the far wall. My hands flew to my neck, checking for any wound that might not have registered yet. There was nothing.

He stood—clearly tense—and went to grab the blade from where it had lodged itself into the wood panels. Without a look back at me, he flipped open the trapdoor with his foot and slid to the floor below.

I stared after him in complete confusion. What on earth was going on? Apparently, I wasn't in hell, and certainly not heaven. Instead, some sort of limbo between life and death.

The arguments downstairs were instant, flowing through the cracks in the floor in muffled fury. It was hard to understand a single word, but one pleading sentence sliced through the air.

"*Please*, Henry!" It was a female, her voice overcome with anguish.

As I shifted to listen closer, the pain flared back to life. With a deep, shaking breath, I settled myself to face my injury. I sluggishly lifted my skirts, as if it would give the wound a chance to hide. The pain that throbbed every second assured me it wouldn't be a simple scratch.

Someone had removed the stocking from my right leg. How had I not noticed that before? As I scanned down the length of my leg, dried blood streaked in all directions, threatening to engulf the pale white. My stomach lurched as I saw it. A large gash spanned my calf, still oozing blood. As if that weren't bad enough, something hard and white peeked out into the faint light.

First, why did I not feel the full pain? Second, how would I manage any kind of escape attempt? There was no way I could walk.

The bone under my knee had shattered in my fall and sat at a horrific angle, showing itself to the world in all its glory.

With the severity of my situation sinking in, there wasn't a way to keep the pain at bay anymore. I gripped the tattered quilt for support, fingers pulling so hard it was at risk of tearing. My breathing quickened and my heart slammed against my chest bone. Every other breath that escaped my lips sounded like it belonged to someone else.

There was no possible way I would get out of this. I couldn't even put up a good fight. It would be impossible to get downstairs. Getting out the window? Unthinkable.

Every ounce of my soul prayed that I would pass out. If the blackness took over again, it would be all done. They would dispense of me without a fight, and I'd wake to my ultimate fate—heaven or hell.

But my body didn't cooperate.

They left me in my attic of misery for so long that I ran out of tears and my panicked breaths slowed to a shaky, acceptable level. The pain faded to a kind of deadly threat, manageable only as long as I didn't move. However, even a breath was too much movement.

When the trapdoor fell open again, I turned to stone. Wrapping the blanket tightly around me, I awaited my fate.

The first man up was the father. Second, my original captor. His eyes were trained on the floor, barely changed from the scolded child from a few moments ago. He held a large, black bag at his side. With slow determination, he lifted his head and made eye contact. My heart leapt in a confused spasm. Was the sparkle hiding in his eyes a promise? Or simply anger?

His father was nothing short of furious. His veins protruded in angry explosions from his clenched fists. His jaw was locked so tightly I briefly wondered if he was in danger of breaking teeth.

He was the hell, I decided.

"You'll be staying here," Hell Man snapped. "You are Oliver's responsibility, and his alone. You are not allowed to leave. Do you understand?"

I stared at him, shock welling inside. So, they weren't going to simply kill me?

"Do you understand?" he repeated, his voice a growl.

My voice was a croak. "Yes."

"Good." He glared from me to Oliver, then disappeared downstairs again.

CHAPTER FIVE

Amputation

As though he was stalking an injured animal, Oliver trudged toward me. Every step he made was slow and deliberate, his eyes fixed on my hidden injury. It throbbed in the most agonizing way, like it knew it had been discovered. I flinched away as he sat on the cushion beside me.

He took his time, scrutinizing my face with his surprisingly compassionate eyes. "I have to fix your leg."

Somehow, I found my voice, hoarse and cracked though it was. "I would prefer a doctor."

He shook his head. "That's not possible."

With a *bang*, the trapdoor slammed open and the youngest brother popped into view. He wasn't too young, probably about fifteen. Even so, adulthood hadn't quite caught up with him. Curly blond hair shot every which way, framing his bright blue eyes. His arms and legs mimicked the hair, too long for his body and not quite ready to be tamed. His body excreted energy—ready to run, ready to fight, ready for anything the world could throw at him.

"I got it!" he shouted, holding a liquor bottle to the sky.

Nerves crashed through my belly like a trapped fish. I wrapped my arms tightly around my middle in a useless attempt to calm it. Was there really anything about my situation that could get worse?

Oliver hardly glanced at him. "Good. Bring it here. What about Bernard?"

The boy hesitated, looking between us as if he were choosing who he could outrun. "Can't Donnell help—"

"No." Oliver held out his hand and waggled his fingers expectantly. "Did Bernard say he would come?"

The boy sighed deeply and dropped the trapdoor closed with his toe. Each movement was just about as slow as he could make it. "He's coming. He's gonna be mad, though."

Oliver rolled his eyes to the sky and shook his hand in the air, still waiting for the liquor. "I'm well aware of that."

"You sure we can't take her—"

"Yes, I'm sure," Oliver snapped. "Now, give it."

The boy handed him the bottle but remained a few feet away, wringing his hands like a worried old woman. His pretty eyes darted everywhere, ready to run or fight at the first sign of movement.

Oliver gestured at his younger brother. "This is Arthur. He'll help." He popped the cork on the poison liquid and pushed it my way.

I didn't touch the bottle. "Please, just take me home. They'll take care of me there."

But what was there to go back home to? My father? The man who essentially sold me to a stranger? Would my family even take me back if I showed up on their doorstep? My injury certainly wouldn't be something they could afford. Besides, how would I find out what town we were in? Let alone get to it . . .

Oliver grumbled under his breath and pushed the bottle so it bumped my clammy hands. Like a parent on his last thread of patience, he eyed me down the bridge of his nose. "You have two choices. Either cooperate or . . ." He shrugged. "Don't."

When I didn't respond, he shoved it again, pressing it to my chest. Liquid sloshed ominously inside. "Drink that, please."

I took a whiff of the foul-smelling stuff. It was likely to kill me on its own it smelled so strong. "I don't drink."

"Remember the two choices? That's not one of them." He tapped the bottle, his nails making a strangely melodic *clink*.

There wasn't much of a choice. I knew very well that being stubborn wouldn't help me in the long run. Besides, there were only so many times they could threaten my life before actually taking it.

So, I took the bottle. I stared at the dark liquid sheltering inside, hoping it would give me a different answer. It didn't. "How much do I have to drink?"

"Just start drinking," Oliver said simply.

Hesitating for a few more moments didn't bring any alternatives. What other option did I really have? I couldn't walk, couldn't escape, and would end up dying of my injuries without any help. They *certainly* weren't going to take me to get the help I wanted.

With a small yet angry huff, I brought the bottle to my lips and took a gulp. The abominable liquid burned the entire way down. I coughed and sputtered, fighting to keep it from coming straight back up and out my nose. I was not successful.

Oliver placed a handkerchief in my hand and gestured to the mess on my face. "Try again. This time, *swallow* it."

I screwed my eyes shut and tried again, drinking until my lungs screamed for air. The resulting cough spurred on the pain yet again. I tried to focus on anything other than the all-encompassing spasm, but it had the upper hand. The agonizing wave coursed through my bloodstream, forcing me to collapse into a twitching ball. My vision clouded, stars sprinkling across the threatening darkness. The lip of the bottle pressed against my collarbone, menacingly cold, pulling me back to the matter at hand.

"More," Oliver said when I finally went silent.

Reluctantly, I swallowed again, eyes clenched as the sharp taste overtook my senses.

My heart did a somersault when the trapdoor crashed open again. A third man poked his head into the room, his alert brown eyes framed by round-rimmed glasses. The moment he spotted me, his shoulders slumped.

"Dammit, Oliver!" he barked, climbing all the way up and slamming the door closed behind him. He dropped a worn leather bag onto the floor, the items inside clanking. "What kind of—you *idiot!*"

Despite his outburst, the man strode to my side. His fingers were warm and steady where they pressed against my neck, vaguely under my ear. Unconsciously, I leaned against him, as if the pain would fade away, absorbed by his kind touch.

"Told ya he'd be mad!" Arthur said.

"This is Bernard," Oliver muttered, though I didn't need the clarification.

I was only vaguely aware that I was releasing a thin whine, breaking only when I would gasp for breath. Already, my movements felt muted, slower, and somewhat like a distant waltz.

Bernard's featherlight touch traveled down the length of my arms, to my hips, then carefully down the length of my legs. I didn't move from my folded position; I was completely immobile for fear of the pain. He lifted the hem of my skirt and let out the longest sigh I'd ever heard.

"That's gonna have to come off," he announced.

"*Pardon?*" I blurted. I might've been a dusty old box with how easily they ignored me.

"Yeah!" Oliver snapped. "That's why you're here. You gonna help me?"

Bernard dropped the skirts and stood, his movements measured and almost apathetic. "Firstly, I shouldn't be here at all! Secondly—"

"*What's* gonna come off?" I demanded. Even to my own ears, my voice sounded like a squawk.

"So you're just gonna let her die here?" Oliver demanded.

"No," Bernard said firmly.

Arthur nudged my shoulder with the liquor bottle. I yelped at the touch. *Has he been here the whole time?*

"You might want more," he whispered. He helped me sit, cradling me while I took another gulp. It didn't seem as bad this time. The burn had faded to a smoke similar to a relaxing campfire—warm but comforting.

The room began its own kind of dance, flowing back and forth. It should have been nauseating, but it somehow . . . wasn't. It felt as though I was the one doing the swaying, and perhaps I was. The fear had trickled down into the back of my mind; there, but difficult to reach.

Oliver crouched in front of me, eye to eye, one hand on each shoulder to steady me. "Before we begin, I have a question for you." His face swirled before me. "What is your name?"

Some deep part of me knew why he would ask such a thing. If I were to die, they would want to put something on my tombstone. That thought didn't surface long enough for the worry to take hold, so I answered easily. "Nella."

He scooped me up like an injured child and, in one fluid movement, had me lying on the table. The pain sparked from the change in position, but like the anxiety, it remained hidden in the back of my mind.

Oddly, I was more concerned about the table. Where had it come from? Had Arthur moved from my side to set it up? It was the only explanation. Perhaps it had been under one of the sheets in the corner of the room.

The alcohol had complete control of my senses, numbing all worry, all feeling. I felt dizzy, giggly, groggy. Nothing made much sense.

The men said a few things, commands here and there, but I don't remember what they were, or even if I answered. Was I laughing? That was certainly possible.

When they touched my foot, I didn't scream. But no amount of alcohol could dull the painful reality. When Oliver placed one hand above my right knee and the other directly above my ankle, the liquor failed. He looked deep into my face, his brows furrowed in worry. Arthur rested his palms on my arms, ready for the impending battle.

Tools clinked against the table as Bernard prepared the area. "When I begin, hold on with everything you've got. I'll have to work fast."

For a brief moment, everything was clear: shining sharp objects beside me, my skirt hiked farther up on my injured leg than remotely acceptable, and a glaring injury I wanted to forget.

Someone mentioned blood loss, and something snapped in my brain. Adrenaline washed over me, and I pushed to get up, to run away, to escape in any way I could. The men were stronger. *So* much stronger. Arthur's grip wasn't nearly as gentle anymore. My body hardly lifted from the table.

My injury wasn't a simple matter; I knew what was coming. A person couldn't place a bone back under the skin and then back into its rightful position. Especially not in an attic.

And definitely not without infection.

"Bite onto this, sweetheart." Bernard placed a rolled rag between my teeth. "Ready?" His voice sang through the room, unwavering.

Everything moved in slow motion. Cold steel touched my leg—precise, threatening. And then a new pain erupted in my limb. Sharp, spreading, all-encompassing. A result of spitting out my gag, my own bloodcurdling screams sliced through my ears. I tried to move, tried to fight them off, but the alcohol had done its job.

There was no ounce of dignity in the way my body fought for survival. Bernard may've moved fast, but every second turned to an eternity.

I caught a glimpse of his dark head bent over my lower half, blood splattered up to his elbows.

Oliver held me steady, his teeth barred against his own demons.

Mercifully, I didn't see anything more before I slipped into sweet unconsciousness.

CHAPTER SIX

I Want It Back

Red-hot agony coursed through my veins before I even thought about opening my eyes.

"Stop!" I heard myself scream. I threw myself to the side, my attempt to escape the unimaginable pain. It stalked me, its claws gripping my injured leg, sinking deeper with every breath I took.

Oliver ran his hand over my sweat-soaked forehead, cooing at me like a child. "Shh, shh . . . it's all done. It's all stitched up, and the bleeding stopped."

My breath caught against my ribs, and my eyes shot open.

My leg.

His blue eyes were a mere inch from my brown ones, the surrounding freckles only accentuating his worry.

"What. Did. You. Do?" I demanded, my voice a growl. Though as menacing as I could make it, it didn't hide the underlying sob. The world around me swayed; nothing stayed in focus for longer than a second. Nausea pricked at my gut, and stars danced along my vision.

He winced and backed away, as though I were liable to spit venom. "I took care of it." Like berries sprinkled across the ground, blood was splattered all across his tan shirt. My blood.

I hazarded a glance at my feet. Or foot. True to my nightmares, there was only one bare foot at the end of the table.

"Where is it?" I whispered. My heart took off at a full run, making my breath hitch. Blood-soaked linen had been wrapped below the knee of my right leg, but there was nothing more.

He had been reaching for the liquor bottle on the floor, but his hand froze in the air. "What?"

"Where is it?" I repeated. Though my vision was far from clear, I let my eyes travel across the candlelit room. Arthur crouched at the end of the table, staring back at me. Not only was his shirt covered in blood, but it had also clotted in his hair. He held a wet rag in one hand, the water dripping from it a glistening red in the faint light.

Murderers.

These men were trained murderers.

With a grunt, I pressed my forearm against the table and fought to sit up. "I'm leaving," I announced. "I need my leg back."

A strange sound escaped Arthur's lips, a strange mix between a snort and a laugh. The room paused its sashay to do one big bow, making everything in my vision blur into a cascade of dulled browns and grays as I tilted toward the floor.

Like a cat, Oliver sprang from his own crouch and pushed me down. Though I wanted to protest, to fight against him, everything was too fuzzy, too . . . too red.

"I want my leg back. Where is it?" Channeling my mother, I fixed him with what I hoped was a steady stare. His face wavered, fading from black, to white, to red.

"I'm sorry, Nella," Oliver whispered. "This is all my fault . . . but it's gone."

"Gone?" I whispered. I turned my head away from him, squinting to take in the state of the room. On the floor was an oblong bundle, wrapped in an old patchwork quilt. The blood had seeped through one end of it, effectively ruining the muted greens and blues of the fabric.

"Put it back?" My voice cracked. Part of my mind knew this nightmare was my reality, that my leg was long gone. Even so, nothing felt real. It *had* to all be a horrible dream. In only a few moments, I'd wake up, back in my own bed, safe and sound.

"I can't," Oliver said. He pushed the hair from my sweaty forehead and tilted my head up. "Drink some of this, it'll help."

I obeyed, swallowing the laudanum with ease. It started as a blossom of pain below my knee, though it rapidly grew to an explosion all its own. As if a red-hot iron had been rammed through me, the agony threatened to clog my senses again.

Mercifully, before my scream reached my ears, the red pressed in on all sides and pulled me back into unconsciousness.

The following days, or maybe weeks, were a complete blur. There was usually alcohol tinged with laudanum in my system, making my memories turn into a melancholy legato. Anything that stuck was filled with pain, tears, and the brief appearance of people.

There was really no way to track how much time passed before I noticed I didn't have that many daily visitors. Eventually, I spent more time awake than I wanted, leaving me to stare at the cobwebs on the ceiling.

Bernard made the trip to check the wound daily, chatting to me about his family to keep me distracted. He lived on the outskirts of town with his wife and twin boys. The five-year-olds were constantly finding mischief, and the daily stories never failed to bring a smile to my face. I couldn't help but let my mind wander back to when I was young, chasing my own siblings around the house.

More often than not, Oliver joined him on these visits, a silent shadow at the edge of the settee. He brought me food that I refused to eat and spooned water into my mouth. He reminded me of a lost puppy, filled with guilt. Dark scabs marred the pink flesh of his lips. He spent the majority of his visits gnawing on them, making it worse by the day.

At one point, Oliver brought me something to occupy my time. It was a worn copy of *Moby-Dick*, the edges of some of the pages wavy and littered with sprinkles of water damage. I could only imagine how many times it had been read while out on the road, a distraction from the rain. Or perhaps a much-needed diversion from the job at hand.

"I always wanted to visit the ocean," Oliver shared with me. "Maybe one day I can go."

Despite the stream of entertainment from the men, my favorite visitor was a woman—their mother.

At first, I thought she was heavyset, but as the haze faded into a firm reality, I realized a baby was the cause of her thickening waistline.

When I first met Rose, she spat fiery words at my semiconscious self and forced food into my body. She even helped me change into a clean chemise (because Lord knew I wouldn't let the men help me with that) and cleaned the debris out of my hair. Her voice a steady pianissimo, she sang in French throughout the entire process, wrapping me in the comfortable blanket of her sweet voice.

Her eyes were the icy blue of an untouched spring, matching Oliver's intense gaze perfectly. Her hair rode the line somewhere between a blond and a light brown, the candlelight glistening from the waves that escaped from the bun at the base of her neck.

There was something about her that stole my heart. Perhaps it was the way she seemed to adopt me as one of her own, or perhaps it was the way she took charge whenever the men were near—not a single one of her children would cross her. I was sure of it.

For psychopathic captors, the majority of them did their best to care for me. The father never crossed my threshold again.

The blank spot under my chemise haunted me, but I refused to look at it. Whenever Bernard changed the bandages, I clenched my eyes. If I didn't acknowledge it, it wasn't there. Even so, every part of me ached. My body refused to realize a portion of my leg didn't exist anymore. Some part of me was still out there, calling for my toes to wiggle, my skin to feel touch.

The day I finally tried to get up, to face my reality, I was spurred on by hunger.

I watched the sun come up in the small window, the pink glow cascading through the dark attic, turning to yellow, then white. There hadn't been the usual breakfast. The sun had still been high in the sky the last time I saw anyone.

Patience wasn't a talent of mine.

Gripping the edge of the settee, I turned my body so my leg hovered over the floor. I stared at my foot for so long without blinking, my vision blurred. Biting my lower lip, I tugged the skirt up. Inch by agonizing inch, I exposed the creamy white skin of my left leg. Bile pooled at the back of my throat as the fabric slithered higher and higher.

The bandage was right where it should've been, tightly wrapped below my knee. It was clean, showing no sign of what hid underneath.

A shrill sound came from somewhere deep inside as I untucked the linen and let my trembling fingers unwind it. With each pass around my leg, the swelling throbbed its caution.

Did I really want to see it? There was absolutely *no* way I would like what I found under the bandages. Yet that curiosity pushed me forward, unwinding the fabric little by little.

Under the knee, the skin was mottled different shades of purple and red. One, two more rounds of linen revealed the first stitch. Then another. Then another. And another . . . When the fabric fell to the floor, I could plainly see the marred skin that once housed my leg.

I clamped my hand to my mouth, forcing the bile back down as I fought to come to terms with it. The skin was angry, swollen, and colorful. The line of stitches was ragged and traced from one edge to the other.

My vision swayed as my breathing grew faster and faster, the tears flowing unchecked down my cheeks and into my lap. I gripped the skirt at my thighs and focused on my breaths. In. Out. In. Out. All the while, I stared.

I could've stared for hours, or even minutes. I'll never know. Eventually, the tears dried up, replaced by the desperate need for escape—for control.

With a small, desperate sort of noise, I held onto a nearby nightstand and pushed myself to stand. It wasn't so bad, other than the rush of pressure to the affected area. I wobbled some, but that had more to do with my mind than my balance.

A growl erupted from my stomach, spurring me on. I let go of the settee and jumped. I made it a few unsteady and extremely unladylike bounces before my hands sought assistance. Though I scrambled to grab anything I could, I had gone too far.

With agonizing slowness, I fell.

Almost as soon as I hit the hard floor, the trapdoor opened with a matching *thump*. Oliver climbed in. I pushed myself up to a seated position and narrowed my eyes at him, not sure what he had planned.

He stood very still, arms crossed hard and one eyebrow raised. Had I really been difficult enough to cause such irritation when only half conscious?

I swallowed hard and crossed my own arms to match his. "*You're* the one who did this to me."

"It certainly wasn't my intention." He hooked an arm behind my back and scooped me to my foot. Any hint of violence was gone from his grip. Instead of being rough and painful as it had been in the beginning, it had become tender and caring.

"If you're not going to let me go, why not simply kill me?" I asked for what had to have been the hundredth time that week.

For the first time, I actually received an answer. "I don't know."

CHAPTER SEVEN

Letter

With great care, Oliver wrapped one arm behind my back and helped me limp back to the settee. My permanent resting place . . . at least, it felt that way.

My stomach growled. "I hate to be a bother, trapped in *your* attic and all, but could I get some food?" Perhaps my tone was a little too gruff, maybe I should have been more grateful to even be alive. That didn't erase the bitterness that crashed inside my empty stomach.

"Ma will get you something when she's finished downstairs, I'm sure." He pulled over a rickety chair and sat. "Let me see? Did you land on it?" He scooped the bandages from the floor.

I complied, exposing my deformity to this stranger. He had me trapped, but I certainly wasn't going to wait around like a broken clock on the mantle anymore. "You're not going to tell me what she's finishing?"

He said nothing as he rewound the bandage. Once satisfied, he turned his gaze to me. "Here." He fished a pen, inkpot, and a small pad of paper out of his pants pocket and shoved it in my direction. "We'll be gone for a few days. I figured you might like to send a letter to your folks."

My eyebrow raised of its own accord. This was the *last* thing I expected. "I can write anything I want?"

He shot me that same look. "No. Of course not. I'll be reading it before I seal it up. We leave in an hour, so you'd better get to writing." He held up a finger at me, waggling it like a schoolteacher. "I wouldn't suggest writing anything you might regret."

I ran my fingers over the green and gold pen, wishing I had formulated a secret code with my sister. Of course, the idea had never entered our minds. Who would imagine one of us being trapped inside an attic, missing a leg and hoping for rescue?

I was so lost in thought it took me a full minute to register what he said. "You're leaving?" He wouldn't trap me in the attic, alone and without food for days on end . . . would he?

He shook his head, reading my thoughts. "Ma will be staying home. She'll take good care of you, I'm sure."

I eyed him carefully. "And where are you going?"

He shot me a mock smile as he stood up. "You don't get to know that. I'll be back before we leave to grab your letter." Before he reached the hatch, he froze. "Whatever you do, don't tell anyone about the letter."

Without another word, he disappeared down the ladder. The loneliness didn't settle into my chest this time. I had paper.

I immediately dipped the pen into the inkwell.

Dear Mama and Chris,

Was that right? To exclude Pa? Should I write Miriam one too? A thump from outside reverberated through the room, making the decision for me. There was no time. Pa didn't deserve a letter.

Dear Mama and Chris,

I hope this letter finds you well. I miss you two very much. Little Chris, I miss how your smiles melt through me and bring a smile to my own face. There's a boy here who reminds me of you.

Was that too much? As I studied the words, a small drop of ink formed on the nib and dribbled into a puddle on the page. *Just write. Even if it's all a lie.* I'd redeem myself later.

> *I miss Mama's cooking too.*
>
> *I made it safely to Mr. Murray's vineyard. The staff is large, but there is still plenty to do. I stay busy. When I first arrived, I was ill, but you shouldn't worry yourself about it. I recovered well.*
>
> *Mama, you always told me to take my future into my own hands before someone else does it for me. I remember that every day as I head downstairs to begin my mornings. I suppose, in the end, that's what happened. I didn't make my own path, so one was decided for me.*
>
> *My duties are simple, as I learn my new role here, but I think I could be happy. Though I do believe what I miss the most is my piano. There isn't one here, and my fingers cry daily to feel those keys.*
>
> *One day, I hope to have a piano again.*
>
> *Please give my regards to Pa.*

I love you all,

Petronella Dowling

My heart ached as I stared at the words, knowing my family would take each sentence to mean I was truly happy. But everything was a lie. Other than the piano. Well, and the boy who reminded me of Little Chris.

Mama will turn into a steaming kettle when she notices I left Pa out of the letter, but I needed more fury than that. She *should* be mad about it all—about the situation I'd ended up in. About the fact that a part of me was gone forever.

Speaking of which, where had they taken my leg? It was a valid question, was it not? The stub throbbed ominously, but I still refused to lift my skirt and view what remained of the limb.

What would my life even be like without a leg? Certainly not much. I wouldn't get a husband, and therefore would never have children. I'd be a spinster forever. My father's biggest fear.

It was really all his fault. I wouldn't have been in this position at all if he hadn't sent me off. Sure, we would have eventually lost our house after we ran out of belongings to sell, but at least I would be home.

With two legs.

Even the debt was his fault. It would've been easier to rip my soul out and feed it to the dogs than to forgive him.

The thump of the trapdoor made me clutch the paper to my chest.

"It hasn't been an hour yet!" I protested as Oliver climbed up.

"It took less time than I thought." He shrugged, plucking the letter from my fingertips.

"The ink hasn't even dried yet," I protested.

"I'll be careful," he promised, eyes scanning the page with ease.

Even though the majority of it was a lie, the idea of someone outside of the family reading a letter of mine just seemed wrong. Intrusive.

"Did you want to write your Pa his own letter?" Oliver asked, looking over my words one more time.

"No." My tone was too harsh, slicing through the air. "He doesn't deserve to hear from me."

Oliver arched an eyebrow but didn't question it. "All right then." He handed me the envelope and waited as I addressed it. Once done, he folded everything up neatly. "I'll deliver this whenever I have the chance."

My shrug was so sluggish he must've read it as reluctance. He narrowed his eyes, watching closely enough to observe each individual breath I took.

"Aren't you glad to be sending a letter to your family?"

I shrugged again, faster this time. "I suppose. None of it is true. I can't write what I want to." I dragged my eyes away from him and focused on the place where the floor met the wall.

"Would it help if you said everything you wanted to say . . . to me?"

That caught me off guard. *Was there a hesitation in his voice? How could this man be nervous with someone like me?*

I flipped my brown gaze to meet his piercing azure one, squaring my shoulders with as much bravery as I could muster. He reminded me so much of his mother. Tender at first glance, but with that underlying fight always sparkling. "The only thing that would help is if you let me go."

He glanced at the window, the corner of his lip twitching with just a hint of a smile that accentuated the freckles that danced across his nose. "And what would you do, out there alone?" At the moment, nothing about him looked threatening. Every inch of his body was relaxed, showing off his full cheeks and rebellious slouch.

I crossed my arms. "I'd catch a train back home."

He paused to blow a stray piece of tousled coffee-brown hair from his face. Very pointedly, he let his eyes roam down my body, taking his time on my mahogany braids, my uncorseted middle . . .

I crossed my arms over my breasts and glared at him as he continued his perusal, finally stopping at where my right leg should've protruded from the nightgown.

"Stop that. And it's *your* fault," I snapped. I tucked my good leg underneath me, as though it would hide the reality.

The light faded from his eyes, and lines creased his forehead. "I bear more responsibility than I care to think about."

"You should've just let me go."

"There is no way I could've done that." He sat on the armrest and ran his hand through his hair. "You saw me. The rules are simple."

"Oliver James!" The shout was shrill, unmistakably from an upset mother. Stung, he jumped to his feet.

"Wait." I grabbed his wrist before he could get more than two steps.

He turned only partially, his feet pulling him toward his duties. "I'm sorry, I can't keep you company."

"No, no." I shook my head wildly, hair flying all over the place. Sure, my kidnapping was technically his fault. But if he had followed orders, my reality would be so much worse. I wouldn't have my life.

I took a deep breath, remembering all the sermons on forgiveness I had heard. My father still didn't deserve such a thing, but Oliver . . . I spoke before I could talk myself out of it.

"Thank you," I said firmly. The words flowed easier than I had expected.

He blinked in surprise. "You're welcome?"

"For not . . . well . . ." I glanced at the blade tucked into his belt. "You know."

His finger ran over the wooden handle, his body slack and distracted. "I wish it was that simple."

Gooseflesh ran up and down my arms. "I'm safe though, right? You said—"

He held up one finger. "Hush. I'm *trying* to keep you safe, understand?"

It took everything in me to stay still, not to break down into terrified questions and trembling.

I wasn't safe. Sure, I was trapped in an attic, but I had thought I was *safely* trapped in the attic.

He continued, ignoring my inner turmoil. "As things stand, nothing bad will happen to you—"

I couldn't stop the red-hot anger that flew from my lips. "You took my leg!" I shouted.

Oliver pinched the bridge of his nose. "*Anymore.* This life is unpredictable. All I know for certain is that I have to go downstairs and out with the others for a few days."

The cold feeling remained. "That's not reassuring."

"OLIVER!" This time, the shout came from his father. My mouth went dry.

"It's him, isn't it?" I demanded. The memory of that knife against my neck was too real. "When you're gone, will he—"

Oliver pushed a lock of loose hair behind his ear. "My father? Not much makes him happy. But he's going with us."

"But—" My heart fluttered and my arguments lost all traction as his hand found mine, his thumb tracing my skin. Over and over, like a melody meant to put me in a trance.

"I can't give anything more. Just know that I will do my best to keep you safe." He squeezed my hand. "I have to get down there before he comes up here. Okay? Just . . . just don't tell anyone about the letter."

I nodded, still unsure what reaction to settle on. He sent me a small, slightly useless smile before disappearing down the stairs again.

The scolding voice of his father echoed up into the quiet, making my emotions settle into an anxious mess. I lay on my blanket, my small cries melding into gut-wrenching sobs.

CHAPTER EIGHT
The Melody

It was only a few minutes after the crunch of wagon wheels faded into the distance that the trapdoor flopped open.

My eyes focused on the spot, anticipating the food that would inevitably come with Rose. But she was empty-handed. I wrinkled my forehead in confusion as she bustled to check out the window. Satisfied that her men were gone, she came straight to my side, determination driving each step.

"Are you hungry?" she asked. Her accent was strong, dancing around each word.

"Yes?"

"Up with you." She flapped her hands and scooped up my freshly cleaned dress from the end of the settee. "Get dressed. It's time to be a lady."

"What?" I stared at her as she set the dress in my lap. "But what if—"

She waved her hand dismissively. "Henry's too worried about . . . well, he won't come back yet. *Dépêche-toi.* Get dressed. We're going downstairs."

That word was all I needed to jump to action. Balancing to properly get the corset on took a little extra work, but as soon as I was fully clothed, I almost felt whole.

Once I was finished, Rose held me at arm's length, eyes narrowed and mouth at an angle as she scrutinized my appearance.

With a huff, she apparently determined I was worthy for downstairs. "It'll do for now."

It was a struggle to get out of my attic prison. She climbed down first, ready to help me to the floor. I sat on the edge for a long time, leg dangling as I fought to figure out how I would manage the rickety ladder.

Rose didn't give any encouragement as I struggled. She simply stood there, hands on her hips, her expression sour.

I hooked my foot on the lowest rung I could reach. Taking a deep breath, I inched myself down, using my hands. The final descent was more like a fall, but Rose was surprisingly fast for her pregnant state. She caught me just in time.

Without a word, she propped the ladder against the wall, then wrapped her arm around my waist to help me hop toward the staircase.

The hall was wood-paneled on all sides, with a few sconces littered around for light, and two doors on opposing sides.

When we reached the staircase, I didn't want to move. There was a part of me that just wanted to sit and scoot down like a child. If I were alone, I probably would've done just that.

As it was, I grabbed the banister and hopped one step at a time, Rose hovering nearby just in case.

Halfway down the staircase, she broke the concentrated silence. "Oliver told me you wrote a letter to your parents?"

I froze. Hadn't he told me not to mention it? Not sure what else to do, I nodded, biting my lip to concentrate on the task at hand.

"He said you missed something."

I paused again, confused. "Missed something?"

"Your piano." Her eyes narrowed at me, as though I should have known what she was talking about.

My fingers ached at the very mention of the word. I could almost feel my muscles wasting away with every day that went by without practice. "Yes, I miss it," I said, so softly I hardly heard myself.

"Ah, good." She nodded, her mind apparently made up. She motioned for me to resume my journey downstairs.

When I finally made it to the red-and-white rug below, I turned my full attention on her. "Why good?"

"You'll see." She gestured in the direction of the sitting room. In reality, we hadn't traveled far, but my body ached. The stump of my leg throbbed, feeling as though it would explode like an overfed tick at any moment.

Either Rose didn't notice, or she didn't care. She wrapped her arm around my waist, and the journey continued.

We only got a few steps before the front door opened.

"*Merde!*" Rose slapped her hand against her heart, letting me go as she did so.

Without her support, I crashed to the ground. She didn't notice. She had grabbed a book from a nearby side table and was brandishing it at our visitor, unleashing a string of furious French words.

The owner of the male voice yelped as she hit him, but he sidestepped her anyway and rushed to my side. Placing his arms under my shoulders, he hauled me back up to a sitting position.

It was Oliver. "Are you okay?" His face was flushed from a mixture of both amusement and physical exertion; his hairline was damp from sweat.

I grit my teeth against the shooting pain that coursed through my leg. I hadn't fallen directly on it, thankfully. But the sudden movement still made it feel raw and broken.

"I thought you had a job to do?" I asked. He was the last person I expected to see come through the door. After all, hadn't I watched the wagon leave?

Rose crossed her arms firmly over her protruding middle. "*Oui*, you were to help your father with—" She cut herself off.

Oliver placed one hand on his knee, grunting as he stood. "You were right," Oliver grumbled. "Like a child, I'm to stay home with the womenfolk. Donnell took my place."

"Who's Donnell?" I asked. There was a chance I had met him already, but my mind had been so muddled with pain and drink, I would've forgotten anyone.

"Older brother. Between me and Bernard," Oliver said simply. "Pa's perfect pet. Since Pa doesn't approve of my decisions"—his voice took on a low growl—"Donnell hasn't bothered to introduce himself."

Rose patted his shoulder. "Henry is just trying to protect you, you know that."

Oliver gritted his teeth but didn't release whatever quip was hiding on the tip of his tongue. "As I'm too much of a disappointment, I get to wait for correspondence in town. But I don't have to leave just yet." Oliver shrugged, eyes sliding back to me. "What is she doing down here?"

Rose didn't look the slightest bit ashamed. "You're here, so help me move her into the sitting room. *Maintenant.*"

Without protesting, Oliver bent and scooped me into his arms as easily as if I were a child.

The sitting room was dark and cozy. A tall, oak bookshelf, a worn, velvet blue settee, an impressive window that overlooked the porch, and a beautiful cherrywood grand piano.

"You didn't tell me you had a piano!" I gasped the words, reaching for the beautiful instrument before he even set me down.

Oliver shrugged. "Well, I didn't know you played."

Rose made herself comfortable on the settee, leaning to her side in a particularly unladylike fashion, her bump a mountain on top of her. The moment she caught me watching, she fixed her posture and fanned her hand for me to continue. "Go on."

I maneuvered to sit properly, body moving to its predetermined position. Every muscle knew where to go. My right leg, even the part that was long gone, ached to touch the silver pedal. So much so, I could feel every movement tingle throughout my body. My mouth felt dry as I stared at the blank space, fingers placed at their home position.

Though I could nearly feel that cold touch of metal against my foot, the limb was long gone. My stump wiggled under my skirts in its own frustration, as though it could somehow reach its goal.

A sharp pang speared through my chest as I stared down. Everything was wrong. I couldn't even play properly anymore.

"No matter." Rose waved her hand in the air yet again. "Switch feet."

I obeyed, placing my bare left foot on the pedal. It didn't feel right. The shift pushed my whole body too far into the higher notes.

Swallowing the worries, I pressed middle C. The note filled the air—sweet, simple, welcoming. That simple tone told me it would all be okay, assured me that I'd adjust to my new circumstances. Moving a few inches over on the bench was the least of my worries, after all.

My right hand picked out its own melody, the left adding a few notes of its own. Gradually, the song grew into its own beast, my fingers dancing along the keys.

For all I knew, they had left me alone in the room. Just me and the piano. My paradise.

With each run, each count of four, I traveled further into my mind. My imagination soared somewhere in its own mountain paradise, the animals gathering around to listen to each note.

I was far, far away.

Anywhere but this dark home of killers.

At some point, Oliver rested his hand on my shoulder, bringing me back to the present. Only then did I realize tears had begun to trail down my cheeks.

"Are you okay?" he asked.

I nodded, wiping my cheeks as fast as I could. "I'm all right, I'm sorry." I shook my head wildly to dislodge the emotions. "Just missed this more than I thought." It wasn't a lie, though I knew the real reason my emotions had gotten the better of me; I knew I couldn't just stay trapped in this house, this attic anymore.

At some point during my song, Rose had come over to stand behind me. She rubbed my back, transferring the reassurance that only a mother could. "Come, we'll make supper." She held out a hand for me, and I took it.

I couldn't escape, but at least I could eat.

CHAPTER NINE

Cane

They let me sleep on the couch that night, nestled in an old, tattered family quilt. My temporary perch was right across the room from the piano, giving me unlimited access to the sweet sensation of ivory against my fingertips. I spent the majority of the time there, letting my mind go to its happy place over and over again.

If life could stay like this, perhaps it would all be okay.

As long as I could forget that they were all killers. But I knew that would be impossible. As soon as an opportunity presented itself, I *had* to try for freedom.

Oliver slept on a blanket by the front door, as though he thought I was idiotic enough to attempt an escape after dark. He gave me my space, only coming in to listen to me play.

To my surprise, he was gone before I woke in the morning, leaving me alone with the golden light of the sunrise that streamed through the window.

Well, that and the sound of pots and pans clanking on the stove in the kitchen.

Rose was occupied.

Oliver was gone.

Would I ever get another chance?

I swung my left leg to the floor and stood, using the sofa as a crutch.

I wouldn't get far, I knew that. But I owed it to myself to at least try.

With every hop I took, an audible *thump* echoed across the wood floor. I tried to move silently, but it seemed impossible. To my relief, Rose seemed too preoccupied with breakfast to notice.

The space between the couch and the entryway was hard to traverse. I called upon my best balancing skills and just did my best. When no one appeared to stop me, I made the final hop to my escape.

A turtle would have been jealous of my pace as I opened the door. One creak, and it would be all over. I knew it.

A particularly loud clatter sounded from the kitchen, followed by what I could only assume was a string of French curses. That was the distraction I needed.

I shoved open the door and bounced out, not bothering to close it behind me.

Getting off the porch was yet another struggle. I held onto the railing as if my life depended on it—and it very well could have.

When I made it to the middle of the yard, my stump throbbing ominously, I saw him. Oliver was in the center of the dirt road, framed on either side by the muted greens of the late-summer leaves. He looked like he stepped out of a painting, sitting tall on his horse, attention solely on his escaped prisoner.

My heart skipped a beat, and I turned to run, or rather, hop. My efforts were futile. The horse's hooves pressed into the dirt behind me, slowly, deliberately.

I didn't look back. I just rushed for the barn, hoping it would provide some sort of protection.

Oliver released a long sigh. "Come on, you're gonna hurt yourself."

As if to prove him right, I tripped, careening face-first into the dusty ground. The chickens squawked from their pen, likely sympathetic. I could only imagine I looked similar to an injured chicken, hopping along.

He swung from his horse. "You all right?"

I didn't dignify him with an answer. I didn't even turn to look at him.

The leather of the saddle creaked as he reached for something. I flinched, fully expecting him to put me out of my misery. He'd captured his escaped prisoner. How many more chances would he give me?

"Are you gonna kill me now?" I whispered.

"No." He grumbled something under his breath, then took my arm and hauled me up. "I made you something." He thrust a long stick in my direction. I let my eyes roam over it, noting the way the sun glistened on the polish. It was relatively simple, the only real design from the natural spirals that spanned the whole way to the bottom.

I took it, surprised by its light weight. I traced my fingers down the smooth grains, marveling at how the sunlight brought out the rich reds of the mahogany.

It was a crutch. At the age of twenty-four. The very idea of being reliant on such a thing sent chills down my spine and sparked a queasy feeling in my stomach. As nauseous as I was, I did my best to ignore it. A crutch could be my ticket to freedom. Or at least add to it.

"Thank you," I whispered, meaning the words. But was it just a bribe to get me to obey?

My stomach swirled. I placed the tip firmly against the soft ground and pressed my weight against it. It felt strange, but certainly more secure than a single wobbly foot. Oliver held his hands out like a worried father as I leaned all my weight on it and attempted a hop. Or would it be called a step? Regardless, my success brought a smile to my face.

"Good job." He grinned right back at me, that childlike expression taking over. I could almost imagine what he looked like as a little one, a mess of energy and tangled brown hair.

Before he became a killer.

That queasy feeling came rushing right back as I took another step. My shoulders sagged. More freedom or not, he wouldn't be letting me go. I was the prisoner of a trained killer, and that was that.

His nose wrinkled and eyebrows rose in his confusion. "What's wrong? You hurting?"

I shook my head rapidly. "No, not that." Though the fall had definitely not been good for me. My limb throbbed so hard it felt like it might explode.

He held the horse's reins lightly in one hand as he leaned against the weathered, apple-red wall of the barn, crossing his arms over his chest. "Tell me?"

I hesitated, glancing at the cane. The freedom that I could look at but not touch.

I closed my eyes tightly, gathering up the courage. He'd caught me trying to escape—could I really question him? But I knew I'd never see sunlight again if I didn't at least try to speak up. "I want out."

He froze so solidly he stopped breathing.

"I don't want to live my life trapped up there." I gestured toward the house with my chin, fighting to stand tall, brave, ready to be the one in control. It may have helped me feel better, but it didn't help get the answers I desired.

He sighed, running his fingers through his hair. They snagged in a particularly difficult knot near his shoulders. He avoided my eyes, instead focusing on the detangling. "You have to understand—"

"No," I snapped. "*I* don't need to understand. I'm not some cow trapped in your barn."

His eyes drifted closed, likely debating on how to deal with my stubbornness. "Just a few more steps, and you could at least achieve the barn part . . ." He muttered the words as he scrubbed at his temple. "There is only so much I can do. I'm doing everything I can to keep you safe, keep you *alive*." Without warning, his clear gaze bored straight into mine. "I'll do everything I can to give you freedom."

It wasn't the answer I wanted, not anywhere close. I slumped against the cane. "You can't get me a room downstairs?"

He shook his head solemnly. "No. But I'm doing what I can to change that. Just—" He glanced back down the road, as if checking for witnesses. "Don't get yourself into mischief. When they're gone and it's safe, you're welcome to live life as you please around here. Just as you have lately."

I prayed that my stare shot bolts of anger straight into his heart. His horse stamped nervously, but Oliver didn't react. "That's not good enough. *You're* the one who trapped me here!"

He shook his head, the toe of his boot tapping against the dust. "There wasn't much else I could do. Do you understand? If I let you go, and word got around, it would destroy everything we stand for." He stood straight as the barn itself, looking very much like the murderer he was, strong and opposing with eyes of blue steel. "And I know, killing you wouldn't be what you preferred."

I wouldn't have been surprised if he could see the smoke coming out of my ears. "And what do you *stand* for?" I crossed my arms. "Killing people?"

He threw his hands in the air, grumbling something I couldn't understand. "I can't discuss that, I'm sure you know that. But *you* need to get back upstairs before they get home."

I wasn't giving up that easily. I stood straighter, puffing out my chest. "Did you, though? Did you kill anyone while you were gone today?" Some part of me felt triumphant. I had him. He squirmed under my gaze, if only slightly.

He let out a long breath. "Nella, I can't—"

"You did, didn't you? A murderer is all you are. If I get out, I'll notify *everyone*. I know what you look like. Your posters will be—"

He pressed his hand against my mouth, looking down the road in case his father materialized from the trees. "Hush. I just went to town. Now, get back inside. They're coming home early. Ma will help you upstairs."

I twisted my head to the side to free it, but otherwise, I stayed silent.

He watched me for a long moment, likely waiting to see if I was going to explode on him again. When he finally spoke, his voice was stiff with his forced patience. "I told you I would do what I could. My plan is not to keep you trapped here."

I ran my hand over the crutch again. It wasn't like I could travel very far until I mastered how to use it, anyway. I sighed. "Fine." I tapped the stick with my pointer finger. "I'll go inside like a good little prisoner." Standing as straight as humanly possible with my chin up high, I waltzed past him, my fingernails digging into the wood of my new cane.

CHAPTER TEN

Town

I practically attacked Oliver each time he stepped onto my floor for the next two weeks. "Can I come downstairs now?"

A friendly smirk would cross his face, and he would pass me food, drink, or whatever he came to deliver. He never once came up just to pass the time. "It's not safe just yet."

Each time he said it, my reaction was a little worse. First, I acted simply disappointed. But by the end of the two weeks, I had my arms crossed like an angry child.

I craved the breeze, the smell of fresh morning dew, the sun on my arms. I needed to feel the keys against my fingers, hear the melodies as they flowed through the air.

When he finally came for something different, I must've fallen asleep in the window like a pet cat. I had to bask in the sun however I could, let those rays warm my forever-fair skin. Oliver woke me by shaking my shoulder. The sun had moved during my respite, blinding me as soon as I dared open my eyes.

I jumped, shielding my face from the harsh rays.

"Sleepy?" He grinned. "The morning's half gone already."

I glanced outside, hunting for any sign of change. The trees waved in the light breeze, a mix of greens, reds, and golds. No stranger came down the path, nothing new.

"They left," he announced. "Took the wagon this morning, probably while you were sleeping. Do you wanna come downstairs?"

Instant energy. I practically vaulted upright, the world spinning dangerously as I gripped the crutch. Freedom. Finally.

"Careful . . ." Oliver held out his arms to steady me. "I'll carry you." When he saw my face wrinkle at the idea, he held up one finger. "It'll be easier to get downstairs that way, will it not?"

My eyes traveled down the crutch and to my single bare foot, peering out under my skirt. It would certainly be easier to have his help, but some part of me squirmed at the knowledge that I was nowhere close to the heaviest human he'd ever carried.

He didn't wait for my consent. He crouched low for me to crawl onto his back. I hesitated for as long as I could. He was my ticket downstairs, to the piano. I couldn't do it alone.

"Come on," he urged.

Sighing, I wrapped my arms around his neck and hopped on. He caught me easily. In fact, every step he took with me on his back seemed easy.

All I could imagine was a fully grown man slung over his shoulder. No matter how hard I tried, I couldn't erase the image of the victim's blood dripping down his chest. It would inch its way lower and lower until it pooled at the tip of his limp hair, then finally drip audibly to the floor.

The thought made me shiver and my stomach swirl. He was a murderer. The warmth that radiated from his back as he traversed the ladder, the way he held his breath whenever he had to move with care, his messy locks that tickled my nose—it all belonged to a murderer.

Even so, he would be my ticket downstairs. He had essentially saved my life, right? That had to excuse him for some of those wrongdoings.

Right?

When we reached the ground floor, I moved to dismount. He responded by holding tighter to my legs. "Just stay, it'll be faster."

I pointed over his shoulder to the piano, my forearm against his ear. "I've been practicing with the crutch, I can do it myself."

I could practically feel the answering smirk radiate through his body. "I'd be willing to bet that you'll like my idea better." He waltzed to the front door and scooped up a single shoe. One of Rose's, I assumed.

"You're taking me outside?" My voice resembled the excited shriek of a toddler, but he didn't seem to care. He chuckled and set me down on the nearby chair, handing me the shoe. I bent to put it on, the corset pressing hard into my thighs. I didn't care. Excitement bubbled through my body with every button I closed.

"Oliver." Rose strode from the kitchen, wringing her hands on an apron. "You know full well this isn't a good idea."

His entire body slumped. "I know, I know. We're just going to see if there's a letter from her parents. We'll be back long before they even consider turning home."

She *tsked* her tongue. "You'd better be right."

"They have a two-hour ride one way. *Then* they have . . ." He hesitated and turned his head to look back at me. "The mission. We'll be back long before they are."

I raised one brow, but they both ignored the unspoken question.

Rose huffed. "Unless Martin brings news like last time."

That stopped Oliver's breathing for just a moment.

I poked the back of Oliver's leg with my foot. "Last time?" Again, he ignored me.

"He won't. Everything was perfect. It'll be easy from now on, I'm sure of it."

Rose stared down her nose at him, the picture of a scolding teacher. "It was perfect when you were on the train too."

Oliver rapidly shook his head, as though to dislodge the worries. His voice was a growl when he spoke. "We're not discussing that."

"Just be careful," Rose said. "I'm not responsible for whatever happens."

"I know." Avoiding her gaze, he pressed the cane into my hand. He hardly waited for me to stand before ushering me out the front door.

All of my questions flew from my mind as I struggled to catch up. "I'm not *that* fast!" I protested, grabbing onto the doorframe for support.

He glanced back at his mother, who shook her head as she walked away. "Sorry," he muttered to me.

"I'm still slow," I grumbled, regaining my footing. "There's only so much practice I can get up there."

After he hauled me off the porch, we began the agonizing trek away from the house. The air was just growing cool for the autumn season. Everything smelled clean, crisp. Though, likely anything would smell that way after being trapped in an attic for so long.

My brain replayed what he and his mother said over and over. Even the beautiful weather and simple freedom couldn't push the reality away.

"What would happen if they came home early?" I finally asked.

"Nothing."

I let out a growl of protest. "Something would happen, otherwise your ma wouldn't have been worried."

"They won't come home. That's that." He shot me a firm glare. "I'm finished talking about it."

Effectively ending the conversation, he walked a little faster, leaving me to trail behind.

"Oliver?" I asked breathlessly.

He sighed and stopped, feet side by side like a soldier at attention. "What?"

"I can't keep up."

He waited for me to catch up, then scooped me onto his back. The process was only slightly less awkward than before. At least the outside air helped diminish the vision of a dead man over his shoulder.

"Oliver?" I asked after we had traveled a while longer.

"Hmm?"

"I thought of something I haven't asked you."

"What is that?" He sounded like he was talking to an annoying sibling who wouldn't stop asking "why."

"What state are we in?"

He sighed but otherwise didn't react. "Tennessee."

I brightened only slightly at the idea. At least I had made it to the correct state. "Where at in Tennessee?"

"South. Chattanooga is the closest major town."

"That's where your pa is going?"

"Yeeep." He dragged the word out just a little longer than necessary.

"Why didn't they take you?"

He stopped walking. "I'll make you walk the rest of the way if you keep asking questions I can't answer."

I didn't push him further. He messed up on the train—that *had* to be the reason he couldn't go with them on this journey. Was it simply because he brought me home with him? Or was it because he did something else wrong?

Despite my best efforts, I couldn't stay silent. My imagination swirled every which way, thinking of all sorts of fanciful reasons he wasn't allowed to help.

"But why?"

He froze again for just a moment. His decision made, he stalked to the edge of the trail and released my thighs. I was slow to grasp his plan, so I didn't tighten my grip on his neck. When he leaned back, I fell butt-first into the pile of leaves. I squealed the entire way down.

"Oliver!" I protested, fighting to get myself upright again. "What if I landed on my leg? And you know, I can't keep up with you!"

He shrugged. "I told you not to ask questions like that."

"But you didn't tell me *why*. I know *nothing*." I reached for his hand to help me up, but he didn't make a move to assist.

"You're not to know."

"I can't leave the attic without you by my side. Who am I going to tell?"

"One never knows what could happen."

I struggled to stand, using the tree for balance. "Does that mean there's a chance you'll let me go home?"

Like a hawk on the prowl, he glared down his nose at me, one eyebrow raised. "Stop wasting time. Let's go." Apparently deciding we didn't have time for my limping walk, he scooped me onto his back and continued down the dirt road.

It was a long walk, though beautiful with the rapidly coloring trees that lined either side of the pathway. It took a tremendous amount of effort not to ask him any more ques-tions. Each time my mouth opened to discover more about his world, I had to remind myself that I didn't want to ruin my chance at going to town.

When we broke from the trees, I slipped from his back. Despite its small size, the town was busy. The clang of a black-smith's hammer echoed all around, and the stench of the stable took over the rest of my senses. The mercantile was well stocked and busy. As we passed, I could see several women inside poking around at this or that. A gorgeous dress hung in a window, ready to tempt any woman who might look its way.

Oliver didn't give me much of a chance to dawdle. I wasn't one for drooling over dresses, anyway. There was only one thing on my mind: a letter from Mama.

It didn't take us long to reach the post office. People edged out of our way when we got close. Whether they were curious about who I was, or just nosy about what I did to my leg, I didn't know. It felt like their eyes followed me everywhere I went. I had to have been quite the spectacle.

I did my best to ignore it, though I inched closer and closer to Oliver's side, hoping it would take the attention off me. But maybe, if news of Mr. Murray's death had already traveled, the onlookers would recognize me from a missing poster. If there were any in circulation . . .

As we stepped inside the post office, I examined the adver-tisements tacked onto the wall. Not a single one had my face. I hadn't really expected anything different, but a sad sigh still escaped my lips.

Oliver stepped right up to the counter, his shoulders squared. "Any letters for Petronella Dowling?"

The young girl behind the counter didn't look a day over sixteen. "One moment, I'll check." She gave him a sugary smile before turning toward the wall of well-organized letters behind her.

The advertisements on the wall didn't hold much of interest. A far-off bank robber here, a man wanted for drunk or disorderly conduct there, but otherwise, there wasn't much to pay attention to.

Except one.

WANTED:

Information involving a murder on a passenger train, thirty miles outside Chattanooga. Suspect believed to be six feet tall, brown hair, blue eyes. Any information, contact the sheriff.

I nudged Oliver with my elbow. He ignored me completely until the woman handed him my letter. I hardly noticed.

"I know," he said under his breath as he turned for the door. "Let's go."

He held it open for me as I hobbled on out. "But what if they catch you?" I whispered.

"They don't have any information *to* catch me." He held the letter out for me, most likely to distract me from questioning him further. "You want to read it now? Or wait till we get home?"

Eagerly, I nodded. I practically skipped to the nearest bench and plopped down. It was impossible to get the envelope open fast enough. My heart swelled with more excitement than I had felt in weeks.

Oliver didn't sit beside me. Instead, he stood on the edge of the sidewalk, monitoring everyone else around. At least I wouldn't have to worry about someone sneaking up on me with a guard like that.

Darling Nella,

We were growing worried when we didn't hear from you. It's been months! Each and every one of us is grateful that your reason was nothing too serious. One never knows what could happen on a long journey such as yours.

Little Chris caught a slight chill shortly after you left. It is possible that the two of you became ill with the same thing. I'm just thankful you weren't any sicker.

When your brother was feeling better, he made the decision to move in with Miriam. That way he can help her husband easier. I told him he could easily walk there in the mornings, but he wouldn't listen. I believe he wanted away from the house and its emptiness.

Your sister came over for a few days this week to help decorate the house. As you well know, everything was left in quite a state. She brought a few of the odds and ends from her own home and helped me make a few things. The house doesn't look nearly as lonely now, with a few knickknacks adorning the mantel.

Miriam's baby is growing nicely. I can't wait for the day when tiny feet will grace our floors! I will be a grand-mother, can you imagine? When prodded for what they plan to name the tiny thing, Miriam refused to say. She says it's a surprise, but I truly believe they haven't decided yet. Of course, as you know, we are pushing for a fourth generation of Christopher.

Your father misses you greatly and sends his love. We both hope that one day you will forgive him. One day, you will see he was doing his best for his family. Protecting us all is his God-given duty, as you well know.

I skimmed through the next few paragraphs. It was mainly composed of the same thing: trying to convince me to forgive my father.

"Not gonna happen," I muttered under my breath.

> *Your father has promised me not to go gambling again, and he has been true to his word so far. Every day, he goes to work and comes right back home for supper. I think this finally helped him realize where he needed to be. Praise be to God for that!*

"What in heaven's name are *you* doing out here?" Oliver's voice jerked me straight out of the letter. I wadded it up, hiding it in my palm, eyes darting every which way until I saw who had alarmed him.

CHAPTER ELEVEN

Caught

Oliver focused intently on the imposing figure coming out of the shadowy alley.

The man froze when he registered who the voice belonged to. His ashy blond hair was tied at the nape of his neck with a strip of leather, not a single strand daring to escape. Every part of his appearance was pristine. There wasn't a smudge on his shirt, or even a shadow of a beard on his angled jaw. The complete opposite of Oliver. I'd seen him through the window, but other than the chaotic day of my arrival, he hadn't bothered to come upstairs.

"Oh!" Donnell gathered himself as best as he could, brushing his hands down the front of his pants. "I didn't expect the two of you to be in town."

"Well, we didn't expect you to be here either," Oliver said matter-of-factly. "Why are you here and not in Chattanooga? Is Pa back already too?"

Donnell glanced at me, eyes narrowing. "No . . . he's still there with the others."

Oliver took a small step to the side, partially covering me from view. "Then why are you *here*?"

"My job took me elsewhere."

Oliver scoffed. "Your job?"

"Yes, my job."

Oliver ran his hand through his hair and took a deep, calming breath. "How about you tell me why you're *actually* here?"

Donnell crossed his arms and glowered at his younger brother. The sharp angles of his face made him look all the more dangerous. "You first. You took *her* out." He nodded in my direction.

Oliver spared me the smallest of glances. "What Pa don't know won't hurt him."

A low laugh rattled Donnell's body. "Oh, I see then." His humor was cut short. He stepped so lightly he seemed to glide across the hard ground. He didn't stop until his chest practically touched Oliver's. They were the same height, shoulder to shoulder, nose to nose. "That'll be my answer too: 'What Pa don't know won't hurt him.' Got it?"

Oliver held his chin a smidge higher. "Is that a *threat*?"

"Is it?"

My stomach swirled in a combination of confusion and anxiety as I watched. From what I understood, Donnell was part of the mission Oliver had been banned from. Unless there was some vital reason for him to be dropped off near home, he should be a good two hours from the others.

Oliver refused to back down. "Does Pa even know you're gone?"

"Of course." Donnell rolled his eyes and backed off a step. "I'm not a simpleton."

"Then *why*." It wasn't a question.

Donnell exhaled roughly. "I went to a cabin to gather information, got it?"

"Then why are you here?"

"Finished." Donnell shrugged. "I don't answer to you."

Oliver held his hand to his forehead, rubbing the spot between his eyebrows. He took in several semi-controlled breaths, his jaw clinched so tight that veins popped in his neck. He reminded me of a werewolf, ready to transform at any moment. "When is Pa coming back?"

The grin that spread across Donnell's cheeks sent shivers up my spine. A cold, sickened look spilled across Oliver's face.

With a curse, he gripped my arm and practically yanked me onto his back. My stump hit the edge of the chair, and a squeak of pain escaped my lips. Ma's letter fluttered elegantly to the dirt, forgotten in his rush.

"Hold on, hold on!" I reached as far as I could, throwing Oliver off balance just enough to capture his attention.

Donnell chuckled and scooped it up. His glee spread farther on his face as he scanned the precious words meant only for me.

"Give it back!" I waved my hand in his direction, as though the letter would float into the air and return to my possession.

"Letters too?" Donnell placed his hands on his knees, erupting in sick, horrifying laughter.

"Just give it back and let us go." Oliver didn't wait for him to obey. He snatched the letter out of Donnell's hands and tucked it into his pocket. "I didn't see you here, you didn't see us."

Satisfied, Donnell tipped his hat in our direction and simply wandered off.

Oliver wasn't in a "slow and steady" mood anymore. He practically ran out of town. Or at least, raced as fast as he could without jostling me to death.

We rushed along the dirt road, me clinging to his back like a monkey from one of those exotic travel books.

I held on tightly, nails sure to leave marks in his skin. "Oliver, please! What is it?" The fear that radiated off his back was enough to trigger my own dread. He completely ignored my demands, no matter how many times I repeated them.

I knew very well we needed to beat his father home. I would always think of Henry as a man from hell. There was no way he would be kind, especially considering his initial greeting to me involved a knife to my neck. I could still feel it, thin and cold against my skin. The fear turned to ice, and I shut my eyes against the memory.

"I just want to go home . . ." I whispered, not expecting a response.

I didn't get one.

We were probably around halfway through our frantic flight when the rattle of wagon wheels interrupted the peaceful birdsong.

Oliver let out a defeated sigh and slowed to a walk.

I glanced behind us, seeing the wagon and its tall driver. They weren't far away, and they were gaining on us quickly.

"Why not hide in the trees?" My voice was a terrified whisper, my heart beating nearly out of my chest.

For whatever reason, he didn't listen. Perhaps he knew we'd already been seen. Maybe he knew it was no use, anyway—they would always know.

My eyes didn't leave the wagon as it drew close. The familiar bay horse skillfully brought it right up beside us, stopping almost before the driver voiced a deep "Whoa."

The tension in Oliver's shoulders turned him to stone. His breathing was sharp and shallow; his eyes didn't stray from the path ahead of us—the pathway to safety.

"What excuse do you give?" Henry demanded. His voice was calm, but only in the way of a venomous snake poised to strike.

Oliver's voice was controlled, but nowhere near timid. "I won't give one."

"Where have you been?"

"Post office."

I hadn't realized my hands had turned to fists, balling the back of Oliver's shirt. He gently pried my fingers free before placing me on the dusty ground.

The cover of the trees wouldn't save us anymore, but every ounce of my body yearned for its perceived safety.

"Get in, we're going home," Henry said, though he clicked to the horse to carry on. The mare walked obediently, unaffected by the rapidly rising stress levels around her.

Oliver scooped me up and sat me in the back of the wagon with such ease I didn't have time to protest. He then swung beside his father, silent as death.

Neither of them said a single word. They hardly even breathed.

My own breathing was quick, terrified. I felt like a trapped rabbit, nearly ready to be tossed into a tasty stew. Where was everyone else? Weren't all the boys along for the mission (or whatever it was) in Chattanooga?

By the time we arrived back at the two-story home, I didn't have any more answers. My stomach churned as I focused on the little attic window. It was the last place on earth I wanted to go. A small room with absolutely nothing to do.

I might as well have been in jail.

As Henry jumped from the wagon, he gave very different instructions.

"Basement."

Oliver's instant fear was tangible, even from a good four or five feet away. "I'll just take her—"

"No. Basement."

Oliver hesitated for a long moment. The two men stared at each other, unblinking, unmoving. One demanding and firm, the other horrified.

With a deep sigh, Oliver must've pushed his worries into some dark box, and then he helped me out of the wagon. "Do you want to walk? Or me to carry you?"

With a glance back at Henry, I took the small cane from Oliver. "I'll walk."

Henry ignored us and led the horses into the barn.

With each step, the panic sank deeper into the pit of my stomach. I had to get away. He could easily kill me, especially after being caught in town. What reason would he have to keep me around any longer?

I stopped in my tracks just before the steps to the porch, toes turned to face the trees, heart yearning to run.

"That would be a very, very bad idea," Oliver whispered. His voice felt like ice trailing down my spine.

I took a small step—well, more of a shuffle—toward freedom. He didn't stop me. He knew as well as I did that to run would be the end of me.

"Where are the others?" I asked, my voice barely more than a breath.

Oliver didn't wait for me to turn around. He scooped me up and carried me over the steps and into the house. "I'm not sure. I assume they're already inside somewhere."

I didn't move an inch once he set me in the dimly lit entryway. The front door sealed behind us with a sickening sense of finality. "They're not in the basement?"

"No." His voice was a bitter poison.

The nerves that tickled at my stomach only grew to become their own breed of monster. "Why the basement?"

No response. He pulled on my sleeve to get me moving again. There wasn't another option other than to follow.

The windows were open, sending the rapidly cooling fall air all around to kill off every ounce of stress from the heat of summer. The smell of fresh bread permeated the rooms. Everything was so peaceful inside—almost homey.

Noticing that made me sick.

CHAPTER TWELVE

Basement

The basement stairs were tucked away at the back of the kitchen. Arthur stood in the entryway, one cracker in his mouth and another already on its way.

"Oh!" He shoved the crackers into his mouth and struggled to swallow them, as though no one would know about his snacking.

"Where's Ma?" Oliver asked.

"I dunno." Arthur shrugged. "Think she ran outta flour? Or was it milk?" He scrunched up his nose as he struggled to remember. "She went up the mountain to see if the Marrots have any."

Oliver's shoulders sagged. "If she gets back before . . ." He almost choked on his words. "Make sure she doesn't come inside? If she interferes . . ."

Arthur looked from me, to Oliver, then back to me. "Ooh . . . I'll do that." He grabbed a lantern from the counter, lit it, and then placed it in my hands.

"Thanks," Oliver rasped. I stayed silent, my entire body thrumming with the danger.

Oliver nodded, nearly a statue with how leisurely his movements were as he made his way to the staircase, then into the darkness below.

Oliver gritted his teeth more with every step we took. Controlled by his anxieties, his grip gradually tightened, then relaxed only slightly. As soon as his mind wandered again, the tightening resumed.

My heart thumped painfully, each breath grating at my lungs. I didn't know what I expected, but I knew it wasn't going to be a field of flowers.

I would have taken a field of bumblebees over what awaited us. The lantern's light was barely enough to bring the objects out of the shadows. It was a small space, but it was filled.

After setting me in the corner, Oliver took on the job of lighting the candles throughout the room. With every golden glow that echoed across the walls, the sinking finality of the situation pressed harder on my shoulders.

Without my permission, my body sank to the ground. My chest ached from panting for the breath that I couldn't quite grasp.

Most people kept herbs, onions, and potatoes in their basements. Though this room certainly had those on a shelf over by the stairway, that was where the normalcy ended.

The table closest to me was large, with hinged, wooden slats placed on both the head and foot. It almost looked like a tall, uncomfortable bed, other than the fact that each slat had two round holes. Two on the bottom to trap ankles, and two smaller ones on top to trap wrists. On the opposite wall, other tools of their trade hung. There were different whips with varying degrees of malice, several strips of dirty black cloth, and random objects I could only imagine the purpose of.

In the far corner was a prison cell. There was no chair inside, nothing. It was well cleaned, ready for its next visitor. I only prayed it wouldn't be me. Prayed it wouldn't be me for any of it.

Once Oliver was satisfied with the dancing lights around the room, he came to sit beside me. He cupped my hand in his and just held it. His skin was cold and clammy, which did nothing but cause my body to shake.

My voice came out, choked from the lack of air my panic allowed. "What is he going to do to me?"

Oliver squeezed my hand but otherwise said nothing.

"Tell me!" I searched his face for a clue. There was nothing hiding there, only blank worry. "Is he . . ." I swallowed hard, trying to push the panic into the background. It didn't work. "Is he going to kill me?" My voice cracked and a tear escaped, cleaning a solitary path along my dusty face.

To my relief, he had a response to that. "I doubt it."

"What if he does?" My voice jumped an octave, hitting the wrong note. "I really don't want to die. Why won't you tell me what's going on?"

He wrapped one arm around me and held me close to his side. I leaned my head against him, breathing deeply, taking in the scents of sweat and the freedom of the forest. I would take as much calm as I could from him, though I could feel the tension hiding right under the surface.

"I won't let him kill you," he promised, whispering into my knotted hair.

"But you can't control him."

"No," he agreed. "But I won't let him kill you."

His closeness worked magic. Something about being held close like a child chased the panic away, leaving only the sore ache of worry. No part of me balked about being so close to a man. Considering I lived in an attic, it seemed perfectly acceptable. I certainly didn't need a reputation anymore.

I curled closer against him until the pounding of footsteps on the stairway reached my ears. I sat bolt upright, the panic welling back to the surface. Oliver grabbed for my hand again and held it so tight it almost hurt. The slight pain didn't faze me; it gave me something to focus on other than the man who made his way into the candlelit room.

Henry moved confidently to the center, right by the unidentified table. He squared his broad shoulders; his brown eyes were so dark they looked like they could annihilate anything in their way. Oliver pulled himself to his feet, ready for whatever was to come his way. He left me where I was, cowered behind his unwavering legs.

"Why were you in town?" Henry was calm. Too calm. The growl that laced his voice reminded me of a tiger from the traveling circus. Ready, perhaps even excited, to pounce at any moment.

"I'm sorry, sir. I shouldn't have—"

"Whether you should or shouldn't have is not up for discussion. I asked you *why*." His eyes were shadowed by his brow, only furthering his menacing appearance.

Oliver took a deep breath. "We sent a letter to her family so they could know she is all right." He held up his hand before he could be interrupted. "I read it over. There was nothing about us inside. It was safe."

Henry's single raised eyebrow held enough shock and disappointment to knock a person dead. "You sent a letter?"

"Well, yes—"

"From here?" His warning tone was nothing short of seething.

Oliver shook his head rapidly. "No, we used the address of the post office, and her name."

Henry's sigh was so lengthy it sounded like the hiss of a snake. "I'd tell you to stop the letters, but if you did that now, they'd show up looking for her. Which you would have *known* had you consulted me about this first."

"Yes, sir."

My own nerves relaxed only slightly. Perhaps his lecture would be the only consequence.

When Henry nodded in my direction, I wished I could faint on command.

"Get her up." Without waiting to see if we would obey, Henry made his way to the terrifying instruments on the wall.

Even with Oliver hauling me to my feet, my good leg didn't want to cooperate. It buckled on itself. I couldn't force my mind into a false, calm submission. A patient companion, Oliver helped me every step of the way, letting me prop myself up against his side.

"There were rules about going to town," Henry said. He picked a wooden-handled whip and turned listlessly back toward us.

I clung to Oliver, every ounce of my energy focused on fighting the urge to collapse to the cold dirt floor. He held onto my arm just tight enough to keep me from collapsing. Bile rose in my throat, bitter and sharp. For once, I wanted to be dead. Immediately. Anything was better than being trapped in the corner of such a dingy, horrifying room.

Henry's commanding voice made me jump. "I want you to tell me exactly what our agreement was."

After all the time and energy they had spent feeding and nursing me back to health, we had reached the end. Henry wouldn't let me live anymore. Especially now. I knew how to make it to the house from town, I knew roughly where the town was when compared to Chattanooga. I could bring the sheriff straight to their door, and likely collect a hefty reward.

Oliver squeezed my arm, whether to remind me of the promise he'd made before, or to make sure I didn't say anything that could make it worse, I wasn't sure.

Oliver's voice was strong and unwavering. "She is allowed to stay if, and only if, she remains in the attic. It will be my responsibility to take care of her, my responsibility, if something goes wrong."

It felt as though the lid of my coffin had been sealed, cutting off any chance of freedom I would ever have.

"Good job, you were listening." Henry tapped the handle of the whip against his palm, the thud sounding like an unenthusiastic applause. "My first reaction to this predicament was to make you take care of it. After all, if you can't take on such a responsibility, we won't be taking the blame for it."

Oliver stiffened but otherwise didn't react. I felt dizzy, the world around me fading in and out. This was it. He was going to kill me.

"But in the end, I want you to learn from this." Henry tossed the whip to Oliver, who caught it with terrifying ease. "Fifty lashes."

Oliver stared at the long torture device, turning it over and over in his hands, resigning himself to the sentence in only a few seconds. It took me much longer to grasp it. The moment I understood, my blood ran cold. I pressed my back against the wall as hard as possible, as if I could disappear behind it.

Oliver wouldn't be the one on the business end of the whip.

I would.

"But I didn't know!" My voice was small, a futile squeak in the cold, damp room.

"*He* did," Henry said. "Get to it." He flicked his fingers in my general direction.

Oliver turned toward me, taking his time with his every movement. "I'm sorry."

I set my jaw and stared at him, squaring my shoulders with faux bravery. He promised I wouldn't die, sure. But part of that agreement had been to keep me safe. At least I heard it that way. "You promised."

Pain shot through his shadowed blue eyes, but he held firm. "Let's get this over with." He traced a circle in the air, beckoning me to turn my back to him. He gingerly placed each of my palms against the wall and positioned my torso in the desired place. My knee shook so hard it was a miracle I remained upright.

"You're forgetting something." Henry sounded like a father who was sick of walking his son through a simple task.

"She deserves at least *some* dignity," Oliver argued.

"No, she deserves nothing. She's your prisoner. Do as you were taught."

Taught. It was obvious they'd gone through training for various things, but somehow the idea of being taught to punish people one way or another made my body tremble even more.

Oliver's hand touched my arm ever so gently. He traced up my sleeve to the collar, then around the front until he touched the first button.

"No," I snapped, whirling around so quickly I nearly fell over.

"Please, Nella." Oliver's eyes were pleading, both for forgiveness and cooperation.

No matter how many times I looked around the room, there was no escape. I couldn't run, I couldn't hop fast enough. Escape was impossible. I glared straight at Oliver, hoping he could see my vow to make him pay.

"I'll do it myself," I said, my voice surprisingly strong.

With shaky fingers, I undid the buttons on the bodice. Before I could lose my nerve, I let it fall from my shoulders and to the floor. I was slower with the skirt, my fingers slick with nervous sweat as they worked on the ties. But even that task was done too soon. The petticoat was next, a helpless sob bursting from my body as it pooled on the top rung of the crinoline. I yanked the tie for the hoop skirt and let it fall. It sprang onto the floor before crumpling into the pathetic pile of fabric.

All I had left was the corset and chemise—the very things I wanted to keep the most.

The corset was likely a large reason they wanted me to disrobe in the first place, and I knew it. My fingers moved like they were frozen, each snap on the busk feeling like another step closer to death. When the last hook was undone, I chucked the whole thing to the floor with a shaky sob.

I hoped my anger hid most of my humiliation. They didn't deserve the satisfaction of knowing how exposed I truly felt. But that sickening feeling still bubbled inside, threatening to drown me at any moment.

Henry cleared his throat, drawing another small sob from my lips. I clamped a hand over my mouth to force the emotion back down.

Oliver's touch on my shoulder was so soft, so misplaced in the dingy room. I refused to look at him, just kept my nose pressed firmly to the cool wall.

"It has to be all of it." His own voice wavered as he said the words.

Decisions swirled in my mind. Be stubborn and fight to quite literally save my hide, or give in and pray for it to be over soon.

My response was feeble, my entire soul knowing any resistance was futile. "No."

CHAPTER THIRTEEN

Brutal

I sneaked a glance at Oliver. He closed his eyes and took a somewhat shaky breath, likely to gather any patience he had left. "We don't have that option."

If I didn't do it myself, he would. If he couldn't do it, Henry would certainly take on the job. There really was no option.

"Fuck you." Never before had I uttered those forbidden words. They seethed through my teeth, nearly silent and full of the deadly threat I desired. He flinched but stood strong.

I took the biggest breath I could manage and pulled my chemise over my head, pulled the tie on the drawers, and kicked them both away. This left me standing there shaking in nothing but my stockings and shoes, with my arms clamped over my chest.

The basement air was much colder than I anticipated on my thighs and rear. Whether it was humiliation, cold, or terror that caused me to tremble, I couldn't be sure.

Oliver nudged my hand with such gentleness it was almost laughable, then tapped the point on the wall where he wanted me to place it. He did the same with the other hand. I followed his orders, fingers balling into the tightest fists possible as I fought the urge to cover myself back up.

Oliver took a small step back, shifting around until he found the optimal position. Each nervous turn of the handle of the whip, each anxious breath, sounded as loud as a train. Every moment he waited, my humiliation rose a little higher, threatening to drown me.

When the first strike hit my naked back, I was far from prepared. I twisted and jerked away, a scream sneaking through my tightly pressed lips.

I wouldn't forgive him. Never.

By the second or third strike, my fingernails bit into my palms, drawing a trickle of blood. Each thwack blended into a demeaning, miserable tempest. With each lash, my body slumped toward the ground. My healthy leg shook violently, threatening to buckle underneath me. The sobs racked my body so hard I couldn't have seen straight even if I tried.

At one point, Oliver paused his abuse and leaned over my prone form. His light touch on my arm was almost comforting, but I still shied away.

"I'm sorry," he whispered. The stubble of his sprouting beard teased the edges of my ears, his warm breath against my neck a stark difference to the pain that radiated across my back. My body curled a little closer to his protective embrace, my mind swaying into his perceived safety.

"I need you to stand up." His words felt just like the lash of the whip.

I shook my head wildly, gripping his shirtsleeve.

"*Oliver*," Henry growled.

Oliver ignored him. "I'm doing my best. But I need you to stand just a little longer. Please . . ."

"Stop this right *now*." Henry's footsteps were straight out of a nightmare, heavy and final.

Oliver hardly had time to move before his father shoved him out of the way and gripped my arm.

"No!" I heard myself scream as this spawn of Satan forced me back up. His bony fingers pressed into the flesh of my arm, ensuring they would leave a bruise in their wake.

He shoved me against the wall, knocking the breath from me. "I trained you better than this," he growled. "You do your job!"

Oliver's voice came out hoarse. "Yes, sir."

Henry never once released the grip on my arm, holding me just high enough on the wall that I had to stand on my tiptoes.

Oliver's nervous, clammy hand touched my shoulder and gave me a squeeze. It was likely meant to be a reassuring gesture, but I only wanted to kick him where it counted. Especially when it fell away and back to his weapon.

I was more prepared for Oliver's onslaught this time. Even so, when it cut into my low back, my head fell into the wall and my scream echoed throughout the dimly lit room.

Henry never released me, though I still writhed in my agony. Again, I gradually sank toward the ground, leaving him holding my arm at an unnatural angle above my head.

There was no way we had reached the full fifty when Oliver stopped. I had made it to one knee, my fingernails gripping the wall for balance. He scooped up my chemise and laid it over my shoulder, then returned the whip to his father.

"I won't do any permanent damage to her," he declared.

Henry practically growled. "What makes you think you have permission to stop?"

"You taught us that it's up to us to judge how far we should take an extraction method. Though I am not after information, this is far enough. She's under my care. This is *my* punishment. Not hers. I won't cause any lasting harm."

Henry was silent for a few breaths, likely shocked that his son had the guts to stand up for himself. "Grab your things," he finally barked at me. "Get into that attic. I don't want to see you anywhere else, got it?"

I fought to pull the chemise over my head, desperate for a shred of dignity. Every movement made the pain worse; sobs caught in my throat faster than I could take in a breath. My hair stuck to my face with my rapid movements. I knew full well that if I stopped moving, I'd collapse.

"Let me help—" Oliver started.

"Don't touch me!" I yelped as he helped the thin fabric back into position.

"The stairs," Oliver said. "Let me help you—"

"She can make it herself!" Henry barked.

In a daze, I made my way to the staircase, not looking at either of them. The rest of my clothing remained in a messy pile in the corner. I just needed out as fast as possible—I was clothed enough.

I could feel their eyes boring into me with every step I took, every time I tripped, barely catching myself with my hands. I refused to sit and scoot up one step at a time. I refused to look at either of them, to let either of them see my face. When I fell a third time, Oliver spoke up.

"I gather there's no end to how heartless you can be, but I won't follow in those footsteps." His strides echoed behind me, pausing only as he hooked his hands under my arms to pick me up.

I flinched away from his touch, but he persisted. Like a feral animal, I kicked and bit at him, but he held me at arm's length, keeping the blows just far enough away.

The door to the kitchen opened for us, revealing spindly Arthur with his drawn face. With great care, Oliver set me at Arthur's feet before shutting himself inside again.

Arthur didn't say anything—he didn't have to. He knew everything that transpired below.

He cradled me in his sturdy arms, letting me lean my head against his chest. He didn't question it as I sobbed. He pushed the tear-soaked hair away from my eyes at one point, and said a few words, but I didn't hear a single syllable.

We'd only moved a few steps when the thwacks resumed downstairs, punctuated by a very male grunt of pain.

Oliver.

Arthur's steps faltered for a mere moment, but then he sped up. We made our way through the house with record speed, sobs racking my body the entire time.

We didn't pause before the piano, lounging in the heavenly beam of sunlight. Instead, we just went straight up the mountainous staircase. For once, I wanted to get back to my attic prison.

Every door in the hallway was shut tight, leaving no sign of anyone else in the house. The cool attic air smacked into me as Arthur traversed the staircase.

For once, I didn't care if I was trapped again. I only wanted to be alone. I wanted to let the pain and misery take over, to curl up into a little ball and cry. Any movement I dared tugged the blood-soaked chemise against the fresh wounds.

How bad was it? How much of it would mark my back for the rest of my life?

For a while, Arthur sat on the settee next to me, petting my head. It was obvious he wasn't sure how to comfort me, but he clearly wanted to try. He acted as though he was afraid to move too fast, as if one wrong move would break me into a million pieces. Not that it mattered. I didn't think I could feel any more wounded.

Hesitantly, he placed an arm around my shoulders. When I leaned into the embrace, he relaxed a little. "I'm sorry," he said.

I sniffed and rubbed at my eyes. "You didn't do anything."

"I'm still sorry it happened. You didn't deserve that."

Briefly, I wondered if he had officially joined the family profession, if he was an ordained killer. Hopefully not. He was too kind. Too young. Too sweet. *He* wouldn't kidnap a girl and shove her in the attic.

After a long while, I was finally able to shove the thunderstorm of emotions back into a ladylike box. I took a deep breath and started to speak.

"Why did he do that? Why did he give in?" It surprised me to realize that I had begun to trust him.

Arthur hesitated, taking great care to shift his weight on the cushion. "I don't think he knew how to avoid it."

My voice sharpened to that of a knife. "Instead, I get whipped?"

Arthur squirmed. "No . . . well, yes. But no . . ." He flashed me an apologetic smile. "I think he's trying to fix things. Maybe find a way where you can leave the house. Just there was so much going on with the—"

I glared at him. "With the what? Apparently he, and everyone else in this godforsaken place, believes I know information, so you might as well tell me!"

His blue eyes went wide, and he scooted back a hair. "I can't tell you anything."

Some part of me—likely the part that didn't feel I had any kind of future—snapped. I grabbed his shirt with both fists, the oozing wounds on my back stretching with the sudden movement. I gasped at the onslaught but powered on. "Tell me! If I'm going to be trapped in an attic until I die, at least let me be privy to information!" I gnawed on the inside of my cheek, focusing all of my energy on holding steady. Oliver would *not* win! I would *not* show my pain.

He regained himself in record time and pried my fingers from his collar. "If you know things like that, you'd be in more danger than you are now."

"More danger than being trapped here until I kill myself?"

"Shh." He rapidly shook his head, a perfect golden ringlet escaping the tie at the base of his neck. "You're in danger of never being free of this room at all. No chance. If they discovered you knew a *single* thing, there's nothing Oliver could do to keep you alive."

I crossed my arms over my chest, both to hide the way my hands shook, and to look a little more furious. "He's not doing a great job as it is."

Arthur sighed and stood up, attempting to end the discussion. "I'm positive he's doing everything he can."

"The pain *he* inflicted on me is a solid argument against that," I muttered.

"I'm sorry." Arthur patted my shoulder before escaping to the safety of downstairs.

CHAPTER FOURTEEN

Chamber Pot

No matter how hard I tried, sleep—or even a hint of relaxation for that matter—didn't find me. It hurt to move one way; it hurt to move the other. My leg, or lack thereof, ached, my low back was on fire, and my head pounded from all the crying. All I wanted to do was pass out and forget it all.

My back was to the trapdoor, so when it clapped open, every muscle in my body tensed, preparing to fight. The footsteps plodded toward me, then stopped as their owner second-guessed himself.

"Nella?"

Oliver.

At first, I considered leaning against the back of the couch, pretending to be sound asleep, but the anger boiled inside. After all of that, putting me in such danger, he *dared* come back and use my nickname.

Fire lit anew, I whirled on him, my stumpy leg getting bumped in the process. Seeing his face forced me to ignore the pain, fury, the only thing remaining. I grabbed the flower-painted ceramic pot by my foot and chucked it at him.

My aim was good, but he was faster. With a crash, the chamber pot shattered against the wall. He was lucky it was empty.

"Don't talk to me," I snapped.

"Please . . ." Oliver took a step forward anyway. I likely resembled a feral cat, hunched up and hissing at the intruder. "I can explain—"

"You can explain nothing!" I shouted, hurling the blanket at him. It didn't make it far, fluttering to the ground midway between us. "You did this to me. *YOU.*" Out of items of potential destruction, I grabbed the deflated pillow and threw it at him too. He caught it easily and set it beside the settee, just out of my reach.

"I didn't have a choice," he said calmly, hands up in a kind of surrender. "You see that, right?"

"No." I held my hands up in fists, as if I had a chance in a fight. "Don't touch me. Don't get close to me. I'm done with you. I'm *here* because of you. And then you *hurt* me. You! Not your pa, not some other person we happened upon in town. *You!*"

Oliver stopped his advance, a mere inch from my angry fists. "He whipped me too—"

I spat at him. "I'm *bleeding!* It's gonna scar! For the rest of my life."

"I have something to—"

"You bastard. Get out. Go! I never want to see you again. Go! You should've killed me when you had the chance."

He closed his eyes for a long moment and shook his head. "I'm doing the best I can."

As if called, Donnell popped his head into the room. "No one dead?" He looked back and forth between the two of us. "Good. Ma was worried."

I hunted for something to throw at him. "You get out too! You're just as much to blame as Oliver. You could have done something, *anything* to help! But you didn't, now did you? Go! Get!" I fluttered my hands like I was shooing a naughty dog. "I don't want to see either of you ever again! Arthur can take care of me."

Surprise shot across Donnell's face, but he obediently retreated to the safety of the hall.

"It's *my* job to take care of you," Oliver said. His voice was measured and steady, like he was talking to a volatile child.

"Bull. Go!"

He ignored my swearing entirely. "I have to talk to you about something important."

"No. Get out of my sight. All of this is your fault. All of it! You had your chance to talk to me. And this is where that got me. GO!"

With a long sigh, he turned and left me alone in my prison.

The moment the door shut behind him, I collapsed into a ball on the tattered blankets, sobs taking over every inch of my body.

He left me alone for the next few days. The only person I saw was Arthur. He didn't stay during these visits. He brought me food, emptied my new chamber pot, and gave me books. Of course, he was sure to tell me that Oliver had picked them out just for me. I ignored that information and read them anyway.

The lack of socialization didn't bug me for once. Good riddance. They could all die in the fires of hell for all I cared.

Except Rose. I still liked her. And perhaps Arthur.

On the fourth day, I had blown through two books and had memorized every inch of the outside world I could see through the window. Soon, Arthur appeared with my breakfast, a few kind words, and then disappeared yet again. Just like he did every morning.

I ate in bored silence, watching as the older men, including Oliver, hitched up the wagon. He seemed more subdued than before, falling behind the others, copying what they did instead of taking charge.

Against my better judgment, my heart ached for him. He had been beaten too, and I was sure him whipping me hurt him some as well. After all, it was supposed to be his punishment.

I shook my head wildly. "No, no. Don't give in to those bastards."

"Well, that's kind of you."

The voice behind me made me jump so hard the plate almost slid from my lap.

"You scared me!" I glared at Arthur. "How'd you get in here so quietly?" Like a magician, he disappeared through the trap-door in no time flat.

"Maybe you were just that interested in watching my brother." He smirked, the shine in his eyes an exact copy of Oliver's.

"No." I didn't care if my voice sounded harsh. "He kid-napped me." I looked outside again. Oliver was still there, busy loading supplies into the back of the wagon. He had taken off his jacket and laid it somewhere. This made him the only one not completely ready to go. I wondered if he would stay home this time too.

Arthur made a noise that rode the line between ascent and disapproval. "You wanna come downstairs?"

That got my full attention. "Of course!"

His grin made him look even younger than he already did. He was all teeth and freckles, looking completely harmless. He waited for me to stand before picking up both me and my cane.

"I'm not getting whipped again. I won't go until they leave." The wounds on my back throbbed at the very idea of being caught.

Arthur shook his head. "No, Pa gave permission this time."

Permission. That made me instantly suspicious. What would cause him to even consider giving me permission for anything?

"Why?"

Arthur shrugged. "I dunno. Maybe Ma sweet-talked him or something."

With a sigh, I got up from my perch. Whatever the reason, it didn't fully matter. At least I hoped it didn't.

We made our way downstairs easily, the mixed smells of soap and baking bread taking over my senses. When we reached the ground floor, Arthur set me down and handed me my cane.

"I have to go with the others, but Ma's in the kitchen." He nodded in that direction, though the homey smell of bread had already taken over my senses.

My stomach lurched. Suddenly all I could see was him, freckle-faced and adorable, covered in blood and holding a knife, that smile still on his face.

"You . . ." I bit my lower lip, unsure what to say. Good luck? Or ask if he would be participating? "Are you . . . ?"

His smile didn't reach his eyes. "I turned sixteen this March, so I go with them. If that's what you wanted to know."

I fidgeted with my crutch. "Will you be . . . um . . ."

He laughed, his entire posture relaxing. "No, that's unlikely. Just meeting with some—" He shook his head. "No, everyone lives today."

A clearing of the throat came from the doorway. Oliver leaned against the wooden frame, already looking tired. "Pa's waiting."

Arthur jumped to action, grabbing his hat and jacket from their hooks and giving me a quick wave. Oliver didn't follow, he just stayed there, eyes on me.

CHAPTER FIFTEEN
Shoot the Witnesses

I tried to look serious and glare at him, though my heart beat so furiously I doubted it did any good.

"Got permission for you to come down while we're gone. But there are rules."

I sighed and let myself lean against the stairs' railing. "Of course there are."

"Ma wanted you to bathe, said it wasn't right for you to go without for so long."

Those words made me feel like the dirt and grime grew legs. I'd been doing my best to stay clean by scrubbing myself every morning with the provided water basin, but it only did so much. The very idea of washing my hair again was refreshing. But did I smell *that* bad?

"That was kind of her," I said, my nose doing its own thing and smelling my shoulder.

A small laugh escaped from Oliver, but he otherwise remained serious. "There're still rules . . ."

I let out a long sigh. I already knew what those rules would be. "You have to be there?"

He held his hands up in a motion of helplessness. "Take it or leave it."

Rose chose this time to make her presence known. "I've already got the water heating. And I brought a screen you can stay behind. There won't be any indecency on my watch." She narrowed her eyes at her son.

"I just have to be in the room," Oliver clarified, a smirk on his lips. I didn't find it so amusing.

"Fine," I spat, standing a little straighter. "But you ain't getting a peek, got it?"

His smirk turned to a full grin. I narrowed my eyes at him in hopes he wouldn't mention the fact that he'd seen it all already. He didn't.

"*Dépêche-toi!* We don't have all day! And I'm hoping to clean up too." Rose beckoned us to follow her into the sitting room.

We followed, Oliver taking up the rear. As if I would even consider an escape—I couldn't go far with only one leg.

They set the tub up in front of the fire, half filled with cold water. Oliver filled it the rest of the way with steaming hot water straight from the hearth. His movements were careful, ensuring he wouldn't spill a single drop. My own brother would have dumped half of it in his haste.

Rose dragged the screen from the side of the room to block the tub. Oliver quickly took it from her.

"You shouldn't be doing anything like this right now," he said, nodding toward her protruding bump.

I couldn't help but smile to myself. At least he seemed to care about his mother. Murderer or not.

She touched his arm in an unspoken thanks, then turned to me, all business. "Come on, before the water gets cold."

Though there wasn't a chance of the water cooling any time soon, I obeyed. I leaned my cane against the screen so I could work on the buttons of my bodice.

"Let me help you with that." Rose reached to help, but I flinched away. Though I knew her cold fingers meant no harm, the touch on my neck felt wrong, dangerous.

"No, no, thank you." I shook my head wildly. "I . . . I'd rather do it myself." I felt frozen, forbidden images of the event in the basement flashing through my mind.

Rose cooed something under her breath and patted my shoulder. "Would you feel better if I left you here alone?"

I nodded stiffly. I'd bathed with other women nearby my entire life. As long as the men weren't present, it was fine. Why did this change things? She didn't have anything I didn't. Aside from an ever-growing baby bump, of course.

"How do you know they won't come back?" My voice was hardly a whisper. Gooseflesh popped up on my arms, and I scrubbed at it.

"Oh, *cherie* . . ." She pulled me into a hug so tight I was almost concerned for the child in her belly. "They only just left, but even if they were to come home, they know you will be down here. Henry gave his permission. Nothing bad will happen to you today."

Oliver's shadow slid to sit on the opposite side of the screen, but he said nothing to back up his mother.

"I will give you your privacy," Rose said, backing to the edge of the screen to waggle her finger at Oliver. "Now, if he gets out of line, just yell, and I'll put him right back in his place."

The seriousness on her face brought a smirk to mine. I didn't doubt that she would have the power of a thousand men when it came to controlling one of her sons.

I waited until Rose disappeared into the kitchen before I undressed. Each button sent an unwelcome memory into my mind. The way his fingers felt on my shoulders as he turned me to face the wall, the bite of the whip as it cut into my flesh. The scars would probably never fade all the way. No one would marry me now.

But I would be okay.

No one would hurt me this time.

When Oliver's shadow suddenly shifted, I practically fell over the edge of the tub in surprise, clutching my clothes to my chest. He didn't come behind the screen, though; he just slid a dark object in my general direction.

I stared at it, mouth agape and heart thumping audibly in my ears. "That's . . ." I couldn't even say the word.

"Yes. That's my gun," he said. "I request that you don't shoot me with it."

I gingerly picked it up. I'd never had reason to shoot a gun, let alone mess with one. It was startlingly heavy, the metal cold. It was bigger than my hand.

"Is it loaded?" I whispered.

His shadow shifted, as though he was about to retrieve his present. "Yes," he said. "So don't play around back there. No one wants to clean up any unwanted messes."

"Why would you give me this?" I held it away from my body, flat on my palm, with my fingers splayed away from the trigger.

He moved back to his earlier spot, equal lengths of screen on either side of his shadow. "Because I hope it helps you realize that I won't hurt you. And that—"

"Again." I ground my teeth. "That you won't hurt me *again*."

His shadow didn't move a muscle. "And well . . . well, if I did . . ." He swallowed audibly. "Again . . . you could stop me."

I rolled it over in my palms, fingering each mark on the handle. It had been used so much that the curve of each finger was visible in the weathered wood. Despite myself, I placed a finger in each mark. His hands were much bigger than my own, my fingers floating in each chasm.

My mouth felt dry as I delicately positioned the gun beside the head of the tub. I checked Oliver's position once more before finally letting the rest of my clothes drop to the floor.

It was a struggle to get into the tub itself. I couldn't figure out a graceful way to get in with only one leg, so I put my stump in first and tried to guide myself with my arms. They weren't the biggest fan of my efforts and gave out rather quickly, dropping my body into the water with a splash and a yelp.

Oliver's shadow jerked, ready to jump to my aid, but he didn't move more than an inch. "Are you all right?"

I sputtered as I wiped the water out of my eyes. "Yes, I'm fine." I felt my cheeks redden at the idea of anyone being privy to my mishap.

At least I could shoot the witnesses.

CHAPTER SIXTEEN
Trust

We remained silent for quite some time. I let the water gradually turn me into a wrinkly old woman, but I didn't care. The longer I soaked, the better I felt.

"Did Arthur tell you anything?" It had been so quiet, Oliver's voice startled me.

"Huh? Oh, not really." I eyed his shadow suspiciously. "He just told me they were meeting with some people today, and that he turned sixteen." *And, therefore, is able to kill people.*

Oliver let out a deep sigh. His shadow picked at one of the seams in the wood. "I'll answer one question."

I sat a bit straighter. "What?"

"You heard me."

My mind swirled with the options. I could ask if I could go home, but I already knew that answer. I could ask how many people he'd killed, but I *didn't* want to know that answer. I doubted he would actually give me details on the current case, either.

I formed my words like a wish, ensuring that I would get the most out of whatever answer he gave. "Will you tell me about all of you? As in, are there more . . ." I struggled to find the word. "Groups?"

"Clans," he supplied, his shadow relaxing some. I could almost hear the smile in his voice. "I can tell you about that. What do you want to know?"

I gnawed on my bottom lip. "I want to know everything."

His laugh echoed around the room. "How about you give me a place to start?"

"Will you answer more than one question, then?"

"Yes," he said firmly, but then quickly added, "at least until I can't tell you anymore."

"Illusive," I muttered. I searched the ceiling as if it would provide the perfect question. Of course, it remained silent. "How many of them are there? And are they all families?"

"I don't know how many there are," he began, stretching his legs out in front of him. I could see his foot peering out from the side of the screen. "I'm sure there are a lot. They are usually families. We are the Wedman Clan. We are the first of this name. Though it used to be York." He shrugged.

My nose wrinkled. "Your pa changed his name?"

"Yes. When he married Ma."

I stared right at his shadow, willing him to continue. When he didn't, I gave in and prodded. "Why?"

Oliver hesitated for just a moment longer. "My grandfather didn't want him to marry Ma. He didn't approve that she was an immigrant, I suppose. So, out of anger, Pa married her anyway and changed his name to prove he didn't need his help."

I tried to imagine Little Chris doing such a thing. First off, it wouldn't happen. A family name carried too much importance to be thrown away. Second, I doubted Pa would care who he would marry. Within reason, of course.

"So, we are now the Wedmans," he continued. "There are still Yorks, headed mainly by my uncle Martin. That's who they're going to see right now."

"How many clans are there around here?"

"We all have our own territories. The stronger the clan, the larger the territory. The York Clan is rather large, making them our superiors. As Pa went and began his own, we are only as strong as us in this household. Well, and Bernard's. As all of us marry and branch out, our territory will begin to grow."

"So . . . does that mean you won't be the head of your own clan?"

"Right. Not unless I was to leave and start my own—which is not a suggested practice."

"What is—" I stopped, not sure if I actually wanted an answer to the question.

"Just ask. You know what I do. There's not a question out there that'll offend me."

"I'm not worried about offending you." I ducked my head under the water, partially to think and partially to rinse the soap off the top of my head. The bath was cooling, so I reluctantly soaped up the rest of my body.

"Then what is it?"

"I'm just not sure I want to know the answer," I admitted.

His shadow paused as he thought about it. "Again, you already know what I do. Can the information I give you really be worse than that?"

"Yes," I said without hesitation. Body as clean as it was going to get, I began the journey back to my lonely foot. Sitting on the edge of the tub and bringing my foot around to gain purchase of the floor made it much easier.

"You need help?" Oliver asked, likely listening to the water slosh around as I got out.

"I will bite you if you dare," I replied.

His laugh was full and relaxed. "As opposed to shooting me? Don't think I'll chance it. Ask your question, please."

I sighed and dried my hair as well as I could with the towel. "What is your uncle wanting from you all?"

He ran his fingers through his hair. "You had to ask a question I can't answer?"

"Yes." I pulled my chemise over my head and wrapped the towel around my shoulders to catch any remaining water.

"Fine. I can't tell you much, but I can tell you it is from the same mission we all have been working on for a few years now."

"The same one where you killed my employer?" The words were out of my mouth before I could stop them, bitter and full of poison.

He let out such a loud breath that I might as well have punched him in the gut. "The very same."

I let my eyes close as I tried to force my brain to keep up with my questions. *Think them through first! Don't just ask a murderer the first thing on your mind!*

"Did you *have* to kill him?"

Oliver's shadowy figure was so still he hardly breathed. "No," he finally said.

That answer was nowhere near what I had expected. "What?" My own body froze, halfway into the skirt.

"Earnest Murray was not the target. A man named Richard Williams was."

I could feel the guilt flowing from his voice, hitting me like a knife to the chest. "Then . . . why?" My voice broke on the word, though I tried my best to stop it.

"Are you dressed yet?" He stood with such speed that my hands launched into action, shoving the skirt in place and grabbing the bodice.

"Almost." I checked the way the skirt lay over the hoops before I pulled the bodice into place. "I am decent, though."

He came around the screen then, each movement sharp and precise, eyes alit with some newfound energy. "Come on."

"What?" My voice was a squeak.

He scooped up his pistol and tucked it into its holster, then grabbed my cane. "Adventure time."

"What?" I said again, hopping awkwardly backward. "No . . ." I took another hop but hit the edge of the tub. My body fell in slow motion. Before I even had a chance to scream, he caught me.

He brought his mouth to my ear and whispered, "I can't answer all your questions here. Come with me."

I was reminded of the serpent in the Garden of Eden, tempting Eve with whatever she wanted. But like Eve, I nodded and let him scoop me into his arms, wet hair trailing behind.

"We're going out!" he hollered over his shoulder as he slipped out the front door.

"What? No, Oliver!" came Rose's shouts of protests as she hurried after us. She had hit the waddling stage of her pregnancy, so when she made it to the porch, we were already at the tree line, nearly behind the barn. "Oliver James Wedman!"

As if stung, he stopped and turned around. "We're just going to the lake. We'll be back in half an hour tops."

She shook her head. "If you get that girl in any mischief again . . ." She tsked her tongue. "Thirty minutes. Or else."

He tilted his head, touching where the brim of a hat would be, if he had bothered to grab one. "Yes ma'am."

She looked like a painting, wringing her hands on her apron on the pristine front porch, the flattened clearing stretching out on either side of the house. But a painting would never be able to capture the way the leaves chattered any gossip all the way up the mountain and to the clouds.

Rose stayed put for a few moments, likely debating whether or not she should throttle Oliver herself. Mind made, she stepped back inside with a visible sigh.

"Question," I said as we disappeared into the cover of the trees. "What would she be able to do to you if you took too long to come back?"

Oliver chuckled. "I don't even know. Probably send me out to cut my own switch like a child. Don't think she could do much more in her condition. It doesn't matter, we won't get to find out."

"That's what you said last time," I pointed out.

Even so, the idea of her, nearly ready to pop, chasing around a grown man with a switch made me laugh despite myself.

We didn't have far to go. It was just about a ten-minute sprint away. The tree cover broke, and we were at a lake. It wasn't large, I could have easily swum from one side of the other. Maybe that meant it was a pond instead? It didn't matter. The water was clear and the sun was bright. The change in scenery alone made my heart lift minutely.

"Why'd you take me so far out?" I asked as he set me on one of the rather large rocks, just close enough to the water that I could dip my toes. "You could have easily put me back in the attic if you wanted privacy."

"Trust."

Just one word, said so simply, sent shivers up my spine. "Trust?" Like an animal being led to slaughter? Or simply like one friend trusting another?

"Yes. I want you to trust me. Trust that I'm doing everything I can to get you more freedom, and will do what I can to get you moments like this." His eyes were pleading, like a child who did something wrong, but with the right intentions.

"Moments like this . . ." I repeated, tracing my fingers along the cool rock. "Letting a horse out of the pen for a brief ride doesn't make her free."

He flinched. "I'm doing everything I can! Don't you see that?"

I raked my fingers through my still-wet hair until they got stuck in the tangles. "It's not enough."

He sighed and plopped down on the dirt beside me. "Do you want me to answer your question or not?"

"Yes." I turned my face away from his, focusing as hard as possible on a turtle contemplating a swim. I didn't want him to see what was sure to be a horrified expression come over my face.

He cleared his throat before he began. "I was on the train in search of a man named Richard Williams—"

"Why him?" I demanded.

He made a sound similar to that of a growl. "I can't—"

"Trust."

He threw his head back with a dramatic sigh. "Don't you *dare* tell a soul. Got it?" He waited until I looked back at him and nodded, making eye contact. "Good. Richard Williams is the son of the main target. When my father married Ma, my grandfather took him off the will entirely. Stripped him of all rights to that clan and the lands. This means it should've passed to my uncle, Martin. It didn't.

"Instead of choosing a relative to pass the land to, my grandfather requested that the property be auctioned and the money be given to the local school. Earl Williams is the man who bought that land."

I couldn't stay silent. This was ridiculous. "So you want to kill the man who *legally* bought your grandfather's land?"

He waved his hand at me. "Hush. You won't like much, if any, of this story. It's family land. My uncle is equally upset that it wasn't kept in the family. Earl Williams won't sell the land back, and to make matters worse, he's part of the Harold Clan." Oliver stretched, his back popping slightly. He looked just about as uncomfortable as he possibly could. "So, he got in touch with both his family and the Noris Clan—"

"Oh no . . ."

"Shh. So the Harold and the Noris Clan protect them. In the short of things, we're in a war. Does that make sense?" Again, he waited for me to make eye contact.

I searched every inch of his face. For what, I wasn't sure. "Yes, but why his son?"

"Because it's a war," he said, gaze level with mine. "War isn't kind." When I didn't say anything else, he continued: "On the train, he was supposed to be on there. I had lured him to the cargo car—"

"With what?"

He raised his eyebrows. "Do you want to hear it or not?" I placed my hands in my lap obediently, though I knew the movement wouldn't keep my mouth shut. "It doesn't matter with what. Only, your employer, that Mr. Murray, saw the two of us go in and decided to follow. At that point, it was a simple case of kill the witness."

Unbidden, my eyebrows rose. *Simple* . . . Instead, I said, "And where was the other guy? Richard?"

Oliver shrugged. "He disappeared. A whole lot better than you, I might add."

I shot him a glare. "There aren't many places to go on a moving train, thank you very much."

"That's why you get creative." He gave me a half smile. "Richard Williams has a daughter, who has been seen around the area a few times too. So we've been scouting around for her."

My stomach swirled. "But she's innocent."

Oliver laughed, low and dark. "Far from it. But that's pretty much everything. All of which, you're *not supposed to know*."

My mind swirled with the information, but one question jumped out before I had a chance to stop it. "Had you killed people before that?" I let out a little gasp, shocked at myself for even uttering the words.

He blinked in surprise. "You . . . uh . . ." He wiped his face nervously. "I'm pretty sure you know the answer to that one."

I squirmed, somewhat nauseous at the idea. "And you started when you were sixteen? Like Arthur?"

He nodded.

"Has Arthur killed anyone?" I shut my eyes tight against the answer. I couldn't even imagine such a sweet young man taking a life.

"No," Oliver said firmly. "Just a quick reminder for you. If they find out I told you any of this, they won't hesitate to take care of the problem, eliminate the witness. You understand?"

Shivers traveled over every inch of my backbone. "I understand." My throat felt dry, my fingers numb. What was I looking for? A way to justify that this murderer wasn't such a bad person? Why? My brain warred with itself, confusion boggling up every nook and cranny.

"Do you have any more questions for me right now?"

Only one stuck out. "Why was Donnell in town instead of with the others?"

He made a face and threw a pebble into the water. "That, I don't know."

"Did you ask your pa?"

"Heavens, no!" He shook his head, eyes wide as if the very idea terrified him. "We all have our secrets. I might not know what Donnell's is, but I know he'll have his revenge if I dare expose it."

CHAPTER SEVENTEEN
Sara Williams

Being trapped in the attic again brought me to a new level of depression. There was absolutely nothing to do. At least, nothing that caught my eye. I spent the majority of my time staring out the window, expecting to see nothing but the daydreams that danced around in my head. But one day, there was movement.

Donnell stood, halfway hidden by the barn. He was solid, as always, but there was a bit of a relaxed slouch to his upper back.

The reason was easy to see. He had placed his hands securely on a girl's cheeks. She stood there, motionless, waiting for the contact. They were far enough away, I could only imagine her shivering with anticipation as she waited for that intimate touch.

The attic window I gazed out of was the only one on this side of the house. So unless someone came outside and decided to go on a stroll to the back of the barn, no one would notice the strange blond intertwined with Donnell.

He cupped her chin in his palm and bent for the kiss, pulling back with her lower lip trapped between his teeth. She danced on her tiptoes, every inch of her body yearning toward his.

"I shouldn't be watching this," I whispered. But I certainly didn't turn away.

She stood just a little taller, prepared to seal him in another kiss, her hands reaching around his middle. He took no time to react. He held her forearms securely and turned in an elegant sort of dance, pressing her against the wall.

Even as he tugged at her clothing, I didn't avert my gaze. She worked at the buttons of his shirt, nearly tearing them in her haste. They were like wolves, hungry for just one thing.

My cheeks were on fire, as though the lovers' heat was contagious. She was a pretty girl: slim, fair, and blonde. Their erotic dance had worked loose a portion of her hair, leaving it to cascade down her bare chest, all the way to her waist.

Donnell didn't waste any time in pulling her to the ground. His back muscles gleamed in the morning light, sweaty with his exertion. He still had on his pants, but I doubted that would stop him. The girl was reduced to a pale figure stretched beneath him, fingers tracing each one of those muscles.

I bit my lip, my own body tensing with their excitement.

Turn away . . . you shouldn't be watching this. Obediently, I moved from the window, letting out a long, heavy breath, as if it would absolve me of my sins.

But I wasn't alone.

The ever-stealthy Oliver stood right beside the trapdoor, staring straight at me with one eyebrow raised. "What's that about?" His eyes had a teasing sparkle to them, leaving me certain he knew the details of every single impure thought that had gone through my head.

"Nothing!" I held my hands up in a floppy surrender. "Just didn't know you were there?"

He smirked and sauntered to the window. There was no fooling him. "That look on your face ain't anywhere close to 'surprise.'" His sharp eyes scanned the property, locating exactly what I had seen within a second. He chuckled darkly. "Well, well, well . . . not sure who deserves more of a scolding. You, for watching, or them for—" His mouth snapped shut and his entire body turned to stone.

"What?" I searched both his face and the scene below for clues. Donnell had completely let loose, pants to his knees, hands firmly planted in the dirt on either side of the girl's head. With each movement he made, his body clenched.

No! Stop it! I cleared my throat and forced myself to look at Oliver, my toes curling under. "What is it?"

"That little . . ."

His hands rolled into fists, tighter and tighter until the veins popped all the way up his arm.

I could only come up with one explanation. "Is it . . . is that your girl?" Saying the words out loud didn't do much for the rogue jealousy that circled inside. I really had no reason to be jealous! Besides, if that blonde was *his* girl, she wouldn't be for long.

Stop it! He kidnapped you!

His eyes snapped to me. "No." His voice was firm, final. "I don't have a girl."

"Then . . ." I looked back at the couple. "What's wrong?"

They hadn't taken long with their act, though the potential of being caught likely sped things along. Donnell stood a few feet away, pulling his shirt back over his head. The girl was busy doing the same, struggling to cover herself with her chemise. She was fast, only taking a few extra moments to ensure the corset was on straight. Donnell stood guard, back to her, eyes scanning the area for intruders.

If only he thought to look at the window.

Oliver sighed and stood, likely to avoid being caught spying. "That's Sara Williams."

"Wait. Who?"

"The one I told you about. We're going after her father, remember?" He strode for the trapdoor, throwing it open.

His haste, his anger, the name. My heart skipped a beat. She didn't deserve to get caught and inevitably killed by them. Not after something so sacred. "No! You can't kill her!" I shouted, grabbing his arm and pulling down, as if my weight alone would keep him grounded. His momentum was all it took to pull me off the seat and into a heap on the floor. But at least it stopped him.

He shut his eyes for a long moment, fighting for patience before squatting down to my level. "I'm not going after her."

"Then where are you going? To talk to your pa?"

"No," he said tersely. "I'm going to talk to Donnell. Alone."

"I thought you were wanting to kill her." I bit my lower lip, avoiding his gaze.

He made an unnameable noise of irritation, somewhere between a sigh and a growl. "Yep." He patted my shoulder, narrowly avoiding my attempts to grab him again. "Don't worry, she won't be harmed by me." With some kind of practiced magic, he virtually dove feetfirst down the ladder, the trapdoor falling shut behind him.

I crawled after him, pulling it open and sticking my head through. Though I had wasted no time getting there, I hadn't been fast enough. Arthur was the only soul in the hallway.

The young man blinked in pure surprise. "Oh, hello," he said. If I didn't know better, I would've thought he had forgotten I was even upstairs.

"Can I . . . can I come down?" I couldn't see a single sign of Oliver anymore. Perhaps if I could get down, I could at least make it before there was too much bloodshed.

Arthur didn't see that logic. "I ain't risking *my* hide."

An angry noise escaped my throat. "Well then, I need your help. Oliver is going to see—" I stopped short. Would Arthur be likely to care for a victim if it came down to it?

He raised an eyebrow, looking very much like his brother. "Oliver is what?"

I shut my eyes in an attempt to force my brain to focus. There weren't many options left other than to trust him, or at least *try* to trust him. "Oliver's going to kill this girl . . . Sara? But—"

Arthur's sky-blue eyes sharpened, hard and full of danger. It made my heart skip a beat. "How do you know about that? I didn't tell you."

"Never mind that, just—" I pressed my forehead into my hands. *What are you doing?* "Just go stop him? They're outside." Every inch of my body screamed against my actions. What made me think, even for a moment, that Arthur wouldn't follow his lifelong training and take care of the problem?

A confused form of understanding crossed his face. "Stay there!" He held his hand up in my general direction as he raced off. He had to've known that the doglike command wouldn't be the trick to make me obey.

It was strange to see him run like a young, gangly teen. Especially after seeing the death sentence in his eyes. I half crawled, half scrambled back to the window seat and pressed my face against the glass.

The girl was nowhere to be seen, but Donnell and Oliver were there.

Oliver had Donnell by the arm, glaring into his eyes as he talked. Every inch of his body was rigid, threatening. Arthur came scrambling across the yard, standing like an excited puppy behind Oliver.

Oliver glared back at his younger brother and snapped something in his direction. By the way Arthur's shoulders sagged, I assumed it was something similar to "Go inside!" Every movement Oliver made was sharp and final.

Donnell was the same way. He stood solidly with his feet hip width apart, glaring at Oliver as if his gaze alone could smite him.

Arthur said a few things, likely defending his right to be there, before his older brothers sent him retreating into the house. The moment he was due to open the front door, Donnell threw the first punch.

Oliver must not have been expecting it. The fist connected firmly with his jaw, sending his head reeling back. My gasp came too late. Oliver recovered himself, though, returning the punch.

The slam of the front door was so hard my window rattled. Arthur must have heard the fight as it began and decided against obedience. Another slam. This one produced Henry as he rushed after his youngest son. His hands were fists at his side, each footfall deliberate, terrifying.

A flash of white drew my eye into the tree line. It was Sara, darting from her hiding place to find another one deeper in the trees. Oliver's eyes were better than mine; his feet were already moving in her direction.

"No!" I shouted, though it would do no good.

Donnell vaulted himself at Oliver, knocking him to the ground in a puff of dust. Donnell had the upper hand, pummeling Oliver's face and shouting things I could only imagine.

Arthur and Henry dove into the fray without hesitation, wrenching the two apart and holding them with an iron grip. For a skinny guy, Arthur didn't seem to have much of an issue restraining Oliver. I imagined it was only because Oliver accepted defeat, as he didn't seem to be struggling much.

Henry shook Donnell by the shoulders before releasing him, shouting the whole time. Donnell didn't respond. Neither did Oliver. They both stood stock-still, the only movement coming from their heaving chests.

As they all walked back to the house, Oliver's eyes drifted up to my window. It was only for a moment, but the imperceptible movement was all Donnell needed. His own eyes traced their way up to mine, locking for a long, terrifying moment—an unspoken oath. A threat.

CHAPTER EIGHTEEN

Cold Blade

Oliver didn't return to my room after the fight, as much as I wanted him to check in. I lost count of how many times I peered through the trapdoor, straining my ears for the sound of approaching footsteps. But it was like nothing had happened. Rose was busy in the kitchen, and the men had retreated to wherever they did their work.

Long after sunset, when Arthur finally brought my dinner, I nearly attacked him with questions.

"What happened? What's going on? Is she okay? Did they find her? Did you let her go?" I likely looked like a wild woman, dark brown hair a tangled mess, arms flailing with every word.

He locked his jaw and set the plate on the side table next to the settee. Nothing else.

"Arthur!" I pleaded, trying to grab onto his arm. The fabric of my chemise clung to the wounds on my back, causing me to pause. That brief hesitation was all he needed to grip the edge of the hole and swing back downstairs.

I avoided the urge to throw the plate after his disappearing form. The growing of my stomach was too overpowering to sacrifice my dinner.

With an irritated grunt, I went back to stare out the chilled window to hunt for any signs of life.

Cold, sharp, familiar, deadly.

None other than the feel of a blade pressed to my neck woke me. When I gasped, a large, sturdy hand clamped over my mouth. My attacker pressed so hard, I felt my body was destined to become one with the cushions.

The figure in the dark would have been impossible to identify if not for the moonlight that streamed through the window. All I could see was his basic shape looming over me, his squared shoulders, the angry set of the jaw.

Donnell.

"What did you tell them?" Every bit of his voice was laced with a growl. He released my mouth just enough so I could respond.

"Nothing—"

He pressed the knife harder, my body emitting a terrified squawk. Every muscle I had was tensed, waking the nerves along my back. As if I needed an extra reminder of my mortality, pain caressed each individual wound. Even my residual limb joined in, throbbing with an inescapable itch.

"Let me up and—"

"You can talk just fine where you're at."

Briefly, I wondered if he could kill me by accident, or if he really was in complete control of his weapon. I certainly hoped for the latter. "I saw you with her, that's it!"

"What did he tell *you*?"

Without my permission, my eyes darted away, mind scrambling for a way to signal to Oliver, to let him know I needed help. *Now.* A thin whine escaped my throat as I fought for a story, any sort of lie that would buy me time.

All my hesitation got me was another menacing growl from Donnell.

"He gave in, didn't he? He gave in to the whims of some *bitch* and told all." Donnell shook me twice, then released me, backing two impressively large steps away. "Why shouldn't I just get rid of you right here? You ain't nothin' but trouble."

I struggled to sit, back pressed firmly against my seat, blanket wrapped around me like a protective shield. "I didn't do anything wrong. She got away, didn't she?"

His eyes narrowed to slits, sending shivers up my spine. "Sure, she got away. For *now.* But mark my words, if anything more comes of this, it'll be *you* who'll pay the piper." He pointed the tip of the blade at me, letting the moonlight glint ominously off its smooth surface.

"I don't understand." My voice was so soft I could barely hear anything except the terrified quiver.

"No, you don't understand," he repeated, running one hand over his forehead as a father would do when deciding how to deal with an insolent child. "*You* don't understand. What is it you don't *understand*? The fact that you are privy to information you should never have? Information *no one* is to have? Oh, but then you couldn't simply keep that information to yourself. You had to blab it to everyone you could."

"I only told—" I cut myself off. I told Arthur, who ran out like it was his mission to dispose of the girl.

Donnell flicked the blade in the air very much like a magician, showing the results of his latest trick. "Aha, you see it my way now."

I refused to believe it. "Arthur wouldn't tell anyone!"

He chuckled, low and dark. "And what makes you believe that? I'm quite certain Oliver told you *far* more than he was allowed. Meaning, you should understand one very important thing." He leaned in so close I could feel his breath brush my nose. "Family before bitches."

I kicked out as hard as I could, catching his lower belly as he pulled away. Faster than I ever would have thought possible, he gripped that foot and held the blade against the inner side of my calf.

"You know what I should do? I should make one cut for everyone you told—"

Not waiting for him to act any further, I shrieked and pulled back. He dropped my foot, a cut welling with a thin line of blood from my big toe to the middle of my calf.

"Remember, it only takes *one* wrong person before the whole clan knows. And *you* will be the one who pays if they do."

I cradled my foot in my arms, watching as he faded into the darkness of the floor below.

CHAPTER NINETEEN

To Simply Rise

Oliver popped into my attic prison almost as soon as the sunlight burst through the dusty glass.

"Mornin', sleep well?"

I struggled to sit, a yawn overtaking my features. I'd hardly slept all night. How could I, after Donnell's visit—if it could even be called that? The small cut on my foot stung with the memory. I tucked it under the hem of my chemise, slipping it under the opposite thigh.

I'd created enough problems. I didn't need Oliver to know what his brother had done.

He read my expression far too easily. "What's wrong?" Oliver asked. He squatted down, tilting to the side to peer into my downturned eyes like a curious pigeon.

Despite my anxieties, my lip quirked into a half smile at his birdlike position. "I'm fine," I lied. "You're gonna hurt yourself, hunched over like that."

He grinned and stood. His skills would never cease to amaze me. He didn't prop his hand on his knee, the settee, anything. He simply rose as though his joints were freshly oiled.

Oliver waved his hand in front of my face. "What are you looking at down there?"

I jumped, pressing a hand to my heart. "Nothing! Well, your knees?"

He fell into the seat beside me, laughter vibrating his entire frame. "My *knees?*"

"Yes," I said, poking at the offending body part with my pointer finger. "I've never seen someone simply . . . rise."

His forehead scrunched as he stared at me. "What?"

"I've never seen someone do that so easily. Well, aside from a child. Everyone needs help, you know?" I stared him down, momentarily wishing I hadn't said a single thing. "You didn't even pop!"

He stood, moving to the center of the room. He took his time, stretching one arm across his middle, then the other. "Wanna know why?"

I couldn't help myself; his every movement enthralled me. "Yes."

With a showy clearing of the throat, he held his hands straight out and lowered himself as if he were going to sit. Then he held the position, staring me down. "Gotta keep everything strong."

He lowered the rest of the way until his rear touched the floor, his pants tightening to the limit around his frame. He then stood, slower than before, smoother than I ever thought possible. Once he was all the way up, the laughter took over again.

"You're staring like you just witnessed the Second Coming!"

"My *brother* couldn't even do that if he tried. He'd fall flat!" To emphasize my point, I slapped my hands together.

"I'm sure he could if he practiced. I've just been doing this since I was tiny." He held his hand a few feet from the floor.

"I don't know," I countered. I settled against the back of the settee, a challenge forming in my mind. "What else can you do?"

His grin widened. He looked like a teenager, freckled and almost adorable with his amusement. Even with the bruising on his cheekbone. "You really wanna know?"

I nodded.

In the time it took to blink, he was before me, hands pressed into the cushion on either side of my head. I squealed involuntarily, my breathing slowing to a trickle.

"I'm fast," he whispered.

He had me trapped. If he wanted to, he could've done anything to me. Though I was well aware of it, I still felt myself relax. If he wanted to harm me, he would've done it a long while ago.

I surprised myself by releasing a nervous giggle. "You're insufferable."

"Maybe," he admitted, backing up with a grin. "You don't do something your whole life just to be bad at it."

My throat went dry. "To kill people . . ."

He grunted as he jumped for the rafters, grabbing the closest one and hauling himself up like a cat. "I didn't choose my lot in life," he pointed out.

It unsettled me how intrigued I was to stare at him, high above in the shadows. "Stop showin' off and get down," I scolded.

"Psh." He settled himself along the rafter, letting his arms hang on either side. "Used to hide up here from Arthur when we were kids. He never found me."

"How'd you even get up there when you were little?" I countered.

"Boxes make decent stairs."

As if summoned by mischief, the trapdoor fell open and Rose stuck her head into the attic space. Oliver's eyes widened.

"Oliver James Wedman!" She didn't even bother climbing into the room. "Get down here right this instant before you bring the house down!"

I clamped my palm over my mouth to stifle the laughter as the big man fumbled for a better grip to lower himself to the ground. As he slid his legs to the side, his fingers betrayed him. With a stifled "argh!" he crashed to the hard floor.

Rose grumbled something under her breath and shuffled her way to stand over him. "You have chores. So if you're not broken, get downstairs."

Oliver scrambled to his feet and cleared his throat. "Yes ma'am." He gave me a sheepish smile before disappearing down the ladder.

I didn't want to know how bad the fight would be if Oliver knew Donnell had visited me.

CHAPTER TWENTY

Notebook

Nightmares overtook my dreams, both waking and otherwise. Each time I closed my eyes, I saw the blade and its glint in the moonlight.

Mercifully, the wound on my foot was so shallow it hardly bled. I still kept it hidden. Oliver seemed distracted with each visit, so it didn't seem like he would've noticed anyway.

Donnell's visit wouldn't leave my head. On one side of things, if I told Oliver about it, he could potentially keep me safe. On the other side, he would most likely confront his brother and make it worse.

"How are you holding up today?" Oliver asked as he came into my attic cage a few days later.

He had caught me squirming like a maniac on the settee, trying to relieve the obnoxious pain that shot through my body. "My leg itches."

"Then scratch it?" His eyebrow was raised, noticing the crazed state of all the blankets and pillows.

"It's not *that* foot that itches." I pointed at the blank space. "It's that one."

Oliver hesitated for a long moment before setting my lunch on the side table and hurrying to the corner of the room to rummage for something among the boxes. "A great uncle of mine had that problem with his arm after he lost it."

"Does it mean a ghost is tickling my decaying foot or something?" I watched his every move, my lips pursed.

He laughed. "I highly doubt that."

I stared at the blank space, willing the impossible itch to go away. It didn't.

It didn't surprise me that his great uncle had a missing limb. Of course, a bunch of trained killers would likely go through some horrific injuries. That small thought was all it took for the image of a blood-soaked Oliver to creep into my mind. I violently shook my head to dislodge it, my hair flying every which way. "Do you think I can come downstairs today?"

He raised that eyebrow, the sunlight turning the tips to a copper. "Not today."

I twitched in my seat, training my eyes on the floor, stomach swirling. I knew why, but I had to ask. "You're still looking for her, aren't you?"

No response.

I sat a bit straighter, forcing myself to look him in the eye. "You didn't find her, did you?" I could imagine it, her being trapped in the basement, awaiting her death. Or perhaps they would kill her on the spot, then bring her head to whoever needed the proof. I couldn't determine which was worse.

He still didn't give me an answer.

"Why won't you tell me?"

Unapologetically, he focused on my earlier question. "There is to be someone coming for a visit. He's due any day now, and it would be . . ." He paused, biting the corner of his lip as he mused. "It just wouldn't be good if he found you here."

"Who is it?" I studied his every move, hoping he would inadvertently give something away.

His eyes pleaded with me, gentle like an innocent child's. Wordlessly, he pointed at his ear.

I set my jaw, debating on pushing him further. More than likely, it would be some other clan member. The man would come by, complete his business, then leave again. I only prayed it didn't have anything to do with Sara.

If she was dead, or even captured, I'd never forgive myself.

I cleared my throat to dislodge the fear, then lowered my voice to a whisper. "Why can't you tell me who it is?"

In a sharp movement, he pointed at his ear again before changing the topic. "I brought you something."

The idea of a present helped both my discomfort and my questions fizzle below the surface. I bounced like a child, sitting as tall as possible. Startled at how easily distracted I was, I shoved my excitement deep down. Mama would've been appalled to see me act like that. "Something other than food?" Despite my attempts at restraint, my voice went up an octave.

He smirked at my reaction.

Great, even he sees how easy I am to bribe.

"Other than food." He fished for something in his pocket and set the bundle on my lap.

I tore into it, putting more effort than I cared to admit into doing it in a ladylike fashion. Inside was a little leather-bound notebook, complete with a pen and sealed ink well basking on top of it. It was such a small gift, but it brought a genuine smile to my face.

"Do whatever you want with it. Write letters, a journal, anything. I thought it would give you just a little more to do." His smile could be heard in his voice.

I fingered the edge of the papers. "Thank you," I said. I didn't know what to write. I couldn't send the letters I wanted, so it seemed almost pointless to write any. Journals could be found and inevitably read. I also couldn't draw better than a six-year-old. That didn't stop me from gazing at the paper, enthralled by the possibilities, and terrified by the lack of freedom I actually had with my gift.

The window seat creaked as Oliver sat beside me. "What's wrong?"

I let my gaze travel up his body until I found his eyes, noting the way his hands rested on his knees. He didn't look threatening at all, even with the way his muscles tensed under his shirt.

I *almost* trusted him not to hurt me. But I knew he'd do whatever was needed, whether I got hurt in the process or not. "I don't want to be in the attic," I said flatly.

His mouth twitched. "I'm working on that. It'll just take some time—"

I blew roughly through my lips, fixing him with what I hoped was a threatening stare. "I don't want more *time*. There's nothing to do up here. No life to live, nothing to do except make the same pyramid out of books over and over again. Oh, and now I have this." I ran my hand over his gift. My tirade sounded ungrateful, but I didn't care. "It's not enough."

Oliver sighed, patting my shoulder as he stood. My glare hadn't fazed him one bit. "I'll keep working on it. Just try to stay occupied for now?"

"Occupied for now?" I sighed deeply in a useless attempt to keep my real feelings inside. It didn't work. My anger came flying out like a misplayed scale—jarring and sharp. "Does that mean this is just a gift to keep me busy while the guest comes? Keep me occupied and out of your hair? What will happen next week when . . . I don't know . . . your ma goes into labor? You going to keep me up here then, too?"

Oliver remained silent as he mulled over his words. "You know very well how dangerous this life is. Especially for you. I have to do what I can to keep you out of harm's way." He held his hand up to stop me before I could argue with him. "I know I haven't done the best at that so far. But right now, the best I can do is give you a gift to keep you entertained while I try to figure something else out."

My mouth worked before my brain. "Entertained like some child."

He let out a sharp breath. "I can't do this today. Do with it what you will. I have things to do." As he turned to make his way down the ladder, guilt trickled into my stomach.

"I'm sorry, it really is a nice gift."

He was already halfway to his freedom. His eyes met mine, firm and commanding. "Stay away from the window." And the trapdoor closed tightly behind him.

Of course, his warning did nothing but make me go straight to the forbidden window. Had he really expected anything else?

Everything looked exactly the same as it had before. No new wagon, no visitor. A few birds hopped around in the middle of the clearing, fighting over some unfortunate bug, but other than them, the space was completely still.

With a sigh, I opened the notebook to the first page. I wanted to draw the trees as they danced, but my abilities were only good enough to be considered doodles. I wrote the words "Dear Mama" between the scribbled tree line, but quickly struck them through.

I couldn't send a letter to them. Well, I could, but it wouldn't be honest. I'd have to lie again; I'd have to pretend my life was completely fine. Maybe in this fairy-tale life, I would have met the perfect man? A butler, perhaps? Or the heir to the vineyard?

I traced the nib into the paper in tight circles, enjoying the subtle rebellion as the ink spread from one line to the other. It filled the space perfectly, darkening as it seeped through to the next page. I lightened my grip on the pen and drew a tail on the right side of the circle, adding a wing at the very top.

An eighth note.

Despite myself, a smile crept up my face as I got to work. I drew the five uniform lines of the staff, then tried the swirling treble clef on the far-left side.

The staff stared at me, waiting for the music. I let my eyes flutter closed as the song filled my head. I tapped my fingers on the imaginary piano in my lap. I tried to ignore the imperfections in my plan, but a basic idea of the tune was better than nothing.

I scrawled the notes across the page, working one measure at a time, filling it with whole notes, quarter notes, rests, chords. I hoped beyond anything my memory was correct, and everything was in their rightful place. As soon as I was allowed downstairs, I'd bring my creation to the piano and make the necessary changes.

My childhood teacher would be proud to know that I spent my isolation perfecting my music.

CHAPTER TWENTY-ONE

Visitor

The sunset was beginning to fade into darkness, leaving me squinting at the page when a creaking noise floated up to me.

The visitor had arrived.

I held my body in the shadow of the wall and peered through the glass. He'd warned me to stay away from the window, so I at least wanted to try to remain out of sight.

A wagon stopped directly in front of the steps, expelling a stocky man and his carpetbag. He wore gray pants with a knee-length black frock coat and a mustard-yellow waistcoat. His top hat matched his coat, a satin ribbon wrapped around the base. He held himself tall, his height accentuated by the silver-tipped cane that he pulled from under the seat. The top looked to be shaped like an animal's head, but I couldn't be sure from this distance.

He was a man of business, that much was obvious. His salt-and-pepper mustache was neatly groomed to hang down to frame his lips and chin, giving him a look of power.

There were no hugs as the men came to greet him. A handshake from Henry, a handshake from Donnell, a nod to Oliver and Arthur. I envisioned Rose waving from the porch as they all filed back inside, though I didn't catch a glimpse of her. Arthur took the horse and wagon to the barn, his job predetermined by his age.

I shimmied closer to the glass until I had my forehead pressed against it, straining to see anything else as they disappeared onto the porch.

"Who are you?" I whispered.

It was likely the relative Oliver had told me about. I certainly didn't want to be discovered by him.

But . . . I gritted my teeth as my thoughts took a rebellious turn. *What if he's friendly?* Not all of them could be trained, merciless killers, right?

But if he was really from another clan . . .

I tugged on my loose hair to try to force my brain to work properly. Oliver would keep me locked up whether the visitor was kind or not.

If he was a killer like all the others, and he caught me, that would be it. No more attic, no more loneliness, no more life.

If he wasn't, I could be saved.

Was it worth the risk?

I slammed the book shut and left it on the seat. I couldn't solve the mystery by staying still, that was for sure.

I couldn't let myself think about it anymore. Gnawing on my lower lip, I hopped my way to the trapdoor. I placed my palms firmly on the dusty floor and lowered myself to the ground to fling it back. It did so with a loud *bang*. I paused, listening for any signs that someone had heard me.

There wasn't any movement, at least not that I could see. Though, I could certainly hear conversations. Laughter, mixed with good-natured banter, floated up the stairs to my confused ears. I couldn't grasp anything other than a word here or there, no matter how hard I tried. No one seemed upset, so I let myself relax, cradling my chin in my hands.

I listened for hours. The smells of dinner eventually wafted to me, making my stomach growl in protest.

I hadn't touched my breakfast. That was my own fault. The flies circling the solidified porridge made it look pretty unappetizing. Perhaps, when they were finished downstairs, they would bring me some leftovers. I'd take what I could get.

You have sunk so low . . . waiting for leftovers like a dog.

I scooted even closer to the opening, practically leaning out of it. My braid dangled in the air, ensuring that if anyone dared come upstairs, I would be seen instantly.

I gripped the floor so tight, my knuckles paled. My back stretched under the chemise, the wounds threatening to burst.

I gritted my teeth against the discomfort, instead listening to the call of food as it beckoned me closer. The sweet smell of corn, the homey smell of bread and meat—I didn't want to wait for that meal to be cold too.

If I were to be trapped with them, was there really any harm in my sharing their food with them at the dinner table?

The clatter of dishes soon followed, but no one brought dinner to their pet. The men's chattering grew stern, but no one came to care for me.

The moon had a firm hold on the night sky by the time anyone thought about coming upstairs.

Rose was first, dark circles under her eyes and hair disheveled. Entertaining while nearly about to pop had done her in. She saw me leaning through the hole and made a small gasp, hand delicately to her lips.

"No, no, no, no." She waved her hands at me like she was shooing away a bad cat. "You must go back. You can't be seen!"

"Why?" I asked, matching the volume of her near whisper.

She shook her head dismissively. "No, no, no. It would be bad. Go, go, go." She waved her hands at me again.

"But I'm hungry." I moved out of the hole just enough to where I could roll completely out of sight in an instant.

She sighed and placed her hand on her forehead. "I'm sorry, not now. One of the boys can later. But for now"—she shook her head rapidly—"please, *s'il vous plaît*, just go."

I wanted to protest further, to beg and plead, or even get her to bring me downstairs, but I knew any efforts would be futile. Of all the people in this household, I trusted her most.

I didn't have a chance to say anything else.

"FIRE!" came Arthur's screech from somewhere outside.

Rose's face paled, and she rushed for the stairs. "Stay there!" she commanded.

I rushed for the window, the trapdoor flopping shut behind me.

Being trapped in an attic was getting more dangerous with every passing day.

CHAPTER TWENTY-TWO

Catlike Sneaking

The fire was small, lapping at the back side of the barn. Its red and orange tongues inched their way along the side, claiming more of the barn for itself.

I could hear the panicked whinnies through the window, shrill and heartbreaking. How many horses were in there?

Arthur was drawing up water from the well with impressive speed. By the time he had two buckets filled, Oliver and Donnell were at his side, grabbing them from him and hurrying straight to the offending flames.

Though I could hear Rose's instructions as she shouted them from her position in the grass, I couldn't understand a word of them. Everything sounded muted, the urgency syncopated by the horse's cries. Rose pointed from the well, then to the barn itself. "Stand in a line! Pass it, ah, there you go!" Though, I knew she was likely shouting at them in an intense French.

Henry took no time at all to get outside, joining the firefighting frenzy. He also shouted a few words toward the boys. The three of them instantly stopped with the water and rushed for the barn door.

The flames had made it to the roof, moving faster and faster with every minute that passed. Dark smoke rose to the sky, spinning and twisting in its own oddly peaceful dance.

My hands swirled round and round each other as the young men disappeared into the building. They took no time at all to emerge, each of them dragging an animal behind them. Arthur had an angry heifer, while Oliver and Donnell each had a horse.

As soon as they released their charges in the round pen, they hurried right back to the barn.

As they rescued the livestock, Henry threw water on the fire. At some point, Rose had taken the position by the well, drawing up bucket after bucket.

I could only imagine how difficult it would be to do that in her condition. What if it sent her into labor?

The visitor had also joined the fray, dropping his cane in the grass. He took bucket after bucket from Rose and passed each one straight to Henry. Henry then tossed the water on the roaring monster and returned it for more water.

It didn't take more than a few minutes for Donnell, Oliver, and Arthur to rejoin the line. Henry directed Rose back to the safety of the porch, and they fought on.

Whether it was the way their mouths were set in grim deter-mination, or the direction of the wind, they seemed to have the upper hand. One bucketful of water landed on the flames, sending it hissing back little by little.

They didn't stop until every potential flame was snuffed out.

That entire corner of the barn had changed from red to sooty black. Part of the ceiling had caved in, but from my standpoint, it almost looked repairable.

As far as I could tell, they had won without a single loss.

But the men didn't stop to rest. Henry pointed at various points of the tree line, and each of his sons rushed in that direc-tion, checking that they had their pistols.

This made me stiffen even more than the fire itself.

Henry gave instructions to the visitor, then disappeared after Donnell.

The man stooped to rescue his cane from its resting place, then stood there, firm, strong, ready for action.

He looked just as strong as the others, and I wouldn't have been surprised if the cane were only a ruse. Perhaps he had it only to make someone suspect a weakness. When he would be attacked, he would use it as a weapon, beating them down to instant submission.

Rose didn't seem to care either way. She waddled right up to him, said a few words, then went to check on the still-bellowing livestock.

It never occurred to me to back away from the window. If the guest ever bothered to look up, he could've easily seen my pale face in the moonlight.

Luckily for me, he never took his eyes from the trees.

The men filed back to the house in the inky black of the night, ghosts floating along in the moonlight. Only four returned.

They had no prisoners.

Murmurs woke me.

No, not murmurs. They were too loud to be considered such a thing. Loud, angry exclamations from one husky-voiced individual. It certainly didn't belong to anyone I knew.

Momentarily confused, I rolled from the settee and flattened to my stomach. I pressed my ear to the old wood of the trapdoor.

Their guest. It couldn't be anyone else.

As quietly as I could, I lifted the wooden door and set it to the side. It still made a distinct thump. I froze, my hands hovering above the hatch, ready to slam it back in place before they saw me.

When the vibrations of their conversation didn't diminish, I let myself relax.

Gnawing on my cheek, I leaned as far into the opening as I dared, straining to hear what they were saying. The murmurs arranged themselves into words here and there, occasionally producing a half-sentence or two. "How dare you!" or "Don't presume . . ." But otherwise, I couldn't understand a thing.

And then my stomach growled.

Startled, I vaulted back like a sly—though slightly wounded—cat. I rolled my eyes at my idiocy. There was no way they heard my stomach from two floors down. I still listened closely, just in case.

As expected, the arguing didn't cease.

My stomach, on the other hand, swirled in on itself, threatening to resort to cannibalism if I didn't do something to solve its dilemma.

You're not gonna die . . . I poked at my stomach and glanced at yesterday's abandoned breakfast. The porridge had congealed into some kind of inedible mush, and three flies buzzed happily around it. They certainly weren't keen to share, and I wasn't *that* desperate.

But no one had brought me supper. They had been too preoccupied by the fire.

They're too upset to notice you. The little voice in my head startled me, echoed by another growl. I flattened back to the ground to peer out.

No one would notice me if I sneaked into the kitchen.

Well, it depended on where they were, of course. But maybe, just maybe . . .

I gnawed on my lip, letting my thoughts jump around the potentially suicidal plan.

Another painful growl of my stomach decided my fate. If I waited much longer, I would start vomiting, or even get dizzy and faint. I needed to be alert! After all, whatever the men had been hunting for in the trees could come back.

Or the men themselves could come up to me.

Besides, if the men were where I couldn't sneak around, maybe I could just get Oliver's attention? Or even Arthur? They would be able to sneak me a snack, right?

On the other hand, if they catch you downstairs . . . I shuddered to stop that thought in its tracks.

However, some deep part of me was beginning not to care. I was trapped in an attic for the rest of my life. They needed to learn that they couldn't keep me cooped up like a wild animal.

What were they really going to do to me? Strap me to that piece of wood and whip me into submission?

Kill me?

My wounds throbbed and my stomach flipped at the mere thought. Those were perfect reasons to avoid doing anything other than sitting in the window seat. But I could feel the bile rising in my throat as it hunted for food.

Besides, Oliver had yet to come up with a real plan to give me a life again. He'd had plenty of time, hadn't he?

As much as I wanted to believe that, the doubt grew inside. He would have to fight a whole family of trained killers to gain freedom for his kidnapped witness. The odds would always be stacked against him.

And me.

I took a deep breath and focused on the pristine plank floor below.

I set my jaw, mind made up. "I can't just stay trapped in here like a naughty cat."

I just had to make it out of the attic. If I hung by my arms and dropped, it wouldn't be that far. And if I managed to land on my foot, my escape would be nearly silent.

Hopefully.

Before my conscience could caution against it, I dropped my cane to the floor and pushed my legs over the edge. The clatter as it landed made me freeze, but again, the discussion downstairs didn't pause.

There's no stopping now.

I let my legs dangle and held on with my forearms. The distance suddenly seemed so much farther than a single floor. My heart beat harder with every inch that I lowered myself, and my arms shook with the effort. If someone came up the stairs behind me, I'd be dead.

I didn't plan on letting go so ungracefully, but my muscles had their own agenda. Once I dangled from the hole like a opossum, my weight became too much. My grip slipped, and I crashed into a heap on the hard floor, an unladylike mess of chemise and tangled hair.

I didn't let myself feel the inevitable pain that shot through my limb; I didn't even let myself breathe.

The voices had paused this time.

I pressed the heel of my palm against my mouth, fighting the urge to scream. My back was on fire. My missing leg pulsed, exaggerating every severed bone. Even the original gash on the side of my calf screamed for mercy, though it was no longer there.

I heard nothing other than my inner turmoil for ages. No one spoke downstairs. I didn't dare breathe.

The solid thump of footsteps sounded far off to the right, getting closer to the stairway.

Oliver's voice rose from the foot of the stairs. "Oh, it was just—"

The pounding in my ears overpowered whatever excuse he made. Apparently, it was good enough, as the arguing resumed.

"There was no reason for such a mishap!"

"Some hinderances are unavoidable!"

My stomach rumbled again, reminding me of my suicide mission.

What am I doing?!

I removed my palm from my face, eyeing the perfect teeth marks in my fair skin. I let out a shaky breath and scooped up my cane. As I hauled myself up, I bit my lower lip hard enough to hurt.

Briefly, I wondered if I should just scramble back to my attic hideaway. But one look at my prison showed how that would be nearly impossible.

Can't stop now, I thought.

I walked, or rather hobbled, as silently as possible toward the stairs, my side pressed firmly against the wall. Each limping footfall created a thump that was sure to alert the world to my presence.

The talking downstairs continued on, becoming clearer as I made my way through the hallway to the staircase. After an eternity, I made it. They were only a room away, hiding in the sitting room next to the piano. I could see it, beckoning me to try the notes I had written in the notebook.

I could only see one person, the burly guest. He wore a dark coat and matching trousers. His snow-sprinkled hair had been brushed and cleaned since I had seen him last. He held himself tall, extruding power across the entire first floor.

But a tangible anxiety still trickled up the stairs and straight to me.

Them? Anxious?

"As I said, Henry," the powerful man said, his voice deep and commanding. It was the exact voice I would've given to a professor. "It's been two entire months. You had time. Plenty of time, I might add."

"Yes sir—" Henry started.

"I don't want excuses. You"—he turned on his heel to face someone else—"why is there a holdup?"

Arthur's voice sounded small as he stammered over each word. "W-Well, we determined his location b-but—"

His booming voice interrupted. "You found the location? We knew that last time we talked. You knew what we needed from day one. I want the man who did *this* to me." He pointed to his face. To what, I couldn't see.

"Yes sir," Arthur said. I could practically hear him squirming. "But we haven't seen him again."

"Only because you weren't *looking*! He came right here! A mere few feet from your mother. If he got just a little closer, her death would be on *your* hands!" The man paused, frozen as he scanned the room for his next victim. "Bernard, is it? What actual developments have been made?"

Bernard. My lip quirked in a small smile. I hadn't seen him in so long! When had he arrived? He stepped into my line of sight, his straight shoulders accentuating his height. He was the tallest of them all, Oliver only coming up to his ears.

When he spoke, his voice was deep, confident. "He's been keeping a low profile since the mishap on the train. We found signs of the daughter, and have been pursuing that lead. We saw no signs of him yesterday—"

"The *woman*," the man sneered. "Why would she show her face without her father for protection?"

"We aren't sure just yet," Henry said, moving to stand beside his eldest son. "But we were wondering if there is a plan being put into action against us. And that fire confirms it."

The guest waved his hand dismissively. "I don't have time for this. I need them now. Either of them. I need *blood*. When you left, it put *me* in charge. Did it not? Time to follow orders."

Henry didn't so much as flinch. He held his body firm, staring the man down.

"Now, who was the son of a bitch who killed the wrong man?" He looked from one person to the next, cycling through to see who the ultimate victim would be.

It was silent for a long, uncomfortable moment until Oliver spoke. "It was I, sir." His voice was also strong, though there was the twinge of childlike dread hiding in the back. Could this stranger hear his weakness? "Everything went according to plan. Richard came in, and there was a struggle. Only, someone else came into the car. I didn't have—"

"I do not care about *why* you messed up!" he roared. "I just care that it happened! You killed the owner of that vineyard, bringing the law down on the whole area. Do you know how much of a mess this made for me?"

It was Henry who spoke next. "We sincerely apologize for that, Martin. You know as well as I do, circumstances such as this can create many difficulties. But we have a lead on the girl—"

"A lead is nothing without—"

And that was when it happened. I sneezed. There could never have been a worse time for it. Especially one as delicate and catlike as the one that escaped my body. Every single curse that I had ever heard ran through my mind in that moment.

The powerful man's face swiveled like an eagle's, piercing brown eyes boring straight into my soul.

CHAPTER TWENTY-THREE

The Man with the Cane

I acted immediately, abandoning the cane and crawling as fast as I could for the safety of the attic. I didn't dare look back; I knew what was after me.

I knew my fate.

The heavy thump of feet on the stairs echoed in my wake as the pursuer took the steps two at a time. I reached for the nearest door handle, hoping to slip inside. My fingers barely brushed it as large, calloused hands gripped the back of my neck, pulling on the tiny hairs at the base of my braid in the process.

"I've been kidnapped! You have to help me!" Even as I said the words, I knew they were pointless, but I had to try.

He forced me to stand and half dragged, half pushed me toward the startled group of killers. My stump hit nearly every step, sending raw, shooting pain through every bone of my body. He showed no sympathy as I cried out. I pulled and fought against him when I could, but the agonizing, painful descent made my efforts futile. It was of no use, and I knew it.

There was no saving myself from fate. This man didn't *seem* like an enemy to the family, but he was definitely superior. He certainly wasn't someone who could rescue me.

When Oliver's face came into view, he was perfectly expressionless. The kind that required much training: hollow, unknown, empty.

The perfect poker face.

"Who is this?" Martin demanded, a growl in the back of his throat. No one said a single word. Arthur's eyes darted to Oliver, who stared blankly in my general direction. Everyone else either faced their relative straight on or looked to Henry for orders.

The room was so quiet that the scuttle of a rogue mouse could've been heard in the kitchen.

Henry, to my complete surprise, looked straight at Oliver. Only when nothing was said in my defense did he speak. "That is Donnell's fiancée."

My heart stopped, my mouth went dry. It was as though I had been punched in the stomach. Donnell's? *Fiancée?* My mouth worked before my mind. I opened my mouth to argue but glued it shut almost immediately. *Play along. You don't want to die today.*

I went perfectly silent, panic swelling through my body. *You didn't agree to this. They can't do this. They're just saying that to protect you. They're only words.* I repeated the chant to myself over and over, trying to convince myself that it was just a quick excuse to avoid trouble with Martin York.

But did these people bother making up excuses? Or did they create plans instead?

Wrenching my eyes away from Donnell's threatening gaze, I could see exactly how pale Oliver had become. Fear crashed through his stormy eyes, and his brows furrowed with his secret plans.

These people created and executed plans. Not excuses.

Martin York shook me like a limp doll, regaining Oliver and Donnell's focus.

"Ah, I see." He laughed gleefully. "A little stowaway? A pet? It's no wonder you can't get your job done." He traced my jaw with his pointer finger. "Such a shame. But didn't your parents teach you that when there's a job to do, you must do it? Dawdling over such things"—he tsked—"isn't advised."

Oliver cleared his throat and stepped forward. "It was a slip of the tongue." He reached out to take hold of my arm. Firm, but gentle. "She's *my* fiancée."

I leaned in his general direction, but Mr. York didn't release the painful hold of my hair, neck, and back of my clothes. His hands were so big. So strong. So terrifying.

"*Fiancée*, hmm?" There was a disbelieving sneer hiding under his voice. "There are rules to this organization."

"There are," Henry agreed. His hands were clasped casually in front of him, as if this were a routine conversation. "But every boy, one day, becomes a man and chooses his future. In this case, they will stay here until they can start their own household."

Mr. York shook his head. "And the kidnapping claim?" He directed this to Oliver.

He took a deep breath before beginning, one hand on my forearm, the other in a fist at his side. "Well, sometimes things might not be done . . . legally. So I request, as one of us, that you release my fiancée back to me."

Each word was smoothly crafted, normal. Just another midday meeting. Only, the object of discussion was my life.

You were safer in the attic! My mind swirled, panicked, scolding.

The man let go of me, and I practically fell into Oliver's arms. He wrapped his arm securely around me, letting me lean against him and regain my footing. I wanted to melt into him, hide somewhere where no one could reach me ever again.

"Because of this *situation*," Henry said, "I removed Oliver from this crucial case."

"As you should." Mr. York's eyes locked on mine and flickered with a shred of amusement. It was the most expressive thing I'd seen from him yet. "When's the wedding?"

Oliver stiffened some, but his voice stayed strong. "We have not set a date yet."

"But this young woman is living with you. What would her parents think?" Again, he tsked his tongue. "Ah, I see, they likely don't know. Kidnapping and all. But you keep her here without marriage?"

Henry's explanation was confident. The charade felt so real, so final. "Oliver needed to be sure about such a decision before it was made official."

"Well then, Oliver." Mr. York smiled, the kind of grin that sent shivers up my spine. One furry eyebrow lifted as he stared his nephew down. "As you claim you are *affianced* . . . have you made your final decision?"

"Yes sir." Oliver's voice was noticeably softer, but the hesitation had left.

"And you?" He looked at me but didn't give me the option to respond. "Nah, it doesn't matter." He stretched his arms then, deliberate, measured, counting the moments before he told the end of his own personal plan. "As your father can tell you, I used to help a lot of young couples transition into the glorious land of holy matrimony."

I grasped at Oliver's hand, stomach flipping nearly into my throat. He squeezed, a useless attempt to reassure me.

"Oh, yes," Henry said. He moved to stand beside his brother, unified as only siblings could be. "There was that time in your life. You had your own small church, did you not?"

Martin's voice turned syrupy sweet. Every word felt like he held the key to any divine answer I could ever want. "Yes, a very small town, but it was humble. I was given the job that so few receive, to care for some of God's flock."

My fingernails practically dug into Oliver's hand. He took the pain without so much as a flinch. This man, a pastor. At least at one point. And murderer?

I should've never left the attic!

"You're much more suited in your current position," Henry said.

"Well, of course. God has plans for each of us in the different parts of our life." Martin's head swiveled to look at us. "Now, I know there won't be any guests, correct? So why don't we simply wed the happy couple now? Unless, of course, Oliver has more explaining to do?" He stared down the bridge of his nose at his nephew, eyebrows up in a wordless challenge.

"No sir." Oliver choked midway through, bringing out the teeth in Mr. York's smile.

"Well, then we have a date set." Mr. York popped his neck with calculated slowness. "Arthur, go fetch your ma. She, of course, will want to be here for this *integral* part of her son's life."

Arthur glanced from person to person, ensuring there weren't any other orders before giving in and heading to find Rose.

I opened my mouth to speak but didn't manage a single word before Oliver squeezed my hand. No part of marrying him was okay. None of it.

Perhaps it wasn't binding? Perhaps this Martin York wasn't an *actual* man of God?

It couldn't be real. It couldn't be legal.

But the looming man with the sick smile plastered to his face seemed perfectly okay with toying with us. No matter the consequences.

It took no time at all for Arthur to reappear, his mother right behind.

A young woman trailed directly behind, brown eyes wide and alert. She didn't look much older than me. She reached behind her to grasp the little hand of a child. "You two, go play outside, all right?" The second child in question peered through the doorway. Everything from their outfit to their hair was completely identical.

"Yes, Mama," the boys chorused. Dutifully, they tucked their heads and traipsed through the center of the room. As soon as they reached the entryway, they took off at a full run.

Watching the children escape the stifling room, Rose wrung her hands on her apron. "What is this?"

"Oliver will be marrying dear . . ." Mr. York hesitated. "What's your name, dear girl?"

I considered not answering, or giving him the wrong name entirely. "Petronella." My voice grated against my throat.

"Ah, good," Mr. York said. "Oliver here will be marrying Miss Petronella."

Rose glanced among the faces, searching for the correct response she should adopt. "Oh," was all she could come up with, the word a mixture of strife, confusion, and a hint of excitement.

Mr. York took Oliver's forearm and pulled him away from me, positioning him in the picturesque place to the right of the piano. He then looked me up and down as I fought to catch my balance. He clicked his tongue. "Oliver, are you sure? This one's broken."

Oliver looked pained. "I am aware."

"Well, as long as you're sure. One only gets married once." He laughed at some private joke. "Well, there is always a way."

He roughly picked me up, hands under my arms like he was carrying a muddy child. He placed me across from Oliver, safely leaning against the bookshelf in the wall. It took every bit of me to avoid kicking him in the gut.

"Dear Petronella, you know the family business, I assume? From your spying? Well, not to worry. You *should* be all right. You should know to be cautious, and don't anger him too much." He made that clicking noise with his tongue again.

Everyone except for Henry and Mr. York were like dolls in a playhouse, standing dumb and awaiting instructions. No one so much as breathed too deeply.

"Are we ready? The sooner we get this done, the sooner we can get to something *other* than . . ." He pointed from me to Oliver. "This."

He paused for a long moment, scrutinizing my face. "Now, what is this?" He took his finger and traced the edge of my face, removing a stray tear. "A bride shouldn't look so sad on her wedding day."

I opened my mouth to answer, but Oliver chimed in first. "She's a woman. She has her own ideas about how she wants to be married. As you said, you can only do this once. It's unfair to her to—"

Martin waggled his finger at him. "Unfair to *her*? Well, from what I see, there are *so* many other options. You, dear boy, are *this* close to excommunication." He held up his fingers about an inch apart. "This girl has no options. She knows too much."

"She knows nothing," Oliver spat, a hint of a growl in his voice.

"Now, boy, you know better than that!" He shook his head and turned to face me. "Do you know of the Williams family?"

Apparently, my expression gave away everything he needed to know.

"That's what I feared." He turned back to Oliver. "You have two options. A choose-your-own-punishment adventure, if you will. Only two. I will give you just a few minutes to make your decision. Realize, of course, I know full well this girl is far from your fiancée. I know full well this girl is here because of *you.* Now, here are your options, and they are very simple. End it all now, or fix it."

My stomach lurched. I assumed the choices roughly translated to "kill her or marry her to keep her in line."

Bernard cleared his throat and stepped forward. "Oliver, remember what's at stake. Are you sure she's the one? If you take care of it now, there won't be emotions—"

Oliver didn't look at his brother, but his hands turned to fists at his sides. "That's not an option."

I stiffened just a little more. I had hoped Bernard, of all people, would be on my side.

Donnell smirked. "The feelings ship sailed a long time ago."

"I see." Bernard shook his head, true pity tracing the lines of his face.

"Is that your final decision?"

"Yes," Oliver said firmly, fixing him with a cold, determined stare.

CHAPTER TWENTY-FOUR

Wedding

"*Attends une seconde.*" Rose shoved herself between Oliver and Mr. York, hands up as if it would help clear the way. Her round belly did the work for her. "Oliver." She set one hand on each of his shoulders, crystal blue eyes staring deep into his.

Henry cleared his throat. "Alderose . . ."

She flinched but ignored him. She focused solely on her son. "Do you really want to bring her into this life?"

Oliver darted a glance in my direction, just enough doubt in his eyes to make me bristle.

He got me into this mess in the first place. He can safely *get me out!* I sent him the most threatening glare I could muster, but he didn't react.

"She's already in it, isn't she?" Despite the firm way he carried himself, his voice cracked.

Rose squeezed his shoulder. "Martin," she started, turning on her heel to face her brother-in-law. "Let the boy make his *own* mistakes. Henry has it under control. A wedding really isn't necessary." She spoke with great care, taking her time to ensure she chose the correct words.

Mr. York stared at her, mouth open in astonishment. "Henry, get ahold of your woman, will you? This is no place for the likes of you." With only a hint of compassion, he shoved her out of the way.

The other girl reached out to steady Rose. Bernard stepped forward then, tucking one arm around her and ushering her back to the safety of the assembled group. I could only assume that was his wife, and the twins, his children.

"You won't give her the say in her own wedding?" Rose's accent came back in full force, making it difficult to understand each word.

"No." Martin scoffed. "Of course not. Now, do you wish to be a part of your son's wedding? Or not?"

She fell silent, the stress lines plainly visible on her forehead.

"Good." Martin nodded his approval. "Let us begin!"

"Wait, wait." Rose held up both hands, eyes wrenched shut.

"Rose!" Henry threw his arms into the air. "Let the man perform the dadgum wedding!"

Her shoulders drooped at the scolding, but she still managed to fix a firm gaze on her husband. "I will," she promised. "She can't be wed like this." She gestured to my tattered clothing. I hadn't taken the time to change into the hand-me-down work dress. I only wore my chemise and a stained pink dressing gown, with a long, somewhat ratty braid running down my back.

"And what else do you plan to put her in?" Henry spat. "We don't have time to let you stitch together something fancy."

"No, no." Rose shook her head. "Just something nicer." She took my hand and squeezed it gently. "We will return."

To my surprise, no one stopped her as she assisted me to the banister. No one helped us, either. Each step made my heart beat a little faster, my brain come alive a little more.

They were going to make us get married?

Married.

For better or worse—married.

Once in her room, Rose set me in front of her vanity and went after my hair, deftly working through the tangles. I stayed perfectly silent, eyes wrenched shut against the sharp tugs, brain flying back and forth.

How did I end up here?

Sure, he's attractive. He has a financially stable family. I think. But . . . I said no to Tom! Why would I agree to this?

To save your life.

They won't kill me, though. Oliver wouldn't let them.

Don't be an idiot! He wouldn't be able to stop them if they really tried.

I licked my lips, my mouth drier than a sunbaked towel. "Do I have to?" I wasn't completely sure if I said the words aloud.

Rose mulled over her own thoughts for a moment, working on a particularly nasty tangle at the base of my neck. "*Oui.*"

I winced with each pull but did my best to stay still. "If I don't do this . . ." I paused, gulping back emotion. "They'll kill me?"

She set the old bone comb on my thigh. "*Oui.*"

I traced my fingers over the delicate edges, noting how light the handle had turned from years of use. "Would they ever have let me go home?" My voice came out in a sort of choked whisper.

She squeezed my shoulder. "No. Oliver had only a short time to make a decision."

Chills ran up my spine. "What choices did he have?"

"Death," she said the first option so nonchalantly, I wondered for a moment if I heard her correctly. "Or, perhaps, he might come up with something different."

I licked my lips, my syncopated breathing ensuring Rose knew exactly how panicked I really was.

"Chin up, *chérie*." With deft fingers, she sectioned off my hair and started to work on a braided bun. Though she hurried, she ensured every flyaway was carefully tucked in its own place. In no time at all, I had a simple yet elegant hairstyle. The sides of my hair covered my ears, then trailed back to join the braid-wrapped bun.

"Hmm . . ." She traced the circle of hair three times before she snatched the bouquet of slightly wilted wildflowers beside her washbasin.

With each delicate white sprig that she tucked into my hair, I felt myself relax.

A little.

"Alderose! We don't have time!" Henry's voice barreled up the stairs.

Rose jumped but didn't yell back an answer. In fact, she started to hum a little tune to block him out as she searched through her wardrobe.

"This might fit you." She held a multitiered, flower-covered dress out to me, squinting one eye to check the fit. "*Oui, oui.* Close enough. It'll probably be a little long. Hurry, hurry."

I took the proffered dress and let my fingers trace over the different layers. "Thank you," I whispered. At some point, it must've been one of her finest dresses. The sleeves, collar, and layers of the skirt all had decorative lace around the edges.

After lending me a hoop skirt, she helped guide it over my head.

The weight on my shoulders and hips was like a comforting hug. Safe. Home. Happy. I'd worn plenty of dresses like this over the years. But once my father's gambling took over, new dresses became scarce.

"If we had time, I'd take it in so it'd fit you better." Rose clucked her tongue as she ran her fingers along the hem that would inevitably drag the floor.

"Rose!" Henry's voice again. This time, it was accompanied by a loud thump on the door.

"We're coming, we're coming."

He didn't wait for permission. He simply shouldered the door aside and waltzed right in. "Martin is not one who should *ever* be kept waiting!"

Rose cut her eyes at him. "Well, then." She took a deep breath, likely to stifle down whatever comeback she had conjured up. "She's ready."

"Good. Come on, girl." Henry gripped my forearm and pulled, apparently not remotely prepared to be nice to his soon-to-be daughter-in-law.

Will he always be so rough? My shoulders sagged a little at the thought. *Will he even let me out of the attic now?*

Henry pulled me in the general direction of the door, ignoring Rose's rapid French protests and my startled gasps. He didn't even stop when I fell smack on the floor, crinoline flattening uncomfortably against my hips.

Rose rushed to my side, hands whacking her husband's arm. "Stop it! You'll hurt her!"

Before he could pull my shoulder out of socket or even ruin the dress on the weathered wood floor, she forced her pregnant self between us. "She will be down presently. You can tell *Martin* that one does not rush a bride on her wedding day!" She practically spat his name.

Henry released me and sighed. His voice held the growl of unspoken threats. "Mark my words, Alderose . . ."

She stood a little straighter, chin pointed stubbornly in his direction. "A few minutes will do him no harm."

With a huff, Henry turned on his heel and marched out. I watched him go, my mouth dry, thoughts stunned to silence.

"Come on, *chérie*." Rose hooked me under the arms and pulled up, a highly inefficient effort with her poor balance. She tilted forward as I scrambled up, but miraculously, neither of us fell. "He'll be more likely to leave you alone after." She smiled reassuringly.

Because Oliver's done such a good job at keeping me safe so far, I thought bitterly. "Will we stay here?"

Rose patted my shoulder. "I don't know. All of this is too fast. We will figure out the details later. For now, we must go before Martin comes up to get you himself."

She wouldn't be able to stop him for even a moment if *he* wanted to lay hands on me. That was all the information I needed to limp on just a little faster.

When we made it back to the sitting room, Oliver looked just about as nervous as I felt. His hands were clasped in front, fingers twirling together first one way, then another. For once, he didn't stand still. He swayed back and forth, bare feet curling into the rug beneath him.

"It took ya long enough!" Martin scoffed. "You look mighty pretty, though it really don't matter." His lip twitched in an almost smirk. "I'm assumin' you two are already married in the eyes of the Lord." He lifted his head reverently to the heavens, then winked at me. "If you know what I mean."

I bristled. *Be a good girl, keep your head down, and everything will be okay.* But I couldn't listen to the voice in my head. It wasn't bad enough that I was being forced to marry my captor.

I had to do it without my family, without my father to walk me down the aisle. And now this man wanted to bring my virginity into question? "My *virtue* is my business, and mine alone," I snapped, hands in fists at my side. "But if you must know, it is intact."

I hadn't realized I had moved to stand directly in front of the man, glaring like a furious porcupine, until Oliver gripped my shoulders and very carefully pulled me to his side.

Martin York beamed. "Ah, there is some fire to ya, now, isn't there? Good. You'll need it." He pointed to a spot on the rug about a foot or so from Oliver. "Stand there. I'm gettin' hungry and tired of waiting." When I didn't move immediately, he clapped his hands, sending a sharp, booming slap throughout the silent room.

A startled gasp escaped my lips, and I scurried to the designated location.

"All right, all right." He scooped the family Bible off the piano. Making a show of it, he straightened himself and cleared his throat. "We are all gathered here today . . . Little Arthur, Donnell, Bernard, and his wife Anna—ah, Bernard, the little 'uns don't wanna come in for the ceremony?—and their parents, Alderose and Henry Wedman." He took his time on the names, fixing each and every person with the look of a hunter. "We are gathered here today to join these two together in *holy* matrimony."

I felt my eyebrows furrow at the stress he placed on the word. It was like he wanted to ensure we knew he was in charge.

"Though this wasn't the original plan of the day—"

Henry cleared his throat. "Martin, I thought you said you're hungry? Let's get this going."

Martin rolled his eyes. "All right, all right. Oliver, repeat after me."

The ceremony, if it could be called that, went by like a fever-laced blur. When instructed, I repeated the correct words, my brain wandering into some fantasy land.

The kiss was the only part that I knew would live on in my memories. Oliver placed his hands on my shoulders, so gentle, so tender. He stared into my eyes, making me forget the world around us for just a minute. One hand made its way to the nape of my neck—large, cold, and clammy, but strong and full of support.

I gulped, my heart beating like a nervous hummingbird. Then he leaned in, his own eyes fluttering closed. I lifted onto my tiptoes and closed the space between us, aware for just a moment that all eyes were on us.

Mama would have loved to be at your wedding.

Guilt pricked at my stomach. But there was nothing I could do to change the outcome.

Almost as soon as the short but sweet kiss was broken, Martin wrote our names in the family Bible and snapped it closed.

It was official.

If saying "I do" hadn't sealed my fate, *that* certainly did.

CHAPTER TWENTY-FIVE

Written in the Bible

The world tossed and turned in a blurry whirlwind. I couldn't focus on anything, no matter how hard I tried.

Your freedom is over. It's all over.

We sat at the dinner table as a family. Henry at the head of the table; Rose across from him. Their four children and two grandchildren dispersed around, with Martin, Anna, and I sandwiched between.

A potato soup. Fragrant, warm, garnished with freshly picked green onions. It was nice to have a meal straight from the stove, even if the bottom had scorched during the impromptu ceremony. How long had it been since Oliver plucked me from the train? A few weeks? Months?

Nothing ever made its way into my attic prison with steam still dancing from the top.

"You okay?" Oliver asked under his breath. He didn't touch me. In fact, it seemed he was trying hard *not* to touch me.

I nodded mutely and focused on the activity around me.

Bernard laughed at some joke. Arthur made a face at a larger chunk of onion in his soup, resulting in a backhanded swat from Rose.

Bernard chortled, water spewing from his nose. "She might be as big as a buffalo, but you can't pull one over on her!"

Rose must've kicked him, as he yowled and shoved his chair back from the table.

"I *dare* you to try that line on Anna," Donnell said, lips tight with suppressed laughter.

At the sound of her name, Anna's head snapped up, eyes wide and nervous. Her hand had traveled to grip one of her twin's arms. It took her only a moment to recognize the jovial atmosphere, but it took a long while for her hackles to settle.

Rose turned her glare on him. "He won't say that to his wife if he wants to see another sunrise."

Anna let out an almost imperceptible sigh of relief, and she released her son's arm. The little boy acted like nothing had happened and went right back to shoving his brother over on their shared chair.

I felt a small smile play at the edge of my lips. As a result, Oliver instantly relaxed. In a family atmosphere, they didn't seem nearly as threatening.

But perhaps that really made them more terrifying. If *they* could be normal . . .

When the bowls were practically licked clean, Martin shifted in his seat.

"That was a lovely meal, Rose, but we must get back to business."

Rose's face turned to an expressionless mask, but her shoulders noticeably slumped. "Nella, Anna, help me with the dishes while I make the men something to drink."

Obediently, I pushed from the table and followed her into the kitchen. I wasn't sure if I was disappointed that Oliver didn't try to follow, or not.

Once in the kitchen, I shut my eyes for a long moment, taking in the comforting scents of cheese and potatoes. A light hand touched my arm, and I jumped. Anna stood there, a reassuring smile on her face.

"It'll be okay," she said. Her voice was delicate, almost high-pitched like a child's.

"Come on." Rose pushed past us, leading the way to the sink. "Bernard brought in some water earlier. Help me get it on the stove to warm it up."

Before I made it to her side, the woman had already grasped the handle of the nearly overflowing water pail, lips set in a thin, determined line.

Anna and I rushed to take it from her. "No, no, stop," Anna scolded. She took the handles and heaved it up with a grunt. "You know better than to do that." She set it on the stove with a satisfying *clang*.

Rose muttered something in French right back at her, likely griping that she wasn't useless.

I wandered to the pile of dishes to discard the scraps into a bucket for the chickens.

"Where are the boys?" Rose asked.

Anna's entire body seemed to lighten with the new topic. "Told them to go close the chickens up for you and see what else needed to be done outside."

Rose reached across and rubbed Anna's back. "*Merci.*"

I trudged on with my chore, scraping clump after clump of congealed potato into the bucket. I could feel their eyes on me as they worked.

Rose pulled six small glasses from the cabinet, each one clinking as she set them onto the counter. The cork of the whiskey bottle popped as Anna tugged it open, but I didn't turn to them.

As my brain whirled and reality sunk in, my movements faltered. I felt as if I were moving in a dream—slow, steady, numb.

I was married.

To the man who whipped me.

The soup in my stomach turned to steaming daggers, and I leaned against the counter, wincing against the pain.

"Nella?" Rose's footsteps echoed behind me, but I hardly noticed. The world blurred again, and I vomited straight into the bucket of scraps.

"Oh, *ma chérie* . . ." Rose rubbed my back in a way that only a mother could.

As I came up, my emotional shield shattered. "What am I gonna do?" My voice didn't sound like mine; it was childlike, terrified.

"Shh, shh." Rose tucked me into a hug, my face nestled against her neck. "It will be all right."

The drinks clinked as Anna poured out six glasses of whiskey. Cold glass pressed against my arm as Anna nudged one to me. "Take it, you deserve it."

I wrapped my fingers around the delicate drink, studying the amber liquid as it sloshed inside.

"It's really not so bad," Anna assured. "Oliver is a good man. As long as you be careful around the likes of Martin and Henry, you'll be fine."

Rose grunted her agreement. "*Bien sûr.*" She wrapped one arm around my shoulders and squeezed.

My skin went cold. Rose took a risk by standing up for me before the ceremony. "Will he . . . hurt you?" I could hardly force the words from my lips.

Rose sighed, though a flicker of unease passed over her eyes. "Not if I give him enough of this." She tapped the whiskey bottle with her fingernail.

Anna laughed, though the sound was strained. "I'll pour extra then."

I gritted my teeth, and my fingernails bit into my palms. It wasn't an uncommon thing for a man to beat his wife, and I'd already assumed Henry took his anger out on Rose. My stomach lurched at the confirmation. What would Oliver do when he got ahold of me? Legally? "Where am . . . I . . . where will we stay?" The sentences didn't want to form, the confusion taking over yet again. Where was I supposed to sleep? Would Oliver . . . it *was* our wedding night, after all.

"She *can't* stay in that room with all the boys!" Anna gasped at the mere thought.

"No," Rose agreed, absently rubbing her protruding stomach. "For now, the attic will be the safest place."

"Mhm, you can get some privacy there." Anna winked, and I nearly vomited again. She squeezed my arm. "The pain doesn't last long, I promise."

I grabbed the counter for support. My captor officially had every legal right to my body. "If I say I'm on my—"

"Nah, just get it over with. That doesn't deter some men." Anna grinned, and I stared at her like she grew another head.

"I can't do it . . ." I choked out.

"Drink that, *chérie*." Rose nodded to the glass. "It *will* be all right."

The door swung open, mercifully ending that conversation. Oliver cleared his throat. "Anna, Vernon found a snake."

Anna swore under her breath. "I'll be right there." With one last reassuring smile in my direction, she rushed out the door.

Apparently, my confusion showed on my face, as Oliver explained. "The twins. Anton is terrified of snakes, and Vernon will do whatever he can to exploit that."

As if to underline the statement, a shrill scream seeped through the kitchen window.

"That boy . . ." Rose muttered.

"Donnell did the same to me." Oliver's shoulders vibrated in a chuckle.

My eyes didn't leave him. Could I really trust him? After everything? There were still some scabs on my back to remind me of how loyal he could really be to his father.

Rose made a strange noise in the back of her throat to get our attention. It worked. "Oliver, your wife is tired. It's been a trying day."

I stared at her, mouth open in horror. She thought to just send me upstairs and get it all over with?

"Take her to bed, will you?"

Oliver's feet shuffled on the cold floor. "Martin's not done with us just yet."

Rose stood a little straighter and glared at him. "Then come right back down. When you're finished with your meeting, I want to talk with you."

"Yes ma'am." He turned to me and held out a hand. "Ready?"

I took it, my palm sticky with sweat. He moved his arm around my back, letting it rest on the opposite hip to support me. There was something comforting about his protective embrace, I had to admit that.

With his help, I limped out of the kitchen and into the den of trained killers. Every eye turned to us, and I nearly collapsed.

Oliver's voice sounded strained. "I'll be right back, I'm just taking her back up to bed."

"Aw, come on! I'm sure you're better than *that*!" Donnell bellowed.

Laughter erupted from the other men. All except Martin, who stared with a challenge written plainly in his eyes.

Oliver's grip tightened on my waist. "Back off, Donnell," he growled. Standing tall, he carried on through the room and up the stairs.

Once we were out of earshot, he bent to whisper in my ear. "You're shaking, Nella. I'm not going to hurt you. I promise."

I turned my face to his, swallowing down the panic. "I don't want to—"

"Shh." He kissed my forehead, the gesture making both of us freeze for a moment. "I'm only taking you up to bed. I'm not staying. Martin wouldn't let me even if I wanted to. In fact, I'm surprised he's even letting me do that."

I managed to calm the queasiness as he got me into my attic prison. As he promised, he placed me onto the settee, squeezed my hand, then disappeared back downstairs. For once, the cramped, dusty walls felt almost warm and safe.

I didn't plan on sleeping. Instead, I intended to cry until my eyes turned puffy and red. But almost as soon as the first tear hit the stained pillow, I was out.

Gradually, the room darkened until it was lit only by the stars and the mere sliver of a moon. When the sudden lantern light joined in, I jolted awake.

"I didn't mean to wake you, I'm sorry," Oliver whispered.

I went to close my eyes again—at least until the memories slammed into my brain.

We were married.

I sat bolt upright and pointed straight at him. "Don't touch me!"

He blinked, eyes owlish in the flickering light. "I won't."

For some reason, the short, nearly offended way he said it almost felt like an insult. I pushed the confusing dissonance of emotions away. "Why are you up here?"

"They won't let me sleep in my own bed," he muttered, sitting on the window seat and yanking his boots off.

"Why?" I asked dumbly.

He just crooked his eyebrow at me for an answer and peeled off one long wool sock. The way he casually tossed it to the floor shocked me.

When he started to unbutton his shirt, fear pierced my heart. "What are you *doing*?"

He gave me that same look that told me I should already know.

"You can't sleep here!" I scrambled to sit, pulling the blankets tightly around me as I went. Though I knew he'd seen me in far less than my chemise, I wasn't going to give him any ideas. "And you . . . you keep those clothes on!"

He sighed deeply and placed his hands on his knees, watching my every move like a hawk. "I won't touch you. I swear. But I have to sleep *somewhere*. And Martin has the couch."

"Then . . . then sleep outside!"

He rolled his eyes. "Martin is on the couch. He'll know if I so much as go downstairs. I don't feel like finding out what he'll do if he believes I'm shirking my 'manly duties.'"

I gritted my teeth hard enough to ensure I'd have a headache in the morning. "I'll have nothing to do with those *manly* duties. Barbarian!" I curled my hands into fists and held them in front of me, well aware I probably looked like an innocuous, fighting mouse instead of a force to be reckoned with.

His teeth flashed in a full grin. "If you'll allow it, m'lady, I'll sleep right here." He patted the window seat. "I won't touch you. But they won't let me sleep downstairs as if today never happened. You understand that, right?"

My eyes fell to the place where my foot should have been. *None of this should have happened in the first place.*

"Then am I free to go outside as I please now?"

The thoughtful way he licked his upper lip told me all I needed to know.

No.

"So that hasn't changed? Just the 'legalities' of whether or not you can . . ." I couldn't even say it. I waved my hands wildly at him instead.

His foot tapped absently at the floor. "I won't touch you. Not unless you want me to."

The way he cocked his head to the side made my blood boil. I sent my pillow straight at his head. It fell short, brushing his bare feet instead.

"As I said, I won't touch you."

My eyes flickered to the gun at his belt.

He followed my gaze and placed his hand protectively over the weapon. "Oh, *come* on!"

"You won't touch me if I have that."

He grumbled something under his breath as he fiddled with his belt. "I'm not going to give you a loaded weapon while I plan to sleep. How do I know you won't blow my brains out while I sleep?"

I crossed my arms stubbornly. "You gave it to me before."

"Well, I wasn't sleeping then."

I stared him down. "Then you're not sleeping in here."

He groaned and pulled the belt free in one terrifying movement. Despite myself, I flinched. Deliberately, he walked straight to the trapdoor, pushed it open, and poked his head through. "Arthur!"

"What are you doing?" I demanded.

"Neither of us gets the gun," he said matter-of-factly. "I won't touch you. You won't shoot me."

I let out a sort of exasperated noise and fell back onto my well-worn pillow. "Don't touch me."

"I won't," he promised, before tossing the gun to his little brother. "Keep that for me overnight?"

CHAPTER TWENTY-SIX

Sleep

I didn't sleep. At least not very well. My dreams were inundated with blood and screams. I couldn't identify a single person in them. Not the victims, or the killers. But yet, I was sure I knew each and every one.

"Hey, hey, Nella, it's okay." Warm, calming hands clasped onto my shoulders and shook me. "You're okay, it's okay."

My eyes shot open, focusing on Oliver's concerned face.

He probably expected me to smile, or to relax at least a little. I did the exact opposite: I screamed.

"Whoa, whoa!" He backed away so fast he tripped over his discarded boots, barely catching himself on some of the quilt-covered chests in the corner. "You were having a nightmare. I just figured—"

"You said you wouldn't touch me!"

He threw his hands into the air in exasperation and plopped back down on his window seat. The first tinge of red streaked across the night sky, warning of the upcoming sunrise.

"Was this part of your *grand plan*?" I kept my glare on him, waiting to see if he'd squirm. Though, in reality, I didn't think anything could ever make him truly uncomfortable.

"Was *what* part of my grand plan?" he asked, leaning against the window with his eyes half closed.

"This." I pointed rapidly between the two of us. "Did you plan on marrying me this whole time?"

He groaned. "Can we fight about this in the morning?"

"It *is* the morning," I snapped. "It's nearly sunrise."

He groaned again. Apparently, he was *not* a morning person. "It was the only real option, I knew that. But it wasn't supposed to happen this way."

I somehow hadn't expected that answer. "And how was it supposed to happen?"

"I don't know. Pa gave me the ultimatum that day in the basement. Either I marry you or . . ." He made a vague gesture with his hand. "He was giving me time to make the decision."

My hands rolled into fists at my side. "Make the decision to kill me or not? It's that tough of a choice?"

Oliver visibly flinched. "I never planned on killing you. I just wanted to find a better way to talk to you about . . . it. Uh, marriage."

I bristled, though a small part of my brain told me I was being a bit unreasonable. "'Oh, good morning, here's your food. By the way, I have to *marry you* now!' wouldn't have been enough for you?"

He narrowed his sleepy eyes at me. "Really now, do you think you would've taken kindly to that?"

I knew very well I wouldn't have, but I didn't want to give him the satisfaction of being right. "You could have told me what you were planning."

He hit his head against the glass hard enough to make a thump, his disheveled brown hair falling into his face. With exaggerated effort, he brushed it away with his left hand, puffing his cheeks full of air as if it would force him to be calm.

"I'm sorry all of this is so hard for you to understand, but I've been *trying* to save your life this whole time. I'm sorry I just so happened to change it in ways you didn't expect. Now please, can we talk about this tomorrow?"

I opened my mouth a few times, fighting for words to throw in his direction. "I'm not sleeping with *you* in here."

He crooked one eyebrow. "Because you weren't asleep just a few minutes ago?" Like a cat, he curled on the window seat again, arm flopping over his eyes to block out what little light fluttered through the panes.

I glared at him for a long while, watching as his breathing slowed and a light snore fluttered through his lips.

Eventually, I gave in and curled up on the settee, never taking my eyes off him.

"Goodness, sleepy head!" The unmistakable slap of a palm against flesh woke me.

Somehow, I had fallen asleep again.

This time, Donnell stood at Oliver's feet, a huge grin plastered to his face.

Oliver groaned, then rolled in a desperate attempt to escape his older brother.

He was far from successful. In the most ungraceful way imaginable, he fell smack onto the floor. He just stayed there, groaning.

"Don't tell me last night went *so* bad that you're—"

That got Oliver up. He vaulted to his feet and placed his hand firmly on Donnell's chest. He looked like a wolf ready to strike, hair sticking out every which way. "I'm not discussing last night with you, or anyone else. Tell Ma we'll be downstairs shortly." He shoved him toward the door.

"Fine, fine." Donnell held up his hands in mock surrender. "You slept late, though. Food's already gettin' cold waiting for you."

Oliver pulled on his discarded pants, tucking his sleeping shirt inside without a care in the world. His glare never once faltered.

When had he taken his pants off? Hadn't I told him to keep them on? From my blanket cocoon, I watched. They were technically in *my* room, after all. Was there any real sin in watching? I hadn't been able to see anything more than his upper thighs, but that alone somehow sent butterflies scurrying through my stomach.

"You'd better hurry. Pa's got plans for us today." Donnell turned on his heel and started down the ladder, but not before fixing his gaze on me. "Don't worry, darlin'. From what I've heard, it gets easier the more you do it." He winked right before shutting the trapdoor between us.

I scowled at where he had been. *How* dare *he!*

"Ignore him." Oliver lowered himself to sit beside me.

I sat up, tucking the quilt around my shoulders for modesty.

"Was he that rude to Bernard's wife? Anna?" I didn't know what made me ask. I'd never met the woman. I had no reason to tie my experience to hers.

"Anna was raised in the Kennedy Clan over in South Carolina. She would've put a stop to any ribbing like that before it got a chance to get started." A small smile played at his lips at the apparent memory.

I sighed. "How am I supposed to do that?" If I crossed the line, what would stop any of them from just beating me?

"You'll learn eventually, I'm sure." He pulled my dress from its resting place on top of a few crates and set it beside me. "Get dressed, will you? I'm starving."

Without waiting for me to ask, he turned his back to me and went to watch out of the window.

Even so, I didn't take my eye off him the entire time I dressed. He did seem to be trying to win me over, to claim me as his, and that melted my terrified heart just a little. But at what point would he stop? At what point would he give in to his father, and do whatever *he* wanted?

Would I ever be able to trust him?

CHAPTER TWENTY-SEVEN
Wagon Wheel

Once dressed, we made our way downstairs, greeted by the smell of eggs and grits. I did my best to hold my head high as I came into the kitchen, though I felt certain that every single one of them would be imagining my deflowering. To my surprise, no one so much as acknowledged my approach.

Like a gentleman, Oliver held the chair out for me and made me a bowl. Despite the growl in my stomach, I didn't dive right in. What was I supposed to do? It felt impossible to simply act like I belonged.

The entire table was silent, so I assumed everyone else wasn't sure either. Perhaps they were trying to determine if it was safe to talk around me, or if it ever would be. Did they have a rulebook for such things?

Henry answered the question for all of us. "We'll be heading out after breakfast."

Donnell poked at his breakfast mush. "And you don't want anyone to come with you?"

"There's no need," Mr. York said firmly. "The two of us should be able to track her down easily."

Donnell nodded and shoved a spoonful into his mouth. Despite the way he hid his expression, I still caught the glimmer of pure fear in his eyes.

"When do you expect to be back?" Rose asked, scanning the faces of everyone around her as if she could read every thought there was. I doubted anyone would ever be able to keep secrets from her.

"Shouldn't be more than a few days." With a shrug, Henry stood from the table, standing so straight I momentarily wondered if someone had strapped him into a corset. "Oliver, you keep her in line. No more chances."

Oliver didn't bother looking my direction; he simply nodded. "Yes sir. Could we mail a letter to her family? They might want to know about her marriage."

I flinched at the word. Would it ever feel normal? Nerves swam in my stomach. Would I always need permission for something as simple as a letter?

"They already heard from her once. You can't keep them fully in the dark. You know what can and can't be said." Henry nodded firmly at his subjects and marched out the door, completely ignoring the questioning look from Martin York. He didn't ask about it as he followed his brother out. At least not yet.

As soon as the front door closed behind them both, the entire table relaxed.

Shoveling the last bite of his grits into his mouth, Arthur spoke up. "If you're going to town, Oliver, I wanna come."

"No," Rose said sternly as she gathered the empty plates. "You are to clean the chicken coop today."

Arthur made a show of scrunching his entire face in disgust.

I stared, shocked yet again at how *normal* they seemed.

"After you eat, you can write that letter. Okay?" Oliver squeezed the hand that rested on my thigh.

I didn't flinch away. Somehow, I found myself relaxing at his touch.

After breakfast, Oliver brought me to the porch swing to write my letter. The birds sang all around, undisturbed by the wind that howled through the trees.

I ignored them both.

How was I to even tell my family about Oliver?

> *Dear Ma, I married some murderer who both ruined my life and saved it at the same time. You'll love him!*

I wrote it on the page just to get the ridiculous idea out of my head, then spent plenty of time scribbling it out until it was illegible and saturated with ink. On a clean page, I tried again. Serious this time.

> *Dear Ma and Pa,*

It made sense to include him in this one. He'd never forgive himself if he knew what had happened to me as a result of his decision. Besides, I had always envisioned him walking me down the aisle of our little church back home. A wedding felt wrong without my father by my side.

> *I write to you with wonderful news.*

Even that sentence made me grit my teeth. Wonderful.

> *While I have been here, I finally met the one. I realize this is the last thing you will have expected from me, especially so soon. But as my sister once said, when you know it's the one, you simply know. Not God or anyone else under the sun can stop you.*

Dipping my pen into the ink well, I scanned the area for Oliver. He was somewhere out there helping Donnell with a project. From what I could tell, they were fixing the wheel.

Oliver was sprawled out in the dirt, shirt thrown in the wagon, hair free from its restraint. He lifted the wheel easily, every muscle coming to life. Donnell grasped it from the top to help guide it onto the axle. He, too, was shirtless and equally as muscular. He was a larger man than Oliver in general, a few inches taller and wider. But with that sort of strength, I couldn't help but wonder who would win in a fight.

I shook my head to dislodge my runaway thoughts. The letter. I had a letter to write.

> *He's not a bad-looking man. A little taller than Little Chris, with blue eyes and brown hair. He has these little freckles that line the bridge of his nose and accentuate the light in his eyes when he smiles.*

I paused again. I had to remember that Oliver would read it before heading to town. What would he think when he read that part? That I noticed too much of him? What *had* caused me to notice such a thing in the first place? Why did I care?

With a huff, I continued.

> *He's likely the strongest man I have ever met. Which, after my illness, helped significantly. When it is hard for me to get around, he carries me. I do believe he is a good man and will take very good care of me.*
>
> *I will write when I can. Send my love to Miriam and her husband.*
>
> *Love,*
>
> *Petronella*

I gnawed on my lower lip as I stared at the words. It wasn't a long letter. Short and simple. But what shocked me was how nothing other than the farce illness felt like a lie.

I spent too much time at the piano that afternoon. I fiddled with that song I'd created in my notebook. It felt like a lifetime since I'd worked on it.

I adjusted measures here or there, added a few extra notes, and took a few more away. It was a simple melody, flowing one way, then the other. But it just didn't feel complete.

I gnawed on my lip, twirling the pen in my fingers.

It was too airy. Too light. Too . . . joyful.

I pressed a chord with my left hand—solid, firm, lasting. I played another, adding just a little dissonance to the mix. Gradually, my right trilled into place, a stark contrast to the reverberating bass notes.

Perfect.

The clock ticked along from its place on the mantel, the only sign that time was passing. Everyone was outside doing their own chores, leaving me alone.

I could play however I wanted. I could make the song as rough, as peaceful as I wanted. I could be inspired by whatever I wanted, even if it didn't completely make sense.

I glanced in each direction, sitting a little taller to peer from the window. No one.

It wasn't like I was doing anything remotely naughty. But putting my inspiration on paper still felt forbidden. I dipped the pen into the ink well and pressed it to the paper. At the top of the page, in my scrawling script, I wrote the song's name: "For Him."

Satisfied, I returned to the keys, adding more of the solid bass. A beautiful dance of elegance and strength emerged on the page, making relief flow throughout my body.

Sure, it was about *him*. How he'd taken me, hurt me, but also how he managed to rescue me. About how I despised him, but how I was starting to feel safe by his side.

As the minutes ticked on, the song glided through my fingertips. Faster and faster, coming easier with each measure.

"Ah, what's this?" came a gruff voice. I had been so enthralled by my music that I hadn't heard the front door open.

I yelped and grabbed for my notebook, but Donnell was faster. He snatched it from its upright position, holding it out so he could read my sloppy print.

"'For Him'?" He chuckled, eyeing me over the page.

"God," I snapped, trying to retrieve my precious book.

"God, hmm?" He set the book in my lap, pressing it a little too firmly into its spot. He leaned low, hovering so close I could feel his breath on my nose. "I heard you playin' it. Most songs about God aren't that . . . hm . . . *violent*."

I turned away from him so fast, my hair flew from its twist and smacked him in the face.

He didn't stick around to see what I did. With a chuckle, he went back out the front door, humming each of my notes in perfect pitch.

My cheeks grew warm with my blush. I fingered through the pages of the notebook, ensuring I had a hold of the entire song. With a whimper and a surge of regret, I yanked.

The pages separated from the spine with a heartbreaking rip. I wadded them into a ball and shoved them far into my pocket.

I pressed my forehead against the keys, gnawing on my lower lip. It wasn't just the teasing. It wasn't just the fact that he knew who the song was for. It was that he had read my unexplainable feelings on paper.

Whether he knew it or not, he had studied my deepest desires, my forbidden thoughts.

CHAPTER TWENTY-EIGHT

Baby

Days later, the melody wouldn't leave my mind. "For Him" thrummed in my heart, but instead of finishing it, I played the tried-and-true songs from my childhood.

The music flowed around me like a sweet caress, letting me forget that anything was remotely amiss. Rose hadn't been feeling well, so she regularly retired to her room. Over the past week, she was racked with random pains from the seemingly harmless infant inside. Every time I asked if she was all right, she tried to brush it off. But when she leaned against the counter, face contorted into a grimace, I couldn't ignore it anymore.

"Rose!" I practically dove from the seat and rushed to her side. "What's wrong?"

She held out her hand to keep me at arm's length. "I'm fine. It's normal. I've done this many times now. I just need some rest." She patted my shoulder as she waddled on her way, one hand pressed against her lower back.

"Are you sure you're not . . ." I couldn't quite make the word come out, so I waved my hands around in the air, hoping it would fill in the blank. "Do I need to fetch someone?"

"No, no, dear. It's not time just yet. You enjoy yourself for a while."

Ignoring her entirely, I took the dripping plate from her hand and plunged it into the soapy water. "I'll finish this for you."

She nodded, a wince crossing her features. "I'll just go rest." She avoided my gaze as she trudged her way up the stairs, any signs of discomfort or pain hidden behind a set jaw.

I listened for her as I finished the dishes. When I heard nothing except for a light snore, I returned to the piano. I kept the song quiet, barely accenting the crescendos and keeping everything pianissimo. Though I tried to keep "For Him" locked in my brain, it escaped measure by measure, transporting me to my happy place.

Her call yanked me out of my reverie as effectively as if she had slapped me.

"Nella!" Her voice was strained, full of anguish, yet hiding more than I dared imagine.

I scrambled up from the seat and fumbled for the staircase. I was getting faster, but I was certain even a ninety-year-old man would've beat me to her bedside.

I practically fell into the room, momentarily grateful I hadn't crashed down the stairs in my haste. "Are you okay? Is it time?" Though I had no doubt what was going on, I had to ask.

She nodded and waved me over. "I'll need your help. Each one comes faster than the last." She had already dressed down to her chemise. Without any care for modesty, she hauled that over her head as well.

Sweat poured from every inch of her body, making her look like someone had just pulled her from a lake.

"What do you need me to do?" My hands hovered a mere inch above her body, hunting for my purpose.

A low, prolonged groan escaped her lips, and her hands clasped my forearm. I gasped, then gritted my teeth and stood still. My father told me that Mama practically broke his arm when she had me.

Rose's pain faded as quickly as it had begun. Taking a deep, relieved breath, she lay her head back on the pillow. A bead of sweat ran down her forehead, tangling with her lashes.

"How long have you been like this? Why didn't you tell me?" I demanded, helping her push the hair out of her face.

She gave me a weak smile that twisted into a grimace. I braced myself for the stranglehold on my arm.

"I need to go get help. I've never . . . I don't know what to do." I picked up a worn Bible, pushed aside an oil lamp, and peered into a drawer, wishing the midwife's name and address would pop up out of nowhere.

"No, no," she said sharply as the pain subsided. "No one else."

"Bernard? Does he—"

"No!" she snapped.

"But . . ." I shook my head wildly, my braid flying into my face. From the stories I heard, I doubted there would be enough time to get help even if I tried. Resigned, I brushed the wrinkles from my apron and stood tall. "Fine. What can I do?"

She stroked my hand tenderly, as though it would erase the nail marks in my skin. "I'll tell you."

Tell me, she did.

A whirlwind of blood, unnamable bodily fluids, and equally unidentifiable cries.

When the warm, gooey, and all-around icky creature entered the world, I had absolutely no energy left.

Rose didn't look like she had much either, but she scooped the little baby to her chest and wiped away some of the mess on their face.

"Oh, *mon bebe*," she cooed, kissing the little one on the forehead. The tiny thing nestled against her breast, the most heartwarming cry escaping from their lips.

Rose snuggled the new addition for a long while, eyes closed, nearly silent French murmurs flowing over the infant's head. Eventually, she struggled to sit, latching the infant for their first meal. Only then did Rose lean forward to check the gender.

Like an avalanche, the peace and joy crashed from her face, leaving lines of stress crisscrossing from the edges of her eyes and forehead.

"What is it?" I sprang to my knees, teetering on the edge of her bed. She'd delivered the baby, the placenta, was there anything else I didn't know about?

"Oh, nothing, dear." Rose's face didn't match her words. Beads of sweat popped along her forehead like pinpricks, and her shoulders nearly touched her ears as she hunched in on herself. She placed a solid, lasting kiss on the baby's forehead, a lone tear escaping her tightly closed eyes. She turned to a statue, nose breathing in that new-baby scent. It was as though it could disappear in an instant.

Her shoulders vibrated only once with a covert sob.

"What's wrong?" I repeated.

She forced a smile, though it was a farce on her sickly pale face.

She looked like she was in unimaginable pain. "What hurts? What can I do?" I asked, hands fluttering over the bedsheets.

"Nothing like that, *chérie*. I'm just tired is all. Help clean her up?"

Rose held her baby so tight I was almost afraid she wouldn't hand her over. But in the end, she did, one corner of her cheek pulled in where she was likely gnawing it raw.

The tiny creature was beyond precious. All legs and arms with a button nose and shaggy black hair. I couldn't help but smile as I looked her over. Because it was a girl—Rose's first baby girl. The family needed a princess around.

Life would certainly be a lot more fun with a little one.

Oliver and Arthur arrived soon after both Rose and the baby were sound asleep. I met them in the hallway, the ruined apron still tied around my waist. Both men went so still, one might've thought they were being held at gunpoint. Oliver raised a single eyebrow, and Arthur's mouth fell open.

"Is she okay?" Arthur nearly bounced on his toes as he poised himself to dart past me.

"Yes," I said, holding out my arms to block the path. "They're both sleeping now. I'd let them be."

In unison, they shut their eyes and their broad shoulders went slack.

I smiled to myself. For trained killers, their love for their mother was a relief. "It's a girl," I continued.

That relief vanished instantly. They both focused on me like hawks ready to strike, firm frowns on their lips.

"What?" Oliver said the word so precisely, I briefly wondered if he thought I told him I burned down the chicken coop.

My bare toes curled against the chilled wood. "It . . . it's a girl. You have a sister."

Arthur leaned against the opposite wall, sliding down until he perched on his heels, forehead in his hands.

"She's healthy," I assured, but their reaction didn't change.

Oliver hardly breathed, face pale, body frozen. He looked eerily similar to how his mother had when she found out.

"What is it?" I demanded, crossing my arms firmly over my middle. "This is *not* how you react to a healthy sibling!" I pointed straight at Oliver. "So don't you *dare* tell me it's nothing!"

Oliver ran his fingers through his hair until they got caught on a particularly rough patch. He winced as he forced his fingers through anyway, coming away with a few dark strands in his hand. "I . . . I don't know how to tell you," he admitted.

I gritted my teeth. "Tell me."

Arthur practically melted into the bedroom across the hall, moving slower than a turtle. Oliver watched him go, shoulders sagging as he realized he wouldn't be getting any help with the explanation.

"Not here. I don't want to wake Ma. Get changed, and we'll go for a walk." With a resigned sigh, Oliver held his hand out for me, and I took it. His fingers were cold, almost clammy, effectively heightening the anxiety in my belly.

In the attic, I changed as quickly as I could. I didn't bother picking on Oliver or reminding him to keep his back turned while I undressed. He did it automatically, not making a single sound.

In fact, he didn't say a word until we were outside, past the charred barn, and in the forest on the path to the lake.

Every step away from the house made my stomach swirl a little more. "Why won't you tell me? What's wrong with the baby?" I stopped walking and whirled on him in the most commanding way I could come up with.

He sighed and leaned against a nearby tree. "You won't like a single word I say."

I stood in front of him, arms crossed, hip pushed out. I was certain my own mother had faced me with this exact stance, eyeing me down the bridge of her nose. "I highly doubt I will," I muttered.

He pinched the bridge of his nose. "You noticed, I'm sure, how none of us are female."

Ice filled my veins. I hadn't. "I have now."

"We only train males into the family." He cleared his throat, the sound very much like an old man who'd smoked one too many pipes. "Uh . . . business. Not females." He didn't look at me as he spoke. Instead, he stared straight up into the perfectly clear azure sky.

My horrified mind refused to fill in the blanks. "So the girl can't have a job. That's perfectly normal in most families. As you are highly aware, I'm sure."

He made a sort of strangled noise and covered his eyes with one large hand. "You're gonna make me say it?"

I glared at him.

The next words out of his mouth came so fast, I hoped I misunderstood him. "Girls born into the family aren't allowed to live."

Without realizing I moved, my back was against a tree and I slid to the ground, the bark scraping painfully against the back of my head. "Pardon?"

Oliver hadn't moved an inch. "Having a girl is unacceptable. Only men can enter this—"

"No, no, no, no!" I held out my hand to stop him. "A girl can keep a secret just fine if you don't want her to say anything! That's a helpless little baby up there. What are you saying? That's not all right!"

"I'm not saying it's all right!" His hand slapped against his thigh as he let it fall. He knelt in front of me and cupped my chin in his hands. I tried to avoid his eyes, but he was persistent, holding me still until I gave in and met his gaze. "Nothing about it is all right, and that's what's wrong."

I searched his eyes for any sign of a lie. There wasn't one. "But you were raised this way."

"Yes, but . . ." He took a deep breath. "Sometimes you don't have to follow in your family's footsteps. I can't stand by and watch it happen again."

My stomach lurched. "Again." The word felt like it was choking me.

CHAPTER TWENTY-NINE
A Soft Heart

Henry beat us there.

At the sight of his horse, Oliver picked up the pace. He practically dropped me in the entryway and dashed up the stairs the moment we arrived. I wasn't angry that he left me behind. I just felt numb, sick.

What if we were too late? Did I really want to see?

When the cooing from the newborn reached my ears, a strangled sob erupted from my mouth. I scrambled for the stairs.

We weren't too late.

Perhaps Henry would have a heart for once?

No. Hell Man didn't have a heart.

I don't know what I expected to see as I burst into the room. Perhaps Henry with his hands around his daughter's neck? Maybe Henry fighting Rose for access to the baby? Whatever I expected, it certainly wasn't to see him kneeling on the edge of the four-poster bed, stroking the hair out of Rose's face and whispering kind words.

Oliver stood near the headboard, occupying the space between his father and the baby. Nothing about his stance was threatening, but the tension in the air told a different story.

"Why didn't you take care of it earlier?" Henry whispered. The words almost sounded pleasant, soothing.

"I will always be too softhearted," she said. "You know this."

Oliver remained rigid and rotated his body, as if to block the baby from his father's sight.

Hell Man missed nothing. "Oliver?" Henry's eyebrow rose, looking so much like his son. "Are you volunteering?" The threat in his voice was far from hidden.

Oliver flinched. "No."

Rose sat as still as a statue when she noticed me. She stared directly into my soul. If she had a way to transfer her thoughts straight to my brain, she would have figured it out then. What she wanted was important, that was for sure. I stared back, fighting to understand her imploring gaze.

It wasn't until her eyes darted to something under the bassinet that her mission made sense.

A red-and-blue bag made of crocheted granny squares lay underneath. With bravery I didn't know I had, I made my way into the room and bent to pick it up.

"Get her out of here, Oliver!" Henry boomed. "She's the last person we need in here right now!"

My fingers trembled as I stood, tucking the bag against my chest.

"What is that?" Hell Man demanded.

I had no choice but to trust that Oliver would protect me long enough to check. I pulled the drawstring just enough to see inside. There was a tawny crocheted bear, a note, and a bottle with just a little of that precious, early golden milk. I looked back at Rose, hoping I understood. She nodded firmly and gave an ever-so-small smile.

I gnawed on the inside of my cheek. I prayed I read that look correctly. The bag, the look, the family's "duty." If I didn't . . .

The men missed nothing. Their eyes were on me, waiting for my move. Oliver shifted his weight, taking up just a little more of the space between me and his father.

Rose dipped her head in a covert nod and mouthed, "Run."

I took in a steadying breath. It grated against my lungs, filled with warnings and fear. My movements jerky, I shut the bag, looped it over one arm, and jumped to action.

I scooped the infant to my chest and started for the door. If Oliver didn't help, I wouldn't make it, and I knew it. But I prayed that somehow, someway, he would be ready to fight.

I didn't have a plan. I didn't even know where I would go to keep myself safe, let alone a helpless newborn. But unless Oliver stepped up with a different plan, what other choice did I really have?

I pressed the cane to the floor, then hopped my foot forward. One step at a time. Slowly. Deliberately. Nothing seemed to move behind me, though I didn't look back.

The sound of a fist slamming into skin echoed through the silence, followed closely by an "oof!" from Henry. Rose was on the warpath, I assumed. Before I disappeared into the hallway, I risked a glance back just in time to see Oliver jump into the doorway, blocking his father's path yet again. Smoothly, he reached one foot behind him and slammed the door shut.

This was the only chance I would ever get, and I knew it.

I picked up the pace. Cane down, step. Cane down, step. At the stairs, I gripped the banister and jumped, clutching the infant just a little tighter and hoping I didn't lose my footing.

I had just reached the base of the stairs when Arthur stepped out from the kitchen. He looked much older suddenly, stress lines streaked from the corners of his eyes. Everything about him looked sad. His gaze slid to the little baby, and a deep frown settled onto his face.

"Please . . ."

The upstairs door slammed open, sending unintelligible shouting echoing down the stairs. Before anyone could make progress toward us, Arthur made his decision. He scooped the two of us into his arms and raced out the front door.

CHAPTER THIRTY
Runaway

Arthur didn't take me far.

As we burst into the barn, Donnell's head swiveled in our direction. He looked very much like a cougar, wound up to pounce on his prey. He had been occupied by putting the horses up from their earlier trip.

Completely ignoring him, Arthur went straight to work. He chose a horse that Donnell hadn't started on just yet and lifted me into the saddle.

I pressed the infant to my chest, refusing to look away from Donnell. I didn't trust him not to do the "right thing" by his father. Especially not after his threats.

Arthur wrenched the reins out of a startled Donnell's hand. "Go!" he commanded.

I did nothing. I just stared at Donnell, the bile rising in my throat and my mouth going bone-dry. He looked just like he did when I had seen him last: prepared to kill me at any given minute.

"Go!" Arthur slapped the horse's rump. Completely caught off guard, it lurched forward. I grabbed her mane with my free hand and held the baby tight.

Donnell reached for us, his hand just barely brushing the mare's rump as she left him in a cloud of dust and old hay.

"What are you doing?" He sounded like he was in a dream as he faded into the background.

The mare sped on, spurred by my adrenaline.

The baby made a small, pitiful cry and squirmed inside her swaddle. I forced myself to release the breath I had been holding and tried to relax for her sake. She didn't know what was going on, and if she was to survive, she wouldn't remember a thing. Best not make it traumatic enough *to* remember.

I steered the horse into the trees, ducking to avoid being whacked with any more branches than was strictly necessary.

I assumed my pursuers would go down the road to find me first. I had to become invisible.

Though I knew it wouldn't make a difference. These people knew how to track almost anything. The property belonged to them. They likely knew every inch, every leaf, every blade of grass. A girl and a newborn with only three legs between them wouldn't be hard to find.

Eventually, I pulled the mare to a stop in the shade. She had to be tired from the burst of energy. Especially after she had just finished bringing Henry home.

"I'm sorry," I whispered, patting her neck. "Just . . . just don't go home."

We had to make it to the train station. Maybe they'd let me board without a ticket. I looked fragile enough, plus I had a baby. Perhaps they would take pity on me.

But I knew better than that.

Every seat cost money, and I didn't have a penny to my name.

"What do we do?" I whispered to the burbling infant. She looked straight at me, clear, gray-blue eyes full of wonder and not an ounce of fear.

How would I even feed her? She wouldn't stay content for long. I sat up straighter and rummaged through the bag. At the bottom were a few fabric scraps for diapers, a long, white christening outfit, and a little broach. I hunted until I found that glass bottle. There wasn't much of the golden milk inside, but Rose hadn't had much time to provide much more.

It wouldn't keep the baby happy for long, I knew that. But it was a start.

I ran my fingers over the pristinely folded letter. In the most beautiful handwriting I had ever seen was one name: Felicité.

The baby made a faint mewling sound, followed immediately by a scrunched-up face and the start of a cry.

"Oh, no, no, sweetheart," I said, pressing her to my chest and rocking back and forth.

Food. She needed food. She pecked across my collarbone, leaving slobbery kisses in her wake and confirming my suspicions.

I grabbed the bottle again. "This is the best I've got, sweetheart." Felicité didn't seem to care. She just got louder as I ran the bottle's nipple over her lips. It took her a few seconds to figure out what I wanted, but when she did, she grabbed ahold as if she were half-starved.

I winced, imagining how that would feel if I had to feed her at the breast. As adorable as the tiny thing was, she ate like a wild animal. Pushing the thought aside, I wrenched my eyes shut and breathed against the mounting stress.

How would I feed her if she got hungry again?

One thing was for sure: we couldn't hide in the forest and wait for imminent death to find us. Because they *would* find us if she cried much more.

Balancing the infant in the crook of my arm and holding the bottle and reins with the opposite hand, I urged the mare forward. We needed to stay close enough to the road to avoid getting lost, but we needed to stay far enough away to avoid notice. Hopefully.

We plodded along, my heart thumping its rapid dance against my breastbone, Felicité falling into a milk-induced slumber. Just as I started to relax, a twig snapped somewhere behind us.

I jumped in the saddle, nearly losing my balance. Felicité startled, legs and arms shooting out in all directions despite the confining wrap. I twisted to look behind, gripping Felicité to my chest. It was over. They had found us.

Felicité took the extra snuggles to mean we were safe. She nuzzled closer and was out within just a few heartbeats.

To my relief, tussled brown hair appeared through the trees as Oliver made his way up to us.

I stared at him dumbly. He had the reddish start of a bruise on his cheekbone and dried blood packed on his lower lip.

His eyes roamed down my body, the gesture not unlike the way someone might check the quality of a horse. He was ready for business. His scrutiny froze momentarily on the infant. Impulsively, I held her a little tighter.

"Come on," he said gruffly. "We can't stay here."

So, he had made his choice.

Me.

I let my guard drop and scooted back so he could swing into the saddle. He wasted no time urging the mare forward. I clung to her with my thighs, leaning against his back. Felicité gurgled and adjusted herself in my arms, perfectly content. I gritted my teeth. If she cried again, we would all be in trouble.

Oliver knew exactly where he was going. He moved farther from the road, pressing himself to the mare's neck in order to avoid the branches. We moved with unnerving speed as he headed for town. My ears thudded with every hoofbeat as I clung to my lifeline.

I really hadn't expected Oliver to come after us. I knew I wouldn't have had a chance alone, but I had to at least try. What made him decide to run after us? To betray his family?

With his help, we might actually make it to safety.

Flying through the trees, we made it to town faster than I thought possible. The sight of the wood-framed buildings brought me a strange mix of nervousness and relief.

Oliver kept us on the edge of town, staying as far away from people as possible. He never stopped searching the shadows. His head swiveled from side to side, ensuring he would notice the first sign of danger.

My voice cracked as I spoke. "Will they be here yet?"

"I dunno," he admitted. "I hope not. I tried to buy us some time."

When he didn't bother to elaborate, I pressed. "How?"

His head fell forward with his exasperated sigh. "Pa fell down the stairs . . ."

"Did he . . . is he . . . all right?"

He shrugged mutely but didn't comment further.

Once we found the train tracks, Oliver turned the horse to follow them toward town. He sat rigidly in the saddle, every muscle ready to spring him at the first sign of danger.

As we reached the rickety train station, he slid from the mare and swung the reins over the hitching post.

I bit my lower lip as the memories of that station flooded my brain. The last time I was here, I was sure he was going to kill me.

I could almost feel the way the splinters from that very hitching post burrowed into my palm. I would never forget the numbing pain that shot through my shoulder as he pressed his fingers into the muscles of my arm, preventing any chance of escape.

Oliver cleared his throat to get my attention, focused on the baby. She was still sound asleep. "Come on." He held his arms out for me. I let him pull me to the ground, Felicité still sound asleep against my chest.

"Stay here," Oliver commanded. He didn't wait to see if I obeyed. He sauntered straight onto the platform, standing tall, shoulders squared as he walked to the ticket counter.

I only stayed put for a few seconds, peddling my feet on the dusty ground. But I couldn't stay still, not with the ever-increasing chances of the Wedman family crashing through the trees.

As soon as Oliver disappeared inside the ticket booth, I started after him. I slipped my cane from its nook in the saddle and used both it and the wall for balance, cradling Felicité in the opposite arm.

The bell above the door announced my arrival, making me freeze. Felicité jerked, and her eyes sprang open. I stared at her, not daring to even breathe.

She stretched, toes pointing underneath the loose swaddle, fists straight above her head. She opened her mouth in the most precious yawn I had ever seen. Then, completely content, she snuggled back into her spot and fell asleep.

She had the blue-gray eyes of a newborn, with healthy, reddened skin. Her cheeks were just about as chubby as they could be, giving the impression that she just wanted a kiss. She didn't have much hair yet, only a few wispy black strands.

Asleep, she seemed to be the most perfect angel imaginable.

I breathed a sigh of relief and continued on my mission. Oliver stood beside the ticket booth, eyes narrowed in a predator-like fashion, lips pursed. He jerked his head toward a nearby bench, pausing for a brief moment to ensure I noted both his displeasure and his command. Apparently satisfied, he turned his attention back to the frazzled-looking man behind the counter.

"When does the next train leave?" Oliver asked. His voice held not a single shred of fear. Confident, determined, strictly business.

"Where would you like to go?" the man asked, eyeing us both over his glasses. He was a wiry man with bugged-out eyes, accentuated by the glasses that were far too big for his face. He reminded me of some kind of flying insect.

Oliver dropped the businesslike tone and took on one of pure ice. "That was not what I asked, now was it? I need the next train." He placed his palms flat on the counter, his stare boring straight into the little man.

Bug Man blinked once, twice, then finally pulled out a ledger. He took his time scanning it, one shaky finger tracing the entries. Oliver's own fingers curled into fists, then flat again. He looked like he was about to pluck the book from this man at any moment.

"Well, next train will take ya south. But it won't leave for another hour."

Oliver's shoulders sagged, and Felicité let out a hiccupping cry.

"Shh, shh," I whispered, bouncing in my seat to try to get her to settle. She did, but only after releasing a small, yet potent, pop of air. I wrinkled my nose.

"Would you like to buy a ticket?" Bug Man asked.

"No," Oliver muttered. He turned on his heel and walked out the front door, leaving me to rush to catch up.

Felicité was done with travel. She opened her eyes again, stared at me for a mere moment, then scrunched her body to release an ear-piercing scream.

"What now?" I resumed my bouncing. Her mournful cries filled the air, breaking my heart nearly in two.

"Take care of that." Oliver gestured with his chin in her direction. "Her crying will lead them right to us." He helped me back onto the horse, then swung into the saddle with ease.

"She's not a '*that*'!" I snapped. "She's your sister."

He didn't bother reacting to my comment. He just directed the horse down the dusty street and into town.

CHAPTER THIRTY-ONE

Milk

Felicité continued her tremoring, pitiful cries, despite my best efforts. I held her to my chest, rocking her side to side, praying with everything I had. Was she hungry already? Or did she need a change?

Answering my unspoken question, she grabbed at the bodice of my dress with her spindly fingers, begging for the milk she was sure I had.

Seemingly ignoring his sister's distress, Oliver plodded on. He took us straight to the stables, not even getting off the horse before he located someone. A scrawny young man, not much older than Little Chris. The boy turned his head toward us with questioning eyes.

"How can I help ya?" he asked.

"Would you happen to know if there is a wet nurse somewhere in town?" Oliver asked, braver than I could ever be.

"Uh . . ." The boy looked this way and that, as if one would materialize out of the worn wood of the barn. "I'm not . . ." He trailed off and cocked his head to the side as he questioned his own answer.

Oliver sighed and took on a lighter tone. "You see, the baby's ma died, and we're doing everything we can to take care of it. But there's only so much we can do without milk, as I'm sure you understand." He tried a small laugh to lighten the strained mood that radiated around the room.

The boy frowned as he thought. "Well . . . there was . . . There's a lady, Mrs. Eaton, she's down the street. She had a baby a few weeks ago. Maybe she'd be willin' to help ya?"

Despite this news, Oliver didn't relax; he sat ramrod straight in the saddle as Felicité yowled on behind him. "That would be mighty helpful. Will you point us in her direction?"

"Yes sir." The boy moved to the barn's wide entrance, leaning out and pointing down the street. "That way. The house with the green shutters and the wind chime out front." He gave Felicité a wary glance. "I'm sure she'll be able to help some."

Oliver thanked him and nudged the horse along, leaving the boy to stare after us.

The house stood out from the rest, exactly as the boy described. Green shutters and a little bench on the porch. Securely hooked to the ceiling was a set of wind chimes singing their peaceful tune.

After helping us from the horse, Oliver went straight to the door. He knocked firmly, ensuring it would be heard throughout the house. Even so, we waited for the longest possible minute before he gave it another rap.

The door opened almost immediately to reveal a frazzled woman. Her brown hair was askew, dress stained, and she had a baby pressed tightly against her chest.

"Can I help you?" she asked, eyes narrowed at Oliver.

Felicité wasted no time in unleashing another scream. The woman's gaze slid over us, taking in everything in one quick sweep.

Her entire posture changed in that instant. She relaxed and opened the door wide. "Oh, that poor dear! Come in, come in. What can I do to help you?"

"Well, ma'am," Oliver began, supporting me as I made my way up the two steps onto the porch, and then into the house. "We were told you might be able to help us with this little—" He stopped short, likely so he wouldn't call her a *thing*.

"Felicité," I supplied.

"Felicité," he echoed, shooting me a questioning look. "Her ma passed away, and we're trying to care for her as best we can as we travel back home, but we don't have a way to feed her."

Mrs. Eaton kissed her own baby on the top of the head and placed him into the bassinet. The little guy made a mewl of protest, but apparently decided the mobile above him was an adequate distraction.

"Here, let me see what I can do." She took Felicité from me and wasted no time in bearing a blue-veined breast. She placed the baby straight on, not acting surprised in the slightest as the newborn attacked. Felicité's little fists gripped on tight while she nursed like her life depended on it.

"She's not very old at all!" The woman brushed the dark hair on the top of her head with her finger. "How old is she?"

"Not very," I agreed, sitting on the settee. Oliver gave in and lowered himself next to me, giving one last glance to the window behind us. "She was born this morning."

"This morning!" Mrs. Eaton's eyes went wide. "Oh, the poor dear!" She cooed unintelligible words to Felicité and held her close. "Was she able to get anything at all from her mama?"

"Yes," Oliver said. He fidgeted with the edge of his shirt, obviously ready to be gone as soon as possible. "The mother died a little after giving birth, but she was with us long enough to . . ." He trailed off and just gazed down at the squirming bundle.

"That's a good thing. Very, very good." She said this in a high-pitched voice, petting Felicité's head with such care that it made my heart ache. "Do you know what you will do with her from here on out? Do you have family to take her to?"

Oliver glanced at me from the corner of his eye. "To be perfectly honest, we aren't too sure what to do just yet." His sigh was a bit more dramatic than I expected. "We can't take care of her, and don't know where she could go."

Mrs. Eaton kissed the top of her head and gave us a sympathetic smile. "I wish I could be of more help to you, but we have our hands full with that little guy over there." She gestured at the cooing baby in the bassinet, a warm smile lighting her face.

"Are you sure you and your husband couldn't—" I started.

"No," she said sharply. "We've reached our limit. An extra mouth to feed is expense enough. Taking on yet another one just won't work. I'm sorry."

I opened my mouth to argue, but Oliver put his hand on my thigh to stop me.

"We understand," he said, the stiffness of his posture the only thing to betray his stress. "I pray we will find someone who can take her in soon."

Something in the pit of my stomach spasmed at the idea of giving Felicité to someone else. But who was I kidding? We didn't have the ability to care for an infant. We needed to find her a home. A safe home.

Felicité released her prey and lay sprawled out in the most dramatic fashion—arms out to the side, legs limp over Mrs. Eaton's arm, and lips open in a perfect "O."

"I pray so too." Mrs. Eaton kissed the baby's head and adjusted her hold. Felicité's nose twitched in annoyance, but she remained in her semiconscious state.

"I'm sorry I couldn't be more help. Perhaps someone at the livery could give you some milk to take on your journey. I won't have enough to give you after feeding these two." To underline her point, she gave her breast a delicate prod, then tucked it back into the dress.

"We will ask," Oliver said. "Thank you again." He watched me with more scrutiny than was warranted as she handed the baby to me.

I held her close, a warm, cozy feeling spreading through my body as she snuggled into my chest.

CHAPTER THIRTY-TWO

No Ticket

Within minutes, we were on our way back to the train station, Felicité sleeping peacefully with a full stomach. My own stomach swirled. Where were they hiding? I would've expected to see at least some sign of them by this point.

"Where are they?" I whispered, just loud enough to ensure Oliver could hear me.

He shook his head. "I'm not sure. For all I know, they're probably watching us now."

Once at the station, he hitched the horse up just as before and helped me down. The train was there, steam rising from the engine, people milling all around the platform.

We didn't go unnoticed. All eyes were on us, questions swarming from one ear to another. If only they knew what was really going on with the one-legged girl, the tall, hatless man, and a sleeping infant.

Oliver didn't take the time to explain his plan to the strangers. He didn't even bother going into the station. He picked up the pace as he made his way down the length of the train. I had to hop to keep up, holding the tip of the cane off the ground so I wouldn't trip and squish Felicité.

"Where are we going? What are you doing?" I demanded when we reached the end of the platform. All that was ahead of us was the never-ending track.

He stopped and swiveled to face me. "Of all times, I really need you to be quiet now."

I narrowed my eyes at him. "I'd appreciate it if you at least told me what you're planning. The ticket office is that way." I gestured at the building.

He let out a long sigh, his eyes scanning every inch of the platform behind me. "Last I checked, tickets cost money."

"But you asked for one earlier," I argued. He stepped into the grass, but I didn't follow.

"I needed to know the schedule. I wasn't gonna buy one then, either."

Before I could argue any further, his face drained of all color. I didn't have to look behind me to be terrified of whatever he saw. He scooped me up and practically yanked me from the platform. Oliver slipped between the nearest boxcars, his body board-stiff.

I craned my neck to see what he had, though we were far enough in the shadows that I could only see the empty corner of the platform.

He gripped us against him, so much so I could feel his heart pounding beneath my ear. I opened my mouth like a fish multiple times, planning to ask what was going on, what he planned, but each time, I decided against it.

He set me firmly in the gravel and pointed at the ground before taking Felicité from me. I started to protest, but he knelt to crawl under the train's coupling. With one last glance behind me, I followed him, my skirts making it a little harder to move quietly through the space. He waited for me in the shadow of the train, ready to defend me at the first sign of trouble.

Knee, foot, knee, foot, knee, foot. Each stone felt cut into my knee. Each movement felt like some kind of acrobatic stunt that belonged to a circus. Or at least a boy.

Before we stood again, Oliver took his time checking for any witnesses. There was not a single soul.

We were only a few feet away from the forest that spread up and across the mountain. There was nothing but darkness behind the leaves; anything could hide back there.

Oliver nudged my shoulder to direct me into the sunlight. I did as he asked, trying not to let the nerves take over. Sure of himself, he stood tall and yanked open the door to the nearest boxcar. Without asking, he scooped me up with one arm and set me inside, shoving my cane after me. He passed me the slumbering baby, then vaulted in behind us, slamming the door shut and engulfing us in darkness. The only light filtered in from the edges of the door.

Crates lined the car from one side to the other, leaving hardly enough space for stowaways like us. Oliver didn't seem concerned about it. He led the way to the back corner, rearranging the boxes as he went to create a little nook out of sight of the doors. He gestured for me to hide inside the space. Without question, I did as he asked. Everything smelled dark, damp, and vaguely of dirty diaper.

I opened my mouth to ask him something, but Oliver put his finger to my lips.

The sounds of people milling around outside on the platform echoed through the car, accompanied by the slam of the boxcar doors down the way, then the crunch of footfalls in the gravel as someone moved closer. When the feet stopped right outside our hiding place, Oliver squeezed himself into the space with us.

I could feel his measured breathing as he remained calm. His eyelids were closed firmly, as though he was just pretending to sleep. I tried to copy him, closing my own eyes and dreaming that I was anywhere else. Anywhere other than a boxcar without a ticket.

I imagined the lake outside the Wedmans' house. Peaceful, open, safe. The picture wouldn't stay in my mind; all my worries returned in a swarm. What would happen if they found us? Would they throw us in jail? Would they just kill us all?

Not nearly as practiced as Oliver, my heart beat wildly and my breathing raced ahead. I held it as the door banged open. The man outside paused, likely looking into the corners for stowaways. Apparently deciding no one could fit inside of such a space, he shut it firmly and latched it again.

"All clear!" came the shout.

Both of us relaxed. Oliver backed against the wall to give Felicité and I room to breathe. The whistle of the train came shortly after, followed by a jerk as it surged forward. Only then did Oliver let his body slouch in the corner, hand pressed to his forehead.

CHAPTER THIRTY-THREE

Train

"Do you know where this train is headed?" I asked, sliding down the wood-paneled wall to sit across from him.

"South," Oliver said simply, leaning to peer through one of the slats.

I resisted the urge to grumble aloud. "Do we know *where*?"

He shrugged. "This train'll go all the way to Savannah. I doubt we'll stay on long enough to get there."

Felicité gurgled her opinion, then snuggled closer to my chest.

"That's a long way . . ." I sighed and closed my eyes. The last time I'd been to Savannah, I'd been courting Tom. A lifetime ago.

I let myself imagine what life would have been like. By now, I'd likely have my own baby. The thought didn't sound as exciting as it once did, but being trapped in an attic changes things. If I had married Tom, I would've been settled. Safe.

Oliver interrupted my thoughts. "Here." He took the gurgling baby from my arms and held her close. "Go ahead and sleep. It'll be a while yet until we make it anywhere."

I fell asleep easily, shoulder pressed uncomfortably against a crate and Felicité cradled in my arms. To my surprise, I woke with my head on Oliver's arm.

Felicité gave me no time to wonder how I'd drifted to him. She'd been the one to wake me in the first place. She cater-wauled loud enough to make my ears feel like they would bleed. To make matters worse, a foul smell permeated the air.

Rubbing at my eyes with my shoulder, I swayed from side to side. "Why, Felicité? Why?" She hiccupped into silence and bobbed her head like a drunk chicken against my chest, searching for the answer to all her problems. The moment she figured out I didn't hold the solution, the screaming resumed.

"What do we do?" I asked through gritted teeth. "You were such a good, quiet baby!"

Oliver's forehead was in his hands, fingers digging at his scalp. "I don't know." His voice was scratchy, his face pained.

I switched to bouncing her for a few moments, only receiving more screams in exchange for my efforts. "Here." I nearly thrust her at Oliver. He took her without argument and watched as I used one of the crates to pull myself up.

"What are you doing?"

My response was quick. "Looking."

The train jerked and rocked, making me grateful that I was wedged against a wall. How were we going to survive multiple hours with her screaming? She had to be hungry, right? It had already been a few hours since we'd left Mrs. Eaton's house.

When the train hit a rather rough spot, I tilted precariously. Oliver held up his hand and pressed it against my hip to steady me. I didn't even think to scold him.

Slightly more stable, I pulled on the boards of the crate, hunting for something, anything inside. The space between the slats gave me no information other than that they contained off-white sacks.

"What are you expecting to find in there?" Oliver nearly shouted, voice higher pitched than normal.

"I don't know!" I gave up on pulling at the wood and pulled on the canvas bag itself. I achieved nothing in my desperation other than getting the bottom corner of it out.

"Nella," he said, voice lowered with a kind of forced patience.

"Hmm?" I pulled again on the sack.

"You realize those are dry goods? They're not gonna help."

With an exasperated sigh, I leaned against the wall. "I don't know what else to do."

He tugged on my skirt. "Sit, please. Before you hurt yourself."

As I lowered myself again, the car swayed. Instead of landing on my rear, I fell in a cascade over Oliver and the baby, scraping my hands against the worn wood of the wall as I tried to catch myself. I succeeded only in avoiding Felicité.

The train car was silent for the smallest of moments as I lay there in a heap, partially on his shoulders. Felicité blinked at me with her little gray-blue eyes, curious, silent, and very aware. We didn't dare breathe. Immense sadness filled her little face again as she scrunched it up and let out another ear-shattering scream.

Oliver and I let out a long sigh, and I rolled off him to sit.

"She's so loud!" I held my head in my hands, fingers inching up my jawbone to plug my ears. "How do mothers do this?"

"They feed them."

I shot him a glare over my palm. "Well, I can't very well do that, now can I?"

"Well, one day . . ." The moment Oliver realized his eyes had traveled to my chest, he jerked back, as if stung. "Sorry . . ."

At his embarrassment, a smirk made its way onto my face. "Well, last I checked, you *were* my husband."

"Well, last I checked, nothing was official," he shot back.

I squirmed as a tingling feeling traced from my chest all the way to the space between my thighs. My voice cracked as I spoke. "Only because you're a decent man."

"Why, thank you." His smirk turned to a grimace as the screaming continued. The cries echoed across the car, the boxes making the space feel smaller and smaller with every passing mile. Unless I pressed my eye to one of the gaps, there was no way to see out. This, in addition to the overwhelming smell of long-damp wood, made everything worse.

We're going to be trapped in here forever. "Where do you think we are?" I asked, leaning my head against the crate with just enough force that it thumped.

"I have no idea." He gave Felicité his finger to help distract her. She sucked on it for only a moment before spitting out the offending object and resuming her yowling.

So we just sat there, surrounded by our own stress and misery. Every once in a while, Oliver would mumble a curse, rubbing his forehead. Eventually, Felicité hiccupped and switched to a mournful sort of mew. My ears felt startlingly empty with the silence as she fell into a restless, miserable sleep.

In the sudden quiet, my ears rang so much that I hardly heard Oliver's whisper. "We'll get off at the next stop."

Satisfied, I moved my head back to his shoulder to try to go back to sleep. He didn't question it. He *was* my husband after all, right? Besides, his shoulder was much more comfortable than a crate.

I woke with a start when the train squealed and began to jerk to a stop. Felicité did the same, her screaming starting with new vigor.

Oliver grumbled something as his eyes fluttered to an irritated wakefulness. After a break, the screaming didn't seem as bad. As soon as we got off the train, we could find a wet nurse.

The midday light still flowed in through the cracks. Once we emerged from the car, it would be easy to be seen. Too easy.

The train squealed a few more times, and the clacking of the tracks slowed little by little. Until, with one final squeal and a jerk, the train stopped.

"Hurry," Oliver said, shuffling to his feet and grabbing Felicité's bag. He held his hand out for me. "We have to hurry."

I took it and nearly jumped up. "How? What are we going to do?"

"I dunno." He helped me hobble to the door. Felicité didn't miss a single beat with her cries.

Oliver cracked the door and peered out. "Dammit."

My stomach dropped. "What? What is it?"

"Hush." He took a long, deep breath, looking this way and that through the small crack. "There's a chance . . ." He sighed, deciding against further explanation. "Be ready to run."

My eyes fell to my single foot and cane. "I . . . I can't."

He looked wildly at the opposite side of the car, as if a door had materialized. "Dammit."

My heart pounded hard and fast. "What?" I demanded.

"We're facing the platform. There are people." He tried to bounce Felicité a few times, though it did no good.

I pressed my nose against the slats and squinted. The platform stretched before us all right, people milling all about in the afternoon sun.

I strained my eyes to read the station's sign, but only made out an "A" before Oliver pulled me back and placed his fingers on the handle.

I didn't need anything else to know exactly where we were. "We're in Atlanta!" I said, excitement bubbling in my belly.

"Yes, yes," he said dismissively. "I'm going to put you down first. I want you to hurry off and get lost in the crowd. They'll likely follow the little one and I, or at least I hope they do. If they do, hide. I'll come find you as soon as I can."

I opened my mouth to ask a million questions, but there was no time. He moved so quickly I had a hard time following. He set Felicité on the floor, whipped the door open without a care for the squeaking hinges, and picked me up under my arms.

I felt on display as he lowered me to the platform below. Where was I supposed to go? Every eye seemed to swivel to us. Wouldn't someone step forward to take us in? It was obvious that we were stowaways.

"But wait!" I protested as he handed me my cane.

"Go," he growled, nodding toward the more crowded area of the platform.

"But—" I cut myself off as I saw two men striding toward us. Each wore a dark suit and the telltale hat of someone who belonged to the railroad. I didn't need any more prodding.

I hurried in the opposite direction of them, the crowd parting just enough to allow me to slip in. I didn't look back until I had a good few families between us. The men had picked up the pace. One peeked into the car where we had just been, while the other headed in my direction, scanning the area.

Oliver and Felicité were nowhere to be seen.

I turned my back to the men and hurried along. With a cane, I was sure to be an easy target.

"There!" one of them shouted. I picked up speed, nearly hopping with one foot instead of fiddling with the cane. I knew exactly where we were, and that brought me more confidence than anything else could have.

I dove around the corner, hunting for my hiding place. A whistle blew behind me, shrill and startling. I ignored it. There was no time.

The only place I could think to hide was inside the main building. A lady could blend in, right? Even if her hair was messy and she lacked a leg? As I hopped inside the door, I smoothed my palm over my hair to tame it as well as I could. I sat next to the closest lady I could find and fought to smooth my skirts. She gave me a comical look of confusion, scraggly eyebrows arched, forehead crinkled. Otherwise, she ignored my presence.

If only I had been brave enough to steal her hat, my plan might've worked.

Unfortunately, the man's eyes went straight to me. I refused to look his way as he sauntered in my direction. If I didn't acknowledge him, perhaps he would turn and go away?

I could never be so lucky.

He cleared his throat and knelt before me, looking into my face as one would a scared child.

"Miss, are you okay?" he asked.

I hunted for an escape. Nothing. I couldn't run. I swallowed hard to try to control my voice. "Yes, yes. Thank you, sir."

"Would you be so kind to come with us?" he asked, standing and reaching his hand out for mine. "We have a few questions to ask you."

I looked left and right. No sign of Oliver. Only a room full of people I was sure were staring right at me. "I'd rather not, please." My voice cracked.

He sighed. "It's really not a question. I need you to come with me." His deep hazel eyes were pleading, begging me not to make a scene.

You should tell him the truth. All of it.

But how could I? Felicité's life took precedence to mine. If I told the truth, what would happen to her?

What would happen to Oliver?

I swayed where I stood, shakiness overtaking my leg. The officer put one arm around me for support as I hobbled forward.

How was I supposed to answer his questions?

He took me to a small room in the corner of the building. I'm not sure what I expected to be inside, likely something similar to a jail. Instead, the room was a simple office. There was a desk pressed against the wall with a chair in its rightful place. The man grabbed it and slid it my way, gesturing for me to sit. I did so as the door closed behind me with a final *thump*.

"Would you mind telling us your name?" he asked, leaning against the edge of the desk.

I certainly couldn't tell him my real name. First off, if he knew my father and his incessant gambling, that could identify me for all the wrong reasons. But it would open me up to tell the truth . . .

"Your name?"

I sat a little straighter and grabbed the first name that popped into my head. "Elizabeth Long."

He narrowed his eyes, disbelieving, but continued. "As I am sure you are aware, we are concerned about your earlier whereabouts." He paused, waiting for some kind of confession from me. He got nothing. "You wouldn't happen to be able to tell us why you were gettin' out of that train car?"

Without my permission, my fingers fidgeted. "I . . ." What would they believe? That I was traveling with my husband and his sister to escape his father's wrath? Definitely not. That I was hiding in the car of my own free will and deserved to be arrested? I had to play the victim. Somehow.

Doing my absolute best to make eye contact, I grabbed the first, semi-convincing lie I could think of. "I was trying to see how the cars were connected. You see, I've always been curious . . ."

The man crossed his arms firmly over his chest and cleared his throat. "Ms. Long, we don't have time for such nonsense."

I took a steadying breath and let myself fall completely into my story, praying they didn't find Oliver and Felicité. "I know it sounds like nonsense, sir. But I've always wondered about how trains work and all. But you see, when I crossed too close to that car . . ." I trailed off and added a shiver for emphasis. He leaned forward, grabbing on to every word. "That man, that man grabbed me." I made a show of placing my hand on the opposite forearm and took another breath to calm myself. "I'm only glad I was able to get away while I could!"

I sneaked a glance through my fingers. His eyes were wider than before, a cloud of confusion circling through them as though he couldn't decide whether to believe my story or not.

"I'm so sorry that happened to you, miss," he said, standing stiffly. "I'm so sorry to have detained you under false pretenses. It just appeared, as I imagine you are aware, that you came *out* of the closed car."

"Well, you know how—"

The door opened, effectively derailing every lie I could've ever created.

CHAPTER THIRTY-FOUR
"He's dead."

An older man waltzed right in, moving like he owned the place. And he did. He had a snowy white beard, black cap, and black buttoned coat with the golden chain of his pocket watch hanging out the front. I felt queasy when his hazel eyes locked on mine.

Mr. Richards.

An old friend of my father's.

"Ms. Dowling!" He held his hands out wide as though to snatch the inevitable joy from the air, then clasped them together. "It's so good to see you! It's been too long, too long!" He made his way toward me to shake my hand, then froze, eyes locked on where my foot should have been sticking out from under my skirts. "Ms. Dowling?"

My fidgeting began again, but I swallowed hard and held my head up a little higher. "Mr. Richards. It's good to see you too." I took my cane from its resting place against the wall and pulled myself up.

"Your . . ." His eyes wouldn't leave the blank spot under the hem of my dress.

Irritation niggled at me. "I had an accident shortly after I left. I assure you, I am just fine."

He backed the smallest of steps, and his eyes leapt back to my face. "I'm so sorry, that was impolite of me. Especially now, with all that has befallen you and your family!"

A dark cloud made its way into my heart, trailing its fingers around, ready to squeeze at any moment. Did the news finally get out about Pa's gambling? Did he lose the house after all? Were we officially disgraced?

"The Lord always has a plan . . ." I managed, hoping it would get him talking.

It did. "Ah, yes, he always has plans. But sometimes, it's just so hard to see what they really are. Especially in cases such as this." He shook his head, tsking his tongue.

Pa lost the house. He had to've.

"It's a wonder you made it here so fast! I know your ma will be mighty glad to have you here to help—"

I held out a hand, palm flat to stop his words as the dark fingers of dread closed around my heart. It wasn't the house. "Pardon?"

He didn't say a word, only inhaled sharply.

"Mr. Richards." I turned my gaze to stare straight at him, searching his bloodshot, golden eyes. Impending panic clung to my throat, threatening to overtake me. *What happened?* "What are you talking about?"

He blinked slowly, emotions flitting across his face faster than my heart could beat. "You didn't know?"

I reached to grip the back of the seat. It wasn't the house. It wasn't our fragile reputation. What else could've happened? "I don't believe I know, no." Each word tasted bitter in my mouth.

Mr. Richards turned to the other man. "Earl, please give us a minute, if you will."

Earl looked between the two of us, mouth open as if to spill my earlier lie, then turned and walked out without a word.

"You might want to sit for this," Mr. Richards warned.

I obeyed, plopping right into the seat without any regard for being ladylike. My skirts fluffed around me as if to exaggerate my ever-growing hopelessness.

"It was only two days ago, you see."

My heart thudded hard against my ribcage.

"No one knows what musta happened. But they found him at the saloon down the street—"

"Who?" I hardly breathed the word. It couldn't be Little Chris. It couldn't be Pa. It was bound to be some other person. A family friend. Even possibly a *close* family friend. Anyone but—

"Your father, dear. I'm so very sorry."

My mouth went dry. My heart felt numb. The wooziness threatened to overcome me. Nothing mattered, everything felt black. I fell forward into my lap, corset jabbing into my hips as a shocked sob racked my body.

No. No . . . It's not real. None of this is real!

But then, I knew this man had no reason to lie to me.

"I'm so sorry to be the one to tell you, dear." Mr. Richards patted my shoulder with a light, unwilling sort of touch. Satisfied with his attempt at comfort, he backed up and stood a few feet off, waiting for me to put myself back together.

My brain swirled round and round like a tornado, unable to make sense of what was real. Occasionally, the reality would punch me straight in the gut: Had I ever forgiven him? To his face, I certainly hadn't. That alone pained me greater than anything ever could. I didn't have the same anger in my heart as I had before, but did I ever *really* forgive him?

He was my father. Impulsive, sure, but still my father. And I was his Nella Bug. Maybe he really was just trying to give me a life of my own? Why had I never tried to forgive him? To give him one last hug?

Did he deserve my forgiveness?

My stomach twisted inward, and I held tighter onto my middle. I didn't know the answer.

"Can I . . ." Mr. Richards stumbled through his words. "Could I escort you to your home?"

Without thinking, I nodded. It was only when I wiped the tears from my eyes and regained myself that I remembered.

Oliver. And Felicité.

I stood so fast Mr. Richards jumped like I stuck him with a pin.

"Ms. Dowling?" he asked, concern plainly written in each wrinkle on his forehead.

I took just a moment to be sure my voice came out level. "Thank you for your time, and I apologize for my outburst. But I have some things to attend to before I make my way to visit my mother."

How long will it take to get home? Should I find Oliver first? Or just let him find me? And Mama . . . I need to get there. Now.

His face didn't move one bit as he stared at me, mouth agape and eyes wide. "But, miss, you need an escort. I know you're in shock, but—"

The panic in my gut threatened to disarm me again, twisting and punching me to the point of my vision going fuzzy. I swallowed it down. *Just get out of here!* "Oh, that's perfectly okay." I plastered my sweetest smile onto my face, though I was sure every emotion looked as fake as they felt. "I am actually traveling with someone. One of the other servants from Mister"—it shocked me how long it took me to remember his name—"Murray's vineyard accompanied me here."

His mouth shut with a click, but he looked just as confused as he had before. "Then . . . if I may ask, where is he?"

I bit the inside of my cheek as I hunted for an acceptable answer. "There was a . . . misunderstanding out on the platform. Apparently, they thought we were stowaways. Can you imagine?" I laughed, mimicking the high-pitched, fake ones I heard women use all the time.

He smiled in response, but his mouth caught on the edge, like he'd eaten something sour. "I see. Well, if you wait here, I can go find—"

"No!" I said, too quickly. "Please, let me find him. He has a past, you see. He won't come out to just anyone."

One eyebrow shot up. "A past?"

No! No! Wrong move! "It's not my story to tell." I waved my hand dismissively. "But I should go find him. He's bound to be worrying by now." I tried the fake laugh again.

"All right." Mr. Richards opened the door for me. "If you need anything, you know where I am."

"Yes, thank you." I plastered what I hoped was a convincing smile onto my face, the stretch splitting my dry lips, and headed for the door. To my surprise, he let me go. Perhaps it had something to do with his aversion to my emotional outbursts. And that was understandable, because I had to outrun my own feelings before they drowned me.

Earl stood idly in the waiting room, looking about as lost and confused as I felt. I flinched as his gaze caught mine, and he straightened. He must've determined I wasn't much of a threat, as he didn't make any kind of move in my direction.

Run. Hide. Get out before you break.

I made my way out of the front door, the fake smile crumbling away. My breathing didn't return to normal when the door slammed shut behind me. With every heartbeat, my breath grated against my chest.

He was mistaken. Get home, it will be okay.

The city stretched out before me, new buildings tracing the roadways every which way. The town had grown by thousands of people since we moved in. It didn't matter, I still knew where I'd need to go to find a warm bed for the night. No matter how much the city grew, I would always know the way home.

I strolled down the sidewalk, still scanning for my companions. He'd said he would find me, right? Hopefully, that hadn't changed with my apparent capture.

The decision was made before I even consciously thought the words: I was going home. I didn't think I had ever walked the route without an escort before. That thought was equally terrifying and freeing. I held my head up high and pulled my shoulders back. No one would touch a woman on a mission, correct?

Just stay brave. Grieve later. Don't think about it!

Oliver didn't waste time in finding me. I had only rounded the first corner when he placed his hand on my shoulder.

My scream was muffled by the hand he'd clamped over my mouth.

"It's me, it's me," he said.

In that instant, all the emotions I had been holding captive crashed out of me. I collapsed into him, sobs taking over every inch of my body. With each breath, my vision threatened to go dark. My thoughts flew by faster than I could catch them. Each memory, each sound, was gone as fast as it had arrived.

I would never hear him call me Nella Bug again . . .

"Nella?" Expertly holding Felicité in one arm, he propped me up with the other. Tenderly, he tucked one finger under my chin and lifted it so he could search my face. "What happened?" Instead of the angry fire in his eyes that I would've expected when I first met him, every line, every freckle contained concern.

He guided me to a nearby bench and set me down so I could lean against his chest like a child. People noticed, eyes growing wide, hands fluttering to their lips before gossiping to one another. I didn't have enough inside my frazzled head to even begin to worry about it. Sure, they likely knew me, but what did it matter? My father was dead.

"Nella," Oliver said, a bite tricking into his voice. "I need you to tell me. What is going on?"

I took a deep, choking breath, but only one word made it out. "Pa . . ."

In a mere instant, Oliver's eyes narrowed, then went wide. But not in surprise, as I would have expected. Anger. He knew?

"Dammit!" he growled.

He knew? How? The questions couldn't quite make it past the one ever-pressing desire. "I need to go see Mama . . ."

Instead of arguing, he nodded. "How do we get there?" Felicité mewled, whether in agreement or protest, I couldn't be sure.

I gestured in the direction of home. "It's not too far."

Glancing at the soon-to-be-angry baby, Oliver made a grunt of agreement. "Good. We need some help."

CHAPTER THIRTY-FIVE

She's Hungry

The walk to my childhood home with only one leg, with a man, and a screaming child garnered far more looks than I wanted. I felt every gaze as the onlookers studied my tear-stained face. It took only a few moments before recognition hit them.

"Petronella, dear!" one elderly woman said, fluttering her arms like an overly excited baby bird. It was the local seamstress, Mrs. Truman. "It's so good to see you! Oh, and look! Oh, wait till I tell Agnes! A baby! Oh, and this must be your husband? I'm—"

Oliver held up his hand to stop her advance as she rushed forward for a greeting. "I'm sorry, ma'am, but we really must be going. We have time-sensitive business to attend to."

She stopped short on the dusty sidewalk, her wide skirts sashaying around her as she blinked rapidly against the rejection. Her muted brown eyes traveled up my body, then widened as they focused on the fussy baby.

It hurt every inch of my soul to leave her in such a rude manner. But what else could we do? I squirmed under her appalled stare as we hurried on down the street. Agnes would certainly have all kinds of gossip to listen to when she saw Mrs. Truman again.

I didn't dare breathe as Oliver knocked on the faded wood door of my childhood home. It wasn't even necessary—Felicité's high-pitched screams announced our presence better than a polite thump.

My thoughts whirled round and round. What would Mama do when she saw Felicité? Or my leg? How would I even explain such a thing? I gnawed on the inside of my cheek, barely seeing the familiar doorframe in front of me.

I was damaged goods. I had a missing leg and a child. Even though Felicité was far from mine, would Ma believe me? And then I had a husband . . . I had Oliver. Had I even written about the marriage? Suddenly I couldn't remember.

In the end, it didn't matter. Every inch of my body ached to see her. I wanted to fall into her arms and cry, let her pet my hair and kiss the top of my head, whispering useless, sweet words.

Every few seconds, I tensed, sure I heard her familiar footfalls as they clicked across the wood floor inside. Over and over, I took a deep breath, fighting to keep myself from falling into a complete panic.

But nothing ever happened.

Oliver knocked again, louder this time. I balled my fingers into a fist around the top of my cane. Where could she be other than home? And where was Little Chris?

They certainly wouldn't have any staff. Pa surely didn't make enough off me to hire a butler again, let alone keep one!

The very thought made me stiffen. Did he even deserve my forgiveness?

Even on the third knock, no one came.

Oliver let out a long sigh and squeezed my shoulder. "She isn't here, Nella."

I whirled to face him head-on, surprising Felicité to a temporary silence. "But she has to be!" I knew I sounded like a child, but I didn't care.

Sympathy flickered across his face, softening his hard features. "Is there anywhere else you think she might be?"

I started to shake my head but froze as the answer hit me. "My sister!"

Oliver didn't hesitate. He placed a hand solidly on my back and gestured to the street with the other. "Lead the way."

I went as fast as I could, somehow managing not to trip over my own foot.

Miriam and her husband, Timothy, lived only a few blocks away. They had a marginally larger, but much better kept place. She married up, making the family proud.

At least one of us made Father proud . . .

The onlookers seemed to have doubled. Neighbors peered through the windows at the spectacle, their stares a mixture of confusion and anger. Felicité hardly stopped for a breath between screams, so I didn't blame them for their curiosity.

I tucked my head, feeling more and more self-conscious with every step I took.

"That's her," someone whispered. "Did you hear about her father?"

Oliver stiffened beside me. He'd heard it too.

The grief sliced deeper into my soul. I wanted it to be a bad dream. I *needed* it to be. Maybe, when I got to my sister's, we would all laugh about the mistake.

But the hole in the pit of my stomach told me the truth. I couldn't hide from reality.

By the time we made it to the two-story brick house, every inch of my body ached. Miriam's husband maintained better control over his money than my father ever could. Every inch of the house was perfect. Flowers hung in baskets under the window, reaching for the happiness of the sunshine.

Oliver knocked firmly, ensuring that if Felicité wasn't enough to alert someone to our presence this time, the knock would.

The door opened within seconds. Miriam's eyes locked on mine, wide and full of questions. She really looked no different than she had before I left, only with no sign of a baby growing inside. That meant she also had a tiny human hiding away somewhere.

"Nella!" She stared at me, Felicité, then back at me. Never once did she glance at Oliver. "What?"

My voice cracked as I tried to force words past my lips. "Will you help us?"

Miriam didn't bother responding. She practically snatched Felicité from Oliver's arms to check her over. As soon as Felicité caught the sweet scent of milk, her cries diminished and she pecked across Miriam's chest.

Distracted, Miriam stepped back, the two of us following her into the house.

"Delilah!" she called out, her voice echoing through the large house.

A middle-aged, thin Black woman came around the corner, vaguely familiar from my visits in the past. "Yes, miss?"

Miriam gestured to the two of us. "Will you please get a bath drawn? Our guests will need to freshen up before dinner, and a cloth and basin won't be enough." Her nose scrunched up only the slightest bit.

Delilah ducked her head. "Yes, Miss." She hurried along with her task.

Miriam bounced, cooing to Felicité. "She's hungry."

I nodded.

A strange, distant sort of look came over Miriam as she extended one finger on Felicité's back, then another, counting something. "She's not yours."

"No," I said, my voice rising an octave, betraying my anxiety.

Miriam stared me down, eyes narrowed. "She's *hungry*, Nella."

I swallowed hard. I knew I needed to tell her everything, but I couldn't find the words. "I know."

Miriam held the baby just a little tighter against her chest as she fought whatever demon raged inside her mind. "I'll feed her."

Not waiting for agreement, she sat on the blue, wood-trimmed settee and moved the infant onto one arm. She freed one breast, biting her lower lip as she fumbled to get Felicité to latch.

Once she figured out what was being offered, Felicité grabbed on tight, little hands balled against Miriam's white skin. The sudden lack of crying made my ears ring.

Miriam winced, which surprised me. Shouldn't she have been used to this by now?

"Nella," Miriam said, distracting both of us from the feeding. "I don't believe you've introduced me to your . . ."

I glanced at Oliver, our questioning expressions mimicking each other. What answer were we supposed to give? If we lied and said we weren't married, we'd have to figure out how to explain why we were together. With a baby. But if we admitted we were married, what then? Would it limit the number of explanations we would have to provide?

We stared at each other for a moment too long, impatience radiating from Miriam's direction.

"It's your decision," Oliver whispered.

Miriam's eyebrows shot up at his words; she looked even more confused than she had before.

I took a deep breath and chose the only truth I could give. "This is Oliver, my husband." Hopefully, the truth would mean we'd have to explain just a little less.

CHAPTER THIRTY-SIX

Home

Miriam's eyes went as wide as an owl's. She looked between the baby and me again, as if she could find an answer for her existence.

A door slammed somewhere in the back of the house, making Oliver stiffen.

"Who's here?" The masculine voice that floated from the kitchen warmed every inch of my soul. Little Chris.

Oliver's hand slipped under his travel-dirtied coat to rest beside his revolver. I nudged him with my elbow a little harder than necessary and shook my head, hoping Miriam wouldn't see. She did.

Little Chris came around the corner, munching on a piece of bread. He had already shed his jacket, leaving him in a patterned yellow waistcoat.

Seeing me, he didn't spare Oliver a second glance. He raced toward me, and I grinned like an idiot. He scooped me into his arms, the cane clattering to the floor as he swung me in a circle like a child.

While I'd been gone, his body had finally received the memo that he was nearly an adult. He didn't resemble a string bean anymore, and his shoulders had begun to widen. My baby brother—a man. The idea warmed my heart.

It took us a moment to realize no one else uttered a sound. I followed Miriam's gaze to the cane resting on the brightly patterned rug, then to the place my foot should've been.

Miriam's voice was a breathy gasp. "Nella!"

Little Chris set me down, childhood inching back into his features as he struggled to register the shock.

The *last* thing I wanted to explain was my leg. It would lead to a lot of other explanations, and I knew it. "I didn't write about that?" A startled giggle erupted from my lips, not helping my case one bit.

Both Miriam and Little Chris shook their heads.

I fidgeted with the edges of my dress, eyes trained on the floor. "Well . . ." I glanced at Oliver, who stood like a statue behind me. He didn't look like he would be much help. "I fell?"

Little Chris crossed his arms. "Uh-huh."

I let out a long sigh and glanced at the settee. It would be nice to sit, but I knew Miriam well enough to know she wouldn't be allowing me to do such a thing while I still resembled a swamp rat.

My squirming intensified. I couldn't focus well enough to determine what I could or couldn't say. *Oh, we're running from his family. They'll probably kill us if they catch us. But that's normal, right?* "Where's Mama?" I asked instead. "Why are you here and not home?" I looked at Chris.

He placed his hand on his forehead for a long moment, eyes squeezed shut as he shifted from foot to foot. "You're not gonna answer our question first?"

I stood a little straighter, anger flaring in my chest. "No, because I'll have to explain it all over again the moment I see Mama. So, as I see it, I might as well wait. I lost my leg, that alone is obvious enough."

"And you have a child . . ." Miriam said, voice so stern it sent a shiver up my spine. "That's *not* yours."

I clenched my fists, my fingernails digging into my palms. I didn't have an explanation for them. What was I supposed to say? Why couldn't they just tell me? Preferably before I had to dig down and find a lie for everything. "Please! Just tell me where Mama is!"

Little Chris plopped down on the spot on the settee that I'd been eyeing, putting his feet on the coffee table. "She went to the market."

"She moved in here after . . ." Miriam froze, studying my reaction.

That pain ignited again, deep in the pit of my stomach. I swallowed it down. "I heard," I muttered.

"She moved in so she wouldn't be alone." Miriam glanced down the hallway, the impatience plain on her face. She didn't want to talk about it, either. "Delilah! Is that bath ready yet?"

"Pourin' the water in now, Miss!" came the call.

Miriam nodded her approval and removed the groggy Felicité from her breast with a pop. "Cuddle her, please? She should sleep now." She handed the baby off to Little Chris, then finally turned to face me. "Come on, we need to talk." She looked just like Mama with the no-nonsense way she held her jaw.

I glanced at Oliver, who shrugged imperceptibly.

Seeing my nervousness, Little Chris chimed in. "I'll keep him entertained. I'd love to get to know my brother-in-law, anyway."

Before I could protest, Miriam took my arm and dragged me down the hallway, silent apart from the thump of my cane against the wooden floor.

I had yet to hear anything from Miriam's own baby.

Worry tugged at my heart. "Miriam?"

"Hmm?" She held the kitchen door open for me.

I squirmed, not sure how to ask such a question. "Your baby . . ."

Miriam froze as if she'd just seen a bear in the hearth, telling me everything I needed to know.

There was no baby.

My shoulders slumped. "I'm sorry."

Miriam's hand fell to her corseted stomach, caressing it in a longing way. "Stillborn."

"When?" I reached out to touch her arm, to give what comfort I could, though I knew it would never be enough.

"A little over a week ago. My milk came in anyway." She said the last part with an ill-placed laugh, like she wanted to take the focus off the tragedy.

Delilah stood beside the freshly prepared bathtub, hands clasped neatly in front of her apron. Though she heard every word, she showed no sign of it.

"Thank you, Delilah," Miriam said. "You can go now."

The slave politely ducked her head and hurried out the side door, likely grateful to get away from where the conversation was sure to head.

"I'm sorry, Miriam." My heart ached. Poor Miriam . . . between that and Pa, it was a wonder she could stand straight.

"It just wasn't meant to be." Her voice was so light, I could hardly hear it. She positioned me so she could work on the clasps of my bodice. "Now, please . . . explain some things for me."

I wrenched my eyes shut against the panic that welled up inside. "I'll try." My travel-worn, dirty bodice slid from my shoulders, making me shiver. The skirt followed almost immediately after, pooling at my feet.

"Whose baby is it?" She gripped the lower edge of my corset and started to work on the many hooks that spanned up the front. Every movement was rougher than necessary, making my toes curl under.

"Not mine?"

I could practically hear her eyes roll. "Unless your parting words with Tom included a little—"

"No." I plucked the corset from her hands and rushed to get the chemise over my head, as though it would quench any thought of that irritating near-husband.

"That's what I figured."

As she helped me into the warm water, my muscles started to relax, despite the question hanging in the air.

"She's Oliver's sister." I leaned my head against the back of the tub, breathing in the relaxing scents of lavender and lye.

"Why is she with you, then?" Miriam prodded as she settled herself to tackle my hair.

It took me a moment to remember the lie we told at the train station. "Her mother died." I peered at my sister to see her eyebrow shoot up in disbelief.

"So, Oliver's mother simply . . . died?"

"Yes?" I cursed myself for making it a question.

"Well, I know you well enough to see through that lie," she muttered, ripping a brush through the ends of my hair. "What are you doing with this apparently orphaned child?"

"I don't know."

"Oh?" She hit a few extra tangles, causing me to flinch away. I was beginning to think she was doing it on purpose.

"So you're traveling with a newborn, a new husband, a missing leg, looking like you slept in a barn, and you *just so happened* to show up in town without a plan?"

"Yes?" My voice climbed an octave when she found another tangle. She was gonna make me go bald at this rate.

"Are you planning on keeping her?"

I let myself think about it for a moment. We couldn't keep Felicité. How would we manage to take care of her on the run? We'd been lucky so far, but we couldn't exactly take a wet nurse with us. One day, hopefully, I'd have a little bundle of my own, but for now, Felicité couldn't fill that empty place in my heart. "No."

"Will you take her to the orphanage?" Miriam pulled on yet another tangle, drawing a yelp from me.

I reached back and grabbed my hair from her. "I don't want to, but I don't know what else to do, okay?"

Miriam perched back on her heels and stared at me, one eyebrow up. She regarded me with the same expression one would when watching the village idiot. "Tell me the truth, then."

I crossed my arms forcefully, causing a splash. "I can't. All I can tell you is she can't go home, and neither can Oliver."

Miriam was silent for a long time, studying me. "Mama will be happy to have you back."

I flinched. "I can't stay, either."

Miriam blew roughly through her lips. "And can you tell me why?"

I shook my head. "I wish I could."

She took my hair back and returned to working on the knots, gentler this time. "I'll take the baby."

My heart skipped a beat. In a whirlwind of water and soap, I spun to face her. "You'll what?"

She still had a handful of my dark hair, focusing all of her attention on a single mat. "You can't very well take care of a baby. I can. I lost my own, didn't I? Maybe . . ." She paused, emotion flickering through every inch of her body. "Maybe this is why?" Her watery brown eyes lifted to find mine.

She was sure.

I let myself imagine Felicité living with Miriam and Timothy. She'd have a happy, peaceful life. I couldn't see anything wrong with the idea.

"I think that would be perfect."

CHAPTER THIRTY-SEVEN
Scars and Mama

I trailed my fingers in the murky water, heart aching. For my nephew or niece, whom I would never have a chance to meet. For my sister's broken heart, a wound that would never mend. For my mother, who may never recover from the shock and heartbreak. And then, for my father . . .

I dared not even think of him. His smiling eyes, the way his mustache tickled when he'd kiss my cheek.

He'd practically sold me off to the highest bidder! Why did his loss hurt so much?

My untangled hair teased my shoulders as Miriam moved it to the side. I'm not sure if she planned on washing my back or massaging the stiffness from my shoulders. I never got to find out.

Miriam's hands slapped into the water so suddenly, it made me jump. "Goodness gracious! Nella!"

"What?" I demanded, reaching to where her hands had been, halfway expecting to find a spider.

Her fingers returned to my back, trailing down my spine to where the scars hid. I'd forgotten about them, and I wanted to keep it that way. I sat a little straighter, hoping they would disappear again.

"No," she commanded, shoving me forward with such force that my nose went under the water. "Petronella Dowling. What happened?"

I didn't bother correcting the last-name issue—it wouldn't help my case. "Is it that bad?" I hadn't looked at them. Each time I considered sneaking a glance, I stopped short. I imagined they traced up and down my back in dark red welts, looking like I had been mauled by a bear.

"Is it *that bad?*" Miriam echoed bitterly, tracing one of the tender spots. I had never felt *naked* in front of my sister before that very moment. "You . . . you're covered in whelps! Your whole back! Your employer. Murray? Was he . . ." She went silent for a moment, reining in emotion. "Did he beat you?"

I twisted to look straight at her, gripping the edge of the tub so she couldn't push me back. "How bad is it?"

She blinked slowly, mouth agape. "You don't *know?*" She shook the confusion away and hooked her fingers under my arms like she did when I was a child. "Stand up. Let me see."

"No!" I crossed my arms over my chest and pushed as far away from her as I could, hiding every inch of my body. Water sloshed in all directions out of the tub, but we both ignored the mess.

"Nella!" She stood, looking so much like Mama it made me rethink my defiance. "Let. Me. See!"

I grabbed for the first thing that came to my mind, not thinking for a moment how hurtful it might be. "Was it a boy or a girl?"

She went stock-still.

My toes curled anxiously. There was no stopping now. "Your baby. Was it a boy or a girl?"

She plopped into a nearby chair, all skirts and golden blonde hair. "I don't know."

The room went so silent, I could've heard a mouse snore from the walls if I listened hard enough. "You don't know? Miriam . . ."

"I like to think I had a little girl. I always envisioned making her a soft, pink blanket that she would carry all around the house." Unchecked tears trickled down her cheeks, and her hand traveled to the lower part of her corset, as though she could still feel her little one inside. "It's all just too much to handle. The baby . . . Father . . ."

I stayed perfectly quiet, waiting, my heart breaking just a little more.

"When the birth was—" She stopped to stifle a sob. "When it was done, everyone was quiet. So quiet. I think I asked if I had a girl, but no one said anything. Then the room started to twist this way and that and I . . ." She shuddered, then turned her piercing eyes at me. She was done reminiscing. "It's of no consequence. The baby just never was. The cord had been wrapped around its neck for too long." She stood, hands on her hips. "Now, stand up."

She looked like an all-conquering tempest, skirts ruffled just as much as her hair. I gulped, wishing my brain hadn't gone completely blank.

"Come on, Nella—"

"Oh! Hello! I didn't know we had guests, Little Chris!" The high-pitched voice that rang through the hallway could belong to only one person. "Whose baby?"

My heart skipped a beat, and I gripped the edge of the tub hard enough that my knuckles turned snow white.

Miriam made eye contact for a split second before bolting for the door, looking very much like she had when we were young and I had just thrown a mud pie at her new dress. "Mama! Mama!"

"Tattletale!" I shouted. I only had a few seconds, and I knew it. I scrambled from the tub, barely catching myself before I fell on my face. I didn't want to answer any more questions without Oliver's help. Especially naked.

That made me pause for only a moment. I actually wanted his help. When had that happened?

I had a hold of the towel when the clip of their heels echoed through the hall. Cursing under my breath, I wrapped it around my body.

My panic faded when she came into the room. Sunlight glowed in her red-blonde hair, and her brown eyes melted at the sight of me.

"Oh! Nella, dear, Nella!" Her voice cracked on my name, but that didn't stop her. She threw herself to the ground and wrapped her arms around me, sparing me no kisses.

Despite my worry, tears welled up and threatened to spill over. Every inch of my body shook with so many emotions, I couldn't concentrate on a single one.

I couldn't fully remember what I had told her in the letters. Did I only tell her I was sick? Did I tell her that I had a leg injury? Did I tell her anything at all?

"Oh, my baby girl." She planted both hands on my cheeks and pushed me away so she could get a good look at me. "I didn't know you were coming. And you made it in time!" She gave me a backbreaking hug.

"In time?" I glanced warily to Miriam, who only graced me with a glare. She still planned on making me pay for bringing up painful emotions.

"For the funeral, of course. That's why you're here, is it not?" Treating me like a doll, she pushed me to arm's length again and stared into my eyes. "You *do* know . . . right?"

Mutely, I nodded.

She breathed a sigh of relief. "Oh, thank the good Lord!"

Miriam cleared her throat, gaining Mother's instant attention, and a glare from me.

"Mama," Miriam began, crossing her own arms and staring us both down. "Back up and look at her. *Really* look at her."

Claire Dowling did just that, standing deliberately and taking a single step back.

Bile rose in my throat. I felt like I was on display at a zoo.

Though it took her a moment to see the obvious difference in my appearance, it didn't take long enough. "Nella?" she whispered, hand fluttering to her heart. "What happened?"

My missing leg throbbed, a strange, forbidden sensation. "An accident," I said. Both women raised their left eyebrows in a startlingly identical motion.

"You said you'd tell when Mama got here," Miriam pointed out.

I couldn't keep the groan inside. "I was wandering near the . . ." I paused, trying to remember all the details of where I was supposed to be. "I was wandering near a big, beautiful lake. There were all sorts of flowers around, and the dragonflies . . ." I shut my eyes, dreaming up this magical place. To my surprise, all I saw was the pond by Oliver's family home.

My throat went dry. They were hunting for us . . . How long would it take them to catch up?

Mama cleared her throat, and I jumped.

"Sorry." I pushed a rapidly drying strand of hair behind my ear. Best to keep the lie as close to the truth as possible. "I . . . well, I fell and broke my leg. And they—the doctor, I mean—said it couldn't be saved." I stared at the place where my foot should've been, praying I didn't have to say anything else.

"Oh, baby," Mama cooed, enveloping me in a hug so tight, I could hardly breathe. "I'm so sorry. I should've been there with you." Down her cheeks tears flowed freely, sparking a few new ones in the corners of my eyes.

"Mama," I started, resting my head on her chest and taking in the aroma of her homemade rose-scented soap. "I missed you."

She kissed the top of my head, nearly breaking my emotional state in two. "But you're back now, even if only for a short time." Her body stiffened with her next words. "I only wish your father was here. You were always his Baby Bug . . ."

My blood ran cold, and nausea threatened to take control. I opened my mouth to speak a few times but never managed to find the right words. He wouldn't be here. I'd never see him again . . .

I nodded silently, not wanting to break the moment with any more questions. All I wanted was to be close to her, soaking in all the comfort that only a mother could provide.

"You gonna tell her about your husband?" Miriam quipped.

Claire's entire body went rigid.

I fixed my sister with the best death stare I could muster. I started to mouth obscenities at her, but Mama pushed me back to arm's length to get her answers.

"Petronella Dowling. Is that who that man is out there?" Her brown eyes were wide and her neatly trimmed eyebrows arched.

"Yes . . ." Like a child, I squirmed under her gaze. "His name is Oliver. Oliver Wedman." I forced myself to stand a little straighter. I knew I had mentioned him in my last letter, but I doubted it had arrived yet. Even so, I knew I hadn't mentioned our impromptu wedding.

Mama let out the slowest exhale I had ever heard. "Well, there's nothing to be done. Is he of good standing?"

"Uh . . ." I had no idea how to answer that question. He didn't have a penny to his name. Not anymore. "He treats me well. It was quite sudden."

She dropped her gaze to my towel-covered stomach, that one eyebrow arched in an unasked question.

"No!" I clutched at my stomach. "I'm a—" I stopped short. Explaining my virginity would only bring on more questions. "I brought his sister, though. Little Chris has her."

"In the sitting room," Miriam added helpfully, an excited glow taking over her features. "Her mama died suddenly. So . . . I told them I would keep her." She beamed so much, I momentarily considered forgiving her.

"Was that . . . ?"

"Yes, Mama. A baby." Miriam gravitated toward the door. "Come on, hurry up. I'll introduce you."

CHAPTER THIRTY-EIGHT

Voice

Much later, we all sat around the dinner table. Oliver had also taken a much-needed bath, leaving him smelling like rose water. His hair was neatly combed into a queue at the nape of his neck, and he wore a clean suit Timothy had lent him. It didn't fit, not in the slightest. It was too wide in the torso and too tight in the arms, causing him to move stiffly.

"We'll get your own clothes washed up tomorrow," Mama promised. "It's a shame your luggage was lost on the way."

"Mhm," I agreed, shoving a spoonful of beans into my mouth. I had been given one of Miriam's old dresses. It was also too large around the waist. I must've lost some weight while trapped in the Wedmans' godforsaken attic. We used to be closer to the same size.

"Tell us how the two of you met?" Little Chris demanded. He was already on his second full plate. I wasn't sure if I'd even be able to finish the one I had, let alone go back for seconds.

"Well," Oliver sat a little straighter. "There's not much to it. We work together, so we saw each other pretty near every day."

Miriam looked up from the nursing baby in her arms. Ever since the bath, she'd hadn't put Felicité down for a single second. "That's not very romantic. What *drew* you together?"

Claire shot her a reproachful look. "Miriam Lynn. You know better than to ask such questions."

I smiled behind my napkin. Thank goodness for manners.

Oliver apparently didn't much care to follow them himself. "Mrs. Dowling, might I ask what became of your husband? The news was that it was quite sudden."

Mama stiffened as though she'd been stung by a bee. "It's a fair question," she said, likely to herself. "No one really knows what happened. He said he quit gambling after our Nella left. He didn't want to end up like . . ." She trailed off. "But the police think he owed someone money. That's the only thing that explains what . . . happened . . ."

The grief twisted itself like a knife in my gut. Of course, the gambling debts would've got him one day. It always did in the end, didn't it?

"They found him on Saturday. He'd already been gone for a day and night." She said it all with such bravery, as though she was talking about a distant relative, but that last sentence struck her with a sob.

I felt Oliver flinch but assumed it was due to the grief-laced emotions that coursed through the air. "I realize this is sensitive, ma'am. But might I ask *how*?"

No one dared breathe. I fixed my startled gaze on him. Who would ask such a thing?

Miriam provided the answer in a mere whisper. "Knife."

Oliver nodded his thanks and slipped another bite into his mouth. The room fell silent, filled only with the nauseating sounds of chewing.

Little Chris broke the silence, leaning forward in his seat until his arms were flat on the table. "Did you pass out? You know, when they removed your leg?"

Mama's eyes darted to him. "*Christopher!*"

Chris shrugged. "I was just curious. Ain't seen one done."

Mama rubbed my back tenderly, inviting me to lean her direction like a content cat. Did we have to leave?

As if reading my thoughts, Oliver patted my hand and stood. "I really wish we could stay, but we have a train to catch."

Mama gasped. "Already? You only just got here! What about the funeral?"

"Yes, what about the funeral?" Chris asked.

Seamlessly, Oliver took over the lie. "Mr. Murray couldn't afford to have us gone long, so we chose to spend today with family and return to work early in the morning. I really wish we could stay."

Miriam's eyes narrowed to slits. She was on to our lie; I knew it. For once, she didn't say anything.

"Oh, I wish you could stay!" Mama held me tight against her.

I looked pleadingly at Oliver, hoping to melt him with puppy-dog eyes. "Can't we stay at least one night?"

"Yes," Mama chimed in. "The funeral is in the morning."

I sat a little straighter, my confidence renewed. "Exactly. He'd understand if we came back tomorrow, wouldn't he?"

Oliver did his best not to react, but a flash of irritation darted over his face. "It wouldn't be wise. You know how he is . . . *unforgiving.*"

The memory of the bite of the whip sprang to life, stopping me mid-breath. If he caught us, the whip would be the least of our worries.

Chris struggled to chew his hefty bite, leaving him wincing as he swallowed. "If you're wanting to catch a train," he chimed in. "The last one left around five." The triumphant smirk was plain on his face.

Oliver's shoulders sagged. There went his way out. "Then, I guess we'd better go find a hotel to stay the night in and hope *Mr. Murray* isn't too angry."

"Oh, you don't have to do that!" Miriam waved her hand dismissively. "We have plenty of room! Stay here! Timothy is out of town, but I'm sure he wouldn't mind!"

Oliver seemed to wilt a little more. "We will have to leave very early in the morning, I don't want to be a bother." This felt directed toward me—a warning.

Miriam reached to squeeze my hand. "Nonsense, she's my sister! And you're my brother-in-law. Make yourself at home. Relax some!"

"After the funeral?" I piped in.

Mama's face nearly glowed. "It's settled then. Nella, come help me with—"

I practically bounced in my seat. He didn't have a choice—I'd won this battle. "Let's just leave right after the funeral. I'm sure Mr. Murray will understand."

Oliver seemed to stare straight through to my soul with his blue daggers. "Mr. *Murray* is the least understanding person we have ever met, remember?"

Felicité started to howl, arms and legs pawing at the air in her tiny fury. Miriam had been distracted enough that the baby had dislodged from the breast, and she was far from finished.

"Well, aren't you an angry little bundle?" Mama cooed, reaching across the table in the most unladylike show. She captured one of the flailing fists and stroked it with her thumb. "It's so nice to have a little one back here again."

Thankful for the respite, I turned back to my food, though not without a cocky glance at Oliver.

Ha! Not happy I have a voice now, are you?

CHAPTER THIRTY-NINE

Visit

I conveniently forgot about our impending doom for most of the evening. Mama kept me busy throughout the house, talking incessantly about how much she missed me, the antics Little Chris had gotten up to, and how much he was enjoying his apprenticeship. Every chance she got, she held Felicité, only relinquishing her for her next round of feeding.

We even made a cake, surely in Delilah's way, as she worked on dinner.

By the time the moon was high in the sky, and Little Chris passed clean out in front of the unlit fireplace, everything felt as though it had been some kind of bad dream.

"We should get some sleep," Oliver said after a yawn overtook my body.

"We can sleep on the train, can't we?" The last thing I wanted to do was let reality catch up with us.

Mama tsked. "That's far from ladylike, Petronella."

It took everything in me not to roll my eyes, but I somehow remained focused on Oliver.

He sighed. "We can't . . . you know that."

Each time I blinked, Henry's smirking face popped into view. If he found us . . . "All right."

Oliver helped me stand and gave a polite nod to Claire and Miriam. "Thank you for letting us stay the night. It will be nice to start fresh again in the morning."

"What time will you be leaving, again?" Miriam asked, switching the sleeping Felicité to her other arm as gently as she could.

"After—" I hardly got the word out. I planned to stay for the funeral.

"We will be leaving at first light." Oliver's words were final.

My heart dropped. "But we agreed—"

"We didn't agree to anything," he nearly snapped. "We'll talk about it later."

"Can't we at least stay until after we eat?" I felt my expression morph into that puppy-dog plead again. It did absolutely nothing but make his face harden.

Mama didn't seem to notice the animosity. She wrapped me in a rib-squashing embrace and pressed her head into the crook of my shoulder. "Please, be safe? Send me a letter as soon as you make it home?"

I nodded, breathing in the familiar scent of her. How long would it be before I got to see her again? I shot Oliver a glare over her shoulder, hoping he understood exactly what it meant. It was far too unkind to take me away from my family *again*. Especially right before a funeral.

Before my *father's* funeral.

He shook his head almost imperceptibly and mouthed, "Not now."

"I love you, my dear baby girl," Mama cooed, running her fingers through my loose hair.

She didn't need to say anything else. Tears pricked at the corners of my eyes, and it was all I could do to blink them back. "I love you too."

Climbing up to the bedroom was just about the hardest thing I'd ever had to do. The pain blossoming in my chest held back my impending arguments. At least until the door to our designated room shut behind us.

I stood just inside the closed door, unable to take another step. The simple domesticity of the four-poster bed, the handmade quilt hanging perfectly on either side of the mattress, the embroidered towel on the vanity—it all broke the tears free of their cage.

"I'm sorry," Oliver whispered. He stood like a statue in the center of it all, watching me.

"You're not," I snapped. Deep down, I knew he didn't deserve my wrath, but I didn't care. He would take me away from my family. Again.

Oliver took a hesitant step in my direction. "If the circumstances were different—"

"The circumstances? I'm here, safe with my family. Why not just leave me?"

To my surprise, he flinched. "Because, as you keep forgetting, my *father* is after us. *Us.* You and me." He pointed at each of us in turn to drive in the point. "And as safe as you feel at the moment, this is the first place they'll check. I'm just praying they think I'm not stupid enough to be here . . ." He trailed off, one hand rubbing his temple. "Besides I'd—" He froze, eyes wide, as if he hadn't meant to speak.

I grabbed onto my chance. "You would what?"

"Nothing. Come on to bed. We have an early morning." He turned away from me, pulling on a stray piece of his hair with more force than was strictly necessary.

I hurried to his side and grabbed his arm. "I'm stuck with you. So if there's something you're hiding, I'd like to know."

In the candlelight, his teeth flashed in a smirk. "It's not anything like that. Forget it. Let's go to sleep." He sat on the edge of the bed and went right to ignoring my angry glare. He pulled his shirt over his head and tossed it onto the chair in the corner. I nearly choked with his bravery. Sure, I'd seen him without a shirt before, but usually he tried to be at least somewhat modest with a lady in the room, staying in a nightshirt and drawers. I turned my back to him, my face heating up.

Oliver chuckled. "If someone saw you now, they'd wonder if you were really married."

I fidgeted, toes curling under. "Well, it's not official."

As if I punched him in the gut, he ceased all movement. There wasn't so much as a sound of rustling fabric. "No, it's not."

I moved to the other side of the dressing screen, first taking a quick look to ensure he wasn't watching me. Also, to get just another peek at the way his muscles rippled down his back. When I was satisfied that he wouldn't crane his neck to get his own glimpse, I started to undress.

I couldn't stop the whisper from fluttering from my lips. "You didn't want to really be married, did you?" To my surprise, a pang of sadness pierced my belly at the thought.

"Hmm" was the only response I got.

"Hmm?" I echoed, folding the borrowed skirt and bodice up and carefully placing them on the chair at the bedside. I grabbed his trousers from the floor and placed them on top. Messy man . . .

Obediently, he didn't move his gaze from the window as I crawled under the blankets.

"What were you saying earlier?" My hand moved of its own accord, poised to poke him in the back. When I forced it back under the blankets, he turned to stare at me with a raised eyebrow.

"It was nothing." He bent to blow out the candle, then positioned himself for the night on top of the quilt.

We remained silent for a long while, both staring into the darkness. It was me who broke the silence first.

"Aren't you cold?"

"Huh?"

"Lying up there only wearing your—" I motioned wildly in the air as though he could fill in the word I refused to say.

"Drawers?" A barely concealed laugh shook the bed. "I'll be fine."

We fell back to silence until I could take it no longer. Here we were, married, and he was sentenced to a cold, sleepless night without a blanket.

And I honestly didn't want to sleep alone.

"Well, dammit." I tugged on the blanket between us.

He jumped to his feet, sputtering in confusion. "What are you doing?"

I pulled the quilt away from his spot and patted the mattress. "Lie down."

He did as he was told, every movement stiff. "What are you doing, Nella?"

"I think I can trust you not to touch me. And you deserve a decent night's sleep too."

Well aware of my apprehension, he remained on the far edge of the bed. Even with his consideration, his leg rested only inches from mine. I could nearly feel his body heat radiating from it.

No matter how long I stared at the dark ceiling, his quiet breathing never changed to his usual snore.

I couldn't stay silent. "Tell me what you almost said earlier?"

He sighed and rolled to face me with such care he didn't move a single inch closer. "You were supposed to forget about it."

"You know as well as I do, there's no chance of that." Resting on my side, I propped my head up on my elbow, leaving me staring down at *him* for once.

He hesitated a moment longer before letting his head fall against the pillow with another sigh. "If you were to stay here, aside from the danger it would put you and all of your family in, I would probably miss you." His voice took on a raspy edge as he choked out the words.

"You'd . . . miss me?" Whatever I had been expecting to come out of his mouth, it certainly wasn't that. If I weren't around, he still wouldn't be able to go back home. Especially not after he helped me escape with Felicité.

"You heard me." He gulped loud enough I could hear.

I stared hard at his shadowy form. "But wouldn't it be easier if I wasn't around?"

He rolled onto his back and shrugged. "Sure, but you're probably the best mistake I've made."

My face flushed hotter than a sunburn. "You mean that?" I bit my lower lip as my heart thumped wildly. My fingers warred with themselves, as though they could find the answer to *why* that made me so happy.

The shadowed look he shot me stopped my thoughts before they could run wild. "Last I checked, I didn't say things willy-nilly. Stop your swoonin' and get to sleep—we have an early morning tomorrow."

"I'm not swooning!" I snapped.

"Ah, so what would you call your fidgeting? And that blush on your face?"

"How would you know I'm blushing? It's dark!"

He made a clicking noise with his tongue. "Well, I was right, wasn't I?"

I plopped down onto the pillow. "You're wrong. I don't *like* you in that way." But even as I said it, I knew it was a lie. The very thought made me squirm more.

"Uh-huh." I could hear the grin in his voice. "Sleep well, Princess."

Though my blush burned hot on my cheeks, and a smile formed on my face, it took every ounce of restraint I had not to punch him in the shoulder.

CHAPTER FORTY

Flight

Who initiated contact? Had it been me? Did I press my lips to his and demand his attention? Or had his hand found my skin under the sheets?

His touch was warm and featherlight against my thigh as he trailed his fingers up, softly, delicately. My breath caught in my throat, and my body acted on its own accord. I tilted toward him, every inch of me craving the attention.

"Does this mean you're ready to be mine?" he purred, his stubble tickling the sensitive space under my ear.

Moving in the slowness only a dream could provide, I pressed my cloth-covered torso against his, lifting one knee up to trap his thighs between my legs. "Yes," I said. My voice was strong, more confident than I had ever heard it.

He smiled against my neck for a mere moment before nipping the delicate skin. I gasped, my body going limp. That gentle hand trailed up just a little more, gripping the hem of my chemise and taking it up. I stiffened as he found my hip and let his fingers travel back to cup one cheek in his solid grip.

"Mine," he growled.

"Yours," I whispered.

That magical hand was on the move again, tracing up my hip and to my lower belly, teasing me. My toes curled under and

I moaned, waiting to see what he could do to douse the forbidden fire inside—

He didn't wake me when he left the bed. He didn't even wake me as he moved the curtain to peer out the window. He did, however, wake me by throwing my cane and yesterday's outfit at me.

The wooden cane rammed into my knee, breaking me out of the not-so-innocent dreams.

"What on—"

"Shh!" he hissed, the finger that he held to his lips a silhouette in the moonlight. "Get dressed. Hurry."

"Can't we stay longer?" I yawned and ever so slowly stood up. "You said first light. It's not anywhere—"

"Nella, please," he begged. "*Hurry.*"

"What's going on?" Grudgingly, I wrapped my corset around my middle and fumbled with the clasps in the darkness. Ordinarily, I would've argued with him, but his urgency sent chills through the room.

He stood by the window, back flat against the wall, eyes trained on something outside. Something near the front door. His hand rested ominously on the weapon that hung at his hip.

"When'd you get a gun?" It wasn't exactly the question I wanted to ask. Of course he'd had a gun throughout our entire journey. What scared me was *why* he needed it.

He didn't answer, only rapidly snapped his fingers at me in an incredibly insulting way to get me to hurry.

I barely had the back of my skirt tied together and the bodice on like a jacket when he motioned for me to stand by him. I did, mimicking his stance against the wall as well as I could. "Who?" I wasn't sure if I truly wanted the answer.

"I think it's Bernard." He took a deep, settling breath. At least, it seemed calming to him. For me, it rattled every nerve I had.

"It can't be," I argued. "He wouldn't—"

"It's his job, Nella," Oliver said patiently.

He had been right: we should've left yesterday. "But my family!" I grasped his hand. "Chris is still downstairs on the settee!"

"Shh!" Oliver snapped, fixing to stare me straight in the eyes. "Listen to me, and listen to me good. He doesn't want them. He wants *us*. The only thing we can do to protect your family is to get out of here. *Now*."

It felt like my heart was lodged somewhere in the back of my throat, cutting off any ability to respond. I gnawed at the inside of my cheek, trying to keep the strangled cry from escaping its hold.

"Here's the plan," Oliver began, checking on the encroaching threat's progress, then back at me. "Are you listening?"

Like a terrified child, I nodded.

"He'll get inside the house as soon as he finishes—"

"Finishes what?"

"Checking the windows. When he finishes that, he'll go inside."

"How? I know the door's locked—"

"I don't know which method he'll choose, just know he will. But as soon as he's inside, it'll be our time to get out."

I strained to see around him, hoping he was mistaken. But deep down, I knew he wasn't. Someone was coming to get us, and all we could do was run.

What have I done?

My voice trembled. "But Chris—"

He held his finger to my lips, strong and steady. I trembled against it, unable to stop myself.

"Chris will have to fight his own battle." Oliver stretched his head from side to side, producing a satisfying crackle. "I'm counting on him to buy us some time."

A trained machine, Oliver was ready. His hands fell to his sides, fingers moving one at a time as one would play a scale, warming up for whatever would come next.

A small sob escaped my clenched teeth, and my hands took a solid hold of his shirt. Little Chris would stand no chance against someone like Bernard.

One finger at a time, Oliver pried my fingers off him. "I'm going to get you out first. Slide to the edge of the roof and *wait*. Do you understand so far?" He waited for my nod. "I'll be right behind you with your cane. No matter what you do, don't make a sound and *don't jump* without my help." Again, he waited for my nod. He took another steadying breath. "All right, be ready."

Like a ghost, he moved to crouch under the windowsill, hands pressed against the bottom of the frame. Without an eye on his brother, he waited for the sounds of his entry.

Without Oliver blocking my view, I could see the looming shadow below.

Bernard didn't keep us waiting long; he stalked from one window to the next, then started his way back, stopping at the dining room window directly below us. He lifted his rifle and smashed the hilt into the glass, sending shards crashing every which way.

Despite myself, I squeaked. Oliver gripped my shoulder, warning me to stay still and quiet. His head was cocked to the side as he listened for his brother. I couldn't tell if he was counting steps or trying to read his mind.

Without warning, Oliver stood and threw the window open. He didn't wait for me to be ready. He grasped me under the arms and shoved me out the window feetfirst, trusting that my instincts would kick in.

They did. I grabbed at the shingles with my bare foot and hands, losing more skin than I dared think about. I barely caught myself at the edge, only a few feet above the window Bernard had just used for his entry.

Agile as a cat, Oliver appeared beside me. He tilted to the side to peer through the entry window, then sprang into action. He tossed my cane to the ground, then listened again. When he was satisfied, he gripped the edge of the porch roof.

Voices rose from inside the house. "What's this?"

Little Chris.

Another sob ripped free, vibrating my body. *What have you done?*

Oliver swung so his body hung from the roof, legs swinging just a few feet from the ground. With more bravery than I ever could've mustered, he dropped lithely to the wooden panels of the porch.

"Come on." Oliver held his hand up in my direction. "Your turn."

I couldn't hear anything other than the thumps from inside as Chris likely wrestled his attacker.

"No!" I moved for the window, but Oliver leapt to cling to the overhang.

His muscles rippled to life all the way from his neck to the tips of his fingers. His voice was pure ice, melting with urgency. "We can *not* help him. *Hurry.*"

I couldn't move. I couldn't breathe. All I could do was stare at the house, willing my family to be okay.

The tussle only lasted for a few moments before silence engulfed the house again.

No gunshots. But Bernard would know countless other ways to kill someone. It would only take a moment for him to dismember a half-asleep Chris.

Another sob shook me.

"Nella!" Oliver's voice cut through the dark. "Come *on*. We don't have time!"

I hardly heard him. My hands were in fists on the rooftop, fingernails digging into my palms.

A shrill scream floated through the bedroom window. Bernard had already made it upstairs. Mama's room was the first in the hallway. It had to be her scream.

"Nella!" Oliver finally shouted, slamming his fist against the roof. "Now!" He dropped back to the safety of the ground, ready for my descent.

I shook myself back to the mission at hand. I couldn't help them by perching on the edge of a roof like a sitting duck.

Without even looking, I slid from the roof and fell like a sack of potatoes into Oliver's arms. We both crashed to the ground. He likely expected me to copy his own dismount so he could assist me—not for me to fall flat on his face.

Even so, he didn't hesitate. He scooped up both the cane and me and ran, darting into the first alley he came across.

On well-trained feet, he raced on, skirting discarded buckets and sacks. He made no noise other than the *plop* of his bare feet on the well-trod ground.

I was far from quiet. All I could imagine was the inevitable blood flying about my sister's house. Bernard would kill them all, even Felicité. After all, no one was there to stop him.

Oliver didn't slow until we were streets away. By that point, I was openly sobbing.

The neighbors would find their bodies, I was sure of it. Their blood would cover every inch of the floor. It would be splattered across the walls, the bed, soaked deep into the quilts, the beautiful settee. My entire family, slaughtered for one bad decision. *My* bad decision.

CHAPTER FORTY-ONE

Bad Decision

He set me on a step of a closed storefront and plopped down next to me.

"Mama . . . Chris . . ." I cried so hard I could hardly breathe.

Oliver scooped me into his arms and let me rest my head against his chest and soak his shirt with my tears.

"They're gone." The words felt trapped deep in my throat, choking me. "They're gone . . ."

He ran his hands over my hair with such tenderness, it was as though he hoped the touch alone could fix everything. "We don't know that."

"But we *do*." I pushed back to search his shadowed face. I could make out his furrowed brows and the sharp lines of his jaw, leading to his pursed lips. "What else would he do?"

"He wanted us. He wasn't trying to prove a point this time—"

My blood turned to ice. "This time?" I stared into his moonlit face, hunting for his unspoken words.

Oliver remained silent for a moment too long, but he didn't try to lie. "Later, please. We have to talk about it later. Right now—"

"This time?" I wound his shirt into my fists. "*This time?*"

"Nella," he said patiently. "Now is *not* the time. We have to get out of here."

I scooted out of his arms, one hand pressed firmly to his chest to keep him at arm's length. The world shook with my dizziness, my fingers felt numb. "No. You tell me now. Now!"

He shut his eyes to maintain his patience and took a deep breath. "If I tell you, you're not gonna be in any state to run."

"And I'm in such a state now?"

"No." He rubbed at his furrowed brow. Finally, he sighed, defeated. "There is a chance, a *chance* mind you, that your father's death wasn't from his debts."

I flinched involuntarily. I knew what was coming next; I just didn't want to believe it. It took every ounce of strength I had to force the words out of my mouth. "Carry on."

We both flinched when something scurried at the far end of the alley. Oliver stared in its general direction, as though it would offer him a way out of the conversation. Finally, convinced that the sound didn't belong to a human, he continued. "It happened around the same time my own father was gone. This is something—"

I tried, but I couldn't stay silent. "You think he did it?"

"It is possible he did it for no other reason than to show what would happen if you left, if you told anyone once you had some freedom."

Like a fish, I opened my mouth multiple times, but nothing came out. Killing my father. A power move. "And you *knew* about this?"

His eyes opened fully, deadly blue daggers barely sheathed in the darkness. "No. I swear to you, Nella. If he did it, he did it to put *me* in my place. Not just you."

I rested my clenched hand on my chest to still my rapidly beating heart. "But . . . if he did that, what will he do now that we're gone? You just said that Bernard wouldn't hurt my family! I *heard* their screams!"

Oliver grimaced, a hand absently tugging at a loose strand of hair. "We don't have any control over what he'll do now."

It felt like someone stabbed me in the chest. "Mama . . ."

Oliver sat a little straighter and placed both of his hands firmly on my shoulders. "You need to listen to me, and listen good."

I glared at him. I didn't like how many times I was hearing exactly that in the span of an hour.

He shook me gently to get my full attention. "Like it or not, we got ourselves into a war. Staying with your family will get them killed."

"But leaving them alone now—"

"Shh." He placed that steady finger to my lips. "Leaving them alone gives them the highest chance we can give them. All we can do is get out of here before *we're* killed."

I glanced back the way we came, my mother's screams crashing through my mind.

Oliver picked me up as gingerly as he would a broken child, one arm behind my back and one under my knees, the cane resting over my torso. "We can't stay here."

I rested my head against his chest and let the tears fall, not caring if he would become soaked through. We made our way through the dark streets, the only sounds coming from our footsteps and the crickets hiding in the bushes.

We should've left yesterday. What have I done?

When we reached the train station, he placed me in the bushes. My mind felt like nothing except goop.

"Your brother said the train comes through again at eight? As soon as they open, I'll grab us a ticket." Oliver stood, an immobile shadow leaning against a tree.

"We have money for a ticket?" Half-heartedly, I raised an eyebrow. "Where'd we get money?"

Oliver patted his pocket absently. "We needed a ticket."

I bristled like a porcupine, glaring into his soul. "You *stole* it from my *sister?*"

Wisely, he didn't answer.

Where else would he have gotten the money? I wasn't sure if I really wanted to be mad at him for it, either. It would be worth it if we didn't have to endure another train ride crammed into the back of a boxcar.

"Just . . . don't do it again." I buttoned up my bodice. Once the sun came up, I needed to look just a little more presentable. He smirked at my scolding, but otherwise didn't move.

As the sun began its crawl over the horizon, people milled about with their daily routines. By the time the golden light glinted off the tracks, people were already waiting in line at the ticket booth.

Each of those people had a life of their own, a family of their own, a purpose. My stomach flipped, and I shut my eyes tight against the threatening tears.

My family had their own lives. If they're all dead, it's my fault.

"I can't do this," I said, gripping the tree and pulling myself to stand beside him.

Oliver's eyes drooped from exhaustion, but he stood a little straighter at my sudden movement. "Do what?"

"Leave. Not yet." Without giving him a chance to argue, I broke from the undergrowth and started the laborious journey back the way we had come.

"Nella!" Oliver's footfalls pounded against the platform as he raced after me. The crowd around us had all turned to stare at the two bedraggled individuals who had simply materialized from the trees. The way he gripped my bicep was surprisingly gentle, halting any further movement. "Nella, we can't—"

"No!" I snapped, yanking free. "I can't leave. Not knowing they might be just lying there . . ." I had to stop before I broke into tears yet again. "You can come, or you can stay."

He shook his head with a forced sort of slowness. "We don't even know how many of my brothers are here. Or even if they brought help. If they find you, they'll *kill* you." As he said this, he leaned in close, his breath teasing the tip of my nose.

I crossed my arms and waited. Deep down, I didn't know what I was doing, trying to go back. The chances of being found were high as it was. Going back felt very much like the final nail in my coffin.

Oliver sighed. "I could pick you up and take you back to the train."

Unconsciously, I gnawed on my cheek. "But *will* you?" I set my jaw and stared him down, hoping I seemed somewhat brave. Inside, I was quivering.

Oliver cursed. "I wouldn't be able to leave, either." He held out his hand, and I took it. "You just need to promise me one thing."

There was no way I'd blindly promise anything. Not now. "What is it?"

He placed his hands firmly on both sides of my face, staring me straight in the eyes. "No matter what we find, we can't stay. If you stay, you'll die."

I flinched. "But what—"

His breathing was measured, purposeful, likely from him fighting to remain calm. "Please don't argue with me, just promise you'll listen. If the worst happened, there's nothing we can do. Nothing except get out of here."

I nodded firmly, stomach swirling. "But if Bernard already saw we weren't there, why would he come back around?"

Oliver nodded toward the two-story general store. "Because I can guarantee they already know where we are."

I narrowed my eyes at the top of the building. "So, that's where they are?"

"No, it's just where I would hide if I was the hunter."

The hunter. A shiver shot up my spine. How many times had he hunted down someone? How many times had he hunted down someone like me?

"If they're watching us now—"

He sighed, exasperated. "I don't know if they are now or not. There's only one rule to follow when you're trying to avoid capture: always assume they know your every move."

Instead of ducking into the next alley, he continued straight on down the sidewalk. There were more people milling about, darting back and forth as they went about their daily duties. Wagons rattled down the street, sending dust flying through the air.

The walk to my sister's house was long. Every few feet I caught myself staring into a different dark corner.

Always watching. They were always there.

We somehow made it to Miriam's house without incident. Summoning up every ounce of bravery I had, I waltzed right to the front door. Before I could grasp the door handle, Oliver's fingers encompassed my arm. "We can't stay, remember? Just look." His voice was so soft, I hardly heard it.

Letting my hand drop back to my side, I picked my way through the trampled plants and knelt in the porch's shadow, right where Bernard had been only a few hours before. Oliver stood behind, eyes trained on anything that had an inkling to move.

I heard someone before I got the guts to look through the broken window.

"Mama! Do you know where I put the baby blanket? The blue one Mrs. Tribble crocheted for me?" Miriam's voice soared like a song, breaking loose my tears yet again.

"It's not in the baby's chest?" Mama's voice chimed back even sweeter.

"No! Did you take it for Felicité this morning?"

"I didn't! I just wrapped her in the afghan after her bath."

My body leaned against the wall, the relief washing over me. At least three of them were okay, likely unharmed. But where was Chris? And Delilah? Mama wouldn't have the ability to sound cheery if something unspeakable had happened to either of them.

I stretched a little farther out of the shadows, straining my eyes to see through the open kitchen doorway and into the front room. Just one sign. I needed just one sign of him.

It took a moment for my eyes to adjust to the darkness. Sure enough, Chris lay right where I had last seen him. He had a blanket roughly thrown over his body, not even covering his feet. The powder-blue baby blanket the women were hunting for was crumpled at the end of the settee. Delilah stood over him, checking a bandage on his head as he winced. His pale face was marred with angry red splotches, his eyes so swollen it would be a wonder if he could see at all.

When Delilah hit a specific spot on his forehead with her finger, he cursed louder than necessary. She carried on, true as always.

He was okay.

They were all okay.

"Nella, we have to go." Oliver's prodding was the last thing I wanted. "Hurry."

Delilah's sensitive ears heard his whisper. She whipped her head in our direction before I could even start to crawl out of the destroyed flowerbed. Seeing me, her expression changed from one of complete fear, to one of resignation. She gave me a half smile as the relief flooded her face. She didn't say or do anything else; she simply turned back to Little Chris.

"Nella, hurry," Oliver said again.

I made my way out of the flowerbed, careful not to squish what end-of-season blooms remained. He took my forearm and pulled me to stand. Before I was fully upright, he pressed his lips to my ear. A tingle shot through my body, squelched only by his words. "Put your arms around my neck and hold tight. He's here."

CHAPTER FORTY-TWO
WANTED

His words were all it took for adrenaline to replace the sadness. Without question, I looped my arms around his neck. He took one deep breath before taking off.

He ran so fast my hair was sure to whip into his face. I tucked my nose into the crook of his neck, peering over his shoulder with horror as a man materialized out of the shadows. He was shorter than Bernard, wearing an ill-fitting, somewhat familiar suit with a black hat pulled low over his face.

"It's not Bernard!" I shrieked.

"I'm aware."

"Who is it?" I squinted, trying to determine who wore the too-large suit.

"Arthur," Oliver grumbled. He didn't sound the least bit winded as he darted into an alleyway, checking the knobs to each back door to see if any of them were open.

The third door on the right was the one. He had us inside before I had time to think, then clicked the lock into its rightful place. Whoever owned the shop needed to learn to lock their doors.

I gathered myself to stand again, but Oliver had other plans.

We were in the back room of a mercantile, sacks of flour stacked in nearly every corner of the room. Threads and other odds and ends were in their own piles, sitting on tables so they wouldn't be covered by the wasted flour. The end result was a messy winter wonderland. The shop owner also needed to learn how to use a broom.

I didn't have time to take in much else. Oliver rushed through the building, making his way to the front door.

When we reached the front room, everyone froze. Including us.

A young man stood on the second rung of a ladder, refilling the spice jars by candlelight. He stared at us, mouth slack in shock. By the front door stood a man I could only assume was the owner. He was around my father's age, with graying hair and an unkempt mustache. He had a poster in one hand, a hammer in the other, and a nail between his teeth. His eyes were as wide as a dinner plate.

"You!" He pointed the hammer straight at us.

Oliver's muscles tensed, and he gripped my cane tighter. He spread his legs shoulder width apart and tipped imperceptibly forward, likely ready to drop me to the floor and fight.

The minimal change in Oliver's stance was apparently enough to terrify the man. "We don't want trouble!" The merchant's hands shot to the sky in surrender. The hammer smashed a mere inch from his toes and the poster floated to the floor, landing face up a few feet in front of us.

None other than Oliver's face stared back at us in midnight-black ink, right under the unmistakable words: WANTED.

Oliver scooped it up with the same ease as if he had simply dropped a handkerchief. He didn't even glance at it before shoving it in his pocket. "Well, fuck."

"Wanted?" I whispered, heart thudding against my ribcage. "You're wanted? Again?"

"I don't want no trouble!" the merchant said, backing himself into the corner. The younger man stayed exactly where he was, clinging to the ladder.

A frustrated sound that resembled a growl erupted from Oliver. "When'd you get the poster?"

"This morning! The sheriff was passing them out this morning! Said it was urgent!" The man shook like a leaf in his corner, probably about to pee himself for fear of being beaten with my cane.

"Thanks," Oliver said absently. He strode to the hammer, scooped it up, and placed it on the table. Each movement he made brought a jerk from the merchant.

Oliver stood a little straighter and waltzed to the front door, stepping through like he didn't have a care in the world. His eyes were the only things that betrayed his nerves. His head swiveled from side to side like a hawk.

A carriage clattered around the corner, halting with precision directly in front of us. The man up front held the reins lightly, but his movements were stiff as he turned to face us.

I recognized both him and the wagon instantly. Oliver, on the other hand, did not.

I let out a yowl of both surprise and pain as Oliver dropped me onto the dusty ground. There was a flurry of movement through the flying dirt above me as Oliver pulled his pistol from its holster.

Little Chris was prepared for this. In an equally smooth motion, he scooped the shotgun from his lap and held it with one hand, mere inches from Oliver's forehead.

"Stop!" I shouted, waving my hands between them to get their attention. It would take too long to stand up.

Neither of them moved.

"Delilah saw you." Little Chris was stiff as a board, likely as useful as a discarded mannequin. "Get away from my sister."

Oliver's gun came down a fraction. The street was filled with people, every single eye on us.

"Oliver! Chris! Stop this—" I started.

Little Chris's hands were shaky on the shotgun, his eyes so swollen I was positive he wouldn't be able to aim properly. He rolled his shoulders back to get a better grip.

Oliver returned his revolver to his holster with an unintelligible grumble.

"Move. Away. From. My. Sister," Little Chris snarled.

"You're not gonna shoot me," Oliver muttered. Whether he said it to comfort himself, or to throw off his brother-in-law, I didn't know.

He stepped forward in an absurdly confident movement. "We'll do whatever you want. When you get us out of town."

"I'm the one with the gun here!" Little Chris waggled it for emphasis.

"I noticed," Oliver said. "But as I said before, you're not gonna shoot me."

He strode right up to the carriage.

"I . . . I'm gonna shoot you! Back off!" Little Chris's voice trembled.

"If you wanted to, you would'a done it already." Like a man who welcomed death, Oliver placed his hand on the latch to the carriage, holding eye contact the entire time.

With a grumble, I hauled myself upright. "Gracious, Chris. He's not the bad guy."

"And how can you be so sure of that?" Little Chris spat.

The door creaked as Oliver pulled it open. "Because my own little brother is just around the corner. And if we don't get out of here *immediately*, your bruises will be the *least* of your worries!"

Little Chris waved the gun in the air again. "What's going on? You'd better start talking, bastard."

"How 'bout we talk when we get out of town?" Oliver countered.

With a groan, I pushed Oliver's back. "Just get in." I turned to my brother. "We'll tell you, I promise. But first, let's go. Now, please!"

Little Chris's nostrils flared. "How do I know you won't spout off more lies?" Despite his fury, he didn't move to stop us.

I glared at him.

Oliver reached from his perch in the carriage to grip me under the arms. "Guess you don't," he admitted. "But if you don't start driving, you won't get to hear anything." I barely made it inside before he shut the door with a decisive *click*.

As expected, the wagon lurched forward, Little Chris grumbling unknown words in the front seat.

Miriam's carriage was cozy, reminding me of days gone by when my own family could afford to travel this way. The seats were well cushioned, with a matching blanket folded across the rear one.

Oliver lifted the red blanket and shook it out. "Under there. In case anyone looks inside."

I obeyed, sliding to lie under the seat. He draped the blanket over me, then crammed his large body under the opposite seat.

"Speed up a little, will ya? They've got no reason to take you prisoner!"

"Fine!" Chris seethed. "But you mark my words, I'm gonna kill you when we stop!"

I peered around the blanket just in time to see Oliver roll his eyes. But his expression fell right back into a state of pure irritation. "I don't like this."

"Well, I don't like any of this," I shot back. "Especially that WANTED poster." I shoved my hand out flat and wiggled my fingers. "Gimme."

Obediently, he fished into his pocket and placed the wadded piece of paper in my hand, letting his fingers rest there for a moment too long. I plucked both the paper and my hand back as if I'd been stung; my eyes found his.

He hadn't meant to do that, had he?

We were in a carriage running from would-be assassins, with my brother threatening his demise for heaven's sake! The tingling in my body couldn't have come at a worse time. To break the spell, I unfurled the paper and stared at his inked face as well as I could in the low light. I could hardly make myself focus. The image didn't diminish the numb feeling that spread over my bottom lip, or the tingle that traveled down my torso. I only hoped he would think the panic in my eyes was due to the poster.

His likeness was perfect, certainly done by his own family. Who was the artist? I imagined Arthur sitting at the table, quill in hand, and the lustful tingle turned to a bout of queasiness. Under his picture were daunting words: "Wanted for the kidnapping of the daughter of Henry Wedman. May also be traveling with a Petronella Dowling."

I crumpled the paper again and chucked it at him. "Your pa did this too, right?"

He nodded.

"Why?"

"To scare me." He pinched the bridge of his nose.

"If you get caught, won't you be hanged?"

His voice was bitter. "No. My family won't let that happen. They'll get me first. This is a warning to me, telling me to come back. Or else."

"What about me?" I was terrified of the answer. Did Henry Wedman even have a purpose for me? I doubted it.

Oliver didn't answer for a long while, eyes trained on the underside of the seat. "Don't get caught."

My nausea increased. "I don't plan on it."

The wagon rolled along for over an hour, the trail growing bumpier with each passing mile. Eventually, the holes in the road grew bad enough to send us skidding this way and that.

When Oliver was sure we were out of town, we righted ourselves in our perspective seats, watching the landscape pass around us.

"Do you know where he's taking us?" Oliver asked.

"I have no idea," I admitted.

Oliver shook his head. "He'd better be smart . . ."

I squirmed. "I trust him." I turned my entire body to stare out the rear window, avoiding Oliver's searching eyes. "How do we know they won't follow us?"

He sat a little straighter to peer out the space above my head. "We don't. I haven't seen a sign of them, but that doesn't mean anything."

The words were out of my mouth before I had a chance to think them through. "Will they really kill Little Chris if they find us?"

Oliver shot me a look that meant nothing short of "You already know the answer, don't make me tell you."

I plopped back into my chair and placed my head in my hands. Each time the silence overtook us, fear gripped at my heart. "Talk about something. Anything."

"Uh . . ." Oliver shifted uncomfortably in his seat. I doubted he was used to calming someone in such a situation. Usually, he was the one causing the panic instead.

He was saved from trivial conversation by us pulling into a ranch. Horses and cattle grazed as though they didn't have a problem in the world, only a few of them looking our way as we passed.

Little Chris halted the carriage right at the entrance to a rapidly rotting cellar. Oliver clicked opened the carriage door closest to the hiding space, looked cautiously around, then jumped to the dusty earth.

It was hard to discern Little Chris's glare past the bruising. "I guess you can hide in there." He nodded in the direction of the cellar. "*After* you explain." He fixed his gaze on me.

Oliver spoke first. "My family—"

"No," Chris snapped. "You're likely to tell more lies. I can see through hers. Speak, Nella."

I wanted to kick him for treating me like a naughty dog. But what was I supposed to say? Another lie? I couldn't even begin to think fast enough for such a thing. I glanced at Oliver for guidance. He nodded, the permission I needed to tell the truth.

So I did, in the fastest way possible. Well, somewhat. I left out the entirety of how the situation started. "His family is after us. They're killers . . ." The word tasted forbidden on my tongue. "So we're running and trying to hide."

Little Chris stared at us both, mouth agape. "That's not all of it," he pointed out.

"We don't have *time* for the rest of it!"

Little Chris grumbled under his breath. "Fine. Rest for a while, but get out of here after dark."

Oliver's entire body slumped as the stress flowed from him. "Do we need to worry about the owners coming into the cellar?"

"No." Little Chris shook his head. "The maid is the only one who will bother you before dinner. And she will keep a secret."

Was that a hint of a smile on his face? "And how do you know that?" I demanded.

"I'm not a saint, Nella."

My mouth fell open. "Are you saying you took—"

Oliver took my hand. "Your brother and his trysts are his business. Come on, get in there."

Little Chris tipped his hat at me. "I guess we both have our secrets, now don't we?"

"Come on." Oliver tugged on my arm and pulled open the cellar.

CHAPTER FORTY-THREE

Cellar

The smells of the moist earth mixed with drying herbs and overripe fruit hit my senses hard enough to spark my hunger. My stomach growled its approval as Oliver helped me into the dark hole in the ground.

My eyes locked onto a basket of crisp apples on the nearest shelf, my mouth watering in response.

Without needing to ask what I craved, Oliver grabbed one and handed it to me. "Theft is okay when you don't know when you're going to eat next." He sat under the rack of drying herbs, closed his eyes, and leaned his head against the wall.

"You're not gonna have one?" I asked, taking the biggest bite I had ever dared out of the juicy red sphere. A simple piece of fruit had never tasted so good.

"Not right now," he said, swiping a candle from the shelf and lighting it with the provided matches.

"You're worried, aren't you?" I let myself sink down to sit beside him.

The smile he gave me didn't reach his eyes. "Some."

It terrified me, him being worried enough not to eat. That didn't mean I planned on starving. I took another unladylike bite. His eyes sparkled with a smidge of amusement. At least that was genuine.

"You think we'll be safe here, right?" I asked, resting my head against his shoulder. In the shadowed corners, my imagination conjured darkly cloaked men, biding their time for the right moment to strike.

"That's my hope," he said. Despite his words, he positioned himself just right so he could grasp the pistol easily.

Each time I moved, the mythical assassins in the corners did the same, causing me to flinch. By the time I jumped at the imagined killer behind the ladder, Oliver spoke.

"No one's here." He moved to his knees, shining the light from the candle into the corners as proof. The only thing that stared back at me were the canned peaches stacked in a pyramid against the wall.

"I know, I can't help it." I shut my eyes for a long moment, but the anxiety just continued to build inside. Oliver was nervous—that alone meant I had a right to be terrified. If they came through the cellar door, that would be it. I highly doubted Oliver's skills with a gun would save us while trapped in a hole. At least not for very long.

After brushing the dust from a somewhat empty shelf with a flourish, he positioned the candle in the middle. He stared at it for a long while, perfectly silent other than the resigned sigh that escaped his lips. I stared at him, waiting for the worst.

Without warning, he whirled on me, his hands shooting out to tickle me under the arm.

Uncontrolled laughter took over my body, making it diffi-cult to breathe. I whacked at his hands, but I might as well've been a fly. "Inappropriate!" I squealed, falling to the ground in surrender and chucking a basket his way.

"Are you going to let *me* stress about it, then?" He didn't relent, despite my squirming and protests.

"Yes! Yes!"

He released me then, the smirk on his face being the only proof of his disobedience.

"Not appropriate," I muttered, peering at him through the hair that had fallen across my face and righting my skirts as well as I could.

"That smile is worth it." He let me lean against him again, tucking his nose in my hair. "Let me worry about it for now. There's nothing we can do until dark."

I hardly heard him. His warmth awoke that forbidden tingle. It erupted throughout my body, warming me to the point of overheating.

Whether I was spurred on by anxiety or lust, I'll never know. I let my hand glide from my own thigh to his, testing his reaction. He stiffened a little, but only for the smallest moment.

Answering my biological call would keep the shadows from coming alive with my fears, and I was considering it. It wasn't wrong, right?

My gaze traveled up his arm, noting every freckle on the way to his face. His eyes were locked right on mine, reading my every expression. I opened my mouth to say something, any-thing, but nothing came out. My heart thudded audibly against my breastbone, threatening to break free at any moment.

We were married. Why did I feel guilty for wanting to lean in?

It's fine. You're man and wife! I scolded myself.

I turned my face up to his and proceeded to do the last thing I expected.

I'll never be sure who closed the final gap between our lips. But once we moved, that tingle became a raging fire. My kiss rapidly changed from a hesitant, featherlight touch to a rough, hungry sort of press. My hands trailed up his biceps and to his shoulders, and my body moved to kneel at his side.

"Hold on," he said under the kiss, breaking the connection by pushing me back a few inches. "I need to know one very important thing right now." His voice was breathy, eyes wild and starved.

"What?" I demanded, toes curling in my mess of skirts, every inch of my body vibrating with the urge to tackle him. I didn't know what to do with the pent-up fire that raged inside.

"What are you trying to do?" He made eye contact, his icy-blue eyes dancing with the same energy I felt. "I want a very truthful answer."

I set my jaw and plopped back onto the dusty ground. "I wanted . . . you know what I wanted!" I shot him a glare.

My expression must've looked comically vicious in the flickering light, as his lips twitched into a smile. He regained his composure and sat a little straighter.

"I know what it *looks* like you wanted. But I don't want to give it to you if you aren't *sure* you want it." His lip slipped behind his teeth as he gnawed on them, as though the sensation alone would force him to remain calm. It must've worked; his body stayed perfectly still.

I forced myself to think about it. I tried to imagine it. Skin to skin. The desperate joining of two adults. My brain couldn't focus long enough to form a complete picture. All I wanted was to close that gap between us.

To escape.

"We're married. And if we aren't going to survive . . . and we're married, anyway."

Oliver perched on his knees and leaned over me, hand tracing down the packed-dirt wall until it rested beside my head. "If you want to stop, just tell me."

I nodded. Why would I want him to stop? Did I really have anything to lose anymore? My hands reached forward, cupping behind his head and pulling him back to me for another, deeper kiss.

"You're sure?" he asked again through kisses. I could feel his resolve melting each time our lips touched.

"Do you not want to?" I backed up just enough to stare into his eyes. Briefly, it occurred to me that I could drive him insane if I teased him with it. I would have to remember that for the future. If I withheld it from him this time, *I* would be the one going crazy.

"On the contrary, Princess. I most certainly want to. I just don't want to do something you'll regret." He hovered so closely that our noses nearly touched.

I didn't hesitate. "I won't regret it."

He released me and sat back on his heels, the ever-controlled mask completely slipping from his face. His lip crooked into a smirk, his eyes sparkling, daring me. I had never seen someone look so much like a predator, and yet I somehow wanted nothing more than to fall into his trap. "Then come on."

Some inner version of myself took over. I took control of this alluring hunter. I hiked up my skirts just enough to place a knee on either side of his thighs, half sitting, half hovering over his lap. I could feel his heart thud under the hand that I pressed against his chest, and I liked it. I wanted it.

He started his fingers at where my right leg began, taking his time caressing the scarred flesh that remained. Both of his hands took their positions at the sensitive skin behind my knees, then danced their way up the backs of my thighs. Inch by inch. "Your move," he whispered.

My own heart skipped a beat, my bravery faltering for only a second. *You wanted this. Right?* The persistent heat traveling throughout my body answered the question before my thoughts had a chance to catch up.

I worked at the buttons of his shirt, fingers shaking more than I dared acknowledge. Each button seemed to take forever. Oliver waited patiently, mouth partially open as he took deep, calming breaths. Before I'd finished the final one, his own fingers found their way free of my skirts and traveled up my back. They traced their way over my shoulders and then rested at my throat. Savoring every moment, he started to work on the buttons of my bodice.

I squirmed, startled at how hard it was to be patient. Once finished, he pushed it from my shoulders, letting his fingers trail over my skin so lightly it made me shiver.

He pressed against me with a kiss as he pulled the ties of my skirts.

Much more skilled than I, he had me untied in a mere moment and had the fabric gathered to pull it over my head. I grabbed it impatiently, yanked my hair free, and threw it to the side. The crinoline and petticoat followed in quick succession. Left only in my chemise and corset, it shocked me how ready I felt to bare it all.

Oliver chuckled as I worked on unfastening the busk of my corset, fingers fumbling as though they'd grown to double their size. Once I threw it to an unknown corner of the room, he took over.

In one swift movement, he leaned forward, pushing me onto the ground where he hovered over me in an impressive show of strength, chest only a fraction of an inch from mine. My heart thudded against my breastbone, loud enough it could certainly lead Bernard to our exact location.

"What now?" I breathed the words, though I didn't know why.

"You still want it?" he asked, keeping his lips just out of reach.

An irritated growl erupted from some unknown part of me. "Stop asking that!" I shimmied out of my chemise before he could say another thing. I held my breath, instantly nervous. He'd seen me before, I knew that. But this was different, intimate.

He smirked before nipping my lower lip. "As you wish, Princess." He moved away from me just long enough to remove the rest of his clothing. Before I had ample time to admire the unseen way his leg curved into his bottom, he was back.

His hands roamed down my body, tracing the curves of my breast, then down my sides. I flinched away only as he hit the ticklish zone on the side of my ribs.

"I'll remember that for later," he promised, leaning to kiss the spot.

"Don't you dare," I breathed, though at the moment, I really didn't care. Any worries I had before were long gone. The fiery tingle had grown to the point I trembled, craving absolutely anything he would give to me.

He traced my side with his tongue, pausing at the top of my hip bone, then moving across to my lower stomach. To my relief, he didn't trace any lower. I wasn't sure I would have survived such a thing. Though that fiery part of me would have certainly welcomed it. Instead, his fingers did the work, traveling up the inside of my thigh.

One touch from him was all it took to make me gasp. He took that as consent and continued his exploration. I let him, pushing the worries to the back of my mind. He kept his eyes focused on my face, reading my every expression, watching for any potential regrets.

There weren't any.

My brain was long gone.

We were married.

It was okay.

I let him take me then, pulling me into a feeling I hadn't expected: pain.

Though he went slow, I yelped. He stopped in his tracks. I narrowed my eyes at him, shocked that I didn't want him to stop.

He lowered his chest to mine, his warm skin like a comforting blanket. "I can stop. Do you want me to stop? Just say the word." He didn't move a single muscle as he waited.

This had to be why I'd never heard a woman speak kindly about what they considered to be their "womanly duties."

"Do you want me to stop?" The stiffness in his voice was the only thing that made me realize I was holding his forearm in a death grip.

"I don't know," I admitted, releasing his arm. "How long till it gets better?"

"No one told you about it hurting, did they?" His breath tickled my neck, making me crave him all the more, despite my worries.

"Well, not exactly? I'd heard . . . but it's not ladylike to speak of, now is it?"

He placed a kiss in the hollow below my ear that turned into the most delicate bite I could've imagined. I shivered. "If it's too much, or if you want me to stop, just tell me? You don't deserve to hurt." His voice was warm and comforting. As though his words were laced with opium, my body began to relax. "Will you trust me? I have an idea."

I nodded mutely, unable to really focus. At some point, his hand had traveled back down to the source of my fire, igniting it again and drawing a sigh from my lips.

Delicately, he brought me into a sweet kind of ecstasy. He took his time, whispering words in my ear that I didn't fully hear. Quite frankly, I didn't care about the pain anymore. I craved it just as much as I feared it. In fact, it seemed to be fading just a little.

By the time it was over, we were both covered in sweat and dirt from the floor. He pulled me into his arms, and we curled up in the far corner.

Though we were in a musty cellar, I didn't want to be anywhere else.

His ever-tracing fingers paused on my hip bone. "We need to get dressed."

I didn't want to move. If I got dressed, would the spell be broken? Would reality come flooding back in? I craned my neck to get a good look at his face. His eyes hadn't relinquished the stress, but the rest of him had relaxed.

Perhaps I was what he needed to erase the fears. Despite myself, the thought made me smile.

"If the worst happens and someone comes in here, I think you'd prefer to be dressed," he said, kissing my forehead.

He was right. With a groan, I moved away, grabbing my chemise and shaking the dirt from it. Oliver stood and began gathering the rest of the clothing strewn across the room.

I didn't want to think of the last time he'd seen me naked, but standing vulnerable in the candlelit room ensured the memories plagued me.

"Oliver," I started.

"Hmm?" He stopped his tidying, giving me his full attention.

"Miriam saw my back." I tapped the area on my lower back, flinching at the sensation.

Apparently, Oliver hadn't been expecting me to bring up his transgressions. His body slumped, and he pursed his lips. "C'mere," he said after a moment of thought. He gripped me around the waist and spun me so my back was to him. Scooping me up in one arm, he dragged his fingers along the back of my legs, over the curve of my rear, then to the tender spot at my low back.

I didn't fight his touch, though it made me shiver. Even his tracing fingers went still as he studied the scars.

"Stand here," he commanded, placing me back on the ground. I didn't argue, though I had to take a deep breath to banish the memories that threatened to drown me.

Not now. You're safe. He's not going to hurt you!

He knelt behind me, hands on my bare hips, his breath teasing my lower back.

"You see," he started, kissing where I assumed one scar began, "I didn't want you to have *any* scars." He kissed again, his lips trailing down the line. "I understand it's no excuse for what I did. I should've run away with you that very moment. I'm sorry. You didn't deserve that."

His fingers marched to the front of my stomach, teasing, promising, making me catch my breath.

The moment there was a thump at the door, his comforting touch was gone.

By the time the door started to open, he already had his gun drawn and ready.

CHAPTER FORTY-FOUR

Captured

I n record time, I tugged the chemise over my head.

The door opened with agonizing slowness, creaking on its hinges. A heavyset woman came onto the first step, humming some folk song. Her eyes crinkled as she caught sight of the lit candle, then tracked to the side until finding Oliver and his gun.

She screamed, her basket clattering down the stairs as she rushed to cross herself. What I could only assume was a curse in Italian flew from her mouth.

I slumped against the cellar wall as I relaxed. It was just the maid. We were fine.

She didn't find anything calming. Little half-formed yelps escaped from her throat. I didn't blame her. Staring straight at a naked man holding a gun wouldn't make me feel very calm either.

"S-Sorry," Oliver stammered. He bent to place the revolver back inside of the holster and jerked his pants back on. "Did Chris not tell you we were going to be here?"

She started to shake her head, but then changed it to a nod. "He did mention there might be someone here, but I did not expect . . ." She motioned wildly at us and the pile of clothing.

To my surprise, Oliver's face had a pinkish tone to it. "Well . . . please, come get what you need. We'll be gone by morning."

She nodded just once, the movement jerky. "Will you . . . um . . . will you hand me four potatoes?" Her voice still wavered, but she stood a little straighter.

Oliver did as she asked, placing the potatoes in her basket, then handing it back up to her. She flinched as their hands touched on the wicker handle. The poor woman would never go into the cellar feeling safe again, that was certain.

After she was gone, I wrapped the corset around my waist. "What kind of mischief is Little Chris up to out here?" I mused.

A barking laugh escaped Oliver's lips before he got it under control. "If I were to hazard a guess, I'd say the same thing we just did."

I stared at him, mouth agape. "No!"

He smirked and pulled his shirt over his head but didn't bother to provide any other details.

It finally hit me whenever I was nearly asleep, head on Oliver's chest.

Nella Bug . . . you'll never hear that again.

The cacophony of emotion slammed through me with such violence, I had no control. A guttural sob broke from my throat. I gripped Oliver's arm with such force, I would certainly leave bruises.

He was up in a mere second, crouched and ready to fight. "What? What happened?"

I didn't have to say a word. Each sob shook me harder than the last, leaving my breaths to grate through my throat like blades.

Wordlessly, Oliver settled back onto the packed dirt, pulling me into his embrace. He tucked my head under his chin, whispering soothing nonsense into my hair. "I'm sorry, I'm so, so sorry, Nella."

"He's gone," I wailed. "And I never . . . I never forgave him. When I saw him last, I never even gave him a hug." I clutched at Oliver, reaching for comfort from the wounds that would never heal.

Did my father really deserve my forgiveness? He essentially sold me to the highest bidder—but he did it to give me a chance at my own life. And even though I didn't agree with his methods whatsoever, he did it because he loved me.

"And I didn't even go to the funeral . . ."

Oliver pressed me closer against him. "I know. I'm so sorry, so sorry!"

He held me as I cried out more tears than ever before, kissed the top of my head as I grieved, rocked me as I desperately sought breath between the sobs.

Eventually, my eyes raw, I cried myself to sleep in his arms.

Oliver kissed me awake long after the sun had disappeared below the horizon. I woke with a start but melted under his lips.

He moved to tickle my ear with the stubble of his beard. "Are you all right?"

I wiped at my eyes. They felt bruised, and my vision was still blurred from all the tears. Even so, I nodded. "I think so."

He kissed me again. "Then it's time to go."

The only sound came from crickets chattering as though they had plenty to gossip about. If any of them knew what we'd been up to, they would certainly have at least a few conversation topics.

"Did you sleep?" I asked, watching as he grabbed a cloth bag from under the stairs and threw random food inside.

He only shrugged, eyes stuck on the canned peaches.

"Thievery is acceptable when you don't know where your next meal will come from, remember?" I grabbed one of the cans and handed it to him. "Just probably shouldn't take all of them."

His eyes locked onto mine as he pushed my hair out of my face. The worry had returned, clearly overtaking his body. He was so stiff he could've been mistaken for a tree stump without much effort.

"What's wrong?" Saying the words allowed the worry to bloom in my chest. If he, of all people, was concerned . . .

"Nothing," he said, kissing the top of my head. "I'm just not looking forward to going back out there when I don't know where Bernard or Arthur are."

I squirmed. "What exactly would they do if they caught us?"

"They wouldn't kill us, if that's what you're worried about." Oliver turned his back to me and sank into a crouch. "Come on, the sooner we get away from here, the better off we are."

I hopped onto his back, a process that was becoming easier by the day. He took the stairs effortlessly but paused at the doorway for a long moment. If he had been a dog, his ears would've been tipped forward to hear the slightest noise.

"We never should've stayed in a place so blind," he muttered to himself. One deep breath later, he flung the door open and stalked into the moonlight like a provoked bear.

No one shot us, no one jumped out at us; nothing but a startled animal moved in the brush.

Satisfied that we were safe for the moment, Oliver gave in and closed the cellar with a resounding *thump*.

"I don't want to do this," he said to himself as he sauntered into the forest of nearly leafless trees.

"We could just go back?" I said.

"We're trapped in a hole in the ground. When they inevitably find us here, it's all over."

A shiver played up and down my spine. "That thought isn't comforting."

"Not much of this situation is."

He didn't relax the farther we made it into what I normally considered to be the safety of the trees. Each time I tried to begin a conversation, he'd simply grunt in reply. Eventually, I gave up and fought to think of anything other than the nerves wafting from him.

If they found us, a whipping would be a blessing in comparison to what we'd get, I was certain of it.

"How many of them do you think Henry sent?" I asked much later. The moon had moved to the far edge of the sky, caressing the tops of the trees.

"Three."

The finality of his answer made my grip falter. I gasped and scrambled for a better grip, but he didn't let me slide more than an inch toward the leaf-covered ground.

"You didn't know how many there were earlier," I said, my voice shaking. My hands began to copy them. *It's okay, it's okay. He has everything under control.*

The only response I got was Oliver touching the tip of his ear.

I strained my own ears to listen, hunting for any sounds outside of the barely perceptible crunch of leaves under Oliver's feet. A lone wolf howled in the distance, its hauntingly minor melody sending shivers up my spine. An owl answered in his own questioning way, but no other animal joined in. In the silence afterward came another footfall. Though nearly timed with Oliver's, it seemed to come from the darkness to our right.

"No, no, no, no . . ." My voice was so quiet, so desperate, but apparently too loud for Oliver. He pressed his finger to my lips, somewhat sloppily due to the angle. It got the point across.

"What are we going to do?" I whispered, not sure if I actually uttered the words or only formed them with my lips.

"I'm not sure yet," Oliver admitted.

I was beginning to miss when he just didn't tell me anything. I could've dealt with some false hope.

My ears could only pick up one set of footsteps, and even then, only every few steps did I hear it. It was so hard to pick out, I almost wondered if I was making it up.

I did, however, notice when it moved closer.

Then Oliver took off at a full run.

"Don't. Let. Go." He didn't bother whispering anymore. He passed the bag of food to me so he had his hands free for whatever was to come. "Aim true."

It was time for me to fight. My heart skipped a beat, but I didn't hesitate. I wrapped my left arm across his chest and used my right to rummage inside the bag for the first apple. I barely had a hold of him. One wrong move, one muscle twitch, and I'd be down. I squeezed my thighs tighter against his sides, my stump throbbing ominously against the strain.

The footsteps multiplied. No one cared anymore about going undetected. There were three sets: one behind, and one on either side.

In the moonlight, the one on my left flitted in and out of view. Each glimpse wasn't long enough to tell who it was, but did it really matter? I adjusted my hold on the apple and chucked it at the runner. It fell short, barely clipping his ankle and producing nothing but a bark of laughter.

I hadn't noticed Oliver had pulled out his gun until he skidded to a stop. He did it so fast, my head bonked the back of his.

The collision didn't faze him, but it left me reeling for a moment.

The three figures materialized out of the trees, effectively trapping us in the middle of their circle. Bernard, Donnell, and Arthur. My stomach dropped at the sight of Arthur. He was dirty from his run, but a big smile danced across his face. He looked like a wild animal about to get his first taste of blood.

But he was so young.

Oliver didn't waste any time worrying about who stood where. He fired. The sound was so loud and unexpected, a scream erupted from my throat. Bernard didn't so much as flinch, his gun held steady and prepared to shoot. If anything, he almost looked bored. Arthur, on the other hand, jumped as if he saw a snake, and Donnell's hands fluttered across his chest before he regained himself and steadied his own pistol.

Wasn't a shot to the chest supposed to knock a person flat? I grabbed another apple and threw it as hard as I could. It hit Donnell in the shoulder, jarring his own gunshot.

An icy wave of fear spread through my body as the wind from the bullet whizzed past my ear. I pressed a little closer to Oliver.

"You can't have her." Oliver's voice was a growl. He shot again. Everything seemed to move in slow motion. The hammer slammed forward, and the cylinder rotated to the next shot.

I didn't get to see if he went down or not.

A weight hit us square on our backs, knocking us to the ground. Without delay, someone ripped me from Oliver's side, despite the way he grappled for my arm. I heard my own shrieks echo throughout the forest. They sounded foreign, like they came from some other poor soul.

Before I could process it, Arthur had me wrestled to the ground, legs straddling my torso, my arms locked above my head.

I kicked at him, which only made him hook his feet over my thighs, securing them to the ground. He wasn't even breathing hard from the exertion.

Only a few feet away, Oliver used everything he knew to get free from the other two. The fight I had seen him in behind the barn had *nothing* on this one. The punches thrown weren't simply meant to hurt—they were meant to inflict damage. Each time a fist made contact with skin, it sunk deep.

If we made it out, Oliver's face wouldn't look nearly as handsome for quite some time.

It'd be worth it.

His two older brothers circled him like wolves, taking turns jumping at Oliver, teasing him.

When Bernard knocked him to the ground with a kick to the back of his knees, I was sure it was all over. But Oliver had other ideas. His feet were under Bernard's hips in an instant, his trapped hands grasping at one of his, holding on tightly as he kicked with all his might. Bernard fell off with an angry growl.

"Just back down!" Bernard shouted as they faced each other with feral determination. They both panted with the exertion, and they both had blood trickling from the wounds on their faces.

Donnell jumped at Oliver next, drawing an "oof!" from his lips. Like a snake, he squirmed out from under him, pouncing to his feet with his back to a tree.

"What do you think will happen if I do that?" Oliver spat a mouthful of blood into the grass.

Bernard moved to the left while Donnell moved to the right, the two of them communicating with silent glances.

Bernard spoke first. "If you just stop this, you'll get your birthright back. You'll eventually be able to have a clan of your—"

"Clan of my own?" Oliver laughed, a deep, terrifying sound. He had stopped moving, his back pressed to the tree, his discarded gun between him and Donnell. "What makes you think that'd make me give her up?"

Bernard registered Oliver's plan before I did. As Oliver dove for the pistol, Bernard was on him. He grabbed Oliver's hand and smashed it into the packed dirt until the weapon fell away and he yelled in pain.

Oliver regained himself, grabbing Bernard's ear and yanking.

"Arthur! Don't just sit there!" Bernard shouted as he rolled away from the counterattack. Donnell fell to the ground, pouncing for Oliver's limbs, attempting to pin him if even for a moment.

I tried Oliver's move on Arthur, fighting to bring my foot around to his hips. When that didn't work one bit, I fought to move my arms to grab his ear, nose, anything. Not one limb moved.

Nothing budged until Arthur hoisted me to a seated position and pressed a blade to my neck.

Everything froze. Oliver went completely still. Donnell gripped his arms and yanked them behind his back, making him wince.

Arthur held my arms behind my back, and my shoulders ached for release. That was the least of my worries. I could feel the sharpness of the blade as it pressed against my skin, feel the warm trickle as my blood dripped from the edge.

"Pa doesn't care if she comes home alive," Donnell said, his voice as sweet as sugar.

Oliver took his time, looking from one person to the next.

Arthur didn't adjust his grip. He held tighter, drawing a whimper from my lips. I didn't want to make any noise. If even a sound moved my neck, that might be the end of me. I wanted to beg, I wanted to plead with Arthur to let me go. We were friends, right? Didn't that count for something?

"Let her go, Arthur." Oliver's voice was that of a man attempting to calm a rabid bear—staccato and at least an octave too high.

Arthur didn't move. He didn't make a sound. He just breathed slowly, chest moving in and out against my back.

The veins stood out on Oliver's neck, his fists clenching and unclenching.

Bernard's sickly sweet voice chimed in: "You know what to do, Arthur."

"*No!*" Oliver screamed, launching himself in my direction.

Arthur stiffened around me, and everything went black.

CHAPTER FORTY-FIVE

Breathe

*I*t's not real.

It can't be happening.

I'm alive.

I'm safe.

We're both safe.

We're at Miriam's house, curled up on the settee while we wait for Mama to come home.

The moment she comes through the door, we'll break apart like we were innocent of any impure acts.

That's it.

Safe.

But the blood . . .

I jerked awake with a strangled cry. Every muscle I had screamed in protest over the smallest movement.

It took a while for my eyes to adjust to the near darkness. The only light came from a lantern on the wall beside an ominous set of stairs on the opposite side of the room. Bars obstructed my view as I forced myself to register where I was.

The stairs were far from the scariest thing in the room. Tools meant only to inflict pain hung on the walls, whips nearly reaching the floor from their designated hooks. A set of shackles were next to them, limp and thankfully unused. I didn't need to see anything else to know where I was, but my eyes still took it all in.

A table stood in the middle of the room, a barely breathing woman strapped so tightly to the top, she couldn't move even if she tried. The petite blonde woman made no noise, the only sign of life coming from the shaky rise and fall of her chest. Dark swatches of blood were smeared across different parts of her pale body, naked and exposed as the day she was born. As if the poor woman needed more to hurt her body and pride.

I gasped in a breath so large it hurt, sending my body into a round of uncontrollable shaking and whimpers.

We were in the Wedmans' torture chamber. And I was trapped in the cage.

"Shh, shh, shh . . ." came Oliver's voice. His icy fingers touched whatever was closest to him—my leg. I jumped.

They had shackled him to the wall, the cuffs low enough to the ground that he could sit, but high enough that he couldn't reach very far. He jerked against the restraints, making the chains clatter their protest as he reached for my hand. I closed the gap, wiggling my hand through the bars and to grasp his. I pressed my torso against my cage to get as close as possible.

"I need you to breathe," Oliver said firmly. I tried to obey, but each breath felt like knives scraping the lining of my lungs.

"Nella!" He squeezed my hand, snapping my attention back to him. "Breathe with me. Concentrate, or else you'll pass out again." He looked me in the eye and exaggerated every breath, hoping I'd follow along.

I didn't.

"Why are we here? I don't want to be here! Oliver!" My voice had risen a good two octaves, resembling a terrified lamb.

"Nella, Nella, Nella . . ." He yanked on the restraints again as he tried to reach far enough to touch my face. He only made it a finger's width inside of the bars. "Close your eyes and breathe."

My fingers were numb, sending shocks of that eerie feeling up my arms. The world swam around me, my eyes couldn't focus on a single thing.

We were going to die.

Like the girl on the table, we were going to die.

"Nella—"

My world went dark.

This time, I couldn't lie to my unconscious self.

I came to, keeping my eyes shut and pressing the heel of my palm against them, fingers digging into my hair.

Oliver tugged at the fabric of my tattered skirt to gain my attention. "Keep your eyes closed, breathe. Just breathe. You understand?"

I nodded, breathing in and out as deeply as I could. I was curled on the ground, face mere inches from the dusty floor. It didn't matter. Nothing mattered. I knew they wouldn't grant me a quick death. They'd make me worry about it for as long as they could, likely inflicting pain all the while. A choking sob shook my body, taking away what control of my breathing I had.

"They're going to kill us," I sobbed.

Oliver squeezed my hand. "Hopefully not."

"What are they going to do to us?" Some part of me knew they wouldn't kill him. Family wouldn't kill family, right?

Especially for a first offense. Right? But they didn't need me. They would consider me to be the cause of all their problems. I would die.

As my breathing hitched and became erratic again, Oliver chimed in. "Talk about something, anything. Just *breathe*."

I choked in a large breath and banged my fist against the floor in frustration. The impact hurt just enough for me to go completely still for a solid two breaths before I rubbed my hand.

I gradually sat up, cradling the bruised appendage against my chest. The room looked just as horrifying as it had before.

"Talk, Nella. Don't think about it. Talk about something else." His voice was so calm it made me want to slap him.

Still, I searched my mind for a normal topic of conversation. Finding none, I let the first question I had out of my mouth. "Who's on the table?"

Oliver's finger froze in its slow tracing of my foot. "Sara Williams."

"Here?" I moved to my knees to get a better look at her. She looked horrible, hands bloody and battered, left leg likely broken based on its angle, and gashes in random places around her body. "Why? The poor thing! Why?" I turned to him, the horror of it truly sinking in.

I'd called her to their attention. What if I was the one responsible for bringing death to her?

Before Oliver could answer, I continued. "They just want the land. I'm sure she'll sell it now!"

"Her name isn't on the title. Her father's is," Oliver said, voice level and without a twinge of emotion. It made me squirm.

"I'm sure he'd sell too, seeing this!" I gestured wildly in her direction, the increased blood flow causing my hand to throb. I pulled it back to my chest. "It's horrible."

"He's trained just like us. Besides, they probably can't find her father. They probably want her to tell them where *he* is."

"She can't tell them if she's *dead*."

Oliver flinched. "Likely, it doesn't matter if she's dead."

I wrapped my fingers around the bars and stared at the poor girl. Much of what I originally thought was dried blood looked more like half-healed burns, likely punishment for the fire itself.

If they did that for the fire to the barn, what would they do to me for taking both Felicité and their son? I let my head fall to press against the bars with a thud. "Please, please get me out of here." It didn't matter if it was God or Oliver who heard me. As long as they made it happen.

"I'll let you know when I come up with something," Oliver muttered. "Don't lose control of your breath. Breathe, remember?"

I obeyed, settling myself back against the wall and clenching my eyes shut again. "When do you think they'll come—" A terrified choking noise cut me off. I couldn't finish the sentence. *When do you think they'll come work on us?*

"That all depends on what they're doing, where things are with the Williams family." Oliver rested his head against the wall with a long sigh. "You can nap if you'd like, just don't panic on me. I don't want you to die if—" He cut himself off, shaking his head roughly, his hair flying every which way.

"If they torture me," I finished, the words catching in my throat.

"Mhm" was all Oliver said.

They let us wait. Whether it was half an hour or several, I had no idea. But it felt like an eternity. I couldn't sleep, but I curled up on the floor with Oliver tangling his fingers in my hair. I leaned into it like a cat, taking whatever comfort I could from him.

The door creaked opened, then closed with a slam. I shot up to perch on my knees, aware of every single shadow in the room. Sara whimpered, the first sign of her consciousness.

Henry strode in, tall and confident. I shrank as far back into my corner as I could manage, but he never came our way. In fact, he completely ignored us. When he lit another lantern and set it on the table beside Sara's head, Oliver visibly relaxed.

I didn't. At least one of us was bound to get it, and I wasn't sure how much more she could take. Didn't mean I planned on speaking up to take her place.

Henry pulled a small metal rod from its hiding place on the shelf and placed it in the flame of his lantern, turning it delicately. Sara's eyes remained fixed on it, her entire body vibrating with fear.

"Are you ready to tell me what you were doing here?" Henry's voice held so much sweetness, it would make anyone sick.

Suddenly it all made sense. They found her outside the house, most likely around to meet with Donnell. She certainly had more willpower than I could dream of, if she hadn't told them everything they wanted to know. I doubted I would've kept the secret.

She didn't say a word, whether from stubbornness or simply because she couldn't, I wasn't sure. She didn't utter a single sound until he pressed the hot iron against her rib cage, leaving a long, searing line across her skin.

I gasped, clawing for Oliver's hand. "You have to do something!"

Oliver's only response was to lift the shackles, clattering the chains against each other.

"She doesn't deserve this, and you know it!" My voice had risen higher than I had intended.

"Hush, Nella," Oliver whispered.

Henry let out a low growl, placing the iron back into the flame and turning to face me. My stomach flipped upside down at the soulless look on his face. He appeared inconvenienced, nothing more impressive than that.

"You have the best seats in the house, dear girl," he purred, turning the key in the lock with a click. "But I suppose you can't live knowing you aren't the main part of the story."

I gripped Oliver's hand so tightly my nails were sure to draw blood.

Oliver's spoke so quickly I could hardly understand him. "None of this is her fault! Just let me take care of her, I'll do a better job at keeping her under wraps—"

Henry ignored him, grabbing my arm and wrenching me to my shaky foot. "You don't have much of a chance, my dear"—he dragged me to the table—"but I would think you would have the sense to stay quiet to earn what favor you can." He took the iron piece out of the flame and ever so slowly moved it in my direction.

I shrank away. This was apparently the response he wanted, as a smile traced across his lips. At the last moment, when I was sure I could feel the heat of the iron, he switched directions and placed it firmly on Sara's chest. He held it there, her alabaster skin sizzling beneath. Her weakened body hardly reacted, the only sign of life coming from the way her eyes fluttered closed.

I whimpered. How much more could she withstand before she passed on?

"Are you really sad that you aren't part of this?" Henry cradled the key in his free hand, running his thumb over the teeth.

I swallowed down the bile. "No," I choked out.

He tsked his tongue and switched his iron poker for tongs. He put the key in their jaws and pushed it straight into the flame. I watched in horror as he waited for it to reach the desired heat.

"She's not your toy!" Oliver shouted from behind me.

"What did I tell you before?" Henry spoke with marked patience. "'Keep your nose clean, and I won't have to take care of her myself.' You lost your privilege." Henry adopted the fatherly tone so perfectly, only in all the wrong ways.

He ignored anything else Oliver said, pulling the key free of its fiery prison and holding it up so it glimmered in the light.

"What do you think? Do you think you should've learned your place a long time ago?"

He didn't wait for a response. He pressed the key straight onto my skin, right above where my bodice ended.

The pain was delayed by the shock and startlingly sweet smell of my own burning flesh. My knee buckled, and I fell back, dangling from the vise grip he had on my arm. Some deep, strange part of me was angry that the scar wouldn't be perfect because of the tongs. There would always be the little bumps on either side of the key imprint.

But I wouldn't get to worry about it for long. Eventually, they'd tire of me and end it all.

"Henry!" The accented, feminine voice came from the stairway, sharp and angry. "Don't hurt them! There's no cause—"

Henry laughed, a deep sort of sound that started in the pit of his stomach. "I'll deal with you in a moment, woman!"

She was silent for two whole breaths before her footsteps sounded on the stairs. "He's *my* boy. Just let them go! You can't forget, you left your own family—"

Henry grumbled something under his breath as he dragged me back to my prison. He shoved me to the floor and locked the door again with that same still-warm key.

"This is *business*, Alderose!" he snarled. He scooped up his lantern and stormed for the stairs. Her light footsteps retreated faster than a deer, the door to the kitchen slamming shut again before Henry made it two steps.

Shivers traversed my body as I hunted the floor for Oliver's hand. Once I located his chilled skin, my body curled into a fetal position around his fist, the sobbing overtaking my body.

This time, he didn't coach me on my breathing.

CHAPTER FORTY-SIX

The Death of Sara Williams

Some time later, the door opened again, making both Oliver and I jump. Henry had to be back, ready to finish torturing me. The burn on my chest throbbed, feeling as though the mark would continue to boil until the end of time.

To our surprise, Rose appeared on the steps with her lantern. She paused, checking over her shoulder to see if anyone came to the door behind her before she hurried to the two of us.

"You two *had* to go get yourself caught," she chided. "Are you all right? Did you get her to safety?"

My terrified heart melted. She was worried about Felicité. "She's okay. She's with—"

"No." Rose held up her hand. "Don't tell me where she is. I just want to know that she is safe. Loved."

"Safe and loved," Oliver assured. The stress that had been radiating off his body melted away, if only for a moment. "She'll live a happy life. I can promise that."

Rose sighed, her entire body slumping in relief. "I've been so worried about her." A dreamy look crossed her face, and a smile played at her lips. "If only life were different . . ."

Shaking her head to dislodge any fanciful thoughts, she rummaged through her pocket to pull out a green, pasty leaf.

"Here, put this on the burn." She passed it through the bars to me. "They won't notice you did anything to it, but it will help."

If only life was different . . . I clenched the leaf in my palm. My life was already so different than before. Perhaps it *could* be different again?

A dark chuckle came from Oliver, interrupting my shred of hope. "How many times have you snuck in here to treat prisoners, Ma?"

"Ah, well." She patted his leg. "I don't tell such secrets. They can't be mad at me for what they don't know. And you're *mon fils*." She wrapped him in a hug, nose tucked into his tangled hair. Her mouth moved quickly, though I didn't catch a word she said.

The unintelligible words were all it took to make him stiffen back up. "It won't—"

"*Chut*," she snapped to silence him. "Trust your mama." Her accent took over. She reached her hand in and patted my shoulder. "Put that on, hurry, *dépêche-toi*!"

I jumped to action, rubbing the sticky substance, aloe I assumed, onto the burn. I winced at the touch. If we made it out, it would leave one nasty scar. When I finished, I handed the leftovers to her.

"*S'il vous plaît*." She nodded to me. "Stay strong, *ma chérie*." She patted me once more before getting to her feet and making her way back to the stairs. She paused at Sara's side, her keen eyes missing nothing as she rubbed her arm. Rose whispered a few words in her direction before disappearing back to the safety of her kitchen.

I turned my attention to Oliver almost as soon as the door shut behind her. "What did she say?"

Oliver held his voice so quiet I hardly heard it. "She's gonna try and get us out."

I blinked in surprise. "How? Won't she get herself in trouble?"

Oliver shrugged. "She wouldn't listen to sense if I tried to argue with her."

We fell back into silence, watching the rise and fall of Sara's chest. It was too slow.

Would they put her out of her misery? Would it be quick? Or would they force her to die tied to the table? No matter if she or her family started the fire or not, she didn't deserve that.

How long would it be before I was in her position?

Another lantern sparked to life at the foot of the stairs. I nearly jumped out of my skin, barely stifling the scream that escaped my lips. Oliver didn't so much as flinch. Of course, he had likely noticed Donnell float down the stairway in complete silence.

Despite myself, I let hope creep in.

Perhaps Donnell was part of Rose's plan? He'd release us and have us back in the open air in just a few minutes. But then, he hadn't done that to Sara when he had the chance.

Like Henry, he completely ignored us as he prowled into the room, setting the lantern on the table by Sara's feet. He traced one of the wounds on her side with a touch so light, she didn't stir. He bent forward and kissed her, a tear glistening on his cheekbone.

That single display of emotion made my heart want to break in two. Sara didn't deserve anything like this. And neither did Donnell.

In the smallest show of consciousness, Sara touched his arm. His chest heaved in what could have been nothing other than a sob. He leaned over her, his nose barely brushing hers. He stared into her eyes, unspoken words flowing over every god-forsaken corner of the room. His lips whispered one more thing before he closed the space for a kiss. It was tender, almost fragile. As he stood, he cleared his throat, erasing any signs of weakness.

He took the two large steps back, never letting his eyes stray from hers, and slipped the keys from their hanger on the wall. With practiced ease, he unlocked her shackles and pulled her to the floor.

She slumped in his arms, too weak to hold herself up. He held her there, whispering sweet words into her blonde hair.

Maybe it wasn't too late. Maybe he would free her after all. Even if only to die in the sunshine. The romantic thought made me smile just a little. Especially as he tilted her head up to press his lips to hers one more time.

But then I saw the blood.

A river of maroon flowed freely from her throat, down her chest, over his hands, to eventually a puddle on the floor.

I suppressed a gasp and grabbed hold of Oliver's hand again. He squeezed it, though his skin had gone clammy.

Donnell held her against his chest as the blood soaked them both. She had already been so close to death, it was unclear when she passed. For all I knew, she could have been gone the moment the blade cut skin. He cradled her in his arms, whispering anything and everything into her ear.

She wouldn't be suffering anymore. She'd never be hunted again. That didn't make my stomach ache any less.

Several minutes passed in near silence, the only sound coming from Donnell's broken cries. When it suddenly stopped, Oliver's hand turned to stone around mine.

Donnell stood with a careful slowness, leaving his forbidden love in a heap on the floor. He didn't look from his feet as he shuffled in our direction. One step after slow step. My heart matched each footfall with a nervous thump.

He would just be letting us out so the same thing wouldn't happen to us. But Oliver's rigid hand told me I had every right to be terrified.

Donnell slammed the key into my cell's lock, turning it with a precise click. His eyes remained trained on the floor.

"I'm sorry you had to do that." Oliver almost sounded firm, but his nerves dripped from each word.

Donnell grunted in response, reaching in and hauling me upright. His fingers dug into the inevitable bruises from Henry's earlier mistreatment, making me gasp.

"What are you doing?" Oliver demanded, yanking on his restraints. "Donnell! You have the keys, just let us go—"

Donnell finally spoke, his voice full of venom. "Let you go? Let you *go?*" He laughed as if it were the funniest joke he'd heard all week. "You certainly didn't help Sara."

"I *couldn't* help her, I—"

Donnell glared right at him. "Your little *toy* reported her. If she kept her damn mouth shut, she'd be alive today. None of this would have happened." He dragged me from the cell. He tossed me against the table, the impact knocking the wind from my lungs.

"Donnell!" Oliver shouted. The chains clanked as he fought against them with all his might. "Leave her out of this! I understand that you're mad, take it out on me! Not her!"

Donnell laughed, a deep, rumbling kind of noise. "I can't touch *you*. You're *family*. Ma convinced Pa to give out second chances. Her?" He pushed my shoulder roughly as I lay, terrified enough to become a statue. "I can do whatever I damn well please."

"Leave her alone!" Oliver nearly screamed the words. He flung himself against his restraints, again and again. The chains clanked so aggressively I wouldn't have been surprised to see them separate from the wall.

But they didn't budge.

Donnell didn't seem to hear him at all. He took a fistful of the back of my bodice and lifted me like a doll. I hovered for a mere second before he threw me into the ever-growing pool of blood on the floor. It splattered as I landed in a heap, soaking between each individual finger, making me feel more ill than I already was.

He didn't give me a chance to fight, or even protest. He dragged me through the blood until my face was only a few inches from her lifeless one.

"What would you say if she could hear you?" When he didn't get an answer fast enough, he asked again, gripping the hair at the nape of my neck. "What would you say?"

I could feel the heat still radiating from her skin. She still seemed so *alive*.

"You shouldn't have died." The words caught in my throat, threatening to kill me before they could make their way into the world.

"Well, of course she shouldn't," Donnell spat, shaking me roughly. "She was meant to have a full life. One of her choosing."

"I didn't do this!" I snapped, trying to pull away. "I'm sorry this happened, but—"

"Oh, shut up!" He hauled me up again, practically throwing me on top of the table. I grabbed the edge, fighting to crawl to the opposite side faster than he could reach me. I didn't need to bother. He flipped me flat on my back before I had enough time to tighten my muscles.

With impressive speed and volume, Oliver spewed profanities. I'd never heard anyone come up with so many of them so fast. Each word was unique, and just as vulgar as the last.

Unfazed by my flailing, Donnell fastened my wrists to the same restraints Sara had been in only a few minutes before.

Nervous sweat gathered on my forehead. "None of this will help Sara!"

He tsked his tongue. "Well, you're the only toy available at the moment. And you just so happen to be the one who sounded the alarm in the first place." His face hovered a mere inch above mine.

Without much thought, I spat at him. The saliva hit its mark, splattering right on the edge of his nose. He wiped it away with aggravated slowness, giving his blood further time to boil.

"You found a nice fighter, Oliver," he said.

Oliver's reply came quickly: "Damn you! I will *kill* you! Mark my words!"

Donnell chuckled. "Like you tried to kill Bernard? Good job, that one. He can hardly see out of his eyes today, they're so swollen. But you'll have to hit harder than that to kill one of us. You should know that, baby brother."

Donnell turned back in my direction, grabbing my foot as I geared to kick him, and tying it down with ease. "You see, it doesn't matter if you submit or not." He twirled a small blade around in his fingers, admiring the way the candlelight glinted off the edges.

I had no strength to use against him, begging and pleading were the only options I really had. "If you let us go, we'll never bother you again!"

Donnell laughed. "Groveling will get you nowhere, sweetheart." The pet name sent shudders cascading throughout my entire body.

Oliver didn't stop his threats as Donnell pressed the blade to my chest, directly where my bodice ended and skin began. The touch was light, a mere threat, only a hair's breadth from the throbbing burn. "By the way, Oliver, how'd you like her? Or have you not taken her as your own just yet?" He tucked the blade under the bodice and pulled. The fabric slit easily with a sound that would have been oddly satisfying in any other circumstance.

"If you touch her, I *swear*!" Oliver screamed.

Donnell chuckled, as though he had done nothing more than steal a lollipop from his baby brother. With one quick movement, he sliced down both the bodice and the skirt, ending at the delicate hem.

"You might consider washing more while on the run. I'm pretty sure this fabric is supposed to be white." He fiddled with the edges of my chemise, peeking over the corset, then trailed his hands down to where my hips began. He yanked on the thin fabric that tied the hoops in place, smiling at the way it ripped. He tore them off and threw them aside.

"Much better," he said. "I don't know how you move with that bulky thing on." He rested his hand against my thigh, only the thin piece of fabric between us. I flinched, but that only spurred him on. He trailed his finger up my skin, dragging the nearly translucent material up with it.

Oliver screamed in the background, but I could hardly hear him over the pounding in my ears.

He'd kill me.

But only after he tortured me like they had Sara. Or worse.

He removed his hand with a suddenness that made me gasp. "Oh, I'm sorry. You're nervous?" He patted my ankle with such care, it could've belonged to a doctor. But his tender touch transformed to that of a devil. He jerked the strap on my wrist until it bit into my skin. I tried to pull away, but the leather cut away at my flesh with each movement, threatening to release the blood beneath.

Even with the restraints, my body shook and trembled. A thin whine echoed around me—my own. Apparently satisfied with his work, Donnell began to hum.

It wouldn't have bugged me if he sang "Clair de Lune," anything by Beethoven, *anything* else. But he chose my song. "*His Song.*" The one I had written for Oliver only a few days after our wedding.

Each note sent chills up my spine, each tone made my heart skip a beat, my breath catch in my throat. Of all things for him to sing.

"Stop it!" I shouted, tugging against the restraints. "Stop singing!"

He hovered over me, a sickening sparkle in his eyes. "It's your song, don't you like it?"

"My song, *not* yours!"

"Music was meant to be shared, was it not?"

So, I spat at him. Again. And it was anything but graceful. I couldn't form a good spitball like a man, but I did my best. It landed in a splatter all over his nose and cheekbones.

The sparkle in his eyes ignited into fire. "Oh? Let's play, then."

Oliver's shouts grew louder, if that were even possible. "When I get out of here, I swear! You're *dead,* Donnell! Dead if you lay a hand—"

"Dear brother, you shouldn't have been so greedy, disobeying the rules. You wouldn't be in such a mess." He gripped the busk of my corset, causing me to flinch. With his other hand, he popped each clasp open, sending cool air across the cotton and my skin beneath.

"Please let me go," I whispered, voice catching.

"Nah," he said simply. "What do you think, little brother? Have you seen what's underneath yet? Ah, of course not. You're too much of a *gentleman* to force her."

Oliver made a noise somewhere between a growl and a scream. Donnell did nothing but laugh, low and melodious.

He hooked the blade under the collar of my shift and pulled swiftly, baring me in a matter of seconds.

The pounding in my ears drowned out any other noise— Oliver's shouting, Donnell's taunting. Though all I could do was stare straight at him and his shining blade, all I could see were Sara's bruises and gashes.

"What do you think?" Donnell asked. His hands floated over every inch of my body, his touch featherlight. "Wish you took her while you had a chance? Crippled or not, she's not half bad!" He swatted my upper thigh.

I flinched. My breathing had turned shallow, my entire body frozen in fear. He traced my collarbone with the tip of the blade, then let it lead the way down my side, over my hip bone, and to rest at the tender flesh between my legs.

A whimper made its way to my ears, but it didn't feel like it belonged to me. I wrenched my eyes shut against the tears that threatened to escape, praying for that sweet peace of unconsciousness.

"I don't think you need this anymore, now do you? *Oliver* didn't care enough to take it." He pressed the flat edge of the blade against the delicate skin. Cold, hard, horrifying. I shivered.

"Damnit, Donnell!" Oliver roared. "This isn't what we were taught, remember? Torture with *purpose*. There's *no purpose* here!"

"Purpose . . ." Donnell pursed his lips as he considered, pulling the blade up and over onto my lower stomach, then back down. All the while, he was sure to keep the sharp edges pointed away. "Ah, but there *is* a purpose."

With the speed of lightning, he removed the blade from between my legs and pressed the tip into my ribs, right below my breast. I gasped, not yet feeling the pain, but well aware of the trickle of blood that meandered its way to the wooden table below. He held perfectly still, the tip of the blade still in my skin, his eyes on mine.

"The purpose," he said firmly, "is to show what happens when you meddle with someone else's business." He ran the blade down, splitting my skin open from my chest to hip bone.

My body reacted this time. Pain seared through every inch, a dampness spread underneath me, and then it all went mercifully black.

CHAPTER FORTY-SEVEN

Rose

I woke to heavily accented fussing.

Rose.

I halfway expected to open my eyes and find her scolding me for falling asleep in the sitting room. Of course, I wasn't that lucky.

She could hardly be seen in the near darkness. The entire room was lit by a single candle that she placed on the blood-soaked table in the space under my arm.

It only took a moment for my brain and body to remember the pain. Panic flowed from my toes to the tip of my hair. How deep was the wound? Was I still bleeding?

Rose leaned in to kiss my forehead. "*Ma bébé*," she crooned, pushing the hair off my sweaty forehead.

That was all the gentleness she had time for. Like a bullet, she flew to action, working the tight knots on my wrists loose with the precision only delicate hands could manage. She worked efficiently, untying me in a matter of minutes, while whispering tender words in French the entire time.

Once free, I dared to sit. The pain exploded throughout my torso, and I cried out. Rose pressed her hand to my collarbone to keep me down. She didn't need to. Darkness swirled through my vision like a vicious cloud, threatening to engulf me yet again.

Wordlessly, Rose made her way to Oliver, pausing only a moment to lay a hand on Sara's head. She clicked his restraints open and dropped the keys at his feet.

"Where's Pa?" Oliver demanded. He wasted no time in scrambling to his feet and rushing to my side. Like a child, I reached for him. He squeezed my hand and placed it back on the table, focusing only on my wound.

"Dealing with the Williamses," she said shortly. "They sent someone to negotiate for her release." She jerked her head in Sara's direction. "Your father doesn't know that we don't have that power anymore."

It was growing increasingly difficult to track anyone's movement. My mind and body felt almost numb, with accents of spasming pain.

Where was Donnell? Why hadn't he killed me? Would he be coming back to finish the job?

Hands grasped my shoulders and pushed me up. An unbidden scream erupted from my throat as my muscles tensed. Had they warned me they were going to move me? Had they said anything? I wouldn't have known if they did. It was nearly impossible to focus on their words.

They wound bandages around my torso, tight and secure. I imagined blood soaking through it within a few moments, then twirling its way to the floor.

"It'll do for a while, but you'll have to take care of it soon," Rose was saying.

Take care of what? My wound? My life? Donnell's?

Where was he?

"Where is he?" I demanded. My voice sounded muddled, like I was speaking through a bucket of mud.

They slipped a clean chemise and worn work dress over my head. Where had that come from?

"Ma sent him on an errand," Oliver whispered into my ear. His breath tickled my skin, and I melted against him.

"What are you doing?" I heard myself ask, as Oliver finally scooped me into his arms. The warmth from his body made me snuggle closer. I rested my head against his chest and breathed in his familiar, comforting scent. But it was all wrong—he smelled of sweat, blood, and fear.

"We're getting out of here," he said firmly, kissing my forehead. "You lost a lot of blood, but you'll be all right for now."

Even I heard the unspoken part of his sentence: *at least I hope so.*

His warmth wasn't enough to keep the cold at bay anymore. I shivered uncontrollably, teeth chattering, muscles as tight as the restraints had been. The pain coursed through me in waves, and I gripped his shirt with all my might.

Oliver jostled me some to hang a bag in the crook of his arm.

Where did he get that? What was even in it?

Why wouldn't anyone tell me what was going on?

"It's so cold," I whispered, fingers working Oliver's shirt into fists.

"I know, I know," he purred.

Rose gave him a one-armed hug and patted my shoulder. "Go, quickly. Get her taken care of."

"Thank you, thank you for everything," Oliver said, his voice raw with emotion.

"I'm your mama, it's what I'm here for. Now *go.*" She made a shooing motion at the stairs. Oliver obeyed, turning his back on the room of torture.

My eyes locked on one thing as we ascended the stairs. Blood. So much blood. It glistened in the candlelight, almost as though it belonged in a fairytale. There were two pools, one that encompassed the body of poor Sara, and one that dripped from the table.

Mine.

The world spun out of focus again, and I clutched Oliver all the more, fingernails scraping skin. "I want to sleep." Did I say that out loud? Did I mean to say it? The words just seemed to materialize in the air.

"Not yet," Oliver instructed as he flew through the front door and into the blinding sunlight.

I couldn't remember the path he took through the house itself. Was I still flitting in and out of consciousness?

I scrunched my eyes against the unexpected onslaught of light. When had the sun turned into the devil himself? I draped my arm over my eyes.

Oliver ran in silence for a while. Hours? Minutes? I had no way of knowing. Every few footfalls, I'd drift a little closer to unconsciousness, tilting to the side. Each time, he tightened his grip to keep me in place. He'd say a few words and shake me back awake. A few curses inevitably leapt from my mouth at this, but he didn't seem to care.

I really didn't even notice.

The trees blurred into a never-ending sonata as we traveled on, one solid page of the same repeating measure. Over and over again. Eventually, the sun transitioned to a moon, accompanied by haphazard stars, shining down like little fuzzy daggers.

"If they fell down, would they stab us? Like a million blades?" I asked at one point.

Oliver's steps faltered at the unexpected question. "If what fell down?"

I simply pointed up.

The world blurred in and out of consciousness. Fear probed the back of my brain, but the overwhelming, woozy peaceful-ness masked it.

CHAPTER FORTY-EIGHT
Dreamland Dance

"No. Abso*lutely* not." A high-pitched female voice cut through my starry dreams.

"I don't have a choice, Anna! Where is he?" Oliver's voice.

"I can't let you in here!" Anna spat. Something thumped against wood, presumably her foot against the porch.

Reluctantly, I opened my eyes. Oliver stood at the foot of a pair of stone steps, held back only by the tiny woman guarding the porch. Anna braced herself against the doorframe, completely unarmed, other than the daggers she had for eyes.

Oliver took one solid step, testing her. She took a matching one, slamming the door shut behind her with such force, the upstairs windows rattled in their frames. She postured up to him, eye to eye thanks to the steps between them.

Oliver spoke with a measured patience. "Anna, where's Bernard?"

She threw her hands in the air. "Your guess is as good as mine! I ain't gotta clue where he is. You? I *know* where you're supposed ta be!"

Oliver adjusted his grip on me as he took the last step onto the rickety porch, ending with him towering over her. "Anna, please let us in."

"I *can't* do that!" Despite her words, her shoulders slumped in defeat. "What's gonna happen if Henry finds out?"

Oliver bent his head to the side to swipe at a stray hair with his shoulder. "Just gonna hope he doesn't." When she didn't move, he pushed past her bustling skirts. He managed to grip the door handle with his fingers and finagled it open.

"Oliver . . ." Anna's voice was a worried whine. She hurried into the little room behind us. "I have *children*, Oliver. You know this! What—"

Oliver ignored her and marched on through the house, turning to the side to get through each of the narrow doorframes.

Bernard's house was decorated in a dainty fashion. Crocheted patterns hung all around, from the edges of the chairs to the walls themselves. The door and window frames were edged in a gentle sage green, a stark contrast to the weathered gray wood that overtook the rest of the rooms. The house could only be described as quaint.

It didn't take us long to make it to a little room in the far corner.

Inside was an opposing wooden table, adorned with worn leather straps and a leather-wrapped cushion, a glass cabinet stocked with various bottles, and a severely worn blue chair under a small window.

Oliver made the move to set me on the table, but I balked. Like a furious cougar destined for a bath, I became all arms and legs. Er, leg.

"No! Oliver!" My scream grated against my throat.

"We're gonna help you, it's all right, it's all right!"

He remained firm, yet gentle, as he tried to keep me down. Despite his insistence, I still managed to kick him. As I did, a sharp pain erupted throughout my abdomen, drawing a screech from my lips.

Anna sighed from her porch in the doorway. "Fine," she spat. "Vernon! Anton!" She turned on her heel, yelling through the house as she went.

The short outburst had been all I had in me. I rested on the table without any further fight, holding Oliver's hand like a lifeline. The burn pulsed under my skin, stopped only by the slicing agony that stretched across my belly.

Oliver leaned his head against mine, his lips brushing my hair. "Bernard will help, I know he will," he whispered against my forehead. "Then we'll go. We'll leave and never come back. I promise. I *promise* I'll do everything I can to keep you safe."

The thunder of miniature footsteps cut off any reply I could've come up with.

"Whoa!" one little voice yelled from the hall. It was followed immediately by an "oof!" as Anna presumably snatched him up.

"Uncle Ollie!" the other voice squealed, rushing past his mother and slamming into Oliver's leg. "I heard Da say that you were—"

"Never mind that," Oliver said gently, though his posture stiffened.

Anna returned through the door, lips set into a grim line, one twin under her arm like a sack of flour. "Anton, Vernon, go fetch your da." She plopped her prisoner onto the floor. "Tell him he has a patient."

Faster than a pair of racehorses, they took off for the back door.

"Wait!" Anna called, whirling in an elegant cascade of skirts. "Don't tell him *who* is here. Do you understand me?"

They stared at her, brown eyes widening and grins sneaking across their faces. "It's a secret?"

"Yes," Anna said with a sigh of defeat. "It's a secret. Now go, hurry!"

They took off again, their retreating footsteps chaotic staccatos echoing throughout the house.

She returned to lean against the doorframe. "You'd better not make me regret this," she snapped. "You *know* what'll happen if he finds out."

Oliver flinched. "I know."

My mind was a cacophony of notes and misplaced images. Even with my eyes wide open, one object would morph into the next; the oil lamp would blend into the wall, the cabinet would sway to the syncopation of the dissonant measures. From where I lay on the leather-clad table, Anna looked eerily similar to an oil painting, blurred along the edges, mainly muted tones with a splash of blue from her dress.

Oliver cleared his throat. "Will you help—"

"Yes." Anna strode into the room and yanked open the cabinet. "Yes, I will, but I won't like it one bit. You got it?"

"Yes ma'am."

Though logic told me I was as safe as I could be, my body had other plans. I shuffled to the far edge of the bed as they approached, cowering like a frightened kitten. Were the predators ready for their final strike? My mind fought way more than my weak body did as Oliver and Anna stripped me down, placing a blanket over me for modesty. As far as I could tell, neither of them said a single word. Though I wasn't completely conscious throughout the entire ordeal. I shivered violently— the cold, the kind that would pierce through even the thickest of blankets.

"Here, go ahead and give her that." Anna's voice floated past my closed lids, gentler than before. "Bernard'll likely have to give her more before he begins."

Oliver's large hand cupped the back of my head, tilting me up just enough to sip the liquid from the spoon he touched to my lips. I tasted the familiar, bitter bite before the added honey and liquor.

"Shh, shh . . . drink it, Nella. Please . . ." Oliver crooned.

Laudanum.

It'll help, you know it will.

With what I hoped was an irritated huff, I obeyed. Part of me didn't want to hide behind the hazy shield of relief that it would provide, just in case I needed to fight. But the other part of me knew the reality—I wouldn't be able to run, to fight, or to do much of anything, anyway.

"Good, good, Princess. It's gonna be all right."

A sharp snort came from Anna's direction, but I hardly registered it. "Come on, help me clean the wound while we wait."

Laudanum is a magical substance. When the haze seeped through the cracks of my consciousness, I felt aware of my surroundings. But nothing was truly right. Sweet melodies caressed my dreams, wrapping me in their familiar embrace.

Though dreamland overtook me, letting me dance with the eighth notes, twirl throughout the measures of my songs, I could still hear them. Just like the jutting accents over a passage, the argument stood out.

"If he finds out you're here, I *will* kill you. I'll kill you myself, you understand me?"

Oliver's groan was full of anguish. "We won't stay. Just . . . just please! I need your help. *She* needs your help. She didn't ask for any of this."

"I *know*. That's why I'm helping," Bernard snarled.

Something pressed against my hip bone, an invading, harsh sensation. Somewhere in my muddled brain, I knew Bernard was stitching me up, but I didn't have it in me to care.

"It's not just me you put in danger. It's Anna! And the twins!"

"I *know*! What other choice did I have?"

"Here, cut that? Thanks." Bernard fell silent as he worked, pushing against the bruised skin of my abdomen. "He likely already knows you're gone."

"I know."

Despite my dance with dreamland, fear prickled at my belly. "I don't want them to die," I mumbled. Or at least I thought I did.

It must've come out in the strange language of dreamland, as Oliver squeezed my hand and Bernard chuckled.

"Now you don't worry 'bout a thing." Bernard patted my shoulder. "You're gonna feel like a bobcat tore you to shreds, but you'll make it. Give her a little more? I don't need her awake yet."

The chilly spoon touched my lips again. I took the drug willingly.

"When can she travel?" Oliver asked.

Bernard muttered something unintelligible that made Oliver groan.

CHAPTER FORTY-NINE

Cut Off

"She shouldn't be on a horse at all. Not for a long while," Bernard argued.

"Oh," Oliver shot back. "We could stay with you and Anna for a few weeks if you'd rather."

I opened my sleep-crusted eyes to peer at them. I was nestled against Oliver's thigh, the two brothers staring each other down above me.

"If you *dare* do such a thing, I'll go and tell them you're here myself," Anna spat. I couldn't tell where she was, but she certainly wasn't in the same room. Her voice was even muffled from the walls between us. "After I put the boys to bed."

Bernard brushed a smirk from his lips with the back of his hand. "Rest the night—"

Anna popped into view at the entryway, face pinched with nothing short of fury. "*Bernard!*" She had one half-asleep child slung over her shoulder. The little one lifted his head, grumbling something about rabbits and dragons before snuggling back against his mama.

Bernard held his hand up to halt her impending onslaught, then cleared his throat. "You can stay in the barn overnight. If they find you, you sneaked in on your own accord. Got it?"

Oliver gave him a nearly comical look, head tilted to the side, one eyebrow cocked impossibly high. "He'd know I can't do stitches like that." He nodded down at me, his eyes locking right on mine. "Hello again," he whispered into my knotted hair, squeezing my hand.

"I didn't say there weren't flaws in my plan," Bernard muttered, ignoring my consciousness. "I'm just gonna hope they don't think you were *stupid* enough to come here first."

With a grumble and the swish of skirts in the doorway, Anna shuffled away to continue bedtime.

Oliver gazed at me for a moment too long, his face drawn and sad, like a dog who just dropped his favorite bone in the river.

Bernard cleared his throat. "All right. Here's the plan."

Oliver's head snapped back up, eyes locking right on his brother's. "Go."

With the sigh of a much older man, Bernard stood to rummage through a nearby side table. "You're going west. Take the train—"

Oliver's eyes fluttered closed as he fought for patience. "I don't have money, Ber—"

Bernard chucked a gray velvet satchel at his brother's chest. Oliver caught it easily, the coins clinking inside.

"You're going west," Bernard repeated. "Take the train. It'll get you to Nashville. Then keep going. Don't stop."

Oliver's hands went limp around mine, a coldness traveling over his skin. "The Williams Clan."

With an *oof*, Bernard sat back in the ruby-red chair. "They're the *least* of your worries right now. In fact, they might be what buys you time. That whole situation with that blonde girl, you understand." He waved his hand dismissively.

Bile rose in my throat as the memory flooded my brain. The way her skin had faded to such a translucent white, the way she drifted from the world in Donnell's arms . . .

I must've flinched, as Oliver pulled me to a sitting position, tucking me against his chest in a hug. I gasped as the pain exploded across my belly.

"Sorry," Oliver whispered, rubbing my shoulders to try to warm me. He kissed the top of my head, then went back to business. "You said yourself that she isn't in any state to travel."

Bernard sighed. "I know. But as you said, there's not much of a choice."

Oliver shifted his weight, drawing a groan from my lips. That was it. I had no intention to spend the evening, night, or whatever it was, slowly falling down into the pit of pain. "Do you have . . . more . . ."

Bernard stood, stretching as he did. "No."

I hadn't expected that response. "What?" I could practically hear my heart thudding against my throat.

"In the likely event that you have to run, you can't be a useless doll on laudanum."

I was essentially useless anyway as they carted me through the night-chilled air and into the stuffy barn. Every step made my torso ache. Each thud of a boot against the path brought back the memories, the reality of who was chasing us.

Of what would happen when they found us again.

"Oliver," I whined as we slipped through the crack in the barn door. "Tell him. I'm not like you, I can't deal with the pain—"

Bernard strode forward, giving the nearest horse a pat on the nose. "My answer wouldn't change if you were the damn Queen of England."

But it wasn't just the pain I wanted to escape. It was the memories. I could still *feel* his hands as they traveled my body, feel each individual finger as it pressed against my hips, the way they caressed me as he gutted me to the core.

A horse whinnied, sticking its head over the door and nuzzling whoever was closest.

"You're a bastard," I muttered.

Bernard cleared his throat as though to mask a laugh. "Don't tell anyone that, 'kay? I stand to inherit this clan." He pushed a dirt-caked bucket away from an old ladder. "Go on. Just don't fall off."

"Thanks." Oliver grunted as he hauled me onto his shoulder like a troublesome child. I yelped at the pressure on my abdomen and grumbled nonsense into his back as he gripped the ladder.

Bernard continued on as we climbed. "The train leaves at eight. I have to go up to the main house first thing, and I'll stop by before you leave. If I can."

Oliver muttered his response and gingerly placed me onto one of the voluminous piles of hay. I winced as my torso bent with the movement, and he squeezed my hand.

"Sorry," he whispered.

Bernard's head popped up over the edge of the loft, squinting in the faint light. "I put extra bandages in the bag. All you can do is try to keep it clean. Please."

I fixed my best glare on him, but guilt speared through my gut. He didn't deserve my anger. After all, he was risking his wife and children to keep us safe.

He sent me a sympathetic half smile. "I'm sorry. I know you hurt."

I lowered my gaze. "I know . . . thank you. For everything."

Oliver rustled around the far corner, kicking straw into three lumpy walls. He took his time, patting one pile here, sprinkling hay there. By the time he was satisfied, the entire structure looked like another haphazard stack. With the gentleness owed to a broken doll, Oliver picked me up and set me into the padded structure. Satisfied, he turned back to his brother.

"Thank you. I owe you."

Bernard rested his head against the side of the ladder. "Nah. Just . . . just don't get caught. Okay?"

Oliver produced a strange, forced sort of laugh. "I don't plan to."

"I'll do what I can to delay them. But it goes without saying, if we meet out there, I can't—"

"I know," Oliver said. Was I mistaken, or did his voice crack with the emotion? "Thank you, again."

The barn fell into complete darkness as Bernard left.

Oliver stepped into our hay-lined prison and lay down, fitting his body around mine. He wrapped his arm protectively over my shoulders, avoiding the bruised flesh.

"Try to sleep, okay? Tomorrow is gonna be a long day."

Oliver must've possessed some sort of magical power, for within minutes, a soft snore tickled the hairs on the back of my neck.

CHAPTER FIFTY

Make It Go Away

I tried to sleep, I really did. But every time I shut my eyes, those memories became tangible. "For Him" thrummed in my ears, louder by the second. I gritted my teeth against the nausea, against the memories of that cold knife as it teased every inch of my body.

Donnell stole that song. He stole it before I could even play it for Oliver. Before I even finished it.

Would those notes ever bring me peace again?

He could've taken every inch of me if he wanted to. He could've raped me right there on the table, taken his time with each step of his sadistic torture. The payment for Sara's death . . .

I clenched my jaw against a spasm of pain that ripped through my torso.

"Go away, go away!" I pleaded.

But it didn't. *He* didn't. He laughed, his oddly sweet breath invading my nostrils. How did I even know the smell of his breath? I hadn't noticed in the moment. But somehow, it managed to burn its way into my memories.

In the present, that arm around my shoulders shifted to my waist, giving me short relief from my waking nightmare.

You're in a barn. With Oliver. And a horse . . . not in the dungeon. Not on the table . . .

"You're shaking." Oliver's voice was as gentle as honey. He pressed his lips to the space below my ear.

"I-I'm sorry I woke you." My voice didn't sound real. It sounded strained, like a piano in desperate need of a tune, every note sounding a bit too high.

Oliver pushed himself up onto his forearm, leaning over my back. "Princess . . . Nella. It's dark, I can't see you. But I can hear you." He placed his hand firmly on my arm, the gesture full of control, full of power. Comforting. "Feel you."

A shiver ran the length of my spine. "I can't stop . . . it won't go away." My breath caught in my throat, threatening to clamp down on my airways.

"What won't going away?" he asked.

I didn't know how to verbalize it. Everything was *wrong*, the notes in my mind flew in every direction, each one staccato in differing keys with never-ending crescendos.

Oliver crawled over me; we lay nose to nose, chest to chest, knee to knee. "I know it's difficult—no, no. Impossible—to make it go away. I wish I could tell you that one day it's gone for good. But . . . it never truly does. It'll always find a way back, sneak in when you're least expecting it . . ." He drifted off, perhaps distracted by his own demons.

I focused all of my effort on my breath, on the way it trembled on the way out, on the way it grated my lungs on the way in. "It hurts." And I wasn't talking about my torso.

He leaned in to kiss my forehead. "I know, love. I know."

"When I close my eyes," I continued, "all I see is *him*. All I hear is *him*."

He tucked me against his chest, my head tucked under his chin. "I know. I'm so sorry."

I pushed away from him, staring at the silhouette of his face. "Make it go away."

He cupped my face in his hands, his thumb tracing the soft line of my cheekbone. "There are only a few ways I know to do that."

"Tell me," I whispered. My breath caught in my throat as he leaned in just a little closer, his own breath teasing my nose.

"Laudanum works well, as I believe you figured out."

I nodded, my toes curling under in anticipation of his touch. I knew his answer, and every inch of me craved his distraction.

He scooted forward, erasing that mere inch of space between us and pressing his lips to mine. I melted into him, my hands traveling up his side to hold him close.

Ever so gently, he bit my lower lip. I pressed into him, grateful for the thin fabric of my borrowed chemise. Where were the rest of my clothes, anyway? Had the men even thought about the need for proper clothing on a trip?

"Want me to distract you?" His voice rumbled against my chest.

I didn't bother agreeing with him. Instead, I copied his actions, nipping at his lower lip. His answering smirk was everything I wanted, craved.

His fingers tangled in my hair as he pulled my face back to his, simultaneously turning me onto my back. He pounced on me then, one knee on either side of my hip.

I reached for the hem of my chemise, even the light touch of my fingertips enough to send shivers up my spine. He caught my hand, pressing it against my thigh to stop my progress.

A long sigh escaped his lips. "It's just a distraction. We shouldn't. I don't want to hurt you."

"I don't care right now," I grumbled, ripping my hand free and hiking the fabric to my navel. "Just *fix it*."

His chest vibrated with his hushed laugh.

The welcomed heat had complete control of my body, sending tingles throughout every appendage.

"Take me," I pleaded, arching my hips up to meet him.

"You're hurt, Nella," he purred. But he leaned close anyway, hovering a hair's breadth from my body.

The stitches pulled as I strove to close the gap, and I gritted my teeth. "I don't care right now." I *wanted* it. Not just for the release, but for the distraction. If he made my world explode in a cascade of colors, perhaps I could sleep. Just maybe I would fall asleep and dream of him, not his brother.

He hesitated for way too long, hovering just out of reach. "If I hurt you, if it's too much, *tell me*."

I nodded, my lower lip trapped between my teeth.

His body heat moved away from me, accompanied by the rustle of clothes as he stripped down.

I had always been told that girls weren't to initiate anything—we were to do the man's bidding. Whatever they desired, we were to lie still. Anything else would be indecent.

But I *wanted* it.

My heart skipped a few beats as he positioned himself over me again. I released my chemise and let my shaky fingers trace the muscles of his chest, all the way to his waistline.

His hand rested on my thigh, caressing me. "I'll be gentle." His voice sounded strained.

"No. Don't." I said the words with more force than I thought possible. Did I really mean them?

"Are you sure? I don't want you making promises you don't want to keep," he cautioned, voice still strained.

I smirked and kissed his chest. "What if I have every intention of keeping them?"

As he positioned himself, I bit my lip, waiting.

He could've taken you roughly. Just a few more seconds and—

"Make. My. Brain. *Stop!*" I shouted, wrapping my arms around Oliver's torso and pulling. My side ached with the effort, but I ignored it.

He didn't lower himself any further, letting our skin tease each other. "Okay, okay." He nipped my neck, following it with a kiss. I didn't have to ask again. The only thing gentle about the way he shoved into me was how he refused to lie directly on me. He perched there, gripping my hips and doing exactly what I wanted—turn off my brain completely.

As the first moan escaped my lips, it only seemed to spur him on. But as they continued, getting progressively louder, he pressed his palm over my mouth. I melted all the more, gripping his forearm with my nails.

He was done far too soon.

"No," I protested as he pulled away. Losing the blanket of his body felt like I was losing another limb.

He gave me a shadowed look that had to mean he really just wanted to sleep. "We shouldn't do any of this. You're supposed to rest." Despite his words, he lowered himself back over me, that touch baiting me again.

"I need—" I gasped as his fingers found my core, swirling, teasing . . .

And then he slithered down my torso, layering it with kisses as he moved down.

"What are you doing?" I craned my neck to watch but gave up almost instantly. My body jerked as his head lowered one final time. He wasn't going to give my brain a chance to think again.

I clamped both hands over my mouth as he tasted and explored the deepest parts of me. No matter how hard I tried to keep the gasps inside, to stay still, my body had other plans. He gripped my hips to hold me down as I lost complete control.

His forbidden kiss was relentless, and that was exactly what I wanted. I couldn't tell which way was up, or even what reality was anymore. My body jerked and rocked with every passing second, sweat pooling under my breasts.

He didn't grant me a sliver of relief until I released one final, muffled scream and went completely still. Only then did he travel upward again, dragging that finger through his own personal destruction, across my belly, to rest on my lower lip.

"Better?" he whispered.

My chest heaved, my body ached, but my mind felt free.

"Yes," I breathed.

CHAPTER FIFTY-ONE

Licorice

I t worked.

Silence and the warmth of Oliver's snuggles filled my dreams, completely eradicating the mere thought of Donnell.

We're gonna be all right. Tomorrow is the start of our life.

But when an elbow jabbed me, all peace was gone.

"Be very quiet," Oliver instructed. He crouched at the edge of the wall of hay, struggling into his shirt without taking his eyes off the ladder for a moment.

There was no way I was sleepy anymore. I sat, pain shooting throughout my abdomen. I yelped and gripped my stomach.

"Shh," Oliver hissed, waving his hand absently at me.

I glared at him. "It's not as though I could help that."

He ignored me entirely. "Get the dress on. Hurry."

"What is it?" I shuffled on my knees to his side, peering over the hay.

Oliver sat back on his haunches to yank on his shoes. "We're gonna have to go. C'mon."

My throat went bone-dry. "They're here . . ."

"I think so." Oliver pulled his hair behind his neck, deftly tying it with the leather strap from his pocket.

Somewhere near the house, a horse nickered. I gripped the discarded dress with both hands, as though that alone would provide safety.

A door creaked, followed by angry voices. Recognizable voices.

"Get dressed, Nella," Oliver whispered, nudging my clenched palms.

I pulled the dress over my head, grunting as the movement yanked on the stitches. "Now what?"

His silhouette held up a hand to silence me.

The barn door creaked open, letting in a shred of lantern light. My blood ran cold. I settled onto my stomach, pressing against the itchy wall. Oliver stayed put, his hand resting on his revolver.

Our guest didn't waste time searching downstairs. The clip of boots on the ladder sounded like a death sentence.

With the gun securely in his grasp, Oliver set it on the hay. His shoulders moved in a wave as he settled down to await our fate, sights directly on the ladder.

"It's me, don't shoot," came Bernard's voice.

Oliver let out a sigh as his forehead fell against the hay. "Heaven help us all," he seethed, his whole body going limp in relief.

I ventured to his side, barely peering over the wall.

"Hmph." Bernard set the lantern on the loft, eyeing the two of us. He didn't waste any more time. "Time to start the search." He flicked a single piece of hay in his brother's direction. "I'll do what I can to lead them the other way, to buy you time." He shook his head, scrubbing at his forehead. "As soon as we're gone, get out of here."

"We will," Oliver said. His voice was raspy. Was that from the nerves?

"Just . . ." Bernard sighed deeply, leaning his head against the ladder. "Don't get yourself caught."

"I'll do my best," Oliver promised. "Now get outta here before they come in here." He waved his hand in a shooing motion.

Bernard gave us one last sad smile before grabbing the lantern and sliding to the ground below.

We waited in silence while Bernard saddled the horse beneath us. He worked fast, muttering the entire time about it being four in the morning. When finished, he didn't come upstairs. He simply left the way he'd come, leading his horse into the night.

Still tucked away in the loft, we remained perfectly silent as the hoofbeats faded away. Only then did Oliver move from his post.

He set the pistol on the ground and stood, winding his holster around his waist.

"You dressed?"

"Uh . . ." I glanced down as if a corset and crinoline had magically appeared. Even in the darkness, I knew how shapeless the dress was. How obvious my chest seemed, unsupported under the thin cotton.

"That'll work," Oliver said. He handed me the supply bag and scooped me up. "Let's go."

Though he'd carried me down the ladder from the attic countless times, I still clung to his neck as we made our way to the barn floor.

Oliver went right to the door and opened it just enough to peer through.

"Where are we gonna go?" I whispered. "The train doesn't leave till eight."

Apparently satisfied with our safety, Oliver pulled the door open a little more and slipped through. "We're gonna hope

Bernard keeps them away from the station," he grumbled. "You can't travel much farther than that."

We followed the road, staying hidden within the trees.

My entire body ached. My head pounded with unshed tears, and my torso felt as if someone had torn me in two. "I'm not dressed well enough for a train," I pointed out.

"Well, you're ill. We'll use that to our advantage."

Though he couldn't see my glare in the sliver of moonlight, I hoped he felt it.

The pain had transitioned to an ache that made me feel downright muddy. If I tried to stay awake by tracking the notes of the ever-chirping crickets, the sounds would swarm over me like a cascade of shooting stars.

Because of this fuzziness, I drifted in and out of a dreamless sleep, as comfortable as I could be in Oliver's arms.

Either Bernard lived closer to town than I thought, or I slept more than I thought. The next thing I knew, we were on the platform. The sunrise trickled through the treetops, teasing us with its rays.

All eyes were fixed on us. I gripped Oliver's shirt and gnawed on my lower lip. My dress was out of style, and way too long due to the lack of hoops. At least that hid my leg. But I was positive they could see straight through the lack of corset to my breasts, to the aching wound on my torso.

We didn't look like upstanding citizens. My hair needed to be brushed, and we were covered in hay.

"It's all right," Oliver whispered, clearly reading my thoughts.

He sat on a bench at the far side of the platform and dug into his breast pocket. "I got you something while you were asleep."

He fished out a tiny cloth-wrapped bundle and placed it on my lap. "It's not much, but I figured it'd make you smile."

As though it had the ability to erupt into flames, I gingerly pulled on the ribbon. The black candies inside did exactly what he hoped: they brought a big smile to my face.

"Licorice. Thank you!" I moved to give him a hug, but the pain shot throughout my body. I gasped against the onslaught and pressed my hand against the wound.

"You're welcome." He finished the hug for me and kissed my forehead. "They had some by the ticket counter."

I raised an eyebrow at him. "You already got the tickets?"

He nodded and pulled the two strips of paper out of that same pocket.

"Where . . . what . . . what'd you do with me?" I doubted he would just leave me asleep on the platform with only the autumn-tinged trees for company, but I had to ask.

"I never let you go." He gripped my hand and squeezed. "If anyone asks, though, you're on death's door and you're on your way to see your mother for one final time."

I could feel my eyebrows knit together as I glared at him. "Really?"

He shrugged. "It worked."

I popped one of the candies into my mouth and rested my head against him. If I tried hard enough, I could forget the reality, let my mind wander to the land of music and peace. I could let the symphonies pirouette with the dancing trees. They would twirl in the soft morning light, each sashay a new note on the ivory keys in my mind.

But even with the candy, even with the sunshine on my face, that feeling of foreboding wouldn't leave. My voice trembled as I spoke. "What are we gonna do if they catch us here?"

Oliver's shoulders went rigid, and he stared straight ahead, grinding his teeth. He offered zero encouragement. "Fight. Die. Preferably with some form of dignity." He said it so simply, as if he were just explaining a daily chore.

I stared open-mouthed at him. "You don't have another plan?"

"All aboard!" came the call. The doors clanked as the conductor opened them for passengers.

Oliver took advantage and stood, completely ignoring my question.

Instead of jumping straight onboard, he held back, his eagle-like blue eyes searching every shadow, every face on the platform.

I followed his gaze, trying to see it through his eyes. Nothing looked abnormal to me. A cluster of men and women all buttoned into their travel attire, complete with hats and bags. The platform was set up similar to a porch, leading right to the train car itself, so everyone was prepared to deal with the worst of the elements. Except for us . . .

The wooden platform was so new, not a single board creaked as they moved for the train car. In fact, I was pretty sure that if I tried, I could probably detect the sharp smell of the red and yellow paint on the boards of the station itself. But at the moment, all I could smell was the hot, acrid steam that caressed the train.

The smell of freedom.

The conductor didn't ask a single question as we boarded, though he certainly gave me a few extra glances.

With every step we took into the car, I felt just a little safer. Oliver was deceptively calm, scanning every seat, every face. If anyone was on that train, we'd know.

When we reached our seats, he finally spoke.

"Think you can sit up for a little while?"

I nodded, bracing for the change in position.

I gritted my teeth against the pain as he positioned me in the chair. He apologized every time I winced.

"Why does it hurt worse today?" I demanded in a whine.

"Just does sometimes." He kissed my forehead and settled himself across from me in his own seat.

Slowly, my body relaxed. I slumped against the window, knowing full well that my mother would come unglued if she knew how unladylike I chose to be.

She'd come unglued if she knew any *of this.*

Safe in a sea of strangers, even Oliver began to relax.

We didn't have to wait long for the train to move. The initial surge made me gasp in pain, but I gritted my teeth.

You can do this. You can do this!

Oliver watched me the entire time, poised to pounce if it would help.

Slowly, the fog cleared. I breathed deeply, eyes shut, savoring the sunlight that filtered through the window.

"Try to rest, okay?"

I forced my eyes open. "But where are we going?"

"Right now? Nashville. We can't stay, though." He glanced at the door behind him. Maybe he had forgotten to check that particular shadow for danger. "We'll keep making our way west. My family is less likely to follow us across the Mississippi. And we won't have to worry about the Williams Clan, either."

He slumped in his seat, shifting to eye the rapidly passing landscape.

The mountains soared in the distance, tipped in early snow. I was glad we wouldn't have to traverse any of them—there was no way I would survive that.

We were going west. It was hard to believe how much my life had changed over the last year.

I smirked, remembering how it all began. "The last time I sat at a table just like this, I thought you were gonna kill me." I let my finger trace the wood grain on the table.

He grinned, teeth shining in the sunlight. "So did I."

I spoke without thinking. "It would've been easier for you if you did."

Like the predator he was, his head swiveled to focus straight on me. He captured my face in both his hands and leaned close, his nose just barely brushing mine. "Don't say that. Life changed, and I'm grateful for it. Got it?"

My lip twitched, threatening a smile under his piercing gaze. "I'm glad too," I said, and I meant it.

CHAPTER FIFTY-TWO

Horse Thievery

The trip to Nashville was blessedly uneventful. I spent much of the time curled in my seat, head against the window with Oliver's jacket draped over me.

I could feel the gazes from the other passengers, but no one said a thing. Whether that was from Oliver's threatening stare or mere politeness, I didn't know. I didn't care.

We were safe. At least for a while, and I was going to enjoy every minute of it.

"Hey." Oliver nudged my arm to wake me. "We're almost there. Might be good to get rid of the hay." He gestured to his head.

I straightened with a groan, the stitches pulling as I moved.

"Here, can I?" He transferred onto my bench seat before I managed a nod. I turned my back to him, letting him tame the brown tresses with his fingers.

"Do you get to travel much?" I found myself asking.

"Hmm?" His fingers froze near the nape of my neck. "Well, yes . . . and no. We stayed close to home. Typically, everything is handled within each clan's land. Though, every once in a while, someone will request our help specifically."

"You mean, someone who isn't part of one of your 'clans'?"

"Right."

"Like who?" I stretched my neck to one side, and then another, savoring the relief the movement brought.

He leaned in close, tangling his fingers in my hair to pull my neck to one side. His lips tickled the exposed skin as he spoke. "Anyone. Think, who might want to help someone like us? Think big."

I shifted my weight back, leaning against his torso. "Aristocrats?"

"Sometimes." He nipped at my neck, then released my hair. With a rough clearing of his throat, he went back to finger-combing my mess of hair. "Anyone with money. Someone wants to climb the ranks? They might send for us. Enemies? Secrets? The reasons are endless."

I sighed. "At least you're done with it all."

His fingers faltered mid-braid.

"Aren't you?" I demanded, turning my head as far as I dared to study his expression.

The unreadable mask spread across his face before I got a good look. "Right now," he started, looking up at the roof of the car as he chose his words. "Right now, we just need to find a place to be safe. Anything else, we'll figure out later."

I opened and closed my mouth a few times, unable to come up with an acceptable response. Would we truly ever be safe if he couldn't leave the family business?

The brakes squealed as the train rolled to a stop at the Nashville station. I could feel the worry settling over my shoulders like a landslide.

"C'mon. Let's get a horse." Oliver patted my shoulder, plopping the finished braid over it for my inspection.

I didn't say anything as I stood, gnawing on my bottom lip with the effort. Now what were we supposed to do? How were we supposed to get across the Mississippi?

"That was sweet of Bernard to give us enough for a horse too," I hedged.

Oliver ignored my comment entirely. "Do you want to walk out? Or do you want me to carry you?"

I narrowed my eyes and crossed my arms, leaning against the table. "He didn't give enough, did he?"

Oliver wiped the frustrated look from his face with impressive speed. "You're blocking the way, *dear*. And people are staring. Let's go." He set his face in a tight-lipped smile as he held his hand out for mine. I took it, transferring half of my weight to him as I hopped along the narrow walkway.

He was right, people were staring. I gritted my teeth and moved on. We made quite the pair with our bedraggled outfits and my lack of leg. In fact, I felt naked without the corset holding everything together. My skirts hung unfashionably, dragging on the floor due to the lack of hoops, and my breasts felt completely exposed—and lower than I wanted them to be. Sure, our neatened hair helped, but we still didn't look like anyone who belonged in a dining car.

I waited to continue my questioning until we were on Main Street, hidden by the streams of people milling about their daily lives. "You *can't* steal a horse," I said.

That single eyebrow rose as if to accept the challenge.

"*Oliver!*"

He turned to stare me down, copying my tone. "*Nella*, we can't stay here. Lord knows we can't afford a coach. A hotel. Or even a horse. But we *cannot* stay here."

"We can't *steal* a horse either! They hang people for that!"

"As opposed to murder?" he demanded.

I closed my lips with an audible *pop*.

"We have to go, and we have to go now. I don't know where they are, but they *will* figure out where we went. The sooner we get out of Tennessee, the better."

"Because they can't follow us there . . ." I whispered, mainly to myself.

"I didn't say that," he muttered.

I don't think he realized I heard him. "*What?*" The word was a gasp.

He placed a hand on his forehead, tugging his hair as he fought for calm. "We like a good hunt, okay? Yell at me about it all you want later. Right now, we need to go." He gestured to a nearby bench.

As I sat, I did everything I could to channel all the fury in his direction. "*Fine.*"

He grumbled something under his breath and turned his back to mine. "Stay put. Don't move. Don't draw attention to yourself. I'll be back." He waited for my nod before waltzing down the sidewalk.

I stuck my tongue out at his back, enjoying the release the childlike sass gave me. "Leaving me here like a pet dog." I wrapped my arms around myself as though it would hide my inappropriate attire.

I waited. Or at least I tried. I really did! But after the fourth disgusted look in my direction, likely due to my lack of proper attire, I couldn't do it anymore—I got up.

As soon as we were in the woods again, I was going to have to find another cane. Hobbling with the help of the storefronts only drew more attention.

I gazed into the shop windows, willing myself to relax as I eyed the beautiful fabric and hats in the first shop. Only a year ago, I wore similar outfits. The puffed skirts, the layers, the way they would swish as I moved. I smiled to myself.

"One day," I promised the light-pink one in the window. For the time being, proper clothing would be enough.

I had just rested my hand on the doorknob when Oliver cleared his throat behind me.

"Now's not the time to window-shop," he chided.

I yelped as I whirled to face him. "Do we have enough for . . ." I poked at the unmarred side of my belly.

Oliver scrubbed at his forehead. "He gave us just enough for the train." He sat upon a bay gelding, saddled and ready.

"Where'd—"

"Later." He swung from the saddle and took my outstretched hand. "Questions later. Right now, it's time to go before we end up with an entire posse on our tails."

He placed me on the horse's rear and remounted with an "umph." "Hang on."

I did as he asked. He instructed the stolen horse to walk through the streets. No one looked twice at us, no one screamed at our backs. But as soon as we hit the road, we moved to a gallop.

I gasped as pain speared through my side, but no amount of discomfort would stop me from holding on for dear life. We had to get as far as we could before they discovered the missing horse; I knew that. But why did our escape have to hurt so much? Eventually, Oliver slowed back to a walk and maneuvered us into the trees.

"Ow," I complained.

"Sorry," he said for probably the millionth time. "I didn't want someone else following us too."

I rested my head against his back and took a slow breath. Even that hurt. "I can't believe you stole a horse."

"I can't believe you wandered down the street by yourself," he quipped.

I poked his lower back, not bothering with a full punch. "You left me."

He ignored my griping. "In a few hours, we'll camp for the night. Can you hold on until then?"

I nodded against the muscles spanning his shoulders.

It was going to be a long ride.

CHAPTER FIFTY-THREE

Like a Deer

Though I did my best to breathe through it, by the end of the first hour, I found myself gripping the back of Oliver's shirt to withstand the pain. It helped some, but not enough. I tried to be brave, to keep him from realizing how much I was struggling. But he'd know. Even if my unbidden tears weren't soaking his back, he would know.

Whenever an anxious whine interrupted my silent tears, he patted my leg.

"I'm sorry," he whispered.

"Can't we stop?" I finally asked through gritted teeth. Even though I fought to get my body to relax again, it was getting harder by the minute. "I'm trying to be strong, really I am. But . . ."

"We have to go farther. I'm so sorry, Nella. I truly am." He ran his hand over my thigh, providing what comfort he could as we traveled through the trees.

I screwed my eyes shut against the pain and breathed. In. Out. In. Out.

With each hoofbeat, Sara's overly white face flashed into my mind. With each spasm of agony, Donnell's half smile flittered in her place.

They had to know we left town by now. What would they do when they caught up with us this time? Did they already lurk in the shadows?

I fought for a different image, picturing the piano in the sitting room. I struggled to hear the notes as my imaginary self pressed the ivory keys. The melody slowly took shape, flowing from one side to the other as it brought me into a kind of sedated trance.

Gentle arpeggios in the bass, one blending to the next. Then a solid held chord in the right hand—ominous. One note. Then another, a slow dance into the unknown.

I clung to the song as Oliver set up camp, swayed with it as he tucked me into the makeshift bed he'd created with his coat.

"I need to change your bandages," he announced.

It was the first thing I'd truly heard him say in what had to be hours. Had he even said anything? Or had I been too far gone to notice?

His touch was gentle against my leg as he pulled the dress up and over my hips. I cried out as he lifted me just enough to tuck it out of the way.

"I'm sorry," he whispered. "I'm so sorry."

He did the same movement with the chemise, tucking the fabric around my breasts for just a sliver of modesty as he went to work on the bandages.

He didn't bother unwinding them around my torso. He pulled his knife from his boot and slipped the cold metal under the bandages. I gasped at the unwelcome sensation, a thin whine escaping my lips at the nightmares that plagued me.

"Shh, shh . . ." he cooed. He worked fast, ripping the bandages free of the wound.

I balled my hands into fists and pressed them to my eyes, gasping for air. The entire time it took me to regain my composure, he spoke nonsensical words and rubbed my arm. Slower than should've been acceptable, a clear thought trickled back into place.

"How bad is it?" I croaked. "He gutted me like a deer." A forbidden sob shook me at the last word.

"No, not even close," Oliver promised. "It's long, but not *that* deep. You'll heal." He pressed a damp rag to parts of the wound, clearing away whatever had seeped free. I bit my lip to stay silent but let him work.

He helped me sit, cradling me in his arms while he wound the clean bandages around me. "Try to get some rest. We'll ride again first thing in the morning."

He wasn't joking about "first thing." The second that first bird opened her beak to sing in the frosty air, he was moving. He donned his clothing, finger-combed his hair into submission, tied it at the base of his neck, and saddled the gelding. All while I stared at him, nestled in his coat and munching on a stick of jerky.

"I thought you didn't like mornings?"

"I don't." He held his hand down for me. "It's not the same out here."

Reluctantly, I took his hand and let him pull me up. The pain was still there, but it was noticeably better than the night before. Almost numb. "Ready for another day in the saddle?"

I narrowed my eyes. "No."

"Me either. Let's do it."

Our pace was relentless. At least I thought so. With every passing mile, he seemed to get just a little more grumpy.

My wound seemed to be healing nicely for those first few days. Little by little, I could sit straighter in the saddle, bend just a little easier. But by day six or seven (I was losing track), that all changed.

It was significantly more sore when I hoisted myself onto the horse, but I could still ignore it. As we plodded on through the never-ending trees, I found myself leaning against Oliver more and more.

"Oliver?" I finally whispered, clutching at the lower section of the wound.

His mindless humming stopped. "Hmm?"

"I . . . can we stop?" I pressed at the wound, wincing as I did so. "I think the bandage pulled a stitch." Or, at least, I hoped it had. I didn't want to imagine what else it could be. I could feel the heat through the dirty cotton. *He said it looked all right last night. It's probably just a stitch.*

Oliver pulled the gelding to a stop. "We can't stay long," he said. He'd likely said that exact sentence a million times already.

"What are the chances they've caught up with us way out here?" I demanded. "We've barely stopped to breathe!"

With a grumble-like sigh, he swung from the saddle. "Let's take a look, then."

I reached for him to help me, wincing at the pull.

He frowned at my expression change. "It didn't hurt this morning?"

I shrugged. "Perhaps a little? I didn't notice."

He pulled the bag from the saddle horn. "Come on, let's look at it."

Obediently, I stood still, bracing myself for yet another bandage change. "It's probably just a stitch."

"Probably," Oliver muttered, though his tone said otherwise.

As he did every evening, he lifted my clothing to get to the bandages below. I held the fabric out of the way, staring up at clouds through the bare trees.

Gingerly, he sliced through the bandages. I gritted my teeth as he removed the lower strip of cloth, expecting instant pain from the delinquent stitch. Instead, I felt relief.

And heard his curse.

I craned my neck to see over the wadded fabric. "What?"

Without replacing the bandages, he stood, his hands in fists at his sides. "You avoided infection with your leg. But *this* gets you?" He leaned against the gelding, resting his head against the saddle.

"What is it?" Though it hurt, I bunched the fabric up and bent to see. Most of it looked fine, pink with the stitches poking out this way and that. But before my hips, the skin had turned a deep red.

Infection.

My voice was soft, breathy. "What do we do?"

To my utter surprise, he turned on his heel and stalked to the closest tree. His fist collided with the bark, a yell erupting from his soul. He then stood there, spouting off sentence after sentence in pure French.

I hadn't even realized he *spoke* French.

The gelding sidestepped the fury, blowing through his lips as though to remind his rider to calm down.

I gripped the closest tree to stay upright. "Oliver . . . what do we do?"

He took the biggest breath I'd ever seen, and held it. The release was like a dragon breathing fire. "You? You stay put."

I narrowed my eyes and opened my mouth to argue, but he held his hand up to stop me. "Do I have to tie you up?"

My jaw went slack. "I'm not a child!"

He took his dragon breath again. "No, you're not. But you need to rest, and I need to get some fresh water to clean you up."

"We have some in the canteen," I pointed out. I felt almost nauseous at the idea of him leaving me alone, but I didn't want to admit it. Even so, I lowered myself into the pile of red-gold leaves, the tree against my backbone.

"Not enough." He swung into the saddle. "Here." He tossed his sheathed knife at my feet. "Just in case. I'll be back soon."

With each retreating hoofbeat, fear rose in my throat like bile. Higher in my stomach, then my throat, threatening to choke me at any moment. I touched the key-shaped wound on my chest, biting my lip hard enough it drew blood.

Why didn't Donnell kill me? Where was he now? How long would it be before they caught up with us? And how long would it be before his wound killed me anyway?

I twirled the blade around in my fingers, both terrified and comforted by its weight.

Dear God, don't let me have to use this thing.

CHAPTER FIFTY-FOUR

Take Control

Oliver was gone much longer than I had hoped. At first, I didn't mind the solitude. The simple fact that I didn't have to ride a horse made my saddle-sore rear happy. But eventually, the nerves settled in. Soon, every bird's call seemed to be a warning, every gust of wind seemed to disguise footsteps.

Each time there was a noise, I jumped. And each time I jumped, pain coursed through my body.

How far had Oliver gone? Was he close enough to notice if someone was watching me from the shadows?

I wanted to think he wouldn't leave me alone without being absolutely sure that we were safe. But everyone makes mistakes.

When an unidentified forest animal squealed a protest in the nearby brush, I jumped so hard I saw stars.

I gripped the edges of my skirt, warring with myself. I had two options: either sit and wait for death to find me, or go find Oliver.

"Fine," I announced to the empty clearing. "I'm not gonna sit here and wait for someone else to take care of me." It wasn't like his *people* had been doing an amazing job of keeping me safe, anyway. My stump throbbed at the thought.

Using the tree trunk, I pulled myself up, the knife clutched in my hand.

If Oliver showed up before I got very far, I could always claim I was looking for a new cane.

I hopped the perimeter of our makeshift camp, scanning the undergrowth for a stick that would work. With all the brush, it didn't take long to find one that would do the trick.

"Well, there goes my excuse."

Using this newfound accessory, I hobbled into the trees, maintaining a circular pattern with the cloth bag in the middle.

If I could see the satchel, I was close enough to find my way back. At least, that was my logic. After the fourth or fifth circle yielded no sign of Oliver, I adjusted the plan.

As long as I moved on straight ahead, I'd find the bag again. *You're being an idiot.*

I kept my path as linear as I could, the crunch of leaves under my foot and makeshift cane scaring away any nearby wildlife.

Still, there was no sign of him.

What if Henry found him first? Or Donnell? Or even a bear? He had a pistol, sure, but I had his knife. What if it had been the only weapon that could save him?

I knew I was letting my brain get the best of me, but that niggling sensation in the pit of my stomach wouldn't leave. I gnawed on my lower lip, fighting to ignore the ever-tightening throb along my side.

Each time the pain dug its fingers into my skin, I saw Donnell's face. My mouth went dry, and my fingernails dug into my palms.

"He's not here. He's not here!" I repeated this over and over again as I continued my search.

Though I did my best, I didn't register another presence until it was too late.

A weather-chilled hand clamped over my mouth, the other hooking under my elbows, effectively restraining them behind my back. I tried to scream, I tried to bite, but my efforts were futile.

When I lifted my leg to kick, I only managed to tip the two of us forward, my captor rolling sharply to keep us from falling flat on our faces.

Despite the sudden movement, the man didn't take time to catch his breath. He flipped me onto my back in expert fashion, releasing my arms just long enough to pin them above my head. I wriggled as much as I could, rolling from side to side in a pitifully unproductive manner. When he freed my mouth, the only noise that escaped was some kind of mewling scream.

They had me. It was all over.

The man didn't move.

I twisted under him, sweat pooling across my forehead. Twigs poked into the nape of my neck, but I hardly noticed. Within seconds, there would be a blade to my throat—I was sure of it.

Still, he didn't move.

When that realization finally hit, I went as still as death and opened one eye. When had I even closed them in the first place?

Lips set into a firm, angry line, eyes narrowed to slits. If fire spewed from his nostrils, I wouldn't have been surprised.

Oliver.

"What part of 'don't leave this spot' don't you understand?" He dropped my hands and backed away a single, large step.

I blinked once. Twice. Three times. All I could do was stare mutely at him.

I had been so sure I was about to die . . .

He bent down and, in one swift movement, pulled the blade from where I had tucked it in my stocking. "You didn't even use this." He waved it in the air for emphasis.

Oops. I'd forgotten I even had his knife. But then, I probably wouldn't have been able to grab it even if I had remembered.

With a sigh, he hauled me to my feet. My fear fizzled into the threat of tears. I scrubbed at my eyes, grinding my teeth.

How *dare* he!

I fixed him with my best glare, though I knew my fury likely resembled that of a hen, newly evicted from the nest—messy hair and all.

"Why'd you scare me like that?" I placed my hands on my hips and stuck out my chin, shoving the residual fear into its own dark hiding place.

Oliver completely ignored my anger. He tucked the knife into his belt, turned on his heel, and led the way to where he had left the horse. I hobbled along behind, glaring daggers at his back the entire time.

When he spoke, he still didn't look at me. "Do you know how easy it would've been to kill you?" His voice was so level, so emotionless, it sent a chill up my spine. "Or worse?"

He didn't have to go into detail on how bad it could've been. Anyone could've sneaked up on me. After all, I made enough noise while walking to attract even a deaf man.

We traipsed back to the clearing, the crunch of our feet on the freshly fallen leaves the only sound.

Oliver went straight to the gelding and took the canteen and cloth bag from the saddle horn, leaving a small carcass behind. He brought supper.

I watched his every move. Was he ever going to acknowledge my anger?

"Lie down. Let's get this over with." He made a sweeping movement to the leaf-strewn floor.

Apparently not.

With a resigned sigh, I lowered myself to the flattest spot I could see.

He made his way to my side and plopped to the ground. Neither of us said a single word as he lifted my clothing to scrutinize the wound. I glared at the sky, curling my toes under as I waited.

His chilly fingers traced the edges of the bruised flesh. Tenderly at first, until he had a plan. He unsheathed the knife, and my entire body went rigid.

"What are you doing?" I demanded.

"Helping you. Hold still."

I clenched my eyes shut as the blade teased the edges of my skin, but I held still. I trusted him not to hurt me.

He placed his hands on either side of the infection and applied pressure. I whimpered, but again, didn't move. The sensation was a combination of relief and pain. Satisfied, he wiped away the pus, or whatever else he found, and poured water onto the wound. That hurt significantly worse than I expected.

"I know, I know," he said, holding me in place. "Stay still, please. I'm hurrying!"

He worked quickly, finishing his efforts by placing a poultice of herbs on the affected area, followed by clean bandages.

"Done," he said, slapping his hands together as he stood. "Let's eat." He turned on his heel and moved to the saddle, pulling a dead rabbit from its hiding place. He rinsed the blade, then sliced into the little animal. Despite myself, I winced. He yanked the hide. It pulled away from the delicate body with a sickening *rip*.

"I understand you wanted no part of this life." He used the blade to separate a stubborn section. His body looked as stiff as the rabbit itself. "But until you're safe, I need you to trust me and *listen* to what I say."

Another threatening yank on the skin sent bile rising into my throat. How close had I come to being treated just like that rabbit?

He watched me out of the corner of his eye. I wouldn't have been surprised if he suddenly confessed that he could read my every thought.

So, he was still mad at me. I grunted as I stood. With the heated pain radiating from my torso, tomorrow's ride would be miserable to say the least. "I'm gonna go get wood," I muttered. The pain slithered through my middle. Everything felt bruised, as if someone had beaten me.

I could feel his gaze boring into my back.

"Serves you right for wandering off like that," Oliver muttered.

My hands balled into fists at my side, fingernails digging little moons into my palms. "You *left* me!" I whirled on him, skirts flying in what would've been an elegant cascade if they weren't so filthy. "You *left* me here. You can't expect me to just sit down like a good little girl and wait for one of you"—I waved my hand absently in the air, hunting for the right word—"*people* to show up and skin me just like that rabbit!"

Almost delicately, Oliver's eyes shut and his chest moved up and down in the world's slowest breath. "Just sit down, please."

I crossed my arms and stared him down. "I'm *fine*. No thanks to *you*."

He raised that single eyebrow at me and squatted with ease to pick up a stick. "Let me take care of it. You should be resting—not wandering the mountainside."

I gritted my teeth, debating on how stubborn I truly needed to be. He made quick work of the stick gathering. Within a minute or so, he had a pile of wood beside the freshly skinned rabbit.

"Earlier, I made it worse, didn't I?"

I rapidly shook my head, startled by the question. "Hmm?"

"Your wound," he clarified. "Did I make it worse by grabbing you earlier?"

I shot him a look. "Yes," I snapped, the anger flaring right back to life.

He lifted his head to look me in the eyes. "I'm sorry. All I could think about was if someone else found you first." Despite his words, the anger still radiated from him. He squatted by the wood and got to work, lighting it with little effort. He took a particularly long stick and shoved it straight through the rabbit.

I clutched my stomach, unbidden thoughts of being skinned alive wandering through my head.

He ignored me and balanced the rabbit above the young flames.

I leaned against a tree, watching him turn the little creature round and round. Not once did he look back at me. Was he still mad? Or was he just giving *me* time to cool off?

I sank to my seat, not moving from my position. I fidgeted with what little grass remained, plucking it in a circular motion until all that was left was a perfect, plate-sized clearing of damp earth.

When the meat began to smell like food instead of a dead animal, Oliver still hadn't relaxed. His shoulders were tense, almost hunched over his work. His irritation was impossible to ignore.

I heaved a sigh, much more dramatic than was necessary. He paused for only a moment at the sound.

He has no reason to be mad at me!

"I didn't know where you were!" I finally said, making a fist, trapping the remaining grass against my palm.

"I *told* you to stay put." Oliver's voice was nothing short of forced patience.

"I didn't go *far*." I knew I sounded like a spoiled child, but I didn't care. "I knew my way back! Besides, you'd been gone for hours!"

"One. I was gone for *one* hour."

"Okay, one hour! I didn't know where you were. What if Henry found you? Or Donnell! Or—"

He held up his hand to stop my miniature tirade and rotated on his haunches to face me. He took a controlled breath before speaking again. "And if they had found me, I wouldn't want them to find *you*. They won't kill me, remember?"

He hauled himself to his feet and walked to my side. His shoulders slumped with his sigh, the anger now gone. He bent to nudge my side with his pointer finger, uncomfortably close to my wound. Despite how gentle he was, I flinched.

"If you're going to survive this—hell, if we both are going to survive this—you have to *listen* to me. I don't want to come back to find you *dead*." As if to drive home the point, he squatted so his face was a mere inch from my own. "Do you understand me?"

Some deep part of me snapped. "Oh yes, I *understand*." I placed one hand firmly on his chest and shoved him away. "You think to threaten me, to scare me, like a child? I'm *not* a child. And I'm certainly not *your* child. I've had enough of men controlling my every move." I gripped his shoulders to help me stand. "If you're not going to communicate with me like a decent human being, I'll be moving on." I turned sharply, skirts and hair flying through the air. I didn't look back until I tripped on my way to the horse. That's where I stayed, channeling all my fury in his direction.

I was fairly certain he wouldn't lash out at me, but I knew I'd just played my first move in this chess game that I didn't understand.

And now it was his turn.

Oliver let out a long breath through his teeth and watched me, his expressions changing so quickly, they were hard to track. Surprise, confusion, irritation, attraction, then finally acceptance. He turned back to the charred rabbit and flipped it to the other side.

A strange, warm feeling spread through my chest.

I had taken control, and it felt unbelievably good.

CHAPTER FIFTY-FIVE
Memphis

Memphis was so much more active than the previous town. The platform was huge, with an awning stretching the entire way. People crowded everywhere, waiting to head to their destination. Families congregated around their cases and trunks, anxiously awaiting the start of their new life.

They were everywhere, packed with all kinds of goods to be shipped every which way. Despite our bedraggled appearance, we melted into the activity, grateful for whatever invisibility we could gather from the chaos.

For once, we traveled along the road, dodging the wagons and carts, as everyone milled about their business.

It had only been a few days since the infection had made its way to my wound. Every time Oliver cleaned it, he held his lips in a grim line. Though he always insisted that it hadn't spread.

The pain wasn't any worse, but the bruising didn't seem like it would ever let up.

I reveled in the distraction of the city.

All the activity excited me. This would be the new start to our life, our freedom. And it felt perfect.

Stores lined the streets, their windows packed with dresses, fabrics, and other odds and ends. Despite myself, I had to look into each one.

Every few minutes, something caught my eye. A pretty pink dress with lace detailing, an elegant hat, or some beautiful leather gloves. Each time, Oliver had to tug on my sleeve to bring my attention back to the job at hand.

One store in particular had my full attention. A printing shop, complete with books of every genre. But what made me stop, hands gripping the windowsill, was a thin, hardcover book of music sitting on a stand in the window.

I couldn't tear myself away, straining my eyes to read the composer. "Schumann," I whispered to myself.

Oliver's rapidly growing beard tickled my ear as he leaned in to whisper. "I don't want to wait an hour for the next ferry." Stress radiated from his body, but it did little to dampen my excitement.

"Can't we go in and look around?" I asked. "They can't find us in all this mess of people, can they?"

He made a sick, twisted kind of laugh. "I've done it. It's not hard."

The unease about his killing past made me queasy. "Oh."

He took my hand and led me away from the shop.

I didn't have a piano to play it on anyway. But I would've given almost anything to read that music, to let my brain do the playing.

My earlier excitement boiled again when I saw the first steamship make its way around the corner, the steam dancing up to the cloud-dotted sky. As if summoned by the mega-ship, other vessels swarmed around it, bringing supplies and passengers this way and that.

"Are you sure we can't afford to travel on one of those?" I asked, nodding in the direction of an especially pretty ship.

Almost as soon as we arrived in town, Oliver had sold our stollen horse.

Oliver chuckled. "I doubt it. Not if we want to have anything left over to make a life once we get to where we're going."

"Did you decide exactly where that is?" I asked, stopping for a moment to watch a few of the smaller riverboats zigzag around each other. It was a wonder they didn't crash.

Oliver tugged on my arm to get me moving again. "No idea. California? See if there's any gold left? Nah. Maybe we'll hide in one of the territories with the Indians."

I shivered. "I've heard too many stories of that."

"Stories are often exaggerated, remember that," Oliver pointed out. "We'll be fine."

We made our way to the edge of the river to wait for the ferry. It was much larger than I had anticipated, easily fitting a full wagon and a handful of passengers, with plenty of room to spare. It was quick too, making the journey to our side with astonishing speed.

We waited, leaning against a nearby shop while the people filed off and the wagon was unloaded.

It was hard to wait silently for our turn to board. There were enough people around that I felt safe, but I didn't dare talk about our future around them.

When our turn finally came, Oliver shelled out the money for our ticket. The scraggly old man pocketed it with a grin, making me wonder how much we overpaid. It was a straight profit for him—I was sure of it.

I pushed that thought from my mind and stood, gripping the railing, watching the ripples in the water as they teased at the side of the boat. I felt enthralled by all the activity.

There was so much to see. Tiny boats, multistory steamships, little canoes. Everyone was busy at work. A few fancy ladies, adorned with feathered hats and voluptuous skirts, stood on the edge of one of the larger steamships, pointing across the water at something only they could see.

The green hue of envy tugged at me. *If my father had only controlled himself . . . we were so close to that life.* But it was not meant to be. Apparently, I was never meant to be a fine, well-dressed lady. Surprisingly, that thought didn't hurt nearly as bad as it had before.

Oliver stood like a freshly strung bow beside me, also gazing out at all the activity. His body never relaxed the entire crossing. He hunted each and every face for certain death, reminding me of a trapped animal, always ready to fight.

I tried to stay still, but I fidgeted with my skirt. "Do you see them?" I whispered. His mood was contagious, and I certainly didn't want it tainting my excitement of the crossing.

"No," Oliver said shortly.

I searched his face. "You're lying, aren't you?"

"It's nothing," Oliver said stubbornly, making a show of studying the markings of the larger steamboat.

"Nothing," I repeated. "It's not nothing if I can feel your fear from here!"

Oliver sighed and rubbed his hand across his temple. "You really want to know? Fine." He let out a long breath. "There are clans almost everywhere. Not all of them get along with each other. You know that, right?" He waited for me to nod before continuing. "We'll be traveling in enemy clan territory. The Welks Clan."

I stared into the trees on the Arkansas side of the river. They didn't look like a safe haven anymore. "And if they catch us?"

"They'll either capture us, torture and kill us themselves, or decide to use the power to get in good terms with the Wedman Clan—turn us in."

He said it so matter-of-factly, it made me shiver.

"No other options?"

"Not that I am aware of."

I swallowed hard. "What are our chances?"

He lifted his shoulders in a shrug, slow and deliberate. "Don't have much of a choice, now do we?"

I fell silent, scrubbing my clammy hands on my skirt. With the hoi polloi milling around with their day-to-day lives, it was strange to think that certain death might live right on the other side of the river.

When we made it safely to the other side, Oliver didn't lollygag around. He tugged on my sleeve, and I followed obediently, feet hitting dry ground with a sinking realization: We were extremely far from home.

"Welcome to Arkansas," Oliver said softly, leading me through the small crowd. It seemed that most of the people from the ferry had come across for work, and they all trailed off to their jobs. Those who had farther to go found the stagecoaches or their wagons. We, on the other hand, wandered our way to the edge of the trees and disappeared from sight.

Our progress was silent and filled with nervous energy. Aside from the twittering birds in the distance, no one made a sound.

The only soul we saw was a doe that meandered her way onto our path. She flicked her tail, but otherwise ignored the intruders in her forest. Oliver hesitated, hand on his pistol, likely debating whether we could carry the meat with us. Apparently deciding against it, he watched the doe make her way through the trees in silence.

CHAPTER FIFTY-SIX

Surrounded

When a twig snapped nearby, even the birds grew still.

Without waiting for any other sign of provocation, Oliver's pistol was in his hand. Positioning me behind him, he backed up until I was sandwiched between him and a scraggly tree.

My heart thudded against my ribcage, questions bubbling on the tip of my tongue. *Who is it? Is it them? Can't it just be a raccoon? A squirrel?*

But squirrels don't snap twigs.

Oliver waited, scanning the tree line for the culprit. We didn't have to wait long. My heart pounded so loudly that anyone could've likely overheard.

I peered around Oliver, squinting in the hopes I could locate whatever had spooked him. Nothing.

His breathing never changed—it was as steady and as deep as always. Even so, he stood as still as a stone, gun trained into the shadows.

A lone, tall figure emerged from the trees, hands raised overhead in surrender. He stood so straight it exaggerated his height. He had black, curly hair that was cut short but still managed to be unruly. He was made of lean muscle, dressed in a black vest and pants, his holster in plain sight on his hip. Not a single bit of him looked harmless.

"Oliver Wedman," the man began.

A shot rang out, so loud and sudden I screamed. It took a moment to realize it came from Oliver's gun.

In the moment of silence that followed the bang, no one other than me so much as flinched.

Two moments, and still, no one moved. No one bled.

Had Oliver missed? On purpose?

"I'll stay here," the man said steadily. He didn't seem the least bit shaken from the warning shot. He still looked just as relaxed as before, as if he were simply talking about the weather.

"I won't go down without a fight," Oliver vowed, voice low and seething.

"You're fighting the wrong—"

"I don't think so." Oliver spat on the ground. "I know *exactly* who you are."

The man inched one hand to his pistol, keeping the other raised high. Oliver stiffened. I was certain the next shot would ring true. The man smoothly unhooked the holster and bent to the ground, setting it a few feet in front of him. He then took a large step back.

"I'm not here to fight you."

"Bull*shit*," Oliver snapped. "You think I don't see the others?"

What others? I looked all around, heart thumping in my throat. I hadn't seen this stranger, let alone anyone else. But Oliver was correct. To the right, deep in the trees, someone moved. How many were hiding in the shadows?

The man chuckled. "You're on *our* land, and I know why you're here. That doesn't mean I'd dare meet you alone."

"I won't miss this time," Oliver warned, making a show of lining the sights up with the stranger's head.

"Oh, I'm sure you won't," the man said. He still didn't move. "I'll give you one chance, and that's it, so listen close. You know we've never been on good terms with the Wedman Clan. But if you come willingly, you will be treated—"

Oliver let out the yowl of a trapped predator, and I ducked my head, hands clutched to my ears, awaiting the shot that never came.

Oliver's voice was filled with venom. "And now one of your enemies is on your land. You really think I'll trust you?"

"Of course not. But you should," the man said. "What's your move, son? This is your only chance."

To my surprise, Oliver hesitated, his back rising in small increments as he took a deep breath. He took his time making a decision, but when he was sure, he moved fast.

He pressed me even harder against the tree and squeezed the trigger.

Everything moved so quickly I didn't have time to process how the bark grated against my skin, only the scream of agony as the ache of my wound turned to fire. Men leapt from all directions, tackling Oliver to the ground in an instant. One uprooted me from where I'd been planted, not sparing any care about my being female.

My captor held me securely against his body, forearm tightly over my throat. Only, he didn't put any pressure. He didn't hold a knife to my side, my throat, anything. He simply stood there, holding me immobile.

Oliver fought with all his might, kicking out and tripping one man.

My own captor threw a rope in their direction, his pure-white hair freeing itself from the bonds at the nape of his neck. "Here!"

The only difference between the two men struggling with Oliver was that the younger had straight hair, and the older curly. Other than that, they were near copies of each other.

The curly-haired man had Oliver's arms at one point, pressing them into the dirt. How was he able to do that after being shot? Did Oliver miss?

My answer came at the sight of the ever-spreading blood on the man's sleeve. The wound didn't seem to bug him, as he continued trying to hold his prisoner down with everything he had.

The younger counterpart got the brunt of Oliver's kicks as the older lost control of his feet. Curly Hair pressed down with all his might while the younger man yanked the rope tight around Oliver's ankles.

It took them some effort to tie Oliver's hands. Each time the men had to adjust their grip, he attacked like a rabid cougar. All three of them had their muscles in full working order, making it appear as if they were part of an oil painting, frozen as they waited to see whose strength would break first. It didn't feel as serious as it should've; it didn't look like the fight for our lives. Instead, it seemed like the tail end of a sonata, that final ritardando taking down my hero.

Oliver lost the battle. As soon as our attackers had the slightest bit of control, they had him tied so tight, Oliver's skin reddened at the edge of the ropes.

Oliver's spirit certainly hadn't been broken. He vomited a steady stream of curses until someone placed a rope in his mouth, tying it behind his head in a way that was sure to capture a handful of his hair. Even with that, Oliver made plenty of noise.

Fear held me still. I let Mr. Snowy Hair pick me up and carry me behind the others. If I was going to fight, I'd have to get creative. I knew I had no chance against them.

How long would it be before these people killed us?

As they traversed the forest, they didn't seem to care about the crunch their feet made in the leaves. It wasn't far to their cluster of horses.

Beside the horse, Mr. Snowy Hair adjusted his grip on my arms and pulled another section of rope from his saddlebag. "Can't forget you." His eyes were a mixture of blue and gray, a color so light and piercing, it sent shivers up my spine. His skin was the same; pale enough his blue veins shone through. Likely noticing my stare, he tugged his hat a little lower onto his head and came for me with the rope.

"No, no, no, no!" I tried to pull my arms from his persistent hands, but he had my wrists bound within a few seconds. The bonds weren't nearly as tight as Oliver's. There was no way I could slip my wrists through, but I wouldn't have any marks to remember my capture.

Snowy Man sat me almost delicately on the saddle in front of him. In contrast, Oliver was slung over the back of a horse like a dead man. His back moved with each breath, but every other inch of him was completely still. I could practically see the escape plans rising like smoke from his head. The moment they untied him, I knew he'd explode into another furious attack.

And I would do what I could to help him, even with the pain in my side.

It took me awhile before I found the guts to speak. I was the only one who could get any real answers, after all. "Where are you taking us?" I demanded, trying to keep my voice low.

"The main house," the snowy man said simply.

I squirmed uncomfortably in my seat. "Might I ask why?" I certainly didn't expect an answer.

Oddly enough, he gave me one. "So the boss can decide what to do with ya."

My squirming stopped immediately. "What do you think he'll do?"

The man shrugged against my back. "Oliver shot Da— er . . . Josef." He said the name with a "yo" sound instead of the typical "j."

"He doesn't seem so badly injured, he's riding just fine," I pointed out.

The man behind me shrugged again. "Doesn't mean Johannes will take kindly to it."

I fell silent again as we traveled along. It didn't take long for us to come into a large clearing with a two-story wood-framed house, tiny shed, and a weathered barn nestled deep inside.

Oliver didn't even get the courtesy of using his own two feet to go inside. The young dark-haired man swung a gagged Oliver over his shoulder and waltzed up the steps, across the porch, and right through the front door. I expected to follow him, but instead, Mr. Snowy Hair lifted my wrists and held a knife to the rope.

I flinched as he sliced through, freeing me.

CHAPTER FIFTY-SEVEN
Welks Clan

"Why? Why are you doing this?" I asked, staring at the frayed remnants that lay in the dirt.

He didn't respond. Instead, he caught the reins his father tossed his way and led the four horses into the barn. He wore a loose-fitting long-sleeved shirt and a wide-brimmed hat to shadow his startlingly pale features.

I strained my neck to get a better look at the house, waiting for the noises to begin, for any signs of a struggle. Nothing happened.

Snowy Man started work on the horses, stripping off the saddle and bridle of the one closest to him. He completely ignored me.

"Who are you?" I asked, though I was certain I already knew the answer—the Welks Clan.

"Niklas." He said his name so simply, it surprised me. I hadn't expected him to tell me anything.

I narrowed my eyes at him. It wasn't the answer I had been after, but at least I knew his name. "What are you going to do to me?" My voice was so soft, even I hardly heard it. My mind swam with the images of people being dragged to death behind horses. It'd be an effective way to die, but certainly not one I wished to go through. I remained perched in the saddle, not sure if I was ready to face reality from the hay-covered floor.

Niklas said nothing and rummaged through the tack box for something—a brush, I assumed.

The house remained completely silent. Wouldn't there be signs of Oliver's protest by now? If I took advantage of my current freedom and escaped with the horse, what would he do?

I gnawed on my bottom lip as I thought. I only needed to pluck the reins from Niklas, and then I'd be gone. But wouldn't he be after me with another horse?

I watched as Niklas's fingers folded around what he'd been hunting for. I didn't have time to plan anything out—I needed to act.

I reached forward before I could think through anything else that could go wrong. I pressed my thighs against the horse to hang on. In a mere moment, I grasped what part of the reins I could and yanked.

Instantly, I knew how idiotic my plan had been. Everything was off balance. I fell forward, thighs not strong enough to keep me in place. I fell in a glorious mess of skirts and hair over the horse's head. I careened into a pile of hay, a volley of laughter coming from Niklas.

A spasm of pain careened throughout my abdomen. I gripped my middle and breathed deeply. When the agony subsided, I scrambled up to sit, brushing as much hay from my hair and skirt as I could. "If you're not going to kill me, just let me go!"

He grinned. "If you're planning on escaping, you might want to know . . . I could have you on the ground in a matter of seconds." Without another word, he went back to work, brushing the closest horse.

I watched his every move. Nothing seemed threatening about the way he stood, hip cocked to one side, shoulders slumped. He didn't even seem to be watching me. It felt like some kind of horrible dare, one I was sure I couldn't win. "You're from the Welks Clan, aren't you?"

He glanced at me out of the corner of his light eye and stood straight, hands coming together in a slow, mocking clap. "Good job, you paid attention."

I scrambled to stand, using the stall door for assistance. I likely looked similar to a furious hen, covered in as much hay as I was. Many, many retorts spun through my head, but I settled on a more practical option. "Where's my cane?"

Turning his attention back to his work, he pointed at where my cane rested against the wall. Apparently, it had come to the barn on another horse.

"Might I have it back?"

Niklas chuckled and made a show of looking the piece of wood up and down. "Why not? It'll at least give me *some* excitement if you try to escape." Instead of looking at me, his eyes locked on the house in the distance.

Still, there were zero signs of life.

I felt woozy over his apparent longing. He *wanted* to be included in the inevitable torture. "You're jealous you don't get to participate in the mutilation of my husband?" I crossed my arms and shot him my best challenging glare.

He said nothing. He only sauntered behind the three horses and tossed the cane at my feet. He didn't even have the decency to hand it directly to me.

"Some gentleman you are," I muttered, stooping to grab it from the hay.

"Just remember," he crooned as he made his way back to the tack box, "if you take one step in that direction, I'll have you to the floor faster than you could spit." He eyed me levelly, his stare ensuring I understood every bit of the threat.

The rebellious side of me wanted to stick out my tongue, but I didn't dare. I had to at least try to play it safe. "What are they doing to him in there?"

Absolutely no response. He didn't even give me so much as a glance. I narrowed my eyes further, trying to get my glare to sink beneath his skin. It didn't.

With a sigh, I leaned against the stall to wait for his guard to drop. Or something. But he already seemed so relaxed. How would I know if that ever happened?

I knew he was right. I wouldn't make it out of the barn. But who would I be if I didn't at least *try* to save Oliver? If I got into the forest and hid for long enough, perhaps I could sneak in after nightfall and get him out?

Even I knew how idiotic that idea was, but it was all I could come up with.

Niklas didn't alter his movements. He brushed the first horse, turned him out, then stripped the second of her saddle and bridle, and started on her. Not once did he look my way.

If you don't try, you'll wish you did, I told myself. I gripped the cane and took one slow, sideways step toward the door. He didn't react.

Maybe, just maybe, he was too cocky for his own good. He had two horses and half a barn between us, after all.

"I'm obligated to warn you, Petronella—you won't get far." He said the words so quietly, I almost didn't hear them.

My name. "How do you know my name? Do you have the poster?"

He rolled his head lazily in my direction. "Ahh, you lost use of that brain of yours this time. Letters. We are sophisticated enough to communicate through letters."

I wrinkled my nose in confusion. "With whom? I thought you and the Wedmans didn't get along!"

He just raised a shadowed eyebrow, then returned to his work.

"Hey!" I shouted, startling the horse closest to me. Her ears flickered forward and then back, irritated by the sudden noise. "Tell me what's going on? What are they doing to Oliver? What—"

He waved his hand dismissively. "Just try to run already. We both know you will."

With a huff, I leaned against the stall, arms crossed over my chest. My cane dangled from the crook of one arm.

He smirked, which only made me all the more angry.

This went on for quite some time, me staring at him, him working diligently with the horses. The only thing that pushed me to action came from the house. A crash, then shouting.

Oliver.

The torture had begun.

If I had acquired any cane expertise, this was when I needed it the most.

I raced for the door in my sloppy fashion. *Foot. Cane. Foot. Cane.* I had to get to the forest. Or inside. Somewhere. Anywhere.

An explosive laugh came from Niklas. I heard his heavy footfalls behind me. It only took him two or three leaps before he had me. Just like his earlier capture, he didn't play nice.

I squealed in protest as I crashed to the ground, turning into whatever kind of devil I could. I elbowed at his face but didn't manage to hit anything. He grabbed my elbow and shoved my forearm hard against my back. He did the same with the other arm as soon as I moved it.

I tried to yank away but couldn't get the slightest movement out of anything other than my lower leg. "Let me go! They're going to kill Oliver. I can't just sit here and let that happen!" I pulled harder, pain erupting in both my side and shoulder.

"My goodness, stop before you hurt yourself!" To my complete surprise, he turned his torso and swatted me hard on the rear. It didn't particularly hurt, but it surprised me.

"You . . . you indecent son of a bitch!" I shouted, squirming all the harder.

He laughed. "I told you I'd take you down. I *didn't* tell you what I'd do once I got you there."

A feminine clearing of the throat came from the barn door. Both of us froze, eyes slithering to the young woman standing there, hands crossed over her middle, eyebrows raised. She had the same prominent features as Niklas, but long, dark brown, curly hair instead.

"Ah, rollin' around in the hay. Wait till I tell Da you've got a taste for discarded Wedmans." She laughed at her own joke.

We both spoke at the same time.

"You wouldn't—" Niklas sounded like a snake, ready to strike.

I moved to defend myself. "He didn't—" I knew full well what she implied, and that would *never* happen.

"Ah, well then, better stop ridin' her like a horse and bring her inside. Ma refuses to have her under our roof lookin' like she . . ." Her shoulders rose in a shrug. "Well, like she had a rumble in the hay." She smirked at me.

Immediately, I hated her.

Niklas dismounted and yanked me up to stand, arms still pinned to my back. I gasped as the sudden movement pulled at my side.

"Gosh, don't be rough with her, for heaven's sakes. Look, she's already bleeding!" The girl shook her head, tsking her tongue.

I glanced at myself. Sure enough, a spot of crimson had made its way onto the front of my dress—right where the infection had tried to settle in.

The girl didn't care enough to question it. "But then, she married that bastard, so perhaps she *likes* a little pain." She moved right to me, blue eyes sparkling as she scanned my own. I felt like a fox trapped by a hound, she was so much taller than me.

"Poor thing, she's scared." She ran her finger down my jawline, then tapped my nose. Without thinking, I slammed my head against hers. She sprang back, holding her forehead. I fell back into Niklas's tight hold, starlight trailing across my vision.

"Damn bitch!" the girl shouted. "You'd best be sure I tell—"

"Oh, hush," Niklas snapped. "She's not supposed to have a scratch on her, remember? I'll take her to the house. You finish with the horses." He scooped me into his arms like a child, the cane cradled in my lap.

"*You're* meant to do the horses," she pointed out.

"Well, she can't very well walk, now can she? Can *you* carry her the whole way?"

"Most likely I could—"

"Let's not find out." And Niklas took his chance and escaped the barn.

I glared over my shoulder at the brown-haired girl. Fury seemed to rise from every stray curl on her head as she glared at her retreating brother.

Bitch.

CHAPTER FIFTY-EIGHT
Thump

In the kerfuffle, Niklas's hat had fallen from his head, revealing more than just his sharp nose and high cheekbones. His skin was the color of porcelain. But that wasn't what made me stare. His eyes were more than just an unnaturally light blue. With the help of the sunlight, they were nearly translucent, almost red.

"What?" he demanded, glaring at me. His eyes were squinted, as though the sun's onslaught hurt. "You afraid I'm gonna sprout fangs?"

"N-No . . ." I managed.

He carried me straight to the porch, never once looking back at his furious sibling. When we reached the door, he squatted a little, brushing the handle with his fingers.

"Uh . . ." He cleared his throat and shifted me in his arms, trying to get a good hold of the handle again. "Can you . . . ?"

A forbidden laugh sprang from my lips at the sign of weakness. "Nope."

He didn't move. "Please?"

I fixed my eyes on his face and batted my lashes in what I hoped was some form of mock innocence.

"Damn woman . . ." he grumbled. He bit the corner of his lip and adjusted himself little by little to get to the handle and finagle it open. "Thanks," Niklas said bitterly. Once inside, he flung the door shut with his foot, the house shaking as it slammed back home.

He hesitated, head cocked to the side like a dog, as he listened for any repercussions. When none came, he turned on his heel and waltzed down the hall into the kitchen.

Either the house had been holding the noise captive, or the events had only just begun. All the shouting—accentuated by the occasional grunt—came from behind the closed door across the way. Only a few more feet, and I'd be in the same room as Oliver.

My heart skipped a beat. I gripped Niklas's shirt and pulled, forcing him to look at me. "Are they going to kill him?" I demanded, not sure I wanted to know the answer. Were they going to kill *me*? And why would they choose to do the torture inside of the main house?

In a mix between a shrug and a stretch, Niklas pulled his shirt free of my hands. He nodded at the metal bathtub against the wall. "Might as well be clean for his funeral, in case they do."

He set me in the middle of the floor and stalked to the counter. From their hiding place behind a worn cookbook and pile of childlike drawings, he withdrew two sheathed knives. Not bothering to glance at me, he then moved to the curtain and removed yet another one from its hiding place. He did this several more times, ending up with an armload of blades.

I stared, mouth hanging open like a dead fish.

"I'll be right outside the door." The corner of his lip twitched into an almost smile at my expression before he slipped out of the room.

I stared after him, more confused than I had been before.

"Let's take our prisoner, clean her up, then use her as bait. Or kill her," I muttered. It made zero sense.

The door to the hallway opened suddenly, making me jump so hard I almost fell over. Another woman came inside, this one also tall and with brown hair, but about the same age as my own mother. She had beautiful hazel eyes and a gentle face with an elegantly rounded jaw. She looked so kind, motherly.

I still didn't trust her.

"I'm sorry about their hospitality," she said, gliding to the tub and setting a towel, a bar of soap, and a clean chemise beside it. "Niklas and Sofia will harass each other until their dying day." She tsked her tongue. "Now, I can't completely leave you be, don't want you getting into more trouble than necessary, but I'll sit over here." She smiled sweetly and moved to sit in a chair by the door.

From that pile that had contained two knives, she produced a book, crossed one knee over the other, and let herself be drawn into the novel.

I stared, just as confused as before.

"Hurry, dear. Your man will be gettin' cleaned up before he's allowed to eat too. If he ever stops his fighting, that is." She chuckled to herself and shook her head.

Channeling that startled fish yet again, I opened and closed my mouth. They weren't planning on murdering the two of us?

"What?" I finally asked.

"I made a room for you two upstairs. Moved Niklas in with August, though he was none too pleased. Once you're all clean, I'll let you go upstairs and rest. You've had a long journey, I'd assume."

I nodded dumbly.

"You'll be quite safe. Though your man *certainly* hasn't figured that out yet."

Cautiously, I undid the top button of my bodice. "Maybe because they tied him up like a criminal?"

She didn't glance at me, only stayed inside her book. "If we hadn't done that, there'd be many more injuries." Another crash punctuated her words and she sighed, slamming the book shut in her lap. "Why they couldn't take this outside, I'll never know!"

I flinched at each thump from the neighboring room. Fists against skin? A stomping foot? I couldn't be sure of what went on. The grunts didn't make it sound pleasant.

This woman seemed reasonable. And I needed to talk with Oliver to find out what was *really* going on. Decision made, I redid the button. "Please let me go to him. He'll listen to me."

Her elegant head rose to watch me. To my surprise, sympathy shone back from her eyes, accompanied by a sad smile. "Their rivalry goes back generations. As far as he knows, you're in the same position he's in."

I took a step toward the door, but she held her hand up to halt my progress. "And that's what we want," she continued. "He should be fine once he submits a little. You'll be fine too, just don't interfere." Like the tip of a knife, her eyes narrowed to angry slits and her voice hardened on the last words.

"The water's still hot. Not a common thing in this household, y'know. Take advantage of it while you can." She gestured to the tub with her book, her thumb tucked inside to hold her place. "I don't want to threaten you. I want you to feel safe. However, I'm not against forcing you in there if I have to. You smell like you belong in a barn."

I hesitated, ears trained to the struggling across the hall. I wanted to believe her, I really did. But with him fighting so hard in the other room, I couldn't be sure. But I couldn't exactly squeeze past and break into the room. And it would be nice to get the dirt out of my hair.

My fingers traveled to my scalp, worming their way under the tangled mess. I sighed as the water teased the dirt and grime free.

You can't do much yet, anyway.

I went to work on the buttons on my bodice, each of my movements a jerky statement. Just in case she looked up, I wanted her to know I wasn't happy about this arrangement.

Her shoulders vibrated with a concealed chuckle as she returned to her reading, leaving me to bathe in peace.

Once undressed, I sat on the edge of the tub, letting my hand travel the length of my wound, feeling the rough stitches. The skin was still red and swollen toward the bottom, though the ache wasn't nearly as bad as before.

"When did that happen?" the woman asked, her voice that of a cautious mother.

I removed my hand as if I'd been stung. I didn't want to *think* of Donnell. Let alone tell her about my own torture. Not now. Not ever.

"It's been a while," I said shortly, letting my body slide into the water. Partially to preserve a little modesty, partially to avoid dealing with it.

The water was a comforting hug, welcoming and cozy. My entire body shuddered into relaxation as I let it caress my skin.

"It doesn't look good." To my relief, she didn't move from her seat.

"No," I admitted. Another thump reverberated from across the hall, making me flinch. I breathed deeply, fighting to get my body to return to its relaxed state. *Worry about your side later. It's just oozing . . . it'll be fine.*

"Would you like me to take a look at it?" Again, her voice was kind. It only added to the swirling confusion in my brain.

"No!" I snapped, much harder than necessary, so I quickly added, "Thank you."

She went silent again, the tension ebbing throughout the room. She closed the book with a gentle pop and stood to rummage through one of the cabinets. I knew her goal. I let out an irritated sigh and rested my head against the copper wall.

"It's *fine*," I insisted, more harsh than needed.

"You need to realize something," she said firmly as she made her way to the edge of the tub, a small pair of sewing scissors in one hand, a rag and alcohol in the other. "We don't plan on hurting you."

I laughed bitterly. "Don't *plan* on hurting me? Instead, you're torturing Oliver to death in the other room."

She gave me that same sympathetic smile and patted the curled lip of the tub. I didn't move.

"The clan's culture is hard to get used to, I know. But some things, like trespassing, are simply dealt with this way." She patted it again, but to no avail.

"Will they kill him?"

"I don't know."

I shivered. "Will they kill me?" When she hesitated, I turned to look straight in her face, searching. "Is that a yes?"

"No," she said firmly. "Do you think I'd be sitting here, trying to get you to get out of the tub so I can *help* you, if we planned on killing you? Do you think you'd be in this room *at all* if we meant to kill you?"

She had a point. I set my jaw, teeth grinding. "Give us back to the Wedmans?"

A spasm of confusion crossed over her face. "We heard you were on the run, but that's all we knew. There will be a lot of negotiations in that room regarding what to do with the two of you. In the meantime, you will be treated as a guest as long as you're in *my* household."

Her no-nonsense voice made me relax again, but only a little. "Taken care of by beating him?"

She let out a rough sigh and rested her forehead in her hand. "Procrastinating on letting me clean that up will get you nowhere."

"I'm not procrastinating. For once, in all this horse—" I cut off, deciding not to completely lose my dignity and curse. "*Mess*, I'd like to know what's going on. Why is he in there, being tortured for all I know, if they're negotiating?"

"He will be able to explain that a lot better himself. There are clan rules. If you're caught on someone's land without permission, there are certain things that happen. This is one of those things. The negotiation comes afterward. Now, sit up here before I call one of the boys in to make you."

I shouldn't have been surprised by the sudden threat, but it still made me stare in shock. "But I'm naked!"

She raised one eyebrow—a challenge.

"Fine," I muttered. I gripped the water-warmed metal and pulled myself to the edge of the tub. "Before you start, I don't know your name."

She smirked. "Eva."

CHAPTER FIFTY-NINE

The Door

Her delicate fingers worked with impressive speed. I had to admit to myself, she likely caused much less pain than Oliver ever could have. That didn't mean I didn't find myself yelping whenever she pressed the liquor-soaked rag to my abdomen.

My fingernails did their best to dig into the rim of the tub, and my teeth made little marks under my lip.

"It could be worse," Eva said. "If you gave it a few more days . . ." She trailed off, shaking her head at the mere thought.

When she was finished, Eva left me for her book. I sank back into the water, relief washing over every inch of me. My hands shook a little less as I worked the hay and dirt out of my hair.

When an enormous thump echoed through the house, followed by a grunt, another thump, and an anguished scream, I froze. The sound was not one of pain, but one of stubborn energy. Anger.

I couldn't run to him, naked and soaked. Besides, I couldn't even make it to the door before Eva had me. My heart quick-ened to the point that I could practically hear it. The world spun. Desperate for calm, I ducked all the way under the water and held my breath.

He'd be fine. He'd be fine. He was strong enough to withstand whatever they did to him.

Wasn't he?

But the scream . . .

I stayed under the water as long as I could manage, only coming up when it threatened to force itself into my lungs. Momentarily, I wondered if I would welcome it. Instead of entertaining such thoughts, I popped out with a little gasp for air and glanced in the direction of Eva. Though her face remained pointed at her book, her eyes were focused on me.

The bath gave me time to create a plan. I certainly couldn't do much, but I could cause a scene, hopefully let him know I was alive. Perhaps I could even see if *he* was alive. The house had gone silent after the last angry scream, followed by several more thumps.

I highly doubted that they would keep me in the kitchen until they were finished with Oliver. Unless they took me back outside, they'd have no choice but to take me into the hall. And, as long as they let me walk, I could grab the door handles and wreak what havoc I could.

I dressed in an old but clean chemise Eva offered me. She didn't hand me a clean dress, but it sounded like she planned on taking me straight to bed, anyway.

Like a child, cleaned up and sent to bed without dinner, I thought bitterly as she wrapped a knitted shawl around my shoulders and stood back to critique her work.

"Much better. Now we won't have to worry about washing the sheets in the morning." She scooped up my cane from the corner and turned with a swish of skirts for the door. "Niklas, we're ready to go upstairs!"

The winter man came strutting in. He grinned, taking his time to look me up and down.

Eva, I would consider liking. Him? Certainly not. I narrowed my eyes in his direction, hoping it would scare him out of approaching.

It didn't.

He reached to pick me up, his fingertips brushing my arm as I leapt back. I narrowly avoided crashing into the tub. Unbidden images flashed through my vision, ghosts of pain springing to life in my torso.

"I'll walk!" I wasn't sure if I said it out loud, or if the words halted somewhere deep inside my mind. I tried again. "Please let me walk!" If he carried me, I didn't want to know where my brain would wander. I balled my hands into fists at my sides, my fingernails digging into my palms. If I couldn't stay calm, I wouldn't be able to lunge for the door.

Eva held up her hand to stop him as he advanced for me again. "Let her do it."

Niklas hesitated, obviously irritated about the decision. He crouched to stare me straight in the eyes. I did my best not to flinch away, though the bile rose in my throat.

"There are rules. Aside from the obvious, 'don't run' and 'don't go across the hall,' you have to be quiet. Can you walk quietly with that . . . thing?" He flicked his finger at the cane.

Being quiet was the last thing I planned, but I nodded anyway. "Yes."

"You're not gagging her—she's a guest," Eva cautioned, likely reading his mind. Maybe, just maybe I could grow to like her.

Niklas glared at me for a few more seconds. "Fine. Though it'll be *much* faster if I just carry her up the stairs."

"She's a *guest*, Niklas," Eva repeated, sounding like a mother on her last thread of sanity.

Niklas sighed deeply. "Fine, just stay quiet." He loosely held my arm and led the way to the door.

To distract him from the way my limbs trembled, and myself from the unbidden memories, I spoke. "What happened to 'I can take you down in ten seconds or less'?" I did my best to mimic his cocky attitude.

His lip twitched in a toothy smile. "Oh, I certainly could. But in this case, one step is one step too many."

He moved into the hallway first, likely to block the entrance to the forbidden room. Everything I *didn't* want him to do.

I went completely still, trying to adjust my plan. He watched me, waiting. I didn't have time to rethink my strategy, so I did the first thing that came to mind.

I tripped.

Sure enough, Niklas must've been trained to be a gentleman before a killer. He reached to help me up, still somewhat blocking the door, but not as completely as before. The fall had brought me less than two feet from my target.

I fought to remain calm and let him help me up. Once there, I took a moment to right the shawl around my shoulders. "Thank you." It took everything in me not to look at the doorknob.

Heavens, this won't work. Three . . . please don't hurt me . . . two . . . I trained my eyes on his bare feet. *Don't look up . . . one!*

I lunged for the doorknob, throwing my entire body weight into the door. Niklas was certainly quick, but he expected me to behave like a sane person and turn the knob, push the door, *then* walk through. Instead, he got a suicide mission.

He gripped my forearm before I finished my fall. He held it so tightly I was vaguely aware of the imminent bruising. The door slammed open, propelled by my weight as I crashed to the floor, dragging Niklas behind me.

But it didn't open the whole way.

One of the many things I didn't plan on was someone standing guard directly inside. I had just enough time to realize my folly before Niklas succumbed to my dead weight, careening like a downed tree over me. My arm twisted behind me with his fall, and I saw red.

"No!" I shrieked, fear trickling in to replace the small amount of bravery I'd found. If I was going to sacrifice whatever good treatment I had received, I at least wanted to get something out of it.

The other brown-haired giant, August, emerged from his hiding place on the other side of the door, effectively blocking any view I could've had. Like a trapped animal, I moved my head back and forth, trying to catch a glimpse of something, anything, between his legs. Any sign of Oliver. I got nothing but bookshelves and the open-mouthed face of Josef in the distance.

Before I could even determine if he had changed his blood-stained shirt, August wrenched me from Niklas and threw me over his shoulder. The door slammed shut behind him.

"Really?" He nudged the collapsed Niklas with the toe of his boot. "You couldn't handle a *crippled girl*?"

I didn't give Niklas a chance to respond. I'd just given up any chance I had of remaining a guest, and I wouldn't go down without a fight. I kicked my good leg as hard as I could. "Let me go! If you killed him, I swear—"

August swung me off his shoulder like an axe, moving so fast it knocked the air out of my lungs. Without care, he slammed me flat on the floor and pressed his hand over my mouth. His palm was so large, it easily could've covered my face. The entire man looked like a giant.

Like a candle dropped into a lake, my bravery extinguished itself. I didn't move.

"Careful, August," Eva said from her post in the kitchen doorway.

The dark-haired giant ignored her and glared straight into my soul. "Stay quiet, and we won't have to go through with the *original* plan." He held the stare until he was satisfied with the terror in my eyes, then swung me back over his shoulder. He was so rough, it made me cough.

As if nothing happened, he trudged up the stairs.

I craned my neck to try to get a good view of Oliver, but the door was already shut. I reached for the holster on August's belt, but it was out of reach. With a primal scream, I banged my fist into the small of his back. He flinched slightly, so I did it again, this time adding in a hit from my elbow and the other fist. I flailed against his back, imagining each little bone of his spine.

He did nothing until we reached a small room upstairs. Unceremoniously, he swatted my rear hard enough to make me yelp.

"You barbarians!" I shouted.

"If we're barbarians, you're a spoilt brat. A good whoopin' would do you good, I reckon." He dropped me on the bed.

"You wouldn't *dare*," I snapped, but quickly thought better. I scrambled up to where I sat on my knees, as though it would help me leap from one side of the bed to the other just in case.

His eyes turned to fire, ready to pounce. They were trained to kill; beating someone would likely be considered *fun*.

"August," Eva chided from the doorway. "Even though her hollering and screaming would *certainly* assist your father in getting information downstairs—now that he's bound to've heard her—it wouldn't help in the long run."

August slowly shook his head, eyeing me from his peripheral. "Don't *make* me come back in here."

It took everything in me not to react. I wanted to leap onto his back and jab my thumbs into his eyes . . . Or more likely, throw a pillow at his back. Something. Anything. But all I did was wrap my arms around myself as the room turned cold.

Eva shut the door behind him and came to sit at the foot of the bed. "I would advise against irritating the boys too much. They were, unfortunately, trained to require submission. And they will act before they think." She smiled at me. I didn't return it.

"The worst of it will be over soon, as long as he didn't see you." She added the last part with a shake of her head. "I'll go make you something to eat."

"I'm not hungry." More memories flooded my brain. I used to say that very thing to my father as an irritated adolescent. I clutched at the sudden pain in the pit of my stomach.

"All right, then. I'll leave you to rest. Someone will come get you if you're needed." With care, she stood and made her trek back to the door.

"If I'm needed?"

Her smile turned sympathetic again. "As long as he didn't see you, no one should come get you. Don't worry yourself over it."

I stared at the door long after she left, mouth hanging open. Did she mean what I thought she did?

The struggling had resumed downstairs, each thump more violent than the last. Each yell belonged to Oliver.

Emotions washed over my body, the remaining anger overtaken by exhaustion and fear. With a shaking sob, I gave in and curled into a ball of terrified tears.

What was their plan? Why would they bother to treat me kindly but beat him? Perhaps they were torturing him for information on his home clan, leaving me up in the room to become a future wife for one of their sons.

I'd bite very specific appendages off before either of those barbarians had a chance to do anything to me. *That* was for certain.

CHAPTER SIXTY

In the Loop

The sun was long gone by the time the bedroom door clicked open. I barely heard it. I had since cried all my tears, but I had never moved from my tiny ball at the foot of the bed. I shivered there with my eyes glued to the shadows as they traversed the ceiling.

I flinched at his weight as he joined me on the bed. His breathing was slow, even, familiar. He moved with care, crawling under the blankets, then wrapping his arms around my middle to pull me to him. The touch pulled at the wound, but he was gentle.

He tucked me under the blankets, curling around me like a shield. Even though I knew, without a shadow of a doubt, who he was, I didn't dare believe it until he spoke.

"What did they do to you?" Oliver whispered into the space right below my ear.

Relief flooded through my body, and I rolled over, wrapping my arms around him. He froze for a long moment before disentangling himself and crawling out of bed again. I tried to hold on to his arm, but he gave me a reassuring pat on my hand. He rummaged around on the nightstand for a candle, lit it, and motioned for me to get out of bed.

I did as he asked, not daring to look him fully in the face. He certainly looked like the loser of a fistfight. Bruises littered his body, most still in the process of forming, red and swollen. I just didn't want to see if they had done anything that wouldn't heal.

Oliver held the candle near my head and touched the outline of my jaw, turning my face one way, and then the other. He took his time, examining each of my fingers, my wrist, my collarbone.

"They didn't hurt me," I whispered.

He raised an eyebrow and poked at the bruise on my forearm. "What is this, then?"

I flinched. "I tried to get in to you, and they grabbed me. Not the same as . . ." I trailed off, gesturing to his own bruised cheek. "Are you okay?"

His smile was stiff, his lip split. He scooped me up, my thighs gripping his torso. He set me on the bed that way, leaning over my body, his bare chest a hair's width from my own. "I'll be fine, they fed me."

They'd made him bathe too, that was obvious. He smelled of lavender and lye. But why would they beat someone, then take care of them?

I squirmed out from under him and curled into my own spot on the bed. "How? What? I don't understand any of this. Did you know they weren't going to kill you?"

"No," he admitted, getting into his spot and pulling the blankets up to his waist. "They still might, but probably won't unless I force their hand. We're safe for now."

I expected him to say more, to let his hands roam over my body, but his eyes closed and a slow snore rumbled from his chest.

"Abso*lutely* not!" I snapped, sitting and shoving him hard against the shoulder. He jerked awake, looking at me with wide, bloodshot eyes. "What happened?" I demanded.

"I fell asleep, that's what happened. It's after two, you should—"

"No!" I crossed my arms. "What happened to *you*? *Why* are we safe? What's going on?"

His voice came out slurred. "We should be fine. Are you sure they didn't hurt you?"

"Bastard slapped my ass, but otherwise—"

Oliver interrupted me with a coughing sort of laugh. "Sounds like something you'd get into."

I set my jaw and glared in the candlelight. I had expected him to be upset about that. "Well, it certainly wasn't acceptable." Before I could ask another question, his snoring resumed.

I poked him in the ribs, hard. "I'll get my answers, mister," I grumbled. The only response I got was an even more violent snore as the moonlight traced across the room.

"Good morning, you two!" came the cheery voice from the doorway. I cracked one eye open at the intrusion. It had taken me a long time to fall asleep, and the sun was only just barely up.

"We have things to do today, so come on! Get on up!" Eva clapped her hands sharply, the harsh noise making Oliver flinch beside me.

"I brought this for you to wear today until we can get you something of your own." She held a lightly flowered skirt, matching bodice, and a pile of underthings in my direction. When I reached for it, she pulled back as if she were teasing a dog. "There's a cost."

"Here we go . . ." Oliver muttered.

"Put this on your wound. It'll help. Then replace the bandages. I'll check on it tonight." Eva tossed a small container of ointment onto the bed. "After breakfast, Johannes and Josef will talk with you"—she turned her attention to Oliver, practically staring into his soul—"in the sitting room. I wouldn't keep them waiting."

He sat up, showing no sign of shying under her fierce gaze. "Yes ma'am," he said.

"Okay, hurry on up!" She gave me a loving smile—a shocking change from the look she'd fixed on Oliver—and disappeared back into the hall. She walked with purpose, whether that was to continue waking the house, make breakfast, or murder an innocent mail carrier, I'd never know.

"We need to clean that out," Oliver said through a yawn. "I know you're nervous, but—"

I shook my head rapidly, my hair flying free of its sloppy braid. "It's already done."

He blinked slowly, taken aback. The utter surprise on his face almost made me laugh. Almost.

"You got a beating, I got bathed, and Eva cleaned my wound." I pulled the side of my chemise up so he could see.

He delicately unwrapped the bandages and peered at the inflamed skin. "It looks a little better," he admitted, running his finger along the edges. It tickled. "You'll have one hell of a scar when it's all said and done."

"Thankfully, no one but you gets to see it." The idea that I'd have the constant reminder on my body for the rest of my life wasn't exactly comforting, but I shoved that thought into a back corner of my mind to deal with later.

As if activated by him dropping my chemise back into place, my stomach growled.

"Come on, I'm hungry." Oliver hopped out of bed a bit too fast, freezing as the pain from the night before caught up with him. He switched to moving like an old man as he pulled on his clothes.

He had a shadow of a bruise forming all along his jawline, and his lips were torn in places, threatening to bleed with every word he said. For every bruise I could see, I was certain there were a good ten more.

"Are you sure we can trust them?" I asked, fingering the edges of my corset.

"Not much of a choice, but I hope so. If they wanted us dead, we would be dead. If they wanted to keep us as bait, ship us off to my family, or anything of the sort, we wouldn't be bathed and put up in their son's room."

He took the corset from me and beckoned me to stand by the bed. I obeyed, shivering as he ran his fingers down my sides to smooth the chemise. Tenderly, he wrapped it around my body. He pressed his body against mine as he wrapped me in a sort of a hug, clicking the busk into place.

His breath tickled the hollow below my ear, sending shivers down my spine. "Yes, there is always the chance that they'll turn against us. But that's what we will be discussing with Johannes today."

I flinched as the pressure from the corset reawakened a bruise. "They won't hand us over to your father or Mr. York if they show up?"

"That's one of the things I'll be discussing with Johannes." He patted my rear before sliding the crinoline over my head and tying it in place.

I shot him a look, my irritation from the previous night sneaking back in. "You don't know much of anything, then? Josef is the man who caught us, right?" He nodded. "Eva is his wife, August and Niklas are their sons." Another nod. "Who is Johannes? And why do they have a girl? I thought that was forbidden?"

"So many questions." He sighed, scrubbing his fist against his temple. "The girl . . ." He took a deep, dramatic breath. "It is technically forbidden." Oliver shrugged. "Some families don't follow the old rules."

"And that's why the Williams Clan had Sara?"

Pain flickered over his face, but he plodded on. "They choose which ones to follow and which ones to ignore. My clan followed every rule. Sure, there were mistakes made, but they came with their consequences. The Welks have a . . ." He hesitated, looking to the ceiling for the right word. "Freer way of life."

It sounded nice, but I wasn't sure I wanted to tell him that. "And Johannes?"

Oliver started to work on the buttons of my bodice. "He's the leader of the clan. He makes the final call."

I fidgeted. "And he didn't have a say yesterday?"

"Oh, he did," Oliver assured with a bitter laugh. "He was there the entire time they beat me. But left directly afterward. Said it was getting late and he'd deal with me in the morning. Told Josef he knew what to do."

My mouth was dry, my stomach nearly queasy with both hunger and nerves. "Will I like this Johannes?"

Oliver laughed. "If you have anything against anyone else in this clan, I'm sure you'll hate him."

I wrinkled my nose. "Well, Eva is nice. Everyone else . . ." I shook my head quickly. "No."

He smiled and kissed my forehead. "Well, just try not to anger any of them today, and you'll likely be fine."

"Will I get to go with you?" I gazed up at him, contorting my face into what I hoped was an innocent, pleading sort of look.

"No," he said firmly. "But I can assure you, I'll keep you safe."

"And you?"

He didn't answer my question, just handed me my cane. "I'm hungry, let's go."

"And what if that big one, August, decides to follow through with my challenge from last night?" I hadn't realized how much I was worried about it until the words slipped out of my mouth.

Oliver froze and turned to watch me closely. "And that challenge was . . . ?"

I felt the heat rise to my cheeks. "I hit him, so he swatted me like a child. When he threatened a full-on whoopin', I told him, 'You wouldn't dare.'"

He tried to hold it in, his lip twitching a few times, but in the end, Oliver fell into a laughing fit. "He won't touch you unless you actively provoke him. Yesterday's events don't count. Just don't piss anyone off today, okay?"

Oliver and I sat as still as a couple of unused boards at the dinner table, surrounded by the entire Welks Clan. At first, Eva was the only one who paid us any attention. The tension was so thick, I thought it would choke me. The men at the table exchanged wordless glances, telling me exactly what I didn't want to know—no one knew if we'd be there by evening.

Johannes came to the table last. He looked like anything *but* a clan leader. His body was just as lean as his family's, but instead of being made of muscle, he sagged. Bones jutted from his shoulders, obvious even under his shirt. To say he was ill was an understatement. But even that didn't catch me as off guard as the sight of his wheelchair.

I wondered if the chair and sickness combined gave me enough of an advantage. Perhaps I could outrun this one.

"Petronella, this is Johannes," Eva said, standing to assist him to the table. He waved her away like a fly.

"I'm old, not dead, woman!" The harsh Swedish accent should have made sense, considering how they said their names. It still managed to shock me.

Eva backed away, hands half-raised in mock surrender. "Two pancakes or one?"

He paused, eyeing both me and Oliver with a look that could be read as either hate or suspicion. "Two. Looks like I'll need all the extra energy today."

Eva flopped a couple onto his plate and returned it to him wordlessly.

Like a starving inmate, he cut off a chunk of pancake and shoved it straight into his mouth. "As I recall, the two of you are no longer in good standing with the Wedmans." He looked up from his meal, staring straight at Oliver with a look that contained nothing short of a threat. "Though, that's all you gave up in the end."

Oliver inhaled, slow and deep as he prepared to speak. He never got the chance.

"Johannes, give them just this hour of peace before starting that interrogation up again," Eva scolded, sitting in her designated spot beside her daughter.

The old man swiveled to face her. "It's *my* house, *my* clan. I'll do as I please, woman!"

It didn't faze her. "That's all well and good, but it's *my* kitchen. While our guests are in here, they are under *my* protection."

Surprisingly, Johannes simply snorted and shoved a bite of pancake into his mouth.

Eva wasn't done with him. "If you want jurisdiction of this kitchen, you'll be takin' on the cooking. I assume you'd still want that roast for dinner?" She stared him down, clearly the winner of the battle.

He ignored her admonishments. "Of course, we'll discuss things further after breakfast. Eva, did you make coffee?"

"I'll get it," Sofia said, pushing back from the table and hurrying to fix him a cup. "I'm assuming you had a good night, *Farfar?*"

Johannes shot her a glare as he took the steaming metal mug from her hands. "There's only so well you can sleep with an enemy under your roof." That glare slithered its way to us. I squirmed, poking at my forgotten pancake with my fork.

"I doubt he'll do anything at this point," Josef chimed in. "He has the girl to worry about."

A small smile crossed Johannes's face. "Ah, those good old days. It's amazing what a girl can change in a young man's life."

Oliver smirked but quickly hid it with a pancake.

"Are you not hungry, dear?" Eva asked, nodding at my plate.

In all honesty, I had forgotten to take any bites while eavesdropping. "Oh! Yes, sorry." I took a cautious bite, planning to eat like a lady. Partially to maintain appearances in front of these strangers, and partially because my stomach swirled. My body had other ideas. The moment my stomach got a taste of the breakfast, it took everything I had not to shovel the entire meal into my mouth.

CHAPTER SIXTY-ONE

Safe

They whisked Oliver off as soon as he finished his plate. He didn't even have the chance to get the few remaining crumbs into his mouth, though he certainly tried to shovel it all in.

He wrapped me in a hug, kissing me firmly on the lips. "You're safe, I promise. I'll find you later."

It hurt my heart to let him follow the other men into that library across the hall. All the what-ifs swirled in my mind so fast I couldn't discern one over the other.

"If they were gonna kill him, you'd already be dead," Sofia said bitterly. "You're fine."

"Sofie's right," Eva said, giving her daughter a narrowed, warning glance. "She could've said it in a gentler way, but she's still correct. The only thing Oliver was at risk of was being . . ." She hesitated, staring up at the ceiling as she thought of the right way to say it. "Being roughed up just a little. For information, you understand. But don't worry, you being here makes that go much faster."

"How would my being here help at all?" I asked. I pushed from the table to take my plate to the sink, eyes focused on the floor.

Sofia leaned against the counter, arms crossed. "It means somethin's wrong in that clan, that's what. None of *them* would bring their girl into enemy territory."

I shivered. *Being in enemy territory wasn't our plan.* "If you were a different clan, would you . . ."

"Have killed you?" Sofia finished for me. "Depends on what information you had. You trade the right information for your life, y'know? Yesterday was a test for him, see if he'd break, see if he'd fight for you. We'd watch and learn. As expected, he'd fight for you—that meant we have leverage. If he played the wrong card—" She ran her finger ominously across her neck, laughing at whatever horrified expression came over my face.

"Sofia, go work on the garden!" Eva snapped, shoving a basket into her hands.

"Not much's growin' out there this late!" Sofia protested.

"Then work on clearing it. Do *something* outside of my kitchen!"

Sofia didn't argue more. She turned on her heel and stalked out, giving me one final, threatening glare before the screen door slammed behind her.

Eva patted my hand where it rested on the counter. "What questions do you have for me?"

I watched through the window as Sofia grasped one of the dead tomato plants and yanked. That woman had more strength than I ever wanted to play with. "What are they discussing in there?"

Eva plopped a sponge into my hand and went to pour water on the dishes. "They're discussing what to do now. We already knew you were running from the Wedman Clan, we just didn't know *why*. Now we do. We also now know where the two of you stand with them. Neither of you wish to go back. Besides, he's officially cut ties with his family by telling us anything. He did protest some on that, though we expected that. Which is why we kept the two of you apart. He assumed you were in a similar position, and would say anything to keep you safe." She shrugged as though it was just a normal, daily occurrence.

They'd used me as bait to get the information they wanted. I bristled at the thought. "What *will* you do with us?" I asked, halfheartedly scrubbing at a stubborn spot on the pan.

"I don't know," she admitted. "But I assume you'll be here for a while."

I hesitated a moment longer, watching as Sofia tackled an okra plant. Though, with its height, it looked more like a tree. She gripped it so tightly that her muscles popped into view under her sleeves.

When I spoke again, my voice was nearly a whisper. "Will you hold us here until you can give us back to them?"

Eva chuckled, a dark sound. "Nope. And I'm sure of that. If we take you in, it'll wreak more havoc on their side than if we gave you back."

I nodded firmly, still scrubbing the same pan, even though it was already spotless. "What does 'taking us in' mean to you, then?"

"That's what the men'll be figurin' out now. We won't let you go just yet. Oliver's background is enough to keep us on guard. But that doesn't mean it isn't a possibility in the future. We'll see what they decide." She took the pan from me and dunked it in the rinse water. "You're safe here, Petronella. I promise."

"You can call me Nella," I whispered.

Maybe first impressions weren't to be trusted. Perhaps we were actually safe with them.

Not a sound came from the library all day. No one even emerged for lunch. As far as I knew, no one came out at all. The lack of crashes and grunts made me relax a little, but that didn't mean I didn't worry.

Eva kept me busy, asking questions about my family and where I came from, all while doing menial chores. Eventually, Sofia even joined. To my relief, she kept her snide comments to herself. Even so, she watched my every move with her glaring blue eyes. I assumed she watched for hidden tactics of mine. A knife hidden in my bodice, perhaps? I was about as harmless as I could be.

By the time supper rolled around, I felt relatively comfortable in the house. I knew they were right. If they wanted to kill me, I wouldn't have seen sunrise. They wouldn't have bothered to feed me, let alone feed me pancakes at their family's breakfast table.

Even so, when the door finally opened and the men filed out, my heart skipped a beat. Oliver followed, a hint of a smile on his face.

When his eyes caught mine, that smile expanded into a full, childlike grin. He ran to me, lifting me high in the air and crushing me to his chest. "We're safe, Nella. Safe." He said the words over and over, kissing any part of my face he could get to.

Josef cleared his throat. "Figured a Wedman would have more patience than that!" Several laughs from the others echoed his.

Oliver cleared his throat and set me back on the ground. "She's been worried, didn't want her wondering too long."

"*She* was worried, huh?" August laughed. "You seemed mighty worried yourself in there."

"Well, when you feel bruises each time you breathe, you question some things," Oliver shot back.

Josef patted his own forearm, his sleeve bulging from the bandage that hid underneath. "Oh, I understand that."

Point taken, Oliver laughed.

I looked between the men, completely confused. I was really getting sick of being kept in the dark. With the help of my cane, I stood on my tiptoes to whisper in his ear. "What did they decide?"

I wasn't quiet enough. Eva cleared her throat to get our attention. "My kitchen, my rules. Supper first. Discussions later. Come on, I made that roast for you, Johannes."

Johannes rubbed his hands together like a greedy child. "Ah, yes. Worked up quite the appetite!"

The stark difference between him now and his hard, angry self in the morning surprised me.

"Niklas, set the table. August, cut the roast." Eva snapped her fingers, and her sons jumped to action. Seeing that, Sofia grinned.

"'Bout time they pull their own weight 'round here," Sofia teased, grabbing the plates to set the table.

CHAPTER SIXTY-TWO

But . . .

S afe. We were safe. The words were muted in my head, heavy, unreal. It was as if my body were floating on the breeze, ready to go wherever the song took me. The freedom almost made me nauseous.

When had I last felt safe? *Truly* safe? Before my father told us what had happened. Before my father told us what had happened to our money. Before I had to break the news about refusing the engagement. Before we sold my piano.

Before he sold *me.*

I took some effort to back my mind out of that train of thought. We were safe now, and that was all that mattered.

Oliver and I were well behaved all the way up until our bedroom door shut behind us. Almost as soon as it clicked, Oliver tugged at my clothes.

I felt so lightheaded with relief it was hard not to stay strong. "Hold on, hold on!" I giggled, pushing his persistent fingers away from the buttons. "I want to know everything first!"

"Well," he said, sneaking one arm around and popping the top button open. I didn't stop him, letting the fabric balance precariously on my shoulders as he undid one after the other. "We get to stay here—under their protection." Like a viper, he moved in, nipping at my collarbone. I nearly fell back onto the bed from the sheer surprise of it. Smirking, he pushed the fabric from my shoulders. It tumbled toward the floor, catching on the hoops that encircled my hips.

"They'll likely give us a little land so we can have some privacy."

I knew that if I didn't stay strong, I might not ever hear the entire story. I crossed my arms over my corset, blocking him from snapping it open. "But that's not free."

"Well, of course there's a cost. I have to pay them, but they said they'd let me pay it out over time." He paused, hiding his anxious expression by springing another kiss on me, his fingers creeping under mine to fiddle with the clasp.

"Oliver," I whined, backing myself into the bed. "Tell me first!"

He slumped against the bed frame, eyeing me with a mixture of lust and minute irritation. "I'll work for them at the mill. Become part of the clan." He spoke quickly, as though if he said the words fast enough, he could forget about them.

I didn't expect those words to make me flinch. Clan. He'd still be a killer.

"You'll . . ." I fell back onto the comforter, staring at the ceiling. "You'll kill for them."

He grumbled something under his breath. The only thing I caught was, "Least of my worries . . ."

I sat up so fast, the room spun. "You can't trap me in this room like a good, submissive little girl. Not after . . ." I didn't dare say it. If I said the words, the images of what happened would attack yet again. Instead, I motioned wildly at my torso. "Tell me!"

He groaned and moved to crouch in the plush chair by the dresser. He almost looked like a trapped animal, perched on the cushion, ready to spring away the moment the door opened.

"I . . . and you, I suppose . . . can't be a Wedman anymore."

I narrowed my eyes, not understanding. "Meaning?"

His shoulders slumped. This wasn't the part he wanted to share. "Not only do I have to work with their clan, but I can't consider myself part of my home clan. I can't use the Wedman name. And neither can you."

He took a deep, shaky breath.

"This was what took the longest to agree to. Traditionally, I would've been required to take the Welks name, be completely under their clan." He placed his hand over his eyes, rubbing at his temple. "They wouldn't relent. Said their way was the only option, that I didn't have any room to bargain. But it's *my* name, y'know? And the Wedman and the Welks Clans have always been at odds with each other." He took his hand away, staring at me with an expression so vulnerable, so pained, it made me want to rush to his side.

"In the end, we finally agreed that I could take a name of my own choosing. I'll be working for the clan, similar to a son with their own family and holdings. As long as I pay them for the land, that is. Sons usually don't have to do that."

I settled onto the edge of the bed, watching the turmoil of emotions cross his face. Happy, sad, pained, miserable, then back to content.

He'd be losing his last name. His legacy. It was a very important thing to pass on to children, was it not? "Even with how they treated you, it's still your family. I can see how it would be hard."

He nodded. "They brought their conditions up yesterday. I fought them on it." He smirked as though the beating was a fond memory, a badge of honor. "It's where most of the bruises came from."

I traveled to stand beside him, touching his arm so lightly, it made him shiver. "Do you know what name you'll take?" It would be my name as well, after all.

"I don't know yet. It's not something I have to decide right now. But until I do, I have to use theirs when it comes up." He grimaced. "So, I'd rather figure it out soon."

The pain was etched through his cheekbones. A last name was a legacy. I'd always expected to lose mine. Him? That name would always be like gold.

"I'm sorry," I whispered, wrapping my arms around his tense shoulders. He let his knees sink to the cushion, looking a little less like a gargoyle. "Are you sure it's worth it? Would they let us simply pass through?"

He laughed bitterly. "That was what I requested at first. Passing through isn't an option. Either we stay here, go back home, or . . ." He hesitated. "Well, you know. Besides, it wouldn't be safe to take you into the territories, so I didn't push it further. This way, you *will* be safe. If my family comes this far to get us, they'd have to go through the entire Welks Clan. Which, as you might've imagined, spans many other families. Johannes had five or six boys? I can't remember. Each has their own household. They're strong. We'd be safe behind them."

One more question itched at the back of my head. "What if they sneaked onto the land? Like we did? What if one of the other families told them exactly where to find us?"

"Both of those are very possible, and we'll deal with it when it comes. For now, we're as safe as we can be. We have a place to stay, a *safe* place." He gripped my neck and pulled me down into a kiss, not letting me go long enough to get a full breath, let alone ask more questions.

I still tried. "What if—"

"Trust me," he whispered against my lips, reaching back to pull at the ties of the hoop skirt. This took more effort as they hid under the other fabric, but he managed it. Everything fell off in a whoosh, leaving me in a corset, chemise, and stockings.

Perfect for him. He yanked his shirt over his head and threw it heedlessly into the corner of the room. He then set to work on his pants, the buckle of his belt taking just a little more effort than he had likely planned.

I couldn't help but smile at his excitement. My fingers moved deftly against the busk of my corset. Once I was done with it, I let it drop into the pile on the ground.

It was the last thing I managed to get off before he scooped me into his arms, thighs wrapped around his torso. He fell onto the fluffy comforter, me underneath him. The bed creaked ominously as we landed, making both of us pause for just a moment.

He traced little circles on my cheek, his face hovering mere inches from my own. "I plan on taking good care of you. I wouldn't have married you otherwise," he whispered.

I wrapped my arm around his neck and pulled him so close, our noses touched. "I trust you."

"Good," he whispered back, sealing the deal with another kiss. He held it, his tongue tracing my lips delicately, hand traveling down my body to hike the chemise up.

Despite myself, I stiffened at his torturous touch. He was slow, gentle, watching my every move for any sign that he should retreat.

He moved to a crouch, making his way downward, kissing along the line where the white cotton ended before traveling to my navel.

The tender touch made me squirm, but it was certainly nice.

Until his finger touched the wound. He didn't mean to, I'm positive of that. But like a lightning strike, I was destroyed.

"Stop!" I yelped, kicking out at him and rolling away in one sloppy movement. My heel made contact with some part of him, but I didn't notice which part.

"Nella?" He didn't move, likely unsure how to tame this terrified beast.

I curled into a fetal position, chest heaving with a catastrophic mix of heavy breathing and sobs.

I could practically feel the blade as it cut through the skin. So slowly, so carefully. I could see his steel eyes as they savored my pain, my fear.

"Nella, Nella, shhh . . ." Oliver touched my shoulder, rubbing it with so much care, I could feel his safety and warmth radiating throughout my body.

I shied away. Even that touch was tainted. The way he pressed me into the table, the way he tied my arms and legs . . .

I was vaguely aware that I wasn't getting enough air, but I didn't know how to stop it. The world spun, stars sprang in and out of my vision. I couldn't close my eyes, but I couldn't look at the world around me.

"Nella, look at me!" Oliver gripped my shoulders, ignoring the fear-ridden shriek that escaped my lips. He hauled me up, hands planted firmly on either side of my face. "Breathe. You're safe, you're all right. Breathe!"

My frantic eyes found his, a sliver of calm seeping into my panic. His eyes were nothing like Donnell's. They reminded me more of a clear river on a summer's day, while Donnell's had hardened to gray ice.

Oliver took one long look at me before pulling me into a tight embrace, his nose against my neck. "Feel my breath?" He didn't wait for my response—I couldn't have given one if I tried. "Just focus on my breathing, try to join it. All right?"

He held me there while I sobbed and gasped for air, rubbing my back as one would comfort an infant. As time passed, my breathing deepened. Eventually, I was able to breathe with him, my reality settling into place around me.

"I'm sorry," I whispered, voice hoarse.

"You don't need to be sorry." He pushed me out so he could get a good look at my face. With his thumb, he wiped away what tears he could. "I was waiting for . . ." He hesitated, likely hunting for the right words. "It would've been surprising if you came out of everything without a care in the world. *I'm* sorry. I'm sorry to've put you through any of this."

I tucked my head into the space under his chin and snuggled close. "We're never gonna be safe." A single sob shook my body, threatening to take over again.

He stiffened at my words. "We are safe . . . *You* are safe. I won't let anything happen to you." He kissed the top of my head and held on even tighter. I heard his unspoken meaning: that true safety wasn't promised, that we would always either be hunted, or be the hunter ourselves.

A knock sounded on the door, a mix between gentle and commanding. "Are you all right in here?" Eva called.

Oliver cleared his throat, glancing down at both of our near naked bodies. "Um . . . yes. Yes ma'am."

There was a long pause, her shadow just barely visible under the door, dancing in the candlelight. "Nella?"

I cleared my throat to rid myself of the unshed tears. "I'm all right!"

"Good. Let us know if you need anything, okay?"

"We will, thank you." Oliver rubbed my back again. "Good night, ma'am."

"Good night," Eva echoed as her shadow retreated down the hallway.

"Nella?" Oliver whispered into my hair.

"Hmm?"

"Tomorrow, I have to go in to town. One of Josef's brothers owns the mill and might be able to take me on." Absently, he ran his fingers through what hair had come loose from its braid. "You are safe here, do you understand?"

I nodded mutely. *Safe if I stay put . . .*

"I need you to promise me that you'll stay with Eva. She'll make sure you're okay while I'm gone."

Gooseflesh prickled over every inch of my arms. "Can't you work here?"

He hesitated, avoiding my gaze. "I have to bring in money. I can't just work on menial projects. We have to play by their rules." With one hand, he pulled down the blankets, then tipped us both into the space he'd created, pulling the comforter back over us. "Please promise you'll stay with Eva."

"I don't know where else I'd go," I said, more bitterness in my voice than I'd meant. He'd leave me trapped and at the mercy of these people. Again. Even though I knew staying with Eva would be my ticket to safety, it made me want to stage my own revolution. "I'm tired . . ." I meant to end that with "of being trapped," but a yawn cut me off.

"I know. Sleep, okay? I'm right here."

CHAPTER SIXTY-THREE
Fishing Trip

Nightmares plagued my sleep. *He* lurked in every shadow, glinting eyes piercing into my very soul, knife glinting in the moonlight. No matter where I ran, he followed. No matter where I hid, he found me.

When the faint light of morning greeted me, I breathed a sigh of relief. But that sense of comfort only lasted until I rolled over to find Oliver missing.

It took me a long while to remember what he'd said. The mill. He had to go work at the mill.

I groaned and disentangled myself from the blankets. "Leaving me trapped with these people," I muttered, pouring water into the washbasin and splashing my face with it. "They were his enemy only a week ago. How can he be so sure that we can trust them?" I asked my reflection. "They'd just as soon beat us as feed us, I'm sure."

The freckle-faced girl with haphazard hair just stared back, lips pursed.

I shoved away from the vanity with a little more force than needed, rattling the mirror on its stand. I steadied it before it could fall, glancing at the door to make sure no one came running toward the commotion.

They didn't.

I shimmied myself to stand tall and proud, puffing out my chest. I gazed down my nose at my reflection and did my best imitation of Oliver. "You're safe here, safe with *them*." The reflection blinked, wide, muddy brown eyes that of a lost puppy. "Trapped. I'm *trapped* here." I whirled away from the vanity and yanked the crinoline from the top of the dresser. I struggled into the rest of my clothes, one piece at a time.

Would I ever truly be safe? Would I ever really be free?

After taming my hair into a long, simple braid down my back, I started downstairs. *I might be stuck with these people, but I'm certainly not going to stay trapped in that room!*

"Good morning, dear!" Eva beamed at me from her post by the kitchen counter. "I'm about to toast some bread if you'd like to tackle the eggs. Sofie just brought some in. They're over there." She gestured toward the egg pail with her chin.

Wordlessly, I got to work, placing the clean pan on the stove and choosing a white-and-brown speckled orb as my first victim. I could feel Eva's eyes on me as I dutifully cracked one egg after another into the pan.

Did Oliver really mean for us to stay with these people forever? Were they to be our new . . . family? Eva seemed sweet enough, but Sofia certainly didn't approve of our presence. And the men . . . I had no desire to get to know any of them.

Eva placed a freshly sliced piece of bread on the flat surface of the stove. "Are you feeling all right? You look tired."

I shook my head rapidly to dispel the thoughts that berated my mind. "Yes, I'm fine. Sorry." I scrubbed at a piece of egg that was trying to adhere to the bottom of the pan.

I didn't notice Sofia come into the kitchen. When she reached for a couple of plates in the cabinet above my head, I yelped.

"Scared ya, huh?" One corner of Sofia's lip twitched into an almost smile, halted only by the look her mother sent her way.

"Just didn't see you come in." I sprinkled some salt on the eggs and plopped them onto the proffered plate. Not my best work, but they were at least edible.

"We have some mending to catch up on today," Eva announced, settling herself like a mother hen into her preferred seat.

Sofia groaned as she plopped into her own spot. "It's a gorgeous day outside. Can't we—"

"Sofia, we have mending to do. You can't just go gallivanting off wherever you please. Not when we don't know if the Wedmans crossed the river yet. Besides, I need to check Nella's stitches."

My fork froze halfway to my mouth. "They crossed the river?" How long would it take for them to reach us? Would these people actually protect us?

"No, no." Eva waved her hand absently. "There's no need to worry, dear."

Sofia let out a very unladylike scoff. I turned my attention to her, narrowing my eyes as though it would force her to provide an explanation.

"We don't *know* if they crossed the river, okay? No one has caught sight of 'em."

I gnawed on my bottom lip, the eggs completely forgotten on my plate.

Eva cleared her throat, passing a buttered slice of toast to me. "There's no need to worry. If they were close enough to cause any harm, the men would know. Besides"—she sat a little straighter, like a bird ruffling her feathers for a good cleaning—"we have work to do! I have some extra fabric tucked away in the attic. I want you to choose whatever you want for some curtains."

"Curtains?" I nudged the bread with my finger.

"We're gettin' rid of them already?" Sofia asked, sounding much more hopeful than was strictly necessary.

Eva turned her stare on her daughter. "No, Sofie. We are *not* getting rid of them. On the contrary, they will move into the storage shed until they are able to build their own cabin."

I perked up a little at the thought. "Our own place?"

"The *shed?*" Sofia made a face.

"Yes, the shed. As it's temporary, we aren't to cut a window in it or anything, but I figured makin' some curtains will at least help it feel more like home."

"The shed is only the size of a wagon," Sofia pointed out.

Eva sighed deeply, likely unsure of how she wanted to deal with this problem child of hers. "Yes, it is small. But it will give your brother his room back, and give Nella and Oliver a space to call their own."

"It doesn't even have a stove."

"They will still eat their meals here," Eva explained. "Johannes wants to keep them close at hand for a while."

Sofia hid a smirk behind a bite. "Keep 'em close at hand so they don't kill us all," she said under her breath.

"Sofia!" Eva slammed her hands flat on the table, the sound causing both Sofia and I to jump.

Sofia regained herself, puffing out her chest and meeting her mother's furious gaze. "What? It's true! They think they can take in a born-and-bred *Wedman* and mold him into one of our own?"

Eva took a deep, cleansing breath. She looked so angry I wouldn't have been surprised if smoke spewed from her ears.

"Yes, he was born a Wedman. But now his family is after him. He can't go back."

Sofia crossed her arms firmly over her middle, eyeing her mother down with admirable stubbornness. "So we're just gonna take the two of them in like lost puppies?"

Eva pursed her lips and met the stare. "Sofia. Claire. Welks."

I set my fork on my plate, the growl in her voice making me want to run and hide.

"I will *not* hear another word out of you. Do you understand me, young lady?" Eva waited a mere breath before continuing, glaring her daughter into submission the entire time. "Your grandfather took them in. They are our guests unless otherwise noted. If I hear a single snarky remark about them come from your mouth . . ." She tsked her tongue, her eyes flitting to the back door. "Picking a switch will be the *least* of your worries."

Both Sofia and I flinched.

"Yes ma'am." Sofia ducked her head and took a bite of her breakfast.

I hardly spoke the entire morning. After Eva insisted on removing the last stitches from my torso, I chose a pale-yellow fabric to make into curtains. As nice as it felt to be doing something as normal as sewing, I only wanted to escape the stifling house.

The opportunity only came when Sofia was done with her required mending. "I'm going fishing," she declared, stretching with a yawn. "It's too pretty of a day to just sit here."

Eva sighed heavily and rubbed her temple. "Fine. Take a pistol with you and keep your eyes open."

"I will," she promised, grabbing the designated gun from its spot, high on the shelf.

"And take Nella with you? Show her around."

I paused mid-stitch. Sofia froze, pistol held lightly at her side.

Before she could argue, Eva fixed her with a threatening stare. "She needs to learn her surroundings. Teach her something. Teach her to fish, perhaps. Bond a little."

Sofia puffed her cheeks up with air as she fought against her inevitable rebuttal. "Fine. Come on." She crooked her hand in my direction and stalked outside, the screen door slamming shut behind her.

I set my curtains on the side table and scrambled to my feet, grabbing the cane as I went. On the way out the door, I snatched a pen and pad of paper from the entryway table, glancing over my shoulder to ensure that Eva hadn't seen me.

She didn't. She had already curled into her chair, head resting on a decorative pillow. Nap time.

By the time I got onto the porch, Sofia already had a fishing pole in one hand.

Fishing with this woman wasn't something I particularly wanted to do, though being outside was worth it. "I don't *have* to go with you," I said as I got close enough for her to hear.

"You can't stay here either," Sofia pointed out. "Can't leave you alone."

As if that fact was entirely her fault, I glared at her. "I'm not gonna run off!"

"I don't think you'd have the *ability* to run off even if you wanted to." Sofia turned on her heel and marched into the cover of the trees. "Come along, Shed Mouse. Do whatever you want when we get there. I don't care. But I'm goin' fishin'."

I kept my voice to a low grumble. "Bitchy Pants." I followed behind, staying as far back as I dared. She didn't speak to me, didn't even bother looking back. And that was fine with me.

I perched on a nearby rock to watch. I'd never seen a woman fish before, let alone met one who had the audacity to *want* to do it. In some ways, I admired Sofia for it. But I certainly wouldn't tell *her* that.

If something were to happen, she could care for herself. If she knew how to fish, she likely knew how to hunt. She was certainly strong enough to do just about anything she set her mind to. She could easily be unstoppable if left alone in the forest.

Shocked at myself, I spoke. "Who taught you to fish?"

She cast across the lake, the worm on the other end landing in the quiet water with a satisfying *plop*.

"My *farfar*," she said, using the name she'd used for Johannes at the dinner table. "Before he was injured, he taught me everything he could. Took me out here at least once a week. Even took me up the Mississippi a couple a'times."

A pang of sadness sprang into my heart. I'd never known my grandparents. Perhaps they would've made life just a little easier on us all, ensuring we wouldn't have to sell practically everything we owned.

She studied me for a moment, looking very much like a wildcat, deciding if I was food or not. Apparently deciding I wasn't worth the trouble, she pulled her line in and cast the worm far across the water for a second time.

With a sigh, I settled a little deeper into the crook of my rock and pulled the paper and pen from my pocket. What would I even write to my mother? Was I even allowed to do such a thing?

I gnawed on my lower lip, a drop of ink pooling on the tip of the nib, finally dripping onto the blank page. When would I be able to send it off? Could my family send me a letter back?

I glanced at Sofia, noting her watching me out of the corner of her eye.

Would *she* tattle on my letter-writing?

With a heavy sigh, she shoved the end of her pole into the dirt and turned in my direction, one hand on her hip. "I'll bite, since nothin' else seems to want to. What are you writing?"

I wiped the nib on the inkwell. Did I dare tell her?

"A letter," I admitted, following it up with a harsh, "Is that all right with you, sheriff?"

Sofia smirked at my bitter tone. "I don't care what you do. Just don't stab me in the back, and I'll be fine."

Same to you, I thought, placing the pen back on the paper and getting to work.

CHAPTER SIXTY-FOUR

Letter to Mama

Dear Mother,

Firstly, I must apologize that it has taken me so long to write you. We have been traveling ever since I last saw you. Are you living back at home again? Is Little Chris able to help you around the house? How is his apprenticeship going? And Felicité, how is she faring? I can imagine she's getting so big now, and I'm sure Miriam loves her as her own.

I am eternally sorry for what happened when we were there last. I should never have put any of you in harm's way like that. I selfishly wanted some extra time around those I love, and it nearly cost me everything.

Though we should've left straightaway, I convinced Oliver to stop by the house. I knew I could never forgive myself if I didn't know each and every one of you was safe. Even so, I will never be able to forgive myself for leaving you to clean up after my own selfish actions.

I wish I could explain everything to you, go into detail on why that man broke into the house in the first place, why we had to run. Perhaps one day I'll be able to tell you everything. But for now, the most important thing to know is that I am safe. Truly safe.

We are staying with a kind family right on the other side of the Mississippi. I hope that one day soon we'll be able to hop on the train and head back to visit. I can't wait to see how big Felicité has grown!

Please write as soon as you are able. I miss and love each and every one of you!

Love always,

Nella

It took me longer to write the letter than I anticipated. After every line, I had to stop and recite exactly what I wanted to say. Through my words, I needed to portray safety—though even I wasn't sure if that was the truth. Everything on that wrinkled piece of paper felt like a sugarcoated lie, and it made me nauseated.

Would I ever get to visit them? Would I even get to send them the letter?

By the time I signed my name and folded the paper in half, the sun was high in the sky and my stomach was threatening to eat itself if I didn't feed it soon.

Apparently, Sofia had similar needs, as her shoulders slumped in relief at the sight of my setting down the pen. She started winding up the line, popping her neck as she did so. When she was done, she scooped up her catch of one very feisty bass and marched off into the trees.

I shoved my writing utensils into my pocket and hurried after her, grateful for the space between us.

We said nothing on the walk back to the house. Truly, we didn't have anything *to* say. I didn't want to ask her for permission to send a letter, and I certainly didn't want to explain its contents.

Once inside, I slipped the pen and extra paper back on the side table and made for the stairs. I only made it to the second step when I heard Sofia and Eva in the sitting room.

"They'll take care of it when they return," Eva said with forced patience.

Sofia made a frustrated growling noise. "Oh, right. The *mill*. I'll never understand why they insist on calling it that."

"Well, you never know who's listening."

"In our own home? If someone's in our *own home* listening to information about a secret mission, they probably shouldn't be here!"

My heart skipped a beat, and I leaned against the banister.

"Come, come, Sofie," Eva purred. "It's better to be in the habit of calling it that than to slip up in town one day."

Fumbling with my cane, I made my way into the room with them. They both stopped talking as my shadow stretched across the ornate rug. Sofia made a face that said nothing short of, "You mean to keep it from people like *her*?"

"They're on a mission?" I asked, forcing my voice to stay calm.

Eva cleared her throat. "Yes. The men decided that since Oliver would be staying here with us, he could go with them on this mission."

I stared at the floor, my blood boiling. "What did they need his help with?" Perhaps they only needed him for reconnaissance? Though I highly doubted it. They'd need to prove his loyalty.

"Do you *really* want to know?" Sofia asked.

I stood a little straighter, squaring my shoulders to face her. "I can handle whatever it is they are doing, I assure you."

Eva sighed and rubbed her temple, the movement disrupting the dried flour that hid above her brows. "There is a man down south they needed to take care of. We don't know all of the details, for safety, you understand."

I set my jaw, teeth grinding painfully. Did Oliver mean to lie to me about where he was going? Did he even know?

At the very least, I assumed he had an idea of what they wanted from him. He had said he would need to work with the clan. Right?

"Are you all right?" Sofia asked, one eyebrow raised.

"Yeah." I shifted uncomfortably, my hand slipping into my pocket to feel the letter nestled inside. "Do you know if . . ." I trailed off, clearing my throat. "Do you know if they told Oliver what it meant? Before they took him with them, I mean?"

Sofia and Eva exchanged glances.

"I heard Johannes telling him specifically," Sofia announced, receiving a glare from Eva.

My stomach dropped. "Thank you." I turned with exaggerated slowness, feeling ill. Who was he going to murder this time? And how long would it be before this job either took his life, or brought him right back into the grasp of his family?

What if it was just a cover for the Welks Clan to kill him?

I went to bed early that night, still seething. Every time I shut my eyes, my dreams were filled with blood, knives, and the terrified screams of the innocent.

Because of this, I woke before the sunrise. Oliver still wasn't at my side. He hadn't come home overnight.

I didn't move for a long while, eyes fixed on the empty space where he should be.

Did he *know* he was going on a mission to kill someone? Or was Sofia mistaken? Maybe he truly thought he was going to work at the mill?

If he lied to me about that, what else would he lie about in the future?

I pushed that thought away as fast as it came into my mind. If I let myself dwell on it too long, it'd become a never-ending spiral.

I kicked the blankets from my body with a huff and just a little too much force. "Fine," I said to his missing form. "If you're gonna leave me trapped here, I'll take care of things myself."

Without any real planning, I swung my legs over the bed and started my morning routine. I was vaguely aware that the house was completely silent. Likely, no one else was awake.

"Good," I said, snapping the busk of my corset with practiced ease. "Then I won't have to lie."

I grabbed the pocket with my letter and tied it around my waist, shoving a few of Oliver's discarded coins in with it. "I'm gonna go to town, just *try* to stop me." I directed this to the empty bed.

Who were *they* to control every aspect of my life?

"Stay in your room!"

"Marry this man."

"Because you chose not to marry him, you must work as a maid."

"Stay trapped in this attic until we kill you."

I shivered at the last, unbidden thought. And now, I was trapped in yet another house filled with trained killers.

"Fuck. All. Of. This." I chucked a decorative pillow into its place on the freshly made bed.

Once I was fully dressed to my stockings, I started the trek downstairs. I took every step with care, ears trained for the slightest sign that I had been caught. A creaking bed, a footstep, a sneeze, anything.

To my relief, no one stirred.

In the entryway, I shoved my foot into the lonely boot, then opened the drawer in the side table. Sure enough, a little pistol hid inside. These people really did stash weapons everywhere they could. With just a bit of a struggle, I tucked it into my boot.

The door squeaked on the way to the porch; I paused and held my breath. When no one stirred by the time I counted to ten, I continued on my way to the barn, each step faster than the last.

Freedom.

CHAPTER SIXTY-FIVE
Alone Time

Saddling the horse took significantly longer than I bargained for. The barn swirled with inky black and the dust from the hay. Ominous shadows danced around it all, making me squeal like a petrified mouse every few minutes.

When I reached my chosen horse, I purred sweet nonsense to her, running my fingers down her muzzle. "I'm sorry for waking you. We're gonna go on an adventure."

She blew through her lips, eyes wide and straight on me. My anxieties would soar right to her, and I knew it.

I saddled her with care, squinting in the moonlight. She let me, swishing her tail at any touch that she deemed similar to a fly. When I finally finished, I climbed on and we were off.

I kept her at a slow walk, pressed as close to the tree line as I dared, until we were out of sight of the house. Only then did I let her speed up.

A smile spread across my face as the chilly air prodded me along. It blew through my loosely braided hair, making me close my eyes and stretch up tall, enjoying the freedom, no matter how temporary. I spread my arms wide and tilted my head up, basking in the euphoria.

I'd return, that wasn't up for debate. But at least I'd be in charge of myself for a few hours. I had a letter to send, after all.

I wanted to know how my mother was faring. And Felicité. And everyone else. They'd want to know if we were all right as well. They deserved that much after all the chaos I had dumped onto them, didn't they?

Little by little, the chill crept under my skin. I rubbed the gooseflesh from my arms and continued on. I was highly aware that anyone could be hiding in the shadows, but it was a risk I chose to completely ignore. At least for now.

The freedom was worth it.

"I think I can do this life," I told the horse with a little pat. "They need to learn they can't keep me trapped like a wild animal. That's not too much to ask, is it?"

The mare shook her head roughly, mane flying every which way.

"I know, I know. I'm being ridiculous." I sighed and shifted my weight in the saddle. "But it's ridiculous that they think they can keep me trapped in that house, isn't it?"

This time, the mare ignored me. Instead, she shied at something unseen in the shadows. I froze, staring in the direction she had sidestepped.

Had they found me? Maybe this entire venture *had* been idiotic. Heart racing, I bent to withdraw the gun from its hiding place. It was much harder to push the skirts aside than I had hoped. The crinoline was just a little too stiff, blocking access. When I finally managed to wrestle it free, I half expected to see Donnell standing directly in front of us.

He wasn't.

In fact, nothing stirred. Nothing so much as moved. I trained the gun at the shadows, doing everything I could to steady my breathing. The mare sidestepped again, this time agitated by my own nerves.

"All right, all right. Come on, let's just get to town." I spurred her on with a rock of my hips and a nudge to the withers. This time, I kept my head on a swivel, squinting into each and every shadow.

The relief I felt earlier was replaced by an awareness of how alone I was. My freedom could be cut short at a moment's notice, and I knew it.

The closer we got to town, the higher the sun rose. Along with my panic. Sweat pooled under my arms, making the cotton cling uncomfortably. That was certainly *not* the way I wanted to greet the people in town.

When I made it onto the main street, I relaxed. Just a little. I found the general store easily, tying the mare to the hitching post and sliding to the dusty ground. "I'll hurry, don't worry," I said to her, scanning my surroundings to make sure no one heard me talking to the horse.

As luck would have it, the big wooden door was solidly locked, a sign posted right in the middle. Though, of course, I didn't read it until I had pulled on the handle at least three times.

Open—7 AM

"Well, that's unfortunate," I muttered to the mare, plopping down to sit on the sidewalk near her hooves. I didn't know how long I'd need to wait. But by the time seven rolled around, I was certain Eva and Sofia would notice my absence.

But why did it really matter? Wasn't I trying to make a statement by leaving on my own?

My mouth felt like sandpaper, no matter how many times I swallowed. Sure, I wanted to make a statement. But that didn't mean I wanted to deal with the repercussions of said statement—whatever they were.

I laughed darkly. "What are they gonna do, beat me?" The scars on my back throbbed at the memory. I gnawed on the inside of my cheek, fingers gripping my pocket through the skirts.

Though, that was the least of my worries. If Donnell, Mr. York, or anyone else saw me, I'd be dead.

I looked longingly at the door, regretting my rash decision. Time had a way of taking way too long. The sidewalks would soon be bustling with men, women, and children—and every eye would be on me. I knew the freckles had overtaken my face, and my cane was obvious, leaning against the hitching post. I chewed on my tongue until it was sore, then picked every speck of dirt from under my nails.

When the door finally did open, I jumped.

"Good morning, miss," the young man said. He ducked his head politely and held the door open for me. "I hope you haven't been waitin' long? What can I do for you?" He slid behind the counter, a bright smile on his face.

He was well dressed in a navy shirt and gray vest, a mustache adorning his upper lip.

I cleared my throat delicately; it was incredibly dry from my nerves. "No, no, not long," I lied. "I just need to mail this, please."

I fished the letter from my pocket and presented it to him, my heart hitting an extra beat. *Mother will soon know I'm safe.*

"That, I can do, miss." He gave me the total, and I fished the coins out of my pocket as well, glancing over my shoulder. Did they already know I was missing? I assumed so. Would they come after me? Would Oliver have approved of my sending off the letter?

I squared my shoulders at the thought while the shopkeeper took my precious letter to its designated cubby. *I don't give one iota if he has a problem with it. I'm not a dog to be controlled by him!*

"Can I do anything else for you, miss?" he asked, his brown eyes studying my facial features with terrifying intensity.

"Uh, no," I said, shaking my head a little too hard. "That is all, thank you." I ducked my chin in his direction and hurried back out the door.

Relief nearly overflowed at the thought of my mother soon knowing I was okay. But anxieties still sparked in the pit of my stomach. Donnell could already be watching me, waiting for me to lead him to his brother, or just waiting for the right moment to strike and take me in.

What would he do if he caught me this time? Would he filet me like a fish? If he did, where would he start? Would the blade sink in at the collarbone first—

"Miss? Miss, are you okay?"

I gasped, reality crashing around me. I was safe—if only for now. I stood on the boarded sidewalk, gripping the hitching post, sweat pooling on my forehead, while a very concerned husband and wife hovered nearby.

"I . . . um . . ." I cleared my throat, nearly panicking with every blink. Each time my eyes closed, he was there.

"Are you sure you're okay? Here, here." The lady wrapped her shawl around my shoulders, holding me in a way that was both restrictive and protective at the same time.

Like a startled horse, I balked, struggling free. "No, no! I'm fine. Really, thank you for your concern." I stood as straight as possible, forcing myself to look the woman in the eye as I held her shawl out for her. To my dismay, my hand shook.

The man held his own hand out to steady me. "Dear, you don't seem all right at all. Please, let us get you some help. Do you have any family nearby?"

"No, I'm fine." My toes curled in my boot. *The gun is still there, right against your calf. If you grab it, you can make a quick getaway.*

What was I even thinking? These people meant well; all they wanted to do was help. "I'm all right," I repeated, taking the biggest breath I could muster and glancing at my horse. "Thank you for all of your help." I didn't give them a chance to respond. I hurried to the mare, grabbing onto her lead like a lifeline.

I took a hold of her mane and the back of the saddle, preparing to launch myself onto her back. When I looked across the saddle to do just that, I nearly fainted.

Sofia's piercing blue eyes practically stared into my soul.

I yelped and fell back onto my well-padded rear, the mare sidestepping and whipping her mane.

"She's with me," Sofia said to the onlookers. "I'll take it from here." Her smile was as sweet as molasses, ensuring the strangers warmed to her almost instantly.

I didn't move, as my would-be rescuers found their way into the general store.

So they *had* sent someone after me.

"What are you doing here?" Sofia demanded, crouching in a surprisingly ladylike fashion, just out of my reach.

I didn't bother answering her question, I just started the arduous process of getting back to my feet. "You didn't have to come after me, you know."

She laughed, a dark sort of sound. "Don't you worry your pretty little head, I didn't."

Like a dog, my head tilted to the side. "The sun only *just* rose."

Her lip quirked in a smirk. "Astute observation." She said this with a proper-sounding English accent, completely surprising me. She switched right back to her normal accented voice. "You done in town? Or ya goin' back 'cross the river? Really don't suggest that, but I'll be sure to throw a pretty flower out after you, 'cause I won't be able to attend your funeral, you understand."

"I'm done, I assure you." My eyes scanned the horizon, hunting for that blond head, the shine of a freshly oiled gun, anything that might show that they had found me.

"You sure you're all right?" Sofia asked. She didn't touch me, she didn't hover. She simply stood there, studying every inch of my body.

"I'm fine," I snapped. I grabbed a hold of the nervous mare and hauled myself onto her back. She sidestepped, making it harder than necessary. "Just ready to get back to the house."

Her entire body slumping in defeat, Sofia sighed. "I'll go with you. My horse is across the street." Without giving me the option to protest, she took a hold of the reins and led us in that direction. "No one's up there. I woulda seen 'em."

I shifted in the saddle. "I wasn't worried."

She scoffed. "You weren't, were ya?" Never once letting go of my reins, she swung onto her own horse, head held high.

I glanced back up the hill, catching sight of a singular person. Was he watching us? I couldn't be sure. But the hair color was right. That was all it took for my stomach to swirl yet again.

What if . . . "What were you doing in town?" I demanded. What if she made a deal with the enemy?

"It's none of your damn business," she snapped.

I yanked the reins free of her hand, backing the mare out of her reach. "Tell me." I fixed my eyes right on hers, resisting the urge to study the lone figure. Something deep inside told me that it likely wasn't one of the Wedmans—they wouldn't be so stupid as to stand in the middle of the street.

"I don't have to tell you nothin'." Sofia swiped at the reins, but the horse mercifully danced out of her way.

Gnawing on my cheek, I tried to think of a good strategy. Did I plan on going back to the perceived safety of their home? Yes. But what if . . . just what if? Oliver was nowhere nearby to protect me. He wasn't going to swoop down like my knight in shining armor. Especially considering I'd left out of pure, idiotic stubbornness.

CHAPTER SIXTY-SIX

Cat Fight

"Tell me, or else," I demanded, holding her stare. If I looked anywhere else, I knew she'd see my nerves, guess any plan I tried. In reality, I knew she already did. But I had to try.

Go right. Look left, but go right. When I tensed, she did the same. She was studying my every move.

This wouldn't end well, and I knew it. But I wouldn't let her take me. I couldn't *really* trust her, could I?

If you're mad at me, Oliver, this is what you get for abandoning me in yet another damn prison!

"Come on!" Sofia threw her head back in an exaggerated show of irritation. "Don't—"

It's now or never! I kicked the mare as hard as I could, and we barreled into the trees, sticks accosting us from every direction.

"Dagnabbit!" Sofia howled.

I could hear her horse only a few feet from my own, but I refused to look. I crouched as low on my mare's neck as I could and just prayed. "Go, girl, go," I whispered, my heart hammering in my ears.

"Nella! I don't want to do this!" Sofia's groan did nothing to hide her furious scream. The sound came somewhere to the left of us. Did she plan to get ahead and block our path?

I guided my mare to the right, a particularly sharp branch tearing into the hem of my skirt. *It's all right. I'll deal with it later.*

As luck would have it, fate wasn't on my side.

When I craned my neck to check Sofia's progress, a branch took full advantage of my distraction.

In a matter of seconds, it smacked into my torso and whisked me from my mare's back and to the leaf-covered ground.

Sofia didn't let me stew in my misery for long. Like a knight after a problematic prisoner, she leapt from her horse and planted her feet on either side of my hips.

I knew exactly what she was doing. If I so much as took the time to think of a plan, she'd have me pinned to the ground. As she started to kneel, I rolled. This caught her somewhat off guard, making her teeter to the side. She regained herself easily, diving for my shoulders. I responded by rolling the other way.

I kicked and twisted, fighting for my life like a salmon against a bear. I knew I had little chance, but I certainly wanted to try.

Sofia was strong—much stronger than I realized. But I was desperate. And feisty.

"Just let me go!" I hollered, kicking into her skirts to inflict whatever pain I could. I only managed to get my boot caught up in the hoops of her skirt.

Like an irritated mare, she huffed and flattened her body against mine, thighs pressing hard against my torso, arms holding mine over my chest. "Just stop it!" she commanded, glaring straight into my eyes.

I squirmed under her gaze. I'd wait for the first sign of weakness, then I'd attack. How? Did she even have a weakness? I'd have to figure that out whenever the time came.

"What is your problem?" Sofia demanded. "We're just going back to the house! You're not a damn prisoner!"

I set my jaw and matched her glare. "Don't lie to me! I *am* a prisoner!"

She muttered what had to be a curse in Swedish. "Fine! You can be my prisoner, if you want." To my complete mortification, she flipped me onto my stomach with so little effort, she might as well have been maneuvering a sack of flour.

"What are you doing?" I demanded, swinging my arm in an uncomfortable arc to try to hit her. She caught it easily and pulled, stretching my arm to its limits. Before I could react, she wound a thick piece of rope around my wrist.

"Are you *tying* me?" An animal-like scream escaped my throat.

"Well, yeah." I could almost hear her smirk. "You're my prisoner, right?"

I screamed again, the noise a mix between fury and fear.

It made me feel just a bit better that she had to fight to get me to her horse. She gripped my right arm and yanked, putting her entire body weight into each pull. I planted my feet in the dirt, relishing in the thought that it made it just a little harder on her.

"I woulda come back on my own if you'd just leave me alone!"

She grunted. "Highly doubt that!"

When my head was unsettlingly close to my own mare's hooves, I tried to roll again. My efforts got me nowhere, but I wasn't going to give up.

Sofia placed her hands under my torso and practically tossed me onto the saddle. Unfortunately, she didn't plan on letting me sit there. Instead, she draped me over the seat like the dead, leg dangling on one side, head on the other, rear pointing to the sky.

As if I sprang a leak, the fight drained from me. "I'll follow you back. Just let me up, please?"

I could almost feel the side-eye she sent my direction.

"As much as I despise all y'all," she started, her own saddle creaking as she swung into it, "we're not permitted to kill you. Or even mistreat you. Unless, of course, you give us reason to. So if you'd like to help with that, go ahead. I'd *love* to do something other than till that garden for winter tomorrow."

I had to focus all my energy on *not* squirming like a fish. If I did that, I was sure to crash to the earth.

Sofia took her time. Not once did we return to the road. We weaved in and out of the trees, my hair tangling in every bush we passed. It would take me *ages* to get all the debris out, and I knew it.

She never once uttered a word. I bit my lower lip to keep silent. If she planned to play the quiet game, I would too. Though the increasing pressure in my head made that harder with each passing minute.

Once we were in the barn, she tied up the horses and faced me with a swoosh of skirts. "You know how to unsaddle your own horse, Shed Mouse?"

I bristled. "Of *course* I do. Get me down from here, you—"

She patted my back, the movement dripping with condescension. "Shh, you don't want to get caught swearing, now do you?" She gripped my wrists, causing me to stiffen as the joints protested. "They might not think you're so high-bred anymore."

She yanked me down by my arms, pain shooting through my shoulders almost instantly. The pile of hay I crashed into stifled my screams, and I refused to move. Why did I ever think it was a good idea to leave the house alone?

Oh yes, it was because they kept treating me like *this*.

As soon as I felt the pressure on my wrists release, I rolled onto my back to glare at her. "I don't care. You are a *bitch*."

She stood there, a smirk on her lips and hands resting on her corseted waist. Her eyes almost sparkled with the conflict. "Am I, then?"

A primal scream erupted from me as I lunged at her. To my utmost surprise, I caught her off guard. She fell smack onto the hay-covered floor, just a little too close to the horses' hooves for my comfort. But I truly didn't care. What did any of it matter anymore?

"You think you have control over me?" I gripped her shoulders and shook her as hard as possible. She didn't fight back. In fact, she almost smiled. "All of you! I've never had control over my own life! And I'm *tired* of it! TIRED!" Without thinking, I slammed my fist into her nose.

That got her moving again. Like a cougar, she launched to her feet, knocking me back on my rear. She pounced, and I rolled, a yelp escaping me as she grabbed my ankle.

"You think *I* have a say in my life?" She pulled me back to her like a rag doll, skirts flying everywhere. "I'm a trained killer who's not allowed to *kill*." She straddled me with her legs, squeezing just tight enough that it was uncomfortable. "They need an extra hand on a mission? They call for help. They get an *enemy* on their doorstep?" She gripped my shoulders and slammed me into the earth, knocking the breath out of me. "They take *him* and leave me with his useless whore!"

I spat in her face, momentarily impressed that the glob actually made purchase. "You mark my words, I don't want to be here either!"

From then on, we spat, scratched, rolled, and cursed. It was hard to keep track of who was on top, and whose blood was whose. I knew she wasn't fighting me with everything she had. If she wanted to, she would have me tied in a knot in five seconds flat. Deep down, I knew we both needed to get rid of the pent-up energy—even if it was in a way that would've been unheard of for me only a year before.

They broke us apart when I was on top.

Strong arms pulled me straight up as if I didn't weigh much more than a child. I didn't stop my flailing, or my screaming, and she didn't stop hers. In fact, she sprang at me again. Another man stepped in, grabbing her before she could reach me.

"What is the meaning of this?" my captor demanded. It had to be Niklas, as August had his sister nearly in a choke hold.

"She tried to run off!" Sofia shouted.

"I did not!" I screamed back.

Josef waltzed between us, hands held high in what was supposed to be a calming gesture. "Oh, hush! Both of you! We've had a long day—*this* is the last thing we want to come home to."

They were home. Where was Oliver? I twisted to the right, then the left, getting nowhere. I couldn't move my head so much as an inch. What if he hadn't come back? What had they done to him?

Sofia quieted at the sight of her father. Her cheek sunk in where she gnawed on it. I opened my mouth to demand answers, but the glare from the fearless leader stopped me short.

"Sofia," Josef said. "Get yourself inside and cleaned up. I'd send her with you as well, but I can't trust you not to keep fightin' like cats, now can I?"

She said nothing.

"Go on, go. We'll put the horses up." He clapped his hands with such force, the sound made both of us jump.

August released his sister, and she hurried past us and to the door, fixing me with one last glare before escaping the confines of the barn.

Josef let out a long sigh, shaking his head as startled exclamations came from Johannes outside.

"You're lucky she was holdin' back," Niklas said. He still hadn't released me.

Johannes let out a barking sort of laugh. "That is certainly true, Oliver." He crooked his fingers in the direction I assumed Oliver was standing.

My entire body relaxed at the sound of his name. He was back. Safely.

"Take your woman up to your room and get her cleaned up. After dinner, we'll *all* have a meeting in the library." At those last words, he fixed me in a stare. My blood ran cold.

Shit.

"Yes sir," Oliver said, stepping forward and gently taking me from Niklas. He stood as straight as a fence post, tall and on alert.

Nausea tickled at my stomach. Would it all happen again? Would this man take us into the library, beat us to submission? When Oliver tugged at my arm to get me to follow, I couldn't get myself to move.

With the voice of a terrified child, I spoke: "Please don't beat us."

Josef plainly hadn't been expecting that, as his whole body recoiled. "I don't plan on it. You're not my responsibility, therefore, you're not mine to beat." He gestured toward the house. "Get going, I'll see you both after dinner."

CHAPTER SIXTY-SEVEN

Honesty

On the way to the stairs, we passed the open kitchen door. Sofia sat perched on the table, Eva dabbing something on a nasty scratch on her cheek. Oliver must've felt me stiffen, as he tightened his grip on my arm and hurried me along.

"What are you gonna do?" I demanded as we ascended the stairs.

"Clean you up." He said it so simply, so easily, like it was a daily occurrence. Though, I had to admit, taking care of my injuries was becoming a common chore.

He didn't release my arm until our bedroom door clicked shut behind us.

"Are *you* gonna beat me for my disobedience?" I spat, moving just out of reach and crossing my arms.

"Aren't you full of fire today." He walked right past me and to the washbasin. "I'm not gonna beat you."

"What if *he* commands it?"

Oliver sighed, squeezing the extra water out of a rag. "I'll tell him no. Got it? As it stands, you're my responsibility. Those are the clan rules, not his. What I do with you is my business. It's as simple as that."

"When will I be my *own* responsibility?" I demanded. "And why didn't you tell your father no back when you chose to *beat* me like a damn prisoner!" With every word, my voice grew louder.

Oliver pushed the stool out from the vanity with his foot and nodded at it. "Come on, let me clean you up."

I didn't move. Instead, I crossed my arms, leaned against the bed, and stared him down.

He let the rag drop back into the water with a plop. "I didn't know what else to do. I'm *sorry*, Nella. I won't let anything like that happen again."

The words escaped my mouth before I even realized it. "Am I still your prisoner?"

His shoulders slumped as the pain entered his eyes. "Do you feel like my prisoner?"

I opened and closed my mouth, but the words just wouldn't come. My body felt heavy as I moved to sit at the vanity. "No?"

He was completely silent as he squeezed the extra water from the rag and went to work. Every move he made was gentle, caring. But it didn't quench my anger. "You lied to me."

He paused, the cloth a mere inch from my cheek. "About?"

I shoved his hand away and leveled my gaze at him. "About the mill. You lied to me."

He leaned against the vanity and plopped the rag back into the water. "Would you have preferred me to tell you where I was going? Would that have kept you from worrying?" He didn't wait for my response. "You would've been stressing the entire time, worried they were going to kill me."

I didn't want to admit that I was worrying about that, anyway. "You left me trapped up here," I just said.

He sighed. "You weren't trapped in here, Nella."

"I might as well've been!" I threw my hands into the air, the gesture just a little dramatic for the situation.

"All I asked was that you stay close to Sofia or Eva. But it doesn't sound like you did that, did you?"

"Don't turn this on me!" I crossed my arms, the wound along my torso throbbing as to remind me of its existence. "*You're* the one who lied to me!"

He laughed, the sound dark and suspicious. "How about I make you a deal. I'll tell you what I was up to, if you tell me what you were doing?"

Truthfully, I didn't know if I *wanted* to know what he had been doing. "I don't want you killing anyone!"

He smirked. "I didn't kill anyone." The unspoken "today" rested heavily in my brain. "I helped with a dispute down south on the Mississippi. A man—"

I held up my hand to stop him. "Did anyone kill him?"

Oliver raised one eyebrow as if to say, "Do you really want to know?"

"I don't like you doing any of it," I muttered.

"I don't have much of a choice, Nella." He grabbed the rag again, roughly squeezing the excess water into the basin. "When you are raised in this life, you can't simply leave. I can't farm. I can't work in town. I have *wanted* posters of me all around, for heaven's sake! Besides, my family isn't going to stop hunting for me—"

"I thought you said we were safe here?" I shot back. Though I'd known the truth, it felt good to catch him in a lie.

He ran a wet finger over his forehead. "Are you gonna tell me what you were doing in town?"

In response, I glared at him.

"You do realize I'll know soon enough, don't you?"

I did, but I was still too mad to let him turn it back on me.

"Good God, Nella! I asked you to stay here with Eva and Sofia to keep you safe. And you ran off." He didn't wait for me to nod. "What I want to know is *why*."

"Are you gonna torture it out of me? Since that's what you seem so good at doing?" I was taunting him, and I knew it.

The rag splattered into the bowl, and he turned on his heel, marching to the window. He stood there, rigid and silent for a long, terrifying time. "I'm not gonna torture you. I'm not gonna beat you. But I'd like to keep you safe, all right? And I can't do that if you don't let me!"

We were going in circles, and what fight I had left finally fizzled into pure exhaustion. I tucked my good leg up to my chest, hidden under my skirt. I wrapped my arms around my knee, making myself look like a disheveled, fluffy cupcake. I didn't care. "You left me. You left me alone with *them*. I was mad. Well, I *am* mad. You left me trapped with these people to go murder someone!"

His shoulders sagged, but he didn't turn back to face me. "I didn't murder anyone."

"But you helped! You can't deny that."

He didn't even try.

"First, my father told me who to marry. When I didn't, he shipped me off like a slave. Then, you got me and trapped me in an attic. I was at *your* mercy. I'd eat when *you* deemed it okay, I'd go outside when allowed. And now this? I'm not your doll!" Somewhere in the middle of my tirade, tears escaped the confines of my lashes. They flowed down my cheeks, pooling on my chin before crashing onto where I rested my head on my knee.

Oliver sighed. "My goal wasn't to control you. Well . . ." He paused for a moment, chewing over his words. "Well, at least not the entire time. I kept you in the attic to keep you safe—"

"And look at all the good that did!" To emphasize my point, I hiked up the edge of my skirt to show the remaining nub. "I have plenty of scars that show how much you failed!"

He tugged at his hair as if to buy himself time to stay calm. "You know as well as I do, my father would've killed you if given half the chance." He turned back to me, blue eyes imploring. "I didn't *want* to take you with me in the first place!"

"Then why did you?" I demanded.

He grumbled something unintelligible under his breath. "Because! I'd just killed the *wrong* man. And then I was confronted by an *innocent* girl who had nothing to do with anything. A girl I was *supposed* to kill. Despite what you might think, I do, indeed, have a moral compass."

"I know," I muttered, letting my leg slump back to the cushion. "But—"

He held up his hand to stop me. "I'm sorry I lied to you. I didn't know all the details, only that we were going on a mission. I asked you to stay here, not to imprison you, but to keep you *safe*. Which didn't work all that well, now did it?" He gestured to my bedraggled appearance.

I touched the stinging cut on my chin. "You weren't back, so I had to take care of myself," I muttered, knowing full well that it was a shallow argument.

"No, you decided to be stubborn and get yourself into mischief like a child."

I flinched.

"Why'd you go to town?"

I spun in my seat to grab the rag and clean my own wounds. A deal was a deal, but I didn't want him to stare me down like a naughty child while I told my side of the story. "I had a letter to get out."

"And you didn't think to run that by someone? Anyone?"

I met his gaze in the reflection. "You weren't here."

Deliberately, he made his way to my side, bending at the waist to pluck the revolver from its hiding place in my boot. I'd forgotten about it. "So instead of waiting, you took a gun and went off by yourself?"

I wrung the rag out for a third time, focusing all my attention on the water droplets.

The gun clicked open as he checked the contents. "It's not even loaded," he muttered. He placed it on the top of the dresser with a long sigh. "I assume the letter was to your mother?"

"Yes," I said.

He leaned against the vanity, reaching out to rest his hand on mine. "I wouldn't've told you no. I would've *helped* you."

"No one seems to like letters around here," I pointed out.

"For a damn good reason too. Did you put any location details in there?"

"I'm not stupid!"

He held his hands up in mock surrender. "That's all I ask. That, and don't go out there alone, please. More than likely, they know where we are. If not, they're likely watching your family in case we return. So, please, I beg of you, don't run off." He bent to kiss the top of my head.

"Don't lie to me," I muttered.

"Promise."

CHAPTER SIXTY-EIGHT

Repercussions

Despite Oliver's promises, I still did everything I could to delay our descent into the library.

"Are you *sure* he's not gonna beat me?"

Oliver ran his fingers through his hair. I'd lost track of how many times I had asked that very question.

"As I said a thousand times, he won't so much as touch you."

"But he's having us meet in his *torture* room, Oliver!"

Oliver bit his lip, hard. It didn't do much to stifle his laugh. "No. We're meeting in the *library*. In the hall, look to the right. There's a locked room. *That's* where you don't want to go."

This made me relax just a little, though knowing a room like that truly existed still nauseated me.

He crouched at the top of the stairs for me to hop onto his back. I considered insisting on doing it myself, but the fight had taken a lot out of me. My arms hurt. *Both* my legs hurt. My face was covered in scratches that wouldn't stop stinging. And my upper lip was swollen. Gripping his shoulders, I hopped onto his back, holding on with my knees.

"What is he going to do, then?"

"I dunno." Oliver shrugged. "Probably talk about you and Sofia."

I leaned my cheek against his back. "That's not promising."

"Neither is fighting with his daughter," he pointed out. He paused with his hand on the latch to the library. "He won't touch you, he won't make me do anything either. But as the leader of the clan, he can certainly lecture all he wants. I beg of you, mind your p's and q's."

He wouldn't go inside until I agreed, and I knew it. "I'll behave," I promised.

"Thank you."

He pushed open the door in one fluid motion and stood a little straighter as he stepped inside. The entire Welks Clan had already seated themselves in their oddly plush seats. The room looked too elegant to be a torture room. No ropes, no chains. Nothing that could restrain someone to cut them into bits.

"Go on and sit down." Johannes motioned to the empty settee across from him. He positioned himself in the center of the room, able to meet every eye with only the slightest turn of his head.

Sofia adjusted herself across from us, nestled in a spot between both of her brothers. August was in the seat himself, while Niklas perched on the armrest, his own arm draped over the back of the settee. Eva and Josef were in seats beside their leader, both sitting straight and alert.

"As we are all gathered here . . ." Johannes began, his eyes roaming over each of us like a hawk. "I request some answers. Sofia." He turned his chair with surprising precision to face his granddaughter.

"Yes sir?"

Was it just my imagination, or did she sound nervous?

"Why were the two of you in town?"

I sat back, my shock likely evident on my face. She wasn't supposed to be there either?

Sofia shot me a warning look, but not before everyone else noticed.

"Petronella?"

I squirmed, hand finding Oliver's strong one. "I . . ." I swallowed hard. "I needed to send a letter to my mother." When every single male in the room stiffened, I quickly added, "I didn't tell them where we are!"

Niklas barked a laugh, quickly silenced by a glare from his mother. He folded his nearly translucent hands in his lap, as though it was the only way to keep him quiet, but every eye in the room had already focused straight on him.

Josef cleared his throat to regain the attention. "I assume you went to the general store to do this?"

"Yes," I whispered. Nervous sweat pricked at my skin, dampening my palms. Oliver didn't seem to notice, or care. He steadily held on, lending me what confidence he could.

Josef sighed deeply. "Then they'll know. The postmaster stamps all outgoing mail."

My blood ran cold. That was it. They couldn't forgive something like that, could they? "Oh . . ."

Johannes swiveled his attention to his granddaughter. "And you went with her to do this?"

Sofia traced the wood floor with her bare toes, focused on it as though that action alone would save the world. "Yes sir." It was strange to see her cowed, even if only a bit.

I opened my mouth to contradict her, but Oliver squeezed my hand to silence me.

Niklas spoke up, his laughter hardly contained. "And you didn't think about the postmark?"

Sofia opened her mouth to snap something at him, but closed it just as quickly. Her bare feet stuck out under her skirts, toes curling in what I could only assume was anger. "I *did*. What's the big deal if the Wedman Clan finds them? Just hand them over!"

Oliver stiffened, his hand going ridged around mine.

The settee cushions were so worn, they were liable to hold anyone captive. August had to squirm a little to lean forward in his seat as he broke his silence. "They pr'lly already know where they are."

"And why don't we just shove them in that river where they came from?" For emphasis, Sofia stood, pointing toward the Mississippi.

"Sit down, girl!" Johannes pointed at her seat, the power nearly radiating from his finger. "As I told you before, they are under our protection."

"For now," Niklas added under his breath.

"Niklas!" Eva scolded.

The snowy, blonde-haired man didn't look the least bit ashamed of himself. In fact, there was a hint of a smile hiding at the corner of his lips.

"We'll circle back to that later," Johannes said. "What was the fight about?"

Sofia didn't miss a beat. "She ran off."

"I did not!" I curled my hands into fists, ready to stand and defend myself. Oliver gripped my forearm, as if to hold me to my seat.

"You did too! I was 'bout to escort you home, and you took off!"

I narrowed my eyes at her and tried to stand, but Oliver held me steady. "Well, you—"

"E-NOUGH!" Josef stood with such force the entire room stopped breathing.

"Sofia, they are under our protection. Petronella, *you* are under our protection." He turned to point at each of us as he said our names. "No letters leave this clan without approval. Oliver, the two of you will move into the outbuilding first thing in the morning. You'll be happier with some space away from these volatile, insolent *children*."

Niklas snickered. "The shed."

Josef closed his eyes for a long moment, fighting for calm. "Keep that mouth shut, Niklas. Before I move *you* to the woodshed!"

The young man scooted a little farther back in his seat.

A smirk appeared on August's face. He rubbed at his nose to disguise it before he spoke. "There's no furniture in the shed."

"That's why the three of you will help furnish it over the next few days."

Sofia sighed, Niklas groaned, and August nodded his approval.

Josef pointed a steady finger straight at the door. "Get up to bed. All three of you. Before I take you over my knee like the children you are!"

The troublesome siblings scurried from the room like startled mice, August trailing along behind them with a hearty laugh bubbling from his chest.

"I'll help ya tomorrow, don't worry." He winked at Oliver and me before disappearing through the closed door.

I didn't have any idea how to read the wink, so I said absolutely nothing.

"Thank you for your hospitality," Oliver was saying. "I apologize for any difficulties this may have caused."

Johannes waved his hand absently. "No real trouble. August is right, your family likely already knows where you are, anyway."

"But it'd be good practice to *talk* to one of us before mailing a letter," Eva chimed in, focusing her kind eyes on me. "But I'm sure your ma will be glad to know you are all right."

I nodded, choosing to stay silent. Were we really going to get out of this discussion without bloodshed? And with our own space?

Josef looked toward the ceiling, likely listening for the doors to close upstairs. "Go on, then. You need rest after the last few days."

Oliver ducked his head politely and took my hand in his. "Thank you, you all have been too kind."

Eva's smile warmed my heart. "I'm just glad things have worked out the way they have. I don't like cleaning blood out of the carpets."

The shed looked nothing like what I had envisioned. A small, neat building with a little window tucked beside the door—that's what I expected.

No.

First, there was no window. There were a few gaps between the logs that let a few streams of light in, but that was it. Dust and cobwebs clung to every corner imaginable, and there was a snake's abandoned skin behind some old gardening tools. There was no stove. No bed. No chair. Just a bunch of hoes, shovels, and an axe or two.

As if that wasn't bad enough, water had done its best against the bottom of the door over the years, leaving it gaping just enough to invite all the rats and snakes inside.

Hopefully that curtain Eva had made would help with the appearance, if only a little.

I knew I really couldn't complain. After all, we were getting our own place. Did it really matter if it was a vermin-infested tomb?

Sofia bumped against my elbow, grabbing my attention. "What do you think of this, Shed Mouse?"

Eva shouldered her way between us, taking the remaining space of the little room with her skirts. "We'll fix it up nice enough. We can put a mattress over there." She pointed at the corner across from the door, the one with the snakeskin. "And I can bring down the rockin' chair from my own room. I'm not expectin' any babies to rock anytime soon, after all."

I nodded stiffly, rubbing the gooseflesh from my arms.

"We can put a side table here by the door to put your lantern on." She turned in a slow circle, the fabric of her skirt rustling against ours. "The door . . . I suggest we have the men work on that first. What do you say? Don't have any extra glass lyin' around for a window, but maybe, one day, we can cut one in."

I could feel Sofia's eyes on mine, watching for any reaction I might have.

A year ago, you had a leg, a room of your own, and a piano. I absently picked at my nails, doing everything I could to remain grateful. We'd make it work. Right? At least it wasn't a torture chamber.

"Come along, Sofie, let's get all this junk out of here. We can put it against the woodshed for now." Eva scooped up an arm full of tools and marched right out into the sunlight.

"Better watch out," Sofia whispered. "Some'a those snakes are venomous here."

My breath caught in my throat. I grabbed a shovel and sidestepped free of the dark building before she could say anything more.

CHAPTER SIXTY-NINE
The Shed

No matter how much I despised the idea of living in a windowless shed, it would be nice to have some space of our own.

The three of us women crammed ourselves into the shed, our skirts pressed against each other as we eradicated any remaining pests. I lost count of how many spiders I squished with the tip of my cane. At one point, a shrill scream escaped Sofia when a *very alive* mouse rushed for freedom. I do not regret telling Sofia, with a taunting smirk, "I didn't realize you were so scared of a little 'shed mouse.'"

The men didn't help us with any of the cleaning. Instead, they spent their morning making a door. I didn't imagine it would take much effort to piece together a simple rectangle, but apparently, I was mistaken. The unrelenting pounding of hammers filled the air, accentuated by the relentless squeak of a saw.

The noise only stopped when a visitor appeared on the road. He looked very much like Josef, his brother, I assumed. The men stopped their work and gathered around this stranger to hear whatever news he brought. This entire process only took a few minutes. Then, without any fuss, the stranger left and everyone returned to work. No one bothered to tell us what the impromptu meeting was about.

We all took a lunch break in the shade of a nearby tree. I sat across from Sofia, the two of us exchanging petty glares the entire time. Though everyone surely noticed, no one said a word.

Once we got back to work, we swept the place free of every cobweb, dead cricket, and stray leaf.

By the time the blue sky was streaked with the oranges and pinks of sunset, the space was as clean as it could be, a new door was hung, and there was a newly crafted straw mattress in the corner, an oil lamp resting beside it.

"It's not much, but it's a start," Eva said, brushing any stray dirt from her hands.

"And I can stop sleeping in bed with *you*." Niklas punched August in the shoulder.

August's lip quirked into a mischievous smile. "Ah, you know you needed my embrace." Ever so slowly, he leaned toward his brother. When the snowy pale man staggered back, August tackled him to the ground, both of their hats soaring across the grass.

No one moved to break up the playful squabble. Dust flew every which way, laughter floating from the wrestling pair.

Eventually, Johannes wheeled himself to their side and nudged an outstretched leg with the toe of his boot. "Come along," he barked. "We've business to discuss while the women make supper."

My eyes met Oliver's, unspoken questions flying through my head. Almost imperceptibly, he lifted one shoulder in a shrug.

Laughing, the boys rolled off each other and headed straight for the house, exchanging playful pushes the entire time.

Almost as soon as we went inside, Eva whisked Sofia and I off to work on supper, and the men disappeared into the library. When I tried to hang back to listen, Sofia practically dragged me on.

"If they didn't invite us in there in the first place, they don't want to worry us," she said.

"That's *exactly* what I'm worried about."

The meeting seemed to last for ages. By the time we all sat at the dinner table, my stomach felt like it was going to devour itself.

Oliver pulled my seat out for me before sitting at my side. He had dark circles under his eyes, and the lines in his forehead were deeper than before.

"What's wrong?" I whispered.

"Later," he said, nodding to the end-of-season vegetables on our plates.

Like a confined toddler, I couldn't sit still. I picked at the edge of my stained apron, then the stitches of my pocket. "Does it concern us?"

He nodded stiffly but didn't say anything more—no matter how many whispered questions I sent his way.

"Psst!" Niklas's whisper nearly made me jump out of my skin. I hadn't expected him to say a single word to me. Working in the sun all day had made his translucent skin turn the shade of a newly ripening tomato.

I glanced at him but said nothing, ready to hear whatever sort of abuse he'd hurl my way.

"Did you see any sign of Sofie's beau while in town?" He looked almost like a puppy, eyes wide and excited.

"Her beau?" I dared a look across the table at Sofia. Though I was certain she knew there was a conversation going on, she didn't so much as look at us.

"Yeah, Da caught them a few weeks ago—"

"Niklas!" Eva slammed her fork against the table. We all jumped in unison, mouths slammed shut. "If you're gonna talk at the table, talk so everyone can hear ya."

That little smirk appeared at the corner of his lips. He'd been waiting for this very moment, I was sure of it.

He locked eyes with his sister. "Did you get any good kisses from Edmund yesterday?"

Sofia's mouth fell open. "Niklas!"

Josef cleared his throat. "Niklas, why do you think she saw Edmund?"

Eva slammed her silverware against the tabletop again, the dishes clattering as she did so. "We're not having this discussion at the dinner table. That is final!" Chills scrawled up my spine at the mere look of the glare she shot Niklas.

Josef nodded gravely and poked a shriveled piece of squash with his fork. "Sofia, I'd like to speak with you in the library after dinner."

"Yes sir." Sofia ducked her head, but her piercing eyes had a message just for her brother—he would pay.

"And Niklas," Eva chimed in. "I'd like to speak with *you* in the kitchen."

"Yes ma'am," Niklas said, shutting himself up with a quick bite of food.

As soon as the dishes were cleared away, Oliver and I practically sprang outside. Freedom, no matter how small, couldn't come soon enough.

Oliver walked at my side, hand intertwined with mine. He leaned his head back to stare up at the stars, a long sigh escaping his lips.

I rested my head against his arm. "Do you know who Niklas was talking about? That Edmund?"

"Nah. I'm assuming she has a forbidden lover. That was probably why she was in town at the same time as you." He squeezed my hand. "I wouldn't worry about it."

"I'm not *worried*. Just curious." But there was one thing to be concerned about. "What about the library business? What'd they say?"

This time, his sigh was anything but peaceful. He pulled open the door to our shed and ushered me into the darkness. I refused to move until he had the lamp lit, sending peaceful light dancing across the walls.

Oliver plopped onto the pallet, kicking his boots off one by one. Seeing that I hadn't budged from my spot at the door, he gave in. "Come on . . . Do we have to talk about it tonight? I'm beat."

"Yes. Because you'll avoid telling me then too." I crossed my arms over my chest and prepared to stare him down.

"Ugh, fine." He collapsed back onto the mattress. "But if I tell you now, you likely won't get any sleep."

That pushed me to action. I left my cane in the corner and hurried to sit beside him. "Now you *have* to tell me."

Oliver draped his arm over his eyes and shifted back and forth to sink into the mattress. "Josef has a brother in town, Thomas. He came by this afternoon to warn us. He says he'd seen someone from my family cross over on the ferry yesterday."

I pulled his arm away so I could study every inch of his face, hoping that would tell me if he was lying or not. "Who? Who'd he see?"

My blood flowed like it was made of ice. It was Donnell. I knew it.

"Come on, Nella. Just lie down and get some sleep." He absently patted the spot between him and the wall.

"Not until you tell me who it was. And don't pretend you don't know!"

Looking bored, he gently pushed me off his chest and stood. With agonizing slowness, he started to unbutton his shirt. "It was Arthur."

I went completely still. "Arthur?" That was good, right? Arthur wouldn't hurt me. Right?

"Yes, Arthur." Oliver watched me closely, apparently reading my thoughts. "And he's just as dangerous as the others, you understand?"

"No, no. He's not. He's just a kid! Maybe he can help us? We can all—"

Oliver blew roughly through his lips, his fingers catching in a particularly rough knot in his hair. "Petronella, listen to me, please. Arthur was trained exactly as I was. He's had his taste of blood. He's working to get that coveted approval from our father. He will *not* help us."

The bile rose in my throat. I knew Oliver was right, though I didn't want to believe it.

Oliver's hand rested lightly on mine, his fingers untangling the fabric I'd gripped in my fist. "If they just came over yesterday, they likely won't do anything yet. This is a big mission, and they will want all the information they can get before they strike."

Before they strike.

I fought to keep my breath under control.

He placed one hand firmly on each side of my face, forcing me to look him in the eye. "Listen to me. Thomas and his family are keeping watch in town. Johannes, Josef, Niklas, and

August are taking turns in the house. I'll join them tomorrow. There will be at least one set of eyes open at all times."

The world swayed ominously, my barely healed wound throbbing in my abdomen.

"Nella, come on, Nella." Oliver leaned in to kiss me, tenderly at first, then with just enough force to guarantee my attention. "You. Are. Safe. They won't do anything tonight. I promise."

"Arthur was trained just as you were," I whispered, avoiding his gaze. "Doesn't that mean they'll know your every move?"

"Well . . . yes . . . they will. But that also means I know theirs."

I bit my lower lip, fighting for calm. He didn't release me, just held me securely in his arms.

"Then let's go." I sat a bit straighter, taking a deep, cleansing breath. "We can go to the territories like you planned. Get away from all of this."

Oliver raised one brow. "And have at *least* two clans on our tail? Princess, we started a clan war. And it has to be finished one way or another."

CHAPTER SEVENTY

Fire

Slowly but surely, life took on a regular cadence. We'd wake in the morning, clean ourselves in the washbasin by the door, then head into the house for breakfast. Every morning, without fail, Johannes would command every male to meet in the library after they finished their meal. And after that, every morning, they went off to the "mill."

Once, I asked Oliver what they were doing every day, and he just shrugged. "Patrolling the property. It's quite boring, I must admit. We haven't seen a sign of anyone."

"Maybe that means they aren't there?" I asked, a sliver of hope blooming deep inside.

Oliver laughed bitterly. "No, they're out there. I can promise you that."

I almost regretted demanding that Oliver tell me the truth. After all, did I really want to know that they were watching our every move? I wasn't entirely sure. But I was certain that it contributed to my lack of sleep.

They made their move one suspiciously clear, crisp evening.

I didn't notice a single change in the air. Just like every night, an owl hooted somewhere high in the trees, and the coyotes composed their songs off in the distance.

Oliver, on the other hand, either had precise, animal-like hearing, or just felt their presence.

He vaulted from the little blanket nest in our bed, placing a finger firmly to his lips to keep me silent. He glided to a chink between two logs and leaned close, peering out at whatever hid in the trees.

"Blow out the lantern," he instructed, voice nearly inaudible.

I didn't question him. My heart thudded against my breastbone as I scrambled to the edge of the mattress, lifted the glass globe, and blew. The room fell into complete darkness, making my stomach swirl.

"Who is it? Is it them?" I whispered, straining my eyes to see what I could of his shadowy form.

He didn't answer me. Like a ghost, he glided to the opposite wall, peering through yet another hole. At some point, he'd grabbed his discarded pants from their place on the chair. While hunting the landscape outside, he struggled into them, tucking the night shirt inside. He never once took his eyes from whatever hid outside.

I tucked my good leg up into my chemise, wrapping my arms around my knee and pulling it to my chest. "Oliver, tell me, please."

"Shhh," he hissed. Based on his shadow, it looked he was pressing his finger to his lips again, but I couldn't be sure. He left his position by the wall to rifle through the rest of the clothing pile. Doing so, much of it fell onto the dusty ground below. I stiffened, resisting the urge to scold him for making a mess of things.

After a few barely audible curses, he had what he wanted: his belt and holster. With practiced ease, he buckled it around himself and removed the revolver from its position. With an ominous click, he popped open the chamber. Apparently satisfied with what he saw, he snapped it shut and put it back into its home.

"Oliver . . ." I said, my voice a wavering sort of growl.

Absently, he waved his hand at me, bending to peer through the first hole in the wall.

Too restless to stay still for long, I hauled myself out of bed, gripping my cane more for emotional support than physical. "Dammit, who is it?"

He whirled on me, the sudden movement making me take a stumble back. "It is important that you listen to me. Especially right now. Do you understand?"

I nodded mutely.

"You need to stay here—"

I bristled. "No."

He went completely still, shocked at my refusal. It didn't take him more than a beat or two to get himself back under control. "Nella . . . I need you to stay in here while—"

I held up my hand to stop him. "I'm not staying trapped in this damn shed while you go do God knows what!"

"Shhh!" He leapt to my side, pressing his entire hand over my mouth. He leaned in to whisper in my ear. "There are times to be stubborn, and this is *not* one of them. You can be independent and powerful later. But for now, someone is in the trees. I need you to *stay put*." He pushed me to arm's length, his hands cupping my face with a tenderness that didn't quite match the situation. "*Please.*"

Toes curling into the hard-packed dirt, I nodded. "I'll stay," I whispered.

"Thank you." With an almost panicked ferocity, he pressed his lips to mine. I melted, leaning into his embrace, savoring the warmth that flowed between us. The kiss didn't last nearly long enough. Delicately, he slipped a familiar, leather-clad object into my hand, squeezing my fingers around it. "If the worst happens, don't let them take you."

He didn't let me question him further. With one enormous step, he made it to the door. Inch by inch, he pushed it open just enough for his body. Just as slowly, he squeezed through the space and clicked the door shut behind him.

The second the door latched, cold sweat pricked all across my body.

It was them. Who else would it be? Why else would he give me a knife?

How many were there? How close were they? Had they seen Oliver escape our little shed? I wrung my hands on my chemise, pressing my eye to the crack to hunt for what he'd seen.

There was nothing. The owl still sang his nightly song. The coyotes continued their chant somewhere in the distance.

It took me two steps to reach the opposite side of the shed. I repeated the same steps, looking out in the direction of the big house this time. Lonely candlelight danced in Sofia's room, and the brighter light of a fire shone from the sitting room downstairs.

At least someone else was awake. Oliver would go for help, I was sure of it. Had they planned out exactly how they would contact each other in case of an emergency? They had to've! Right?

I sat back on the mattress, picking at a loose stitch in the quilt. Within a matter of minutes, Oliver would have at least four men to help him defend the household.

I leaned against the wall, briefly wondering how Johannes would fight if the moment presented itself. I knew *I* would certainly never cross the man—wheelchair or not. Perhaps that made his perceived weakness a strength? An attacker was bound to underestimate the old man's power.

If I learned to fight even half as well as Sofia, would people underestimate me too?

Something rustled outside. My breath stopped in my throat, and I gripped my knees, fingernails threatening to break the skin.

When nothing else sounded, I got up again to peer out the nearest hole.

The light had gone out in Sofia's room. I could see two shadowy figures along the back side of the house, moving as only a ghost could. Was one of them Oliver? I liked to think so. I squinted into the darkness, searching for anyone else.

There.

Niklas's hair glowed in the moonlight for the briefest moment. He was on the front side of the house, heading for the trees, swallowed by the darkness as quickly as he'd appeared.

Good. Oliver wasn't alone.

I breathed a sigh of relief but didn't move from my post.

What would I do if whoever was outside made it to our little shed? It wouldn't take any effort to get inside. The door didn't lock, and it was impossible to prop it closed from the inside.

Perhaps Oliver had been wrong, and no one was out there. Maybe he just heard a raccoon hunting for scraps?

I went completely still, the only sound coming from the blood rushing through my veins. When had the owl stopped his hooting?

Something crackled in the corner near the rocking chair. Directly afterward, there was a step.

Firm.

Unmistakable.

A footstep.

My hand flew to my mouth, squelching the scream that threatened to escape. I reached for Oliver's blade, hooking it onto the collar of my chemise.

Don't let them take you.

They'd found me. They were here. Who would be the one to take me to the grave? Donnell? Little Arthur?

A familiar, yet foreboding smell rose from the corner. I didn't realize what had changed until it was too late. Whether it was because I refused to believe they had done such a thing, or because I was simply tired, I didn't grasp what was going on until I coughed.

Smoke.

Smoke twirled for the ceiling, a dry sort of crackle creating the music for its dance. I stood frozen to my spot as the first lick of yellow flames slid into view, caressing the wood like a long-lost lover.

"Fire," I whispered, the reality not quite settling in.

I whirled in a circle, searching for a way out. Of course, there was nothing. Nothing except for the door.

More flames joined the first, dancing faster and faster with each passing moment. Already, they had made it halfway across the short wall, inching toward my only escape route.

I didn't have a choice. I couldn't stay put a moment longer.

With a desperate yelp, I dove for the door, taking my cane with me. I threw it open with a bang, refusing to look back as

I bolted for the trees. The crackling was deafening outside, the heat all the more obvious as it faded behind me.

I could feel their predatory eyes on me, feel their anticipation. I was the injured one—these hunters could take me down with ease.

I ran as fast as I could, using my cane as I would use a second leg to move just a bit faster. If I faltered for even a moment, I knew I'd fall flat on my face. But I couldn't think about that.

Just run.

CHAPTER SEVENTY-ONE

To the Death

Viselike fingers dug into my arm, jerking me to the ground like a shot deer. I screamed as my body skidded across the rough dirt. The trees were only a few feet away; if only I had made it there, maybe I could find safety somewhere?

If only . . .

My captor reached for his downed prey, unrecognizable in the near blackness of the night. He intended to incapacitate me, and I knew it.

Fight! Be like Sofia. They don't need you alive.

Gripping my cane so tight that the wood grains speared my fingertips, I slammed it against the side of his head, releasing a war cry as I moved. The broad figure jumped back, startled. I did it again, this time aiming for his knees.

He grunted at the impact, then held me even tighter. His broad chest rippled as the muscles activated.

My stomach dropped to my knees, my vision blurred. Even through the darkness and haze, I knew who it was. His hair had grown enough that it teased his brows, and he had the start of a beard, but there was no mistaking the way his lips moved with his smirk.

No. No. Anyone else! Anyone but him.

As fate would have it, those steel-gray eyes glistened in the dancing firelight as Donnell stared straight into my soul.

"So, we meet again." He grinned, giving me a full view of his crooked teeth. One had broken at an angle, leaving a strange gap along his bottom jaw.

I gasped for air, fighting to regain my own senses.

Smoke swirled around us, preoccupied with its unique waltz, but I no longer cared about the fire.

He was going to kill me this time, and I knew it.

"It'd be in your best interest to be nice to your brother-in-law, would it not?" he taunted. Somehow, he'd twisted both arms behind my back, holding my wrists with one hand. In a manner very similar to stroking a cat, he crooked his finger up my chin. Chills ran up and down my spine at the absurdly tender touch, and I nearly vomited straight on his dirt-smeared shirt.

Fight, Nella! Fight!

My breathing was too fast, I couldn't see straight. Each breath grated against my lungs, filled with smoke and fear. My eyes darted this way and that, hunting for a savior. But there was no one—just the nearby trees and the flames that lapped at the shed.

I fought to control my breathing. If I passed out from sheer panic, I wouldn't be able to do *anything*.

As soon as I had it under control, I dove headfirst for the ground, bringing my leg to my chest as I did. Either he'd drop me, or keep me from breaking my own teeth. Either option was a success.

I didn't move a single inch.

With impressive ease, his hands flew to keep me in his embrace, his free arm wrapping around my shoulders.

"Oh, c'mon, sweetheart," he purred into my ear. His whiskers tickled my earlobe, sending those shivers all the way to my toes. "I'm a *whole lot* stronger than you could ever be, and you know it. What do you think you're gonna do? Really now, I'd love to know."

When I didn't respond—I couldn't've, even if I had a clue what to say—he took his first steps toward the cover of the forest, dragging me along. My bare heel sunk into the dirt as I fought to stop the process, squirming every which way, yelping the entire time.

His laugh vibrated against my back. "Keep that up, 'kay? Those sounds are *perfect*."

When we were far enough into the trees to suit him, he released my arms but retained a tight grip on my torso. "Be good for just a moment?"

I had to take advantage of what I could. My hands scrambled for his belt, searching for a weapon that I knew would be there. He laughed again, gently shoving my hand away.

"Now, dear pet. You think I'll let you have this?" Cold iron touched the fragile skin of my neck, and I went deathly still. "Don't worry, I made sure you can't reach the gun, either. Now, now, stop your squirmin'. I don't want to nick you by accident." He paused for dramatic effect, gasping. "Like that, see?"

I craned my neck to look down, getting a clear view of a thin trickle of blood as it trailed between my breasts to disappear beneath my chemise. I didn't move a muscle.

"Please, please let me go!" I begged.

"Nah." He adjusted his grip on me, being sure I felt every inch of that blade. "Why would I do something like that? Especially after what *you* did."

The broad shape of Oliver stepped into view, framed by the swirling smoke. He held his gun steadily, not a bit of fear in his stance as he pointed it right at us. Or rather, at his brother.

"Let her go, Donnell," Oliver growled.

Donnell tsked his tongue. "Why would I do that, little brother?"

Oliver never removed his gaze from us. No emotion. He was cold, hard, and, quite frankly, terrifying. I knew he wouldn't shoot me, at least not purposely, but I certainly didn't feel comfortable being on the wrong side of his gun.

They moved fast. Donnell tensed, breaking Oliver's concentration for a split second. Like a gunshot, he lunged for us, screaming.

My heart thumped painfully against my ribcage.

Donnell didn't move a single muscle; he remained over his prey without an ounce of visible fear.

Someone else did.

Springing from the smoke like a crazed bear, a young man flung himself onto Oliver's back with a rabid scream, blade drawn. He was a lithe creature, lanky and made of pure muscle. His brown hair fell all around his shoulders in a messy veil, hiding the expression that I knew would never leave my mind.

Arthur looked exactly like the wild animal he'd been trained to become.

Oliver went down in a puff of leaves and disrupted smoke, his gun discharging as it careened into the air. I heard my scream slice through the chaos as the two of them fought.

Brother against brother.

Killer against killer.

Oliver swiped a blade from his waistband, ready for whatever the fight brought. They were well matched. Arthur was only on top for a moment or two before Oliver threw him off, leaping to a crouched position to face his attacker. Just like a predator, Arthur was on his feet in half a second, a big, crooked grin spanning his face.

"We don't have to do this!" Oliver shouted.

"Sure we do. It's been a long time since we've had a good fight!" Arthur popped his knuckles dramatically.

They crashed together again, their muscles rippling under their shirts as they fought for control. At one point, Arthur used his leg to knock Oliver down. At another, Oliver was pinned to the ground until he kneed his brother between the legs, sending Arthur scrambling back with a yowl.

Nothing was off limits, that was for sure. They fought with their knives, slicing here or there, never once making a fatal cut.

I knew the fight would only end when someone tired out. They could roll around like that forever, evenly matched.

Apparently, Donnell knew this as well. With an inconvenienced sigh, he tightened his grip on me, propped me against his chest, and carried on his way, dragging me with him. I screamed and kicked, but he didn't care.

"Ah, good. You got her."

I hadn't seen the silky-voiced man approach. He stood directly beside his son, arms crossed firmly over his middle. "How long should we let them go on with that?" Henry nodded toward Arthur and Oliver.

Donnell shrugged against my back. "Dunno."

"Remember," Henry said, moving to stand in front of me, just out of reach of my foot. "Don't kill her. She's the best punishment we'll ever have for him." He leaned so close I could smell his stale breath. With his pointer finger, he traced my collarbone, then up to my chin. He paused right under my lip, taunting me. I took the bait, chomping at his finger without a second thought.

Henry yowled as blood flowed freely between my teeth. "Damn *bitch*!" He raised that same hand and slapped me hard across the face, likely painting my skin red.

At the sound of the slap, Oliver's attention faltered for a fraction of a second, letting Arthur get the upper hand. He let out a solid "oof!" as Arthur's fist landed against his nose.

Henry turned slowly, observing his younger children. "Give it up, boy," he called to Oliver. "You can only fight your own blood for so long. And when you're done with Arthur, you've got us to deal with."

With one solid punch, Arthur collapsed to the ground. Oliver rose above him, eyes alight with the fire of a trained killer. "I know," he purred as he stalked toward his father. "And it's time to finish this once and for all. This is my life. And *she's* my family. You're no blood of mine."

From behind us, someone cleared their throat. Deep and strong, August spoke. "And he's not alone, now is he?"

Donnell flinched; Henry stiffened.

"Give it up, *Wedman*!" Niklas growled, stepping out of the trees. "We've got you now!"

From where Donnell held me, I could see the exchange. Henry raised both his eyebrows in a wordless gesture, then rolled his eyes to his right. I didn't get a chance to scream, speak, or even breathe before Donnell followed the silent instructions.

As he shifted his weight to his right, August made a similar movement, both of them at the ready. Perched as if ready to pounce, Donnell did just that. He threw me over his shoulder and ran the opposite way. As he moved, Henry whirled around, gun at the ready.

Niklas dove for Henry. "You go after—"

Bang.

CHAPTER SEVENTY-TWO

Whisked Away

If I ever had a chance to use my voice again, I knew it would be hoarse from all my screaming.

I didn't get to see where the shot landed. I didn't even get to see who did the shooting.

Two more gunshots echoed through the trees, the sounds ricocheting straight into my ears.

Who was gone? Was it mischievous Niklas? Or trustworthy August?

Donnell nearly glided over the leaves as he ran. He seemed to move faster than Oliver had on our mad dash away from their house. How long would it take before they caught up with me?

Would they even bother trying? I was bait—they were bound to know that.

But they did.

Even I heard the rustle of leaves to the left. Fast, light, and sure, someone was running alongside us. Donnell tucked his head and picked up the pace, one hand wrapped around me, the other fondling the gun at his hip.

"Give it up, *Wedman*. You're as good as toast!" Niklas taunted. He didn't sound the least bit breathless. "You're surrounded!"

Donnell let out a sound somewhere between a laugh and a cough. He was growing tired.

We flew on through the trees. How long would we run before he dropped me? How long would I make it practically upside down?

Apparently, Donnell had other plans.

His horse idled under a nearby tree, flicking her flaxen tail in irritation. Donnell made for her, retrieving his gun and shooting into the darkness where he'd last heard Niklas. A resounding yelp gave him all the answers he needed as the horse moved in beside us.

My toes curled under, and I fought to regain any ounce of fight I had left. What would Oliver do in this situation? What about Sofia?

He tossed me onto the horse, the barely healed wound on my torso *just* missing the saddle horn. Without making sure I was secure, he leapt into the seat. With a shout, he dug his heels into her withers and we began our gallop through the trees.

They wouldn't give up, that was for sure.

So you can't give up either.

The horse traveled fast, weaving in and out of trees like she did it for fun. If I threw myself off, I not only would injure myself, but he would have me again within a minute. If I broke a bone, he wouldn't bother trying to help me like Oliver had.

Donnell's head was on a swivel, pinging from shadow to shadow. Did he see anyone? Was Oliver already out there, trying to save me?

Please . . . please let it be him.

I shifted my weight, trying to lift my head to lessen the painful throb as we erupted from the tree line and onto the rocky lake bed. Gooseflesh raced up my arms as the crashing of the water reached my ears. I craned my neck to see. The Mississippi looked so much larger than it had before.

And he was going to try to cross.

"No!" I pleaded, pushing against the mare as I tried to flop free. "I'll drown!"

He placed a solid hand on my back, holding me down. I could feel his dark chuckle vibrate through his palm. "No, you won't. I have *plans* for you, bitch."

The fishy smell of the bank hit my nostrils right before the mare slid to a halt. The water teased at her hooves, only a few inches away. My premature sigh ended in a squeal as Donnell yanked me from the horse.

He seemed to lift me with more effort than before. Maybe he was growing tired? Maybe that would give me a chance?

"Can't have ya squirming too much, can I?" He searched the saddlebags, pulling out a worn piece of rope. "After all, I have plans for you, crippled bitch." Using my hair as a handle, Donnell shoved me to the rocky ground. I gasped as the gravel dug into my skin.

If he tied me to the horse, I wouldn't have a chance.

No one appeared in the shadows of the trees. No horse whinnied to alert me of an incoming savior.

I was on my own.

Desperately, I kicked out, aiming for between his legs. "Let me go, you big oaf!"

My kick fell short as Donnell gripped my ankle, holding it in the air as he would a captured chicken. "And deprive you of my plans?" he purred.

I squirmed to the best of my abilities, nearly spinning in the stones. "They'll be here any minute! You can cross easier without me. Just drop me here—"

He interrupted me with another laugh. His eyes nearly sparked in the moonlight as he teased the rope along my calf.

The touch made me freeze in pure horror. It was over. I was his. He brought the rope lower and lower, his eyes focused right on mine, a slow smile spreading over his face at my inevitably horrified expression. He made it to right above my knees, fingers caressing my skin, when they arrived.

As the shot rang out, I felt the air as it whizzed past my arm.

Even though it caught him off guard, Donnell didn't hesitate. Forgoing the restraints, he tossed me over the horse and leapt back into the saddle. "Hiyah!" he shouted, digging his heels into the mare's withers.

I craned my neck to see who had come after us.

They were all riding bareback, looking like the true hunters they were. Oliver, pressed close to his mare's neck; August, mirroring that same position, only with an arm outstretched along her mane, a pistol at the end. Josef held his mount back a few feet, Niklas perched behind the saddle, poised to jump.

The cavalry is here! I had a chance after all.

Donnell took the horse straight to the rushing water. She didn't approve of his wishes as he urged her on. She sidestepped the water once, twice, then a third time. He kicked her again, and she practically leapt into the icy depths.

Another shot rang out.

And another.

"No! Stop!" I screeched as the water rushed all around us. I shifted to one side to keep my head out of the water, meaning I clung to the mare like a opossum. The current wasn't just teasing at my legs and torso; it had a vendetta against me. It yanked at my chemise, threatening to take me down to its depths.

Seeing this, Donnell gripped the back of my clothing, grabbing a fistful of hair as he did. "Hold on if you want to live!" he snarled.

I scrambled a little farther onto the back of the horse, daring a look back at shore.

They were all still there, mounted and watching Donnell's retreat. Each one of them were as still as statues, whole notes held indefinitely with the fermata of shock.

It's time to save yourself for once.

I couldn't let Donnell take me.

Why are you holding on? He can't catch you if you just let go.

So I did.

CHAPTER SEVENTY-THREE
Currents

*B*ut I can't swim.

I didn't have to push away from the mare before the current gripped me in its icy embrace, creeping through my veins, spearing into my soul.

But I didn't go far. The pain from his grip felt like fire as he yanked me free of the water. Did I yell? Did I scream? I couldn't see through the water streaming down my face as I clawed at him.

"You're not getting out that easy!" he taunted.

I only managed to sputter a few words. "I would rather die!"

I raked my fingernails down his arm, his face, whatever I could reach as he fought to restrain me. He swore as we tilted far to the side. The horse whinnied her protest as she swam on.

I'm sorry, girl, I thought. *I have to fight.*

His fingers wrapped around the back of my neck as he gripped my scruff, his claws sinking into the skin. Hot liquid mixed with the water. His blood? Mine? Both?

The world slowed to *adagissimo*, even the droplets of water taking their time to gather the moonlight before they met the water below. He pressed his cheek against my head, his body heat sending terrified shivers throughout me.

"If you struggle any more, death will be a *blessing*," he seethed. His breath caressed the tender spot below my ear, sending a thin whine up and out my throat.

My fingers trembled as I pawed at him, reaching for what-ever part of exposed skin I could. But they found something better: the sheath on his belt with the wood-handled blade—so worn it was soft.

My breathing hitched as I gripped it with everything I had.

Now. Now! "I'll never give up!" I screamed as I ripped the knife from its sheath and slammed it into Donnell.

This time, there was no mistaking whose blood it was that spread over my fingers. He roared and dropped me.

Run. Run! I threw myself into the freezing river.

It sucked me into its depths, pulling at my limbs, my hair, my soul. I could still see the moonlight as it reached through the water, stretching its fingers out for me, desperately trying to pull me up.

My lungs squeezed, pleading for the air I could not provide. I kicked blindly for the surface, but I couldn't tell if I made any progress.

I don't want to die. But at least it's on my own terms.

I couldn't tell which way was up anymore. The water tossed me around as a coyote would a chunk of venison. My chest ached, an air bubble creeping to the tip of my nose.

No! Fight a little more. Fight!

But my lungs were done. They gasped for relief, taking in the freezing water around. It burned all the way into my chest, choking me, bending my body to its will.

Is this the way I go? At least I get to go on my own *terms.*

The sweet embrace of unconsciousness teased at the edge of my senses as the water pulled me along. I welcomed it. Warmth. Comfort. Safety. It would be mine once more.

I felt his hands as they clutched at my arm, felt the briefest pain as I was pulled away, his fingernails slicing skin.

My angel isn't very good at his job.

The darkness engulfed me.

Finally. I'm safe.

But that angel had other plans. He attacked me. Something smacked against my chest, forcing my body to come alive again, coughing and sputtering.

I curled into a ball, hiding from it as my body expelled anything inside of me in a spew of watery vomit.

The comforting blanket of unconsciousness was slipping away, replaced by a chilly breeze against my legs.

"No," I moaned. *Out loud.*

Someone pummeled my back. Once. Twice. A third time.

I coughed again, shying away from the impact as I spewed out more liquid.

"C'mon, Nella," someone crooned in my ear.

I went stock-still. I wasn't dead. And it wasn't Donnell.

"We've got you, you're safe."

I opened my eyes.

He had one hand on my shoulder, biting his lower lip as he watched me.

Oliver. He had me. In the moonlight, I could make out the crimson that soaked his shirt, that stained the corners of his face.

Blood.

I gasped and patted down my neck, all the way to my torso. Nothing.

"You're all right," Oliver whispered. "You're gonna be all right now."

"We can't stay here," came Josef's voice. "Need to get her warm."

"Mhm," Oliver agreed. He moved to a low squat, inching his arms under my body.

"I've got her," Niklas said, shouldering Oliver out of the way.

"Thanks," Oliver muttered, standing again.

I flinched away as Niklas scooped me into his arms. Why couldn't Oliver take me?

"He's right there, don't worry," Niklas crooned. "He's brutal, y'know. He wouldn't let me hurt you even if I wanted to." As if to underline his point, he nudged Oliver in the side.

"Here." August appeared at our side, proffering a wool coat. Niklas adjusted his hold to get it wrapped around me like a hug.

Water dripped from August's nose, clung to the ends of his hair. He was soaked from head to toe, wearing only a pair of pants, a rope tied around his waist.

"You . . ." I whispered, realization hitting like a runaway train. He was the angel.

August shot me a lopsided smile.

"C'mon!" Josef barked. "Mount up. We need to get home. Now."

A chill traveled up my spine as all the memories crashed into me.

"Did I get him? Is he dead?" I squinted to search for a body, but there was nothing.

"So far," Niklas grumbled. "Saw him get out on the other side."

At least you left a mark on him *this time.*

We traveled fast, making it back to the smoky clearing at the same time as the first hues of sunrise streaked across the sky. Niklas held me snuggled into my borrowed coat, taking care to keep even my ears safe from the wind.

At some point, August had donned his own coat. Like a turtle, he shrank inside of it just like me.

The glistening frost on the grass mixed with the settling smoke made the place look like a fairytale—definitely not like the blood-soaked battleground that it was.

At the corner of the barn, Josef swung from his mount. "August, take Nella to the fire. You both need to get warm. Oliver, Niklas, help me put the horses up."

The man looked dead on his feet. Whatever he had bandaged his arm with was failing, the blood seeping into the fabric of his sleeve.

Niklas hopped down. "We've got the horses. You need to get inside too."

Oliver nodded his agreement, sliding to the ground. "It's bleeding again." He nodded at Josef's arm.

I peered from my cocoon of a coat, studying each and every one of them. It didn't look like they had just won a battle; instead, they looked like they had *lost*. Eyes weary and cheeks hollow and bruised, each man seemed much older than before.

Not a single one of them had made it through unscathed. Josef had been shot in the arm. August had a bandaged shoulder. Niklas *appeared* fine, but he had a slight limp. Oliver had dried blood pretty much everywhere.

Was it his? "Oliver," I croaked.

"Yes?" He took me from August, pulling me into his cozy embrace.

"What happened?" My brain was still foggy, only made worse by the cold that sneaked through the edges of the coat.

He blinked rapidly. "What?" Following the direction of my gaze, he continued. "Oh. That. I'm all right. I'll tell you later, okay?"

I straightened myself to narrow my eyes at him.

"Right. The agreement." He sighed deeply, rubbing at his temple. "My fa— er . . . Henry, he's . . ." He swallowed hard, eyes wrenched shut as he fought through the unbidden emotion. "He's . . . no longer a threat. I didn't have time to clean up . . . before I came after you, you know."

My entire mouth went dry. Hell Man was dead. "I'm sorry . . ." I whispered.

Oliver cleared his throat. "Go on, get warm before you catch your death out here." He bent to kiss the top of my head. "I'll be in soon."

CHAPTER SEVENTY-FOUR
Annulment

No matter how hard I tried, I couldn't sleep.

Eva made me sit through a piping hot bath before wrapping me in the thickest quilt she could find. She then instructed me to march straight to bed and not come down until morning.

Though I gladly obeyed, sleep refused to claim me. The minutes on the square clock passed, one after another.

He didn't come in until the sun was high in the sky.

As he caught sight of me, his eyebrows quirked in surprise. "I thought you would be asleep by now," he said.

"Me too," I admitted. My voice still sounded hoarse.

He sat in the worn chair by the door, fumbling with his shoes. The whole time, his eyes remained locked on my fidgeting. He was covered in bruises. He had a cut from under his ear to his collarbone, and his lip was split in multiple places. But I didn't see any major wounds. No thick bandages that could hide anything detrimental.

Knowing he was safe, I should've been able to relax.

But I couldn't. *He watched his own father die, and he didn't do anything. Or . . . did he do the killing himself?* I hated myself for even letting the thought cross my mind, though I instantly knew it was the truth. The way he acted, the way he couldn't get through his explanation when asked about the blood.

Then my own blood drained from my face.

Could there have been any other resolution? If he let his father go, what would've happened? When Donnell took me, it might've been even easier to capture Oliver. And then he would've tortured him, making me watch every agonizing moment.

And what happened to Arthur?

"Talk to me, please," Oliver said, his voice level, but still gentle. Like a parent trying to console a lost child.

But I was far from a lost child.

Numb, queasy, emotionless, but not a lost child.

I scrubbed at my temple to erase the panic. He did it to save me, to keep me safe. I knew this, but would I ever be okay with him killing anyone? "Are you sure you're okay?" I asked.

He patted my knee. "Yeah. We made progress today, though I know it doesn't feel like it."

I searched his face just in time to see the pain shoot through his eyes. "No." I placed my palm on his chest. "Your father . . . Are you okay?"

His eyes fluttered closed against the emotion. "It's . . ." He sighed and pinched the bridge of his nose. "Hopefully, this keeps them at home for a while."

My hand ran from his chest, lingering on his thigh. "It doesn't feel real yet, does it?"

He let his eyes flutter open, the pain in plain view. "Right now, it's the job. It's not easy . . . and it won't get easier. But . . . I just haven't—" He shrugged as he fought for the right words. "I haven't felt it deep down yet. I've killed more times than you *want* to know. It's easy to ignore after a while. But some . . . some you never forget. My first . . . and this one." He shuddered almost imperceptibly.

I gnawed on the inner part of my cheek, unsure what to say.

"You know," he began, voice starting off soft. With each word, it grew more firm as he became sure of himself. "There's one way you won't have to deal with any of this."

I sat a little straighter. "How?"

He didn't look at me as he spoke. "If you go back home. Live with your mother and sister, you won't have to worry about any of this."

I raised one eyebrow, my heart thudding just a little faster. "With you?"

He paused, fighting against the word. "No."

I sat up a little straighter, staring him in the face. "We're married . . ."

"Yes," he drawled. "But we could have it annulled." Did I hear hesitation in his voice?

My heart sped to just about as fast as it could, hammering in my ears. "But you . . . but we . . ." I glanced down at myself subconsciously. "It's been consummated!" My voice squeaked on the last word.

"Well." He blushed, which would have made me grin any other day. "But we don't have to tell them that. It's not as though they would *check*. And you're not with child, as far as I'm aware." He studied my every move, gauging my reaction.

"I'm not," I snapped, the edges of my heart shattering as I spoke. "I'm tired of men controlling my life!" I threw my arms into the air and slid from the bed. "If I go there, Donnell will soon follow. You can't argue against that!"

He fidgeted. "I'll make sure that won't happen."

"How?" I demanded. He stared at the quilt, each thought flickering across his face faster than the last. "I thought so—you don't know."

He sighed. "No, I don't." He cupped my face in his hands and stared straight into my eyes. "But if you don't want to be part of this world, have this life, be near . . ." He took a deep breath. "Be near a killer, I want you to have the option. If you choose annulment, I will do everything in my power to ensure your safety. I promise."

My heart thudded once. Twice. A third time. Each beat nearly audible.

"I need to know, Nella," he continued. "What *do you* really want? You shouldn't have so many people controlling your life. It's wrong—I was wrong . . . You're not a prisoner. Mine, or anyone else's. What do *you* want, Nella? Do you want to go home to your family, live the life you were born into? Or do you want to stay here, with me?"

I hesitated, willing the extreme emotions to stay inside, trying to keep my heart from leaping from my chest, attempting to keep the tears locked behind my eyes. They escaped anyway, trailing down my cheeks.

Oliver released my face. He was intent on letting me make the final say.

I swallowed hard and let myself imagine the possibility. I could go home. Mama would take me in without question. She'd keep me safe, I'd help around the house. It would be a glorious homecoming, helping Miriam with Felicité, watching as Chris worked on his apprenticeship and started his own family.

Except . . . it'd only be a matter of time before they married me off. It was inevitable. In their eyes, my womanly duties would never be complete unless I had a man. And if I went home, I wouldn't have a say in that matter. I didn't before, why would it change now?

Or I could stay with Oliver and see what happened, explore whatever the world threw at us. Together. I wouldn't be alone with a husband who didn't care for me. We would be a team.

That very thought was all it took to make up my mind. I took a deep, cleansing breath before speaking. "I feel safer with you." I squared my shoulders and met his gaze. I wrapped my arms around his neck and pulled myself so close, my thighs touched his knees and his shaky breath tickled my nose.

"Is that your final decision?" he asked, straining his neck so his face didn't touch mine.

"Yes, please. I don't have any desire to marry anyone else. I think I'll keep you." *Killer or not.* Before I could let my brain run off with the stray thought, I pulled him to me and kissed him.

He grinned underneath me and tangled his fingers in my hair. "I approve of your decision."

Lust threatened to overcome logic as we fell into a heap on the quilt.

"Will we stay here?" I whispered between kisses.

Almost reluctantly, he shrugged. "For now, yes. We need the support of the Welks Clan. Especially now with Arthur—"

I pushed away with a gasp. How had I forgotten about Arthur? "Where is he? Is he all right? Is he going to help us?"

Oliver raised that one eyebrow, as though it surprised him that I'd even come to such a conclusion. "No," he said firmly. "He's safely . . . or well . . ." He gnawed on his lower lip.

I sat up. "Tell me!"

Oliver groaned and rolled to the floor. "He's downstairs. Safe enough."

"Can I see him?" I blurted.

He stared at me for a long moment, apparently just as surprised as I was to hear that come out of my mouth. "No."

"Are they going to let him go? Eventually?"

He turned for the dresser, grabbing a flask and filling the first of the two delicate crystal glasses. "I don't know, Nella. There's a lot of pieces to this puzzle, and I don't know what the next move will be." He held the glass out to me, his other hand curling into a fist for a brief moment.

I slumped and took it, staring at the amber liquid as it sloshed around. "Well, that brings back some bad memories," I muttered.

He smirked and sank into the quilt beside me, holding his own glass. "I don't know what will happen, with Arthur, or with Donnell." He paused as I flinched. He placed his hand on my knee and squeezed. "But I *do* know, I will do everything I can to take care of you."

I sighed and took a sip. It burned the whole way down, resulting in a pleasant warmth that bloomed in the pit of my stomach.

"Tonight, we celebrate what we can—that we are both alive and safe." He held up his glass in the air, waiting for me to do the same.

I stared at the flower-etched glass, fighting the fear of the unknown that fought for space in my head. Before the worries could drown me, I held it up high. "To safety!"

He clanked his glass against mine, the liquid sloshing dangerously. "To safety!"

I took a deep sip, shivering as the firewater burned down my throat and warmed my entire soul.

Safety. We were trapped in someone else's home, sure, but we were all right. Safe. As much as we could be.

CHAPTER SEVENTY-FIVE

Just You Wait and See

I wish I could say I was a good wife and listened to Oliver. If I did, perhaps I would've avoided at least a little heartbreak.

Nearly as soon as the sun rose above the horizon, each of the men left to check for signs of Donnell's return. Johannes went to ask around town with the help of Niklas. The other three hunted every inch of the property and beyond, checking for footprints, or even crumpled leaves.

I stayed in bed late, partially because I didn't want to deal with Sofia, and partially because I was exhausted. Apparently, the other women were just as tired, as I didn't hear a single peep from the household after the men left.

When I finally emerged from my sleepy tomb, I pulled one of Sofia's old dressing gowns around my shoulders and made my way downstairs.

I didn't *plan* on going to see him. It just somehow happened.

At the foot of the stairs, my body shifted in all the wrong ways until I stood stock-still in front of the door, controlling my breath. The lock was there but unlatched. I really didn't want to see what torturous items lay beyond the wooden door, but I pushed it open anyway.

The room was windowless and pitch-black. Barely daring to breathe, I pulled a match from its sconce by the door and easily lit the lantern hanging beside it.

When I let the glass slide back into place, I forced my eyes to wander the room.

The walls were paneled in wood with various implements hanging all around. Whips, straps, chains, rope, and iron loops secured straight to the wall. They had a flat table against the far side, mercifully empty other than the straps that hung from the four corners.

Arthur sat in an iron chair in the middle of the room, his legs shackled to rings in the ground, his hands bound behind his back. Attached to the straps on his arms was a long chain that led straight to the ceiling. This chain was tight, pulling his arms up just slightly and leaving no room for movement.

Had he been like that all night? I could only imagine how sore his shoulders would be after the constant pressure.

He studied my every move, a small, comforting smile on his lips.

"Nella." He nodded stiffly in greeting.

It's Arthur. You have nothing to be afraid of.

I took a large breath, startled to find how clean the room smelled, and then walked right to his side. "Are you all right?" I knelt behind him, setting the lantern where I could see his hands.

His restraints were so tight, they left gouges in his skin. Arthur wiggled his fingers as if to accentuate the fact.

I touched the leather strap, gnawing on my lower lip. I knew better than to take them off—even if for a moment, just to loosen them.

"Are ya gonna let me out?" Arthur asked, a laugh teasing his voice.

"No," I said, standing back up with a sigh. "You know I can't do that."

He chuckled darkly, sounding very much like his brother. "Yeah, I know."

I moved to stand in front, arms crossed over my middle, lantern hanging loosely from a single finger. "I have a question for you."

"Go on," he prodded.

"Why'd you come after me?"

He blinked slowly, as though he was fighting for patience.

"All right, all right, I *know* why you came after me. But . . . you knew they'd try to kill me if they succeeded, didn't you?"

He groaned, pulling against his restraint as he did so. The chains rattled, igniting pure fear deep in my heart.

I shifted my weight and continued. "*You* wouldn't try to kill me, right?" My mouth went dry at the words. Each individual scar throbbed at the memory. My leg ached, the lashes across my back almost burned, and the scar along my torso felt stretched to its limits, threatening to pop.

Something twinkled in the corner of his eye. "Let me out, and we'll see."

When I took an involuntary step back, he laughed. "I know better. So long ago, when we first found you in that attic, you probably would'a let me go. Now?" He shook his head.

I watched the young killer shift in his bonds, heart thudding against my ribcage.

"This is my life. I was born for this. Born for the hunt. If you raise a cow, don't you butcher it one day? Doesn't mean you didn't like the cow." He shrugged, the chain rattling as he did so.

I bristled. "*I'm* not a cow."

He raised his eyes to meet mine, cold and hard, relentless. "One way or another, everyone is livestock."

A chilly fear traversed my spine and my knee buckled, forcing me to grab the wall for support.

"It's what I was raised for," Arthur continued, voice solid. "It's not *my* fault Oliver brought you into this life. But it is my duty to take care of the problem he caused. You just so happen to be part of it. War is war, and I'll do what I have to."

My blood ran cold, and I wrapped the dressing gown tighter around my body.

"Let me out, or don't. That's all up to how fast you want this to end. But know this, Petro*nella* Dowling, you may think you're a sweet and innocent flower, but you started this battle."

I stumbled back one step, then another.

"We *will* come get you. Just you wait and see."

I turned and blindly rushed for the safety of the hall.

"Thanks for the lantern!" Arthur hollered after me.

The door squealed as I slammed it shut, my breathing so fast that stars swirled across my vision.

"We will come get you. Just you wait and see."

Someone cleared their throat only a few feet away. I yelped as I whirled to face my attacker.

Eva leaned against the kitchen doorway, arms casually crossed over her corseted middle. "Have a good chat?"

I said nothing. What was I supposed to do, lie? What would they do to me as a punishment for this? Take me in that very room and whip me? I could only imagine how much joy Arthur would get from such a show. He missed the last one, after all.

"Calm down, sweetheart. I'm not gonna tell a soul you stepped foot in there." She reached out to take my arm. "Come, come get breakfast before you get sick."

I followed her into the kitchen, my every limb trembling. I stayed silent until I sat at the table.

"I thought . . . he was . . ." I sighed, resting my head in my hands. "He was like a friend to me. He was so kind! He wasn't supposed to turn out like . . . like this!"

Eva patted my arm as she placed a slice of toast in front of me. "Each and every one 'a them has two sides. One is sweet as can be. They'll take care of those they love and consider their family. The other?" She shrugged, letting me fill in the blanks.

"But . . . he acted like I *was* family!" I nudged the toast across the plate with my trembling finger.

"He might've. But you changed sides. Oliver is blood, which changes things somewhat. But if either of you stepped foot on the other side of the Mississippi . . ." She tsked her tongue. "Well, he'd survive, but he wouldn't be unscathed."

I rubbed the gooseflesh from my arms. "And me?"

She shook her head mournfully. "Eat your breakfast, dear. Best you stay busy."

I spent the majority of the morning in silence, staying as far away from that dreary room as possible. To keep my hands busy, I started to embroider some bluebirds on a pillowcase for our future cabin and mended one too many socks. Though I was lost in the menial tasks, my mind was far from calm.

How long would it be before Donnell returned? This time, for both of his brothers. Would he bring in reinforcements?

How long would it be until the Welks Clan handed us right over?

It wasn't long after midday when I stood and placed my mending in the basket.

"You all right?" Eva asked.

Sofia peered over her own sewing. She was busy working on a surprisingly intricate pink dress to entice her forbidden beau, maybe?

"I . . . I just don't feel well. I'm going to go up and rest a little, okay?" I stammered.

"Go on, I'll bring food up to you for dinner."

Each step seemed to take me no closer to the safety of my room. The entire time, I kept my eyes on that dreaded door. I didn't look forward until it slid out of sight.

Oliver woke me by kissing my cheek.

I hadn't expected to fall asleep, especially without an onslaught of nightmares. But that's exactly what happened.

A plate of food sat untouched on the bedside table, likely brought up by Eva or Sofia hours before. It was late, the room lit only by Oliver's candle.

I scrubbed the sleep from my eyes and stifled a yawn. "You're back already?"

He smiled and set the candle beside my untouched food. "There wasn't anything to track. We knew that was a possibility." He shrugged.

I shivered involuntarily. I hadn't taken the time to get under the blankets, and the chill had crept into the room.

"Get out of that dress and come snuggle me," he instructed. He practically dove under the quilt on his side.

With the speed of a turtle, I did just that, removing all clothes other than my chemise and crawling into bed. He tucked his arms around my torso and pulled me against him.

"You saw Arthur today." It wasn't a question.

My breath caught in my throat, and I tried to pull away from his grasp. He didn't release me. *Eva said she wouldn't tell anyone!*

"Who told you?" I demanded.

"Arthur." Oliver shrugged against my back. "I'm not mad," he promised with a quick squeeze. "I just want to check that you're all right."

I sighed and relaxed against his warm body, breathing in his woodsy scent. "I thought he'd help us. See our side of things."

Oliver kissed the top of my head. "I wish it worked that way, I really do."

I lifted my gaze to his. His blue eyes were caring, sweet. There wasn't a single hint of the killer hiding in their depths. "If he turned on us like that, how do I know who to trust?"

He gave me a sympathetic smile. "Me. You can trust me." He kissed the tip of my nose.

I melted just a little more. "If it came down to it, do you think he'd actually kill me?"

Oliver sighed deeply. "Try not to think about it, okay? I'm not gonna let that happen. Not ever. I promise."

CHAPTER SEVENTY-SIX
Nightmare

His finger traced my jaw, so gentle it made the gooseflesh rise to the surface. He held me in his lap, so loose I could've rolled away.

Only I couldn't move.

His blade rested on the leaf-covered ground, just out of my reach. That is, if I could move my fingers that mere inch or two. Instead, I just lay there helpless, dressed only in a dressing gown, sprawled across my captor's lap.

"You look so scared, my dear," Donnell crooned, leaning in so that his overgrown hair danced along my cheek with his every exhale.

I tried to open my mouth, to cry for help, to curse his name, but even my lips were frozen.

"What were you thinking when you saw Sara outside your window?" He pushed a stray hair of mine behind my ear, his breath tickling the hollow on my neck as he whispered. "Were you thinking that you would be free if you turned her in? Well, that's not what happens in the real world."

Something sharp dug into the skin of my neck. The knife had never moved. What was it? Four little points, creeping, slicing to grip the flesh under my jaw. His fingers?

"You're not free, are you? And look what happened. You, yes you, you killed her!"

The world flashed red, then white, and a scream echoed through the forest.

My scream.

"Nella? Nella!" Oliver shook me roughly. He hovered over me, his eyebrows drawn together with concern.

I gasped for air, my hands flying to check the path of his fingers, where those impossibly sharp nails had dug into my skin.

My flesh was unmarred, cold, delicate. I could feel my pulse hammering under my fingertips as I scrubbed away the ghost of his touch.

"You're all right, you're all right," Oliver crooned, pulling me into his protective embrace. He tucked my head under his chin, kissing the top of my head.

I breathed in his scent. He smelled of lavender and lye, comfort and order. With every breath I took, I felt myself relax. Little by little, the reality of the warm, candlelit room engulfed me.

I was safe. Secure. Curled in my husband's arms.

Donnell had escaped, but there were five men prepared to kill to keep me safe from him, or anyone else who dared trespass.

"You're safe, I've got you," Oliver whispered into the tangled mess of my hair.

I took the biggest breath possible, noting how my chest ached as it expanded. "Did I wake you?" My voice was hoarse. Had my screams escaped the dream?

Oliver cleared his throat. "Well, it's awfully hard to sleep when you've got a writhing animal next to you."

I felt the blush creep over my cheeks. "Sorry."

"No, no, don't be." He squeezed me tighter. "You don't have control over your dreams." He pulled me back onto the mattress, still clutching me to him.

"If only I did," I muttered bitterly, adjusting myself so that his bicep was my new pillow. I traced the muscles on his chest, smiling inwardly at the way he twitched with the light touch. Was he ticklish? "I'd kill him myself."

Oliver shifted his weight on the bed so he could focus on my face. I could hardly see his expression in the candlelight, but I knew he was doing more than just making sure I was all right—he was trying to figure out if I was tickling him on purpose.

"Killing someone, even an enemy, comes with its own kind of nightmare—" He cut himself off, gripping my hand before it could stray down his side. "And if you don't stop that . . ."

In my attempt to push the dream completely from my mind, I sat straight up, my eyes narrowed in a challenge. "You'll what?"

His eyebrow quirked. "You wanna play that game, do ya?"

I didn't dignify him with an answer. I swung my leg over his torso and set myself on his lower stomach, hands at the ready.

Oliver smirked. "You know you won't win this, right?"

Again, I didn't bother answering. I let my fingers dive for those lower ribs, tickling for all they were worth.

He gritted his teeth against a laugh and glued his eyes shut. He turned to stone, letting me do my worst. His lips twitched as he mouthed, "One . . . two . . ."

I stiffened. What number would he stop at? I moved my fingers a little lower, lightening my touch. That did it. He barked one laugh, then another, his hands clenching into fists as he continued his count.

By the time he hit "eight," he was struggling to keep his squirming and laughter under control.

"Nine . . ." His clear eyes opened, sparkling with mischief in the candlelight.

I gnawed on my lower lip and tightened my thighs on his torso, readying myself for the fight. I tickled him with everything I was worth.

He spoke the last word out loud. "Ten." He pressed his hips high, gripped my shoulders, and rolled. Effortlessly, he knocked me onto the mattress and sprang on top of me. I reached for the nearest pillow, planning on slamming it against his head, but he grabbed my wrist. He pressed it into the feather pillow, then easily snatched the other one. With just one hand, he held both of mine above my head.

I tried to roll, tried to buck him off as he had me, but he hardly moved. In fact, my struggling only brought a wide grin to his face.

"You asked for it." He lifted his free hand and twiddled his fingers in the air, watching the movement as if he were checking the construction of a wheel.

I gulped and went still. I had asked for it, and I knew I'd do it again.

His hand descended upon me with the speed of lightning, finding that magical spot below my own ribs. I fell into a fit of shrieking and laughter, unable to control it for even a breath. He was relentless, making sure I paid for all ten seconds of my torture.

Someone rapped against the door. "Hush in there!" came Sofia's groggy voice. "They can pr'lly hear your shenanigans on the other side of the river!"

Oliver pressed his palm over my mouth to stifle my nonstop giggling. "No shenanigans here! Mind your business!" he called, a lopsided grin plastered to his face.

Whenever I went outside, I stayed close to the house, eyes trained on the trees. At the first sign of movement, I'd jump, often surprising Sofia.

"Will you stop jumpin' like a skinned rabbit?" she snapped one day, one hand over her heart, the other gripping the hoe a little tighter than necessary.

I narrowed my eyes at the offending tree, making sure it didn't morph into an enemy. "I did *not*," I shot back, slamming my shovel into the hard dirt.

Eva had charged us with marking out an extension to the garden, even though it wouldn't be in use until the spring. Sofia looked like a strangely proportioned cupcake with all her skirts hiked up as far as she dared. Her bare legs were on full display up to her knees, giving just a peek of the ribbon-edged drawers.

"You sure did," Sofia muttered. She pushed past me, shielding her eyes against the accosting light of the afternoon sun to peer into the tree line. "You've been doin' that for days."

I couldn't argue with her on that. I had hardly been sleeping, despite Oliver's best attempts at distraction. I knew he had been staying awake to watch over me until I entered that dreaded dreamland. So I eventually started pretending, rolling on my side and controlling my breathing as well as I could. He deserved to get a little rest.

Sofia let out a long sigh, eyes focused straight on my face. "Do you want me to go check?" She nodded in the direction I'd been staring.

"No!" I said, just a little too quickly. "It's nothing. It was just a branch."

Sofia went back to mutilating a rather large rock, but I couldn't break my stare.

"Fine!" Sofia leaned the hoe against the haphazardly built fence and brushed the dirt from her hands onto her apron. "I'll look."

"Sofia! It's nothing!" I reached for her arm, but she was too quick for me.

"You've been checkin' those trees at least once every five minutes for the past hour. If I plan on gettin' any help from you today, I'll have to show you nothing's there."

"Ugh! Sofia!" I rushed after her, using the shovel as a cane to propel me on.

Fearless, she waltzed right into the trees, armed with nothing but the tiny shovel tucked into the ties of her apron and a small knife in her pocket. I skidded to a halt at the edge of the trees.

What if I was wrong? What if it *had* been something other than a branch?

Sofia kicked at a few bushes, peered behind trees, and strolled aimlessly around in the shadows.

"Feeling better now?" Sofia called.

"Yes, now come on!" I glanced anxiously behind us, half expecting to see our foe watching us from the garden.

Sofia exaggerated her eye roll and made her way to my side. "The men are watching the forest. They won't miss so much as a squirrel." She took the shovel from me and wrapped her arm around my waist, leading me back to our workstation.

I didn't say a word until we were back with our toes in the dirt. "But what if they do?" I whispered.

Sofia reached into her apron pocket and retrieved her knife, sheathed in a dark leather painted with red and yellow flowers. "I'm not useless, y'know."

Despite myself, my lip quirked into a smile. "At least one of us can do *something*." To emphasize my shortcomings, I lifted my skirts to display my dirt-caked foot.

"What does that matter?" Sofia demanded.

I crossed my arms and looked her up and down. "You've had your whole life to learn how to protect yourself. And look at you!" Surprising myself, I reached out to squeeze her bicep. "You're stronger than I could ever hope to be. You're taller, you know *how* to use that knife, and, last I checked, you still have two legs."

She leaned against the neighboring fence post, one ankle crossed over the other. "I'm also a girl. I'm impulsive. I don't have near as much trainin' as my brothers. But I learned. And you can too."

I rolled my eyes at her and retrieved my shovel from its resting place, slamming it into the dusty ground. "I'm broken, Sofia."

Her hoe landed against a rock with an ominous clang. "That never stopped my grandfather."

I couldn't argue with that. With a sigh, I took one more look in the direction of the trees and then returned to work.

CHAPTER SEVENTY-SEVEN

Rustle in the Bushes

"Nella," Eva started, scraping a particularly grimy dish into the scrap bucket. "Could you put the chickens up? And Sofia, draw me up a little water to rinse these?"

In unison, Sofia and I pushed from the table.

"Yes ma'am." Sofia grabbed a bucket from the counter and marched to the back door.

The men had already left, escaping to the library to discuss business. Even though it had been days, they hadn't decided what to do with Arthur. Whenever they went to see him, I strained my ears for any sounds of torture, but I never heard a thing.

I assumed they were discussing his fate, but I couldn't be sure. How long would they keep him tied up in that dark room?

"Psst," Sofia hissed. "C'mon." She nodded toward the yard.

With a resigned sigh, I pushed the thoughts of Arthur from my mind and gripped my cane to go take care of the pesky chickens.

From the looks of it, I wouldn't have to hunt for many of them. They were usually good at putting themselves to bed when the streaks of the red-and-orange sunset fluttered across the sky. But there would always be one or two who chose to nest in the woodpile.

Sofia stuck close to me a little longer than necessary. "I'll keep an eye out, okay? I'll be right over by the well."

Deep down, I appreciated her concern. It was certainly a lot better than her calling me Shed Mouse, but her babying felt almost condescending.

"I'm all right," I said, a little rougher than I meant.

She cocked her head to the side, a movement not unlike a curious hen. "You can't pretend that being out here doesn't worry you. Not after—"

"It wasn't bothering me until you *said* something," I snapped. I pulled my shoulders back and strode toward the wayward hens.

Sofia grumbled something under her breath, then turned to go take care of her own chore.

It *had* crossed my mind, though I had been trying to ignore it.

The little hairs on the back of my neck stood straight up, making me shiver. "You're fine, Nella," I scolded myself. "Just get the chickens in the coop and you can go inside."

That doesn't mean he won't have ways to get you away from there.

As though it would erase the nagging thoughts, I scrubbed at my temples. "Keep your head down, find the chickens. That's it."

There was only one hen hiding in the woodpile. She had created a little nest of leaves and twigs between the pile and the side of the house.

"There you are," I said, scooping her into one arm. She squawked, understandably irritated that I disrupted her evening relaxation.

"It's not safe out here after dark for little ones like you." I ran my finger over the comb on her head. She pressed against the touch, clucking the entire time.

We're all livestock.

"I know . . . it's not safe for me, either."

That was when I broke the promise to myself. I scanned where the clearing met the trees, my skin crawling.

The hen squirmed under my arm, but I held tight.

Just one glance.

I took my time squinting into the shadows, relaxing little by little as no one materialized.

He stood so still I nearly missed him. But my anxious brain reacted instantly.

The chicken fell from my grip, and I clutched my cane with both hands. Our eyes met in the near darkness, his gaze illuminated by the sunset.

My fingernails threatened to slice into my palms. I couldn't speak. I could hardly even breathe.

Donnell hadn't shaved since I'd seen him last. He had that scraggly red-gold beard, complete with a mustache. All it did was accentuate the danger in his piercing blue eyes.

His only movement came from his hand as he crooked it, beckoning me to his side. He didn't have to open his mouth for me to hear the words he longed to speak. "Come without a fight. You know it's inevitable."

I stumbled back, but my body failed to remember that a leg was missing. I fell flat onto my rear, my skirts and the mahogany feathers from the startled hen obstructing my view for a mere moment.

By the time I could focus again, he was gone. Only then did I release the trapped scream from my throat.

Sofia was there in an instant, producing a knife from its hiding place in her apron. A trusty guard, she stood over me, legs placed hip-width apart, ready to strike at anything that dared move.

The screen door slammed open, and each of the men leapt to the packed grass below.

They all rushed to my side, pistols raised, ready for action. They created a circle around me, each focusing on a specific area of the tree line.

"Where?" Josef demanded. He didn't look down at me, he kept his eye on the trees.

I had to swallow a few times to convince my voice to work. "That way." I tapped his leg to indicate the direction. Though he was long gone, I could still clearly see him when I closed my eyes.

"Are you sure—" Niklas started.

Sofia fixed a glare on her brother's back. "I saw him too," she snapped.

August's shoulders slumped in a sigh. "I was hoping to get some sleep tonight! It's been impossible, rooming with Niklas."

I risked a glance back at the house. Johannes sat in the doorway, rifle pointed straight at the space where Donnell had stood. Eva hovered in the background, wringing her hands on her apron.

"Get her inside, Sofia," Josef said.

"Yes sir." Sofia didn't ask permission before she pulled me to stand. She hooked one arm under mine and started for the house.

The circle of men held their positions around us, escorting us the entire way to the door.

No one gave any other instructions until we squeezed past Johannes and into the stove-warmed kitchen. Eva pulled the two of us into a tight hug.

In a gruff voice, Josef wasted no more time. "Niklas, Oliver, get the horses. August, you and I will get the guns."

Oliver glanced over his shoulder at me, sending me a smile that was likely meant to be reassuring. But I could see the nerves that played across his tightly strung face. He didn't hesitate for another second. He and Niklas rushed for the barn, their eyes on the trees. Their long strides were that of hunters, anxious to take down the prey that was nearly in their grasp.

With startling speed, Johannes turned his chair and wheeled back into the kitchen. "I want the girls in the library," he instructed. "Sofie, Eva, arm yourselves. We don't know if he brought anyone back with him."

Eva ushered me back toward the hall, Johannes, August, and Josef following close behind.

My heart thumped painfully against my ribcage, and I fought to regain control. "Wait," I demanded, grabbing the doorframe so they couldn't push me any farther. "What can I do to help?"

August scratched his head and shrugged.

Josef sighed. "Staying where we put you for now."

Johannes ignored my stance and kept wheeling forward, forcing me to either move, or get run over. I moved, reluctantly resuming the trek to the library.

"What are you going to do?" Before I went into the room lined with bookshelves, I dared a glance at the locked door only a few feet away.

"Don't worry about that," August muttered. With the ease of a young cat, he hopped onto a waist-high shelf. He pulled a few books out at the top, tossing them haphazardly onto the settee below. He then pulled out two revolvers and a satchel filled with what I could only assume was ammunition.

The other men did something similar, popping open drawers I didn't realize existed and removing more weapons and ammo than I'd ever seen.

Sofia and Eva helped as well, removing their preferred weapons from their hiding places behind the settee. I stared, open-mouthed and stock-still.

"Be careful." Eva stood on tiptoes and placed a chaste kiss on Josef's lips.

"Always." He gave her a one-armed hug, then hurried from the room, August on his heels.

Johannes wheeled out behind him, shutting the door. Eva slid the iron lock into place with a sickening *click*. She stood tall, ready for anything.

"Now, we wait," Sofia said. She took my arm and led me to the settee. "Don't worry, more than likely, nothing will happen here."

I raised an eyebrow at her. "You've done this before?"

She shrugged. "We know how to operate. *Farfar* will patrol in the house, keepin' an eye on both the prisoner and us. We pr'lly won't have to do anythin'." As if to drive home her point, she set her revolver on the side table. "They'll get 'em soon and be home by morning, I'm sure of it." Interlocking her fingers, she placed them behind her head and stretched, letting her eyes flutter closed.

I dared a glance at Eva. She didn't look nearly as relaxed. A deep frown had adhered itself to her features. She expertly tucked her gun into her apron and moved to the far corner of the room, eyes fixed on the locked door.

"How long do we have to stay here?" I asked.

"Pr'lly just until morning when the men get back. Or if *Farfar* says it's safe enough to come out."

CHAPTER SEVENTY-EIGHT

Canoodle Later

Sofia was wrong.

They didn't return in the morning.

Throughout the night, Eva refused to let either of us out of the room. When I insisted on a trip to the outhouse, she simply hauled a chamber pot from its hiding place behind the settee.

We all attempted to stay busy by reading in the candlelight, but we clearly couldn't pay attention to the words on the pages.

Every sound made us jump, no matter where it came from. Was it Johannes patrolling the hallway? Was it Arthur making his escape? Had the rest of the men returned?

We were given no choice but to settle in our seats and wait it out.

Eventually, we slept, though not on purpose. Sofia was first, her head lolling against the wall and a strangled snore trickling from her lips.

I must've followed her lead, because the next thing I knew, I woke with a numb arm and the sight of Eva sound asleep in the plush red chair across the room.

At some point, we all woke up—groggy, silent, and confused. Eva stretched her lithe frame, yawning in a startlingly unladylike fashion. When her limbs were awake enough, she went to the door and knocked firmly three times. She then waited, one finger to her lips to signal us to silence.

Nothing happened.

Pursing her lips, she knocked the same pattern again, louder this time.

A minute passed before someone rapped a different pattern on the outside. I stiffened, but both Eva's and Sofia's shoulders sagged with relief.

"All right, come on, ladies." Eva gestured to the door and slid the bolt free of its bonds.

Sofia dove from her seat, swaying side to side to unruffle her skirts. I followed, slower, but just as grateful to find some sunlight.

Johannes sat in his chair right outside the door, a rifle resting across the armrests. "No sign of 'em," he announced. "Stay inside and away from windows until they return."

My toes curled anxiously. Where were they? What if Donnell had led them into a trap?

"C'mon." Sofia squeezed my arm. "They'll be fine. They've done this a million times."

I raised my eyebrow at her. "They've fought another clan?"

She hesitated, gnawing her bottom lip. "Well, no. But they're prepared."

"As are we," Eva added in. "Come, let's eat. Then perhaps we can get some real rest."

"They're here!" came Sofia's shout. She practically broke down my door as she rushed into my room. She resembled an overexcited child instead of a woman old enough for marriage.

"All of them?" I demanded, scrambling from my cocoon of blankets and tripping my way to the window.

"Yes!" Sofia followed, and we both pressed our noses to the panes, squinting against the lower light of sunset to count the men as they trailed across the yard.

"There's only three," I whispered, horror gripping my stomach.

"Niklas's in the barn with the horses. I saw him take them before I ran up here," Sofia said.

I squinted harder, fighting to read their serious expressions. Had they been successful? Was Donnell gone? If so, what had they done with the body?

"C'mon." Sofia grabbed my arm and practically dragged me toward the door. I followed, not bothering to fix my skirts. My discarded crinoline sat in a heap at the foot of the bed, leaving my dress long and shapeless.

Sofia's strong arm supported me as we traveled down the stairs, ensuring we made record time to the front door. Eva and Johannes met us there, each and every one of us eagerly anticipating the news.

They're okay.

Josef came in first, going straight to wrap his wife in a hug so tight, it lifted her from the floor. She slapped at his dirt-encrusted arm, muttering something about him bringing such filth into her house. August and Oliver waltzed in next, Oliver having to halt his progress for a single step so he could come in behind August. They were just as dirty as Josef—mud was smeared on their faces and pressed deep into their nails. Oliver even had a leaf trapped in the tangled mess of his hair.

His eyes locked on mine, and a small smile quirked at his lips. Relief flooded through my body, tinged with the over-whelming urge to cry.

He was okay. He was in one piece. He was alive.

Oliver tucked me into a hug, his nose nestled into my own hair. He smelled of horse, dirt, and sweat, and his hug would likely make my clothes smell the same. I didn't care. He was back, and he was safe.

My chest expanded to its full capacity, my back pushing against his embrace as I took in a cleansing breath. His lips traveled down my head to covertly nip at my ear. I held in my surprised yelp to the best of my ability. Did that playful move mean they had been successful?

Apparently, Sofia had the same question. "So? You get 'em?" she demanded, bumping against August with her hip.

Her brother scowled at her. "No." His voice was nearly a growl.

"No?" Sofia went completely still.

Oliver begrudgingly released me just enough so I could turn to face the siblings. He noticeably deflated, his body sagging with the reality of the announcement.

Josef pulled his hat from his head and scrubbed at the line of dirt it left behind. "We saw 'em, gave 'em chase for quite some time."

Johannes's chair squeaked from where he sat, crossing his arms in a show of irritation. "Just the one?"

"That's all we saw," Josef confirmed.

"I bet he had help," August muttered. He shed his jacket and tossed it onto the hook, shifting his shoulders back and forth in a way that reminded me of a bear scratching his back against a tree.

Eva had her arms crossed, just like her father-in-law. "Why do you say that?"

Josef grunted and pushed past us all, heading for the hallway. "I'm gettin' a drink 'fore we get into all that."

Eva glared at his back but followed along, never once removing her stiff arms from their position.

When we made it to the kitchen, we took our various positions around the room. Sofia leaned against the doorframe, one knee poking out like a flag. Eva sat in her seat, head in her hands. Johannes and August hovered near the bucket of water, watching as Josef guzzled one ladleful after another. Eva cleared her throat, but he ignored it.

"C'mon, spill it!" Sofia demanded.

"Sofie . . ." Eva cautioned, though her growl was nearly imperceptible through her palms.

I glanced at Oliver, hunting for an answer. I got none. His face was as hard as stone, unreadable as he waited for his new commander to begin the story.

Finally satisfied, Josef rested against the counter, head back and eyes closed. "He led a good chase. We thought he was headin' straight for the river. We were sure we'd catch him there, as there was no way he could cross that far south."

Oliver's hands slid around my waist, supporting me in what way he could. He kissed the top of my head. I pressed against his body, fighting the numb terror that threatened to take over.

Josef reached into the water bucket and took another long sip. "He disappeared 'round ten miles south. Not a trace. Wiped his tracks clean. We searched for hours, but with it still being dark, he could'a been anywhere."

Johannes's mouth was set in a grim line as he scrutinized his son. "Did he cross?"

Josef lifted one shoulder in a lazy shrug. "Doubt it. Unless there was a boat a'ready waitin' for him."

"That's a possibility," Oliver chimed in, his deep voice vibrating against my back. "Especially after what happened last time."

"Mhm," August agreed. "I bet they a'ready had an escape plan. No tellin' how many people 're gathered, plannin' out their next move."

Sofia let out a long breath, somewhere between a sigh and a groan. "So we stayed in that room all night for *nothing*?"

Eva directed her sharp gaze at her daughter. "In times like these, it's better to be safe so we can fight another day."

Sofia shifted from one foot to the other, biting her lip and avoiding her mother's reproachful gaze. The effort not to sass back was written all across her face, almost making me smile.

The screen door bumped against Niklas's rear as he made his way through the back door. He froze on the braided mat, ready to bolt in case his sister shot off like a cannon.

Eva pushed away from where she stood and walked straight to the water bucket, removing the ladle from her husband's dirty fingers. "Go wash up. All of you. You're back home now, so you'd best act like it. I don't want to catch a single whiff of horse shit by mornin'." Her eyes swept the room, focusing on each individual male for a full second.

"Yes ma'am," Niklas and August chorused. Oliver said it too, but his voice was hardly more than a whisper.

As the younger men made their first step toward the hall, Josef cleared his throat. "We need to discuss what to do with the prisoner." He inclined his head in the general direction of the torture chamber.

"No!" Eva barked. She placed one hand on each of her sons' backs. "Clean yourself up, then discuss it in the library. No more business in my kitchen!" She shoved the boys toward the back door.

Sofia's lip quirked in a brief smile as she watched.

"Go get the tub set up, will ya?" Josef asked his sons.

"No." Eva put her foot down with more force than was likely necessary. "Outside. Look at yourself, you're filthy! You said your hellos, and now it's time to get cleaned up. Out with you!"

Like herding a bunch of chickens, she grasped the handle of the ladle just a little tighter and waved it. Niklas and August practically flew through the back door, narrowly missing the wrath of their mother.

Sofia clutched at her sides as she fell into a fit of laughter.

Josef followed more slowly, a twinkle in his eye as he observed his feisty wife. At her side, he bent gradually, meeting her lips with a delicate kiss.

She smacked his side with the ladle. "Out!"

Oliver had yet to relinquish his embrace around me, but when Eva's fierce eyes found him, he dropped me like a naughty dog.

"That goes for you too! Resume your canoodlin' later. Go, go!" He sneaked a quick kiss on the top of my head, a childlike giggle escaping his mouth right before he dove out the door.

I had to fight not to join the laughter. As much as I didn't want to admit it, these people certainly had grown on me.

CHAPTER SEVENTY-NINE

Promise in a Song

It took an agonizingly long time for the men to wash to Eva's strict specifications. But eventually, she deemed them worthy of the house. They all trudged inside, dressed and smelling like gentlemen instead of sweaty farm animals.

To my surprise, they chose to wait until morning to discuss Arthur's fate. Instead, dispersing into their own rooms to rest. I certainly wasn't going to argue with that.

I waited for him at the window, my teeth grinding against both nerves and nausea.

Sure, we were safe for the moment. But how long would it be until Donnell returned? He knew the defenses now. And he *certainly* knew how defenseless I was.

Oliver wasted no time in getting upstairs. He had a grin plastered to his face as I rushed to greet him. Before I could reach for a hug, he slid from his pants and worked his first arm out of a sleeve.

I smirked at his enthusiasm. "Impatient, are we?" I teased, popping open two of the buttons for him.

"It's been a long couple of days," Oliver said. He let me finish the buttons, then shrugged out of the shirt.

No longer did he smell of the outside world. He smelled fresh and clean, that cross between calming lavender and lye. I could get used to that scent, that was for certain.

His hair was still wet and tussled, and desperately in need of a brush. I made a mental note to tend to it. Soon. But I had other things to do first.

"I'm glad you're safe," I said, pressing my entire body against his bare one.

He grunted in agreement. "We weren't in much danger."

I pushed back just enough to raise an eyebrow at him. "Liar. We had to stay in the library all night. There was certainly *some* danger."

He didn't seem to hear me. Instead, he traced my cheek with his thumb, eyes studying every inch of my face. His breath was even, drawing me into his calmness. I leaned into the hug.

For the moment, the argument didn't matter. He was perfectly safe, without so much as a new scratch or bruise on his body.

I craved every inch of him, wanted nothing more than to sink into his embrace. He seemed to have the same idea. He ran his hand over my collarbone, fingers deftly working the buttons of my bodice. It fell from my shoulders, perching on my hips, stopped by the crinoline. His hands moved lower, popping the skirt's button, then pulling the tie on the hoop skirts and petticoat. With a little shimmy to help them along, they sashayed to the floor in a satisfying *whoosh*.

I trailed my hands along his side, making him squirm as I found a particularly sensitive area right above his hip bone.

"Stop that," he chided, leaning in to nip my neck. I stood in only my chemise and stockings, while he had not a single stitch left.

I was in charge.

"You're mine now," I commanded, shoving him in the direction of the bed. He didn't bother fighting, falling back onto the comforter. I smiled to myself as I hurried after him, pulling the chemise over my head as I went.

Breathlessly, he commanded, "Take your hair down."

I did as he asked, pulling the pins from the twist and tossing them onto the floor. They pinged together as they dove to disappear forever under various pieces of furniture. I didn't care—I had a different mission.

I crawled onto the bed and threw one leg over his torso, straddling him. I really was in charge. His eyes twinkled as he watched me, hair cascading down my chest.

"Take me," he whispered, hands moving to grip my hips, a smirk on his face.

And, with a laugh, I did as he commanded.

When all was said and done, we remained curled on top of the comforter.

"I wanna learn to fight," I whispered into the hairs on his chest.

"You do?" He placed a hand on either side of my head and tilted it up to meet my gaze.

I nodded firmly. "I'm tired of being helpless. Tired of being . . . tired of being so . . . broken! Useless!" My stump throbbed at the mere mention of it.

He studied my face for a long while, choosing his words carefully. "We'll teach you," he vowed. He tucked me back into the hug, his fingers tracing down my bare back, making me shiver at the feather-softness of his touch.

"Oh!" Suddenly he stopped and pushed me back.

My mouth fell open in shock. "Oh?" I echoed.

"I got you something." Like an excited child, he scampered to where he'd kicked his pants, bending to retrieve a carefully folded slip of paper. Though I was very familiar with every curve of his body, I couldn't help but watch the way it moved, study the muscles that tightened as he stood.

My heart skipped a beat. A letter?

"This, it's from your ma." He set the weathered envelope in my hand. Though it felt cool to the touch, I could imagine that I could feel the heat where her fingers had been.

He leaned against the foot of the bed, watching with a satisfied grin as I plopped onto the mattress and tore open the envelope.

> *To my darling daughter,*
>
> *When I saw your name on that envelope, I couldn't wait a single moment to open it. Usually, I would wait for Little Chris to hear whatever news you bring. This time? He had to read it later.*
>
> *Felicité is doing so well! She makes the most darling noises, and the entire street has fallen in love. Not a single soul has questioned her origins. As far as everyone is aware, Felicité is Miriam's natural-born daughter.*
>
> *I must say, the night you left is one I would much rather forget. Yes, we are all right after that horrific night, but we weren't sure about you. We had the police combing the neighborhoods for any trace of you, or our attacker. But there was nothing to be found.*
>
> *It reminded me very much of the night we lost your father: sudden and without a trace. I pray your husband hasn't been caught up in that same gambling ring as your father did. It does a family no good, as you well know.*

On a much brighter note, Little Chris and I have moved back home. It feels empty, quiet, but that's also a blessing—you know how babies cry all throughout the night! I go over to Miriam's house almost daily to help her with that little one. That little thing can eat! And holler . . . but can't all little ones?

Please keep me updated on everything in your life. I want to know it all. For now, I am content to know you are safe and well. We look forward to hearing from you again soon.

Love,

Mother

Tears pricked at the corners of my eyes as I read her words. She felt so far away.

"Do you think I'll get to see her again?" I whispered.

Oliver sighed deeply. "I hope so."

I gnawed on my lower lip. "Will Donnell—"

Oliver held up his hand. "My family won't stop until they are forced to. But that's where we come in." He gestured vaguely at the house around him. "I'm trained. The entire Welks Clan is trained. If anyone can keep you safe, it's us."

The thudding of my heart threatened to make me sick. "Will he hurt Mother? Miriam?"

"No," Oliver said firmly. "They have no reason to." He paused, eyes on the letter. "Well, probably not. You've gotta keep an eye on what you write on those envelopes, though."

I clutched at my stomach. "He's gonna kill them . . . he's gonna kill them all."

Oliver rushed to my side, wrapping his arms around me before I could collapse to the floor. "No. No, he is not. You understand me? Right now, Donnell is more interested in you, more interested in me. He's not gonna waste time going after your family!"

I let him lower me back onto the bed.

"They are okay. You are okay. We are safe. Well, at least as safe as we can be. I will *not* let him hurt you. And I will make him pay tenfold for every moment of pain he has caused you." He lowered himself to lay a feather-like kiss on my lips.

"I know this isn't the life you chose, but I want you to feel safe in it. Soon, we'll have our own cabin, our own space. But for now . . ." The pages in his grip rustled as he set them in my lap.

I didn't bother questioning where he'd pulled them from. My brain felt numb as I looked at the tiny dots that danced across the cream-colored page. They trailed up, down, and together in their own special dance that only a musician could read.

"I'm looking for a piano. Somehow, someway, I'll get you one. Soon. I promise." Oliver gripped both of my hands and waited to catch my gaze. "It's time to make ourselves a life. *Our* life. Not my father's. Not your father's. *Ours.*"

Tears welled in my eyes, blurring the dancing dots and lines. I threw myself into him, wrapping my arms around his neck and placing a solid kiss straight on his lips. "Thank you," I sobbed. "Thank you!"

His smile spread against my lips. "I love you, Nella. I want you to feel safe in this life, feel like it's *yours.*"

I hardly heard him. I lost myself in the tears. My life had changed more than I ever imagined, and maybe, just maybe, it was all worth it.

Because it was time to create our life. *My* life.

Ellie should've died in the accident, and she knows it. Yet she wakes downstream with a head wound.

Instead of her small hometown, she finds herself trapped in land run era Oklahoma—complete with bonnets, corsets, floor-length dresses, and covered wagons.

Realizing this isn't some cruel joke, she's scooped up by a man who's convinced she's his missing sister. Despite her plans to get back to her real time, Ellie takes the place of this missing doppelgänger to survive.

But her newfound family has other plans.

To settle a land dispute, there's to be a wedding with the malicious neighbor.

And she's the bride.

Ellie is determined to escape before they make her say, "I do." But when she meets Sam—the only man who truly believes she's from the future—she questions if running is the only option.

A fast-paced time travel novel set in 1894, *Twins in Time* is brimming with rousing stakes, endearing romance, family tragedy, and stirring imagery of the Old West.

ACKNOWLEDGMENTS

With how long this book took to write, creating an acknowledgments page almost feels daunting. There have been so many people who have helped me with *The Killer's Flaw*, I'm worried I'll miss them all!

First, I must thank my amazing husband. Not only has he been a sounding board for everything from how the clans work to the title itself, but he also was always able to help me run through battle scenes to make sure they would be possible. Spoiler alert, 90 percent of the time, I had to redo them at *least* three times before they were realistic.

Of course, I can't leave out my daughter, Annaleigh. Without her influence, I don't think Anton, Vernon, or even Felicité would be in this story. She has been around for every step of this story's creation. Drafting while pregnant, editing first while in the CVICU (Cardiovascular Intensive Care Unit) and then again (and again . . . and again . . .) throughout toddlerhood. Every time I look back at the creation of this book, I will see my little writing buddy.

I must thank my mom and dad for encouraging me to read and create all of my stories as a child. Sure, there were limits when it came to writing at 2:00 A.M. on a school night, but when there wasn't anything else to do, they would always encourage my latest project. Sometimes this was about a tree in a playground; other times, a tiny house along the highway.

Without that encouragement, I don't know if my writing obsession would've continued into adulthood.

To Rebekah and Nick, you guys have no idea how impactful your support has been over the past few years. Any TikTok I post, you guys are there, cheering me on. Any time I feel as though I can't go on, you're there to make me feel like I truly am living the dream.

And last but definitely not least, I must thank the team behind this story. My glorious editor, always there to fix the pesky commas and find the inevitable gibberish that made it through to the zillionth draft. THANK YOU! I love you! And my beta readers, Amanda, Beth, and Emma, you guys gave me the confidence to push forward and get this story out. Thank you all!

NATALIE GRIFFIN

Natalie Griffin is a historical fiction author, momma, and pianist. She owned her own dog grooming company for ten years before she left to pursue her writing dream and raise her little family.

Born and raised in Oklahoma, she can't stand the triple-digit heat, but she does enjoy the excitement that comes from tornado season. If you talk about the storms, you're guaranteed to have a long, animated conversation ahead of you.

She mainly writes stories set in the 19th century, believing she always belonged there, with corsets and log cabins. She will spend days running down a Google rabbit hole, learning whatever obscure fact she can about her chosen time period.

She stays busy with her hunter husband, two daughters, three dogs, and two cats.

Connect with the Author

Nataliegriffin.com
Instagram.com/natalieogriffin
TikTok.com/@natalieogriffin
Twitter.com/natalieogriffin

Leave a Review

If you enjoyed reading *The Killer's Flaw*, please consider leaving a review on your platform of choice. Reviews help self-published authors finds more readers like you.

BLOOPERS PAGE
[WITH EDITOR'S MARKS]

- *The **calvary** is here!* I had a chance after all.
  - https://www.merriam-webster.com/dictionary/cavalry < not Jesus
  - https://www.merriam-webster.com/dictionary/calvary < Jesus

- He dropped a **weathered leathered** bag. [Say that fives times fast.]

- Instant energy. I vaulted **to up.**

- My **tyrant** sounded ungrateful. [Should be *tirade*, but then again . . .]

- He worked quickly, finishing his efforts by placing a **police** of herbs on the affected area, followed by clean bandages. [So close. We'll take *poultice* for $500, Alex!]

- I **yeeted** the chamber pot at his head.

- The three of us women crammed ourselves into the shed, our skirts pressed against each other as we eradicated any **pets**. [We're looking for *pests* here.]

- Satisfied, he wiped the **puss**, or whatever else he found, away and poured water onto the wound. [I believe the word we're searching for is *pus*, but to each his own.]